man Af

D0352442

'Gripping and compelling from first page to last,
Children of Fire is a . . . spell-binding epic told
with masterful craft'

Tracy Hickman, *New York Times* bestselling author
of the *Dragonlance* and *Deathgate* series

'A rousing quest fantasy . . . a fast-paced action-packed
good and evil thriller'
SFRevu

C333828026

Also by Drew Karpyshyn:

Children of Fire
The Scorched Earth

CHAOS UNLEASHED

Book Three of
CHAOS BORN

DREW KARPYSHYN

DEL REY

1 3 5 7 9 10 8 6 4 2

Del Rey, an imprint of Ebury Publishing
20 Vauxhall Bridge Road,
London SW1V 2SA

Penguin
Random House
UK

Del Rey is part of the Penguin Random House group of companies whose
addresses can be found at global.penguinrandomhouse.com

Copyright © Drew Karypyshyn, 2015

Drew Karypyshyn has asserted his right to be identified as the author of this
work in accordance with the Copyright, Designs and Patents Act 1988

This novel is a work of fiction. Names and characters are the product of the
author's imagination and any resemblance to actual persons, living or dead,
is entirely coincidental

First published in the US in 2015 by Del Rey, an imprint of The Random
House Publishing Group, a division of Random House, Inc., New York.
First published in the UK in 2015 by Del Rey

www.eburypublishing.co.uk

A CIP catalogue record for this book is available from the British Library

ISBN 9780091952884

Printed and bound in Great Britain by Clays Ltd, St Ives PLC

Penguin Random House is committed to a sustainable future for our business,
our readers and our planet. This book is made from Forest Stewardship
Council® certified paper.

MIX
Paper from
responsible sources
FSC
www.fsc.org   FSC® C018179

For my father, Ron, a wonderful and amazing man.
Though he was taken too soon he lives on in the memories
and love shared by his friends and family.

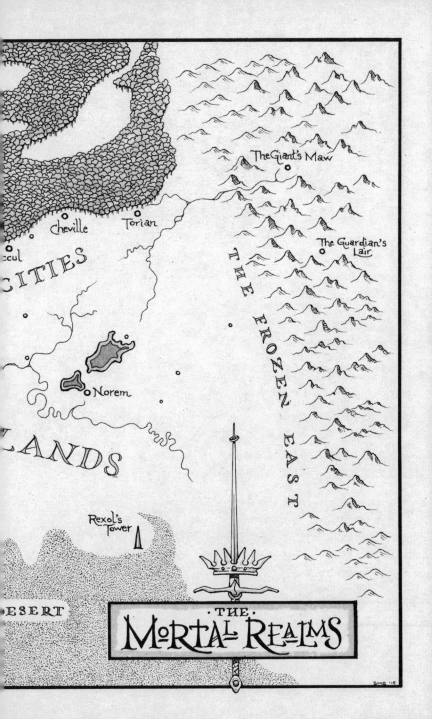

CHAOS
UNLEASHED

Prologue

On the sandy shores of an island at the farthest edge of the sea that bounds the mortal world, four divine, glowing figures stand in a tight circle around an obelisk of black obsidian—the Keystone. It towers above them, fifty feet tall and ten feet across on each of its four sides. Carved into the smooth, dark rock are powerful runes, and shapes and shadows shift below the surface: the living, churning power of raw Chaos.

Hiding in his nether realm far across the Burning Sea, Daemron the Slayer watches the four glowing Immortals intently, images reflected in the still waters of a stone fountain stained with blood.

He is beaten but not bowed. The armies of the Old Gods defeated him on the field of battle, but their victory is hollow. He still lives, as do legions of his followers. Bound to the mortal world they created, the Old Gods cannot follow him here. And so he is content to wait, safe beyond their reach while he plans his counterattack; his armies resting and gathering strength while he uses his own powerful magic to spy on his enemies.

Peering across the infinite chasm of space and time, the four figures appear as little more than blurred silhouettes of golden light. But even at this distance, he can sense that the power of the Old Gods has been diminished. They are wounded, dying. He takes pride in knowing the cost of driving him into retreat is more than even an Immortal can afford to pay. His own wounds are far less grievous. Had he risked more, had he stayed on the front lines longer, perhaps the tide of battle could have been swayed back in his favor. But at what cost? His retreat ensured that he will endure long after the other Immortals are gone. Their end is inevitable, as is his triumphant return.

Still, the ritual he is witnessing gives him pause. Curious, he watches intently as the glowing figures extend their arms and join hands in a circle around the Keystone, their voices rising in a single chorus. In response to their deep, rhythmic chant, the Keystone begins to tremble. A few seconds later it is enveloped by a soft white glow, emanating from somewhere deep within the black obelisk itself.

The pitch of the chant changes, going higher, redirecting and reshaping the gathering Chaos. The glow from the Keystone begins to pulse and thrum, beating like a living heart as it grows brighter and brighter.

The Gods raise their arms, still clasped hand to hand, and a bolt of pure white lightning shoots up into the sky. It streaks higher and higher, growing wider and brighter, stinging Daemron's eyes with its intensity. And then, just as he is about to look away, the white beam fractures, splitting into smaller rays that echo all the colors of the spectrum.

The ritualistic chant of the Old Gods rises in pitch again, a sound so shrill it sends shivers down Daemron's spine. The multicolored rays twist and dance as if alive, then shoot off in all directions, crisscrossing each other over and over as they paint the heavens. Within seconds the entire sky is blotted out by layer after layer of the luminous threads, weaving together and intertwining like a shimmering blanket.

The Gods are no longer chanting. As the spell intensifies, their throats unleash only a keening wail: Immortal screams that seem to leach the color out of the mystical tapestry above them, turning the millions of vibrant threads into a solid mantle of black. And then, before Daemron realizes what is happening, the spell ends, casting his vision of the Gods and the mortal world into utter darkness as the Legacy is born.

Daemron the Slayer wakes with a start, his massive chest heaving with quick, panicked breaths as his mind retreats from the black void. Disoriented, he casts his horned head quickly from side to side, scanning every brick and stone of the bare, circular room that is his innermost sanctum. A single ray of dim light shines down through the circular opening in the dome high above, leaving most of the room in shadow. But his glowing green eyes have no trouble piercing the gloom.

Reassured that he is alone, calm slowly returns. He extends the massive, leathery wings that had enfolded him as he crouched in the center of the empty floor and rises to his feet, stretching the stiffness from the muscles of his bare torso and slowly swishing his long, serpentine tail.

He rarely sleeps, but even a God must rest sometimes, particularly as his power has slowly faded during his exile. For centuries, his infrequent slumbers have been nothing but a time of empty darkness. When the Old Gods sacrificed themselves to create the Legacy, they did more than just cut him off from the mortal realm: They blinded him to the visions of Chaos. Until now.

He knows this was no mere memory, conjured up by a mind desperate to return to the land he should rightfully rule. He never actually witnessed the creation of the Legacy, but he knows it happened just as he has seen. The images running through his head were too detailed, too vivid, and too intense to be figments of his imagination. He was once a great prophet, and though it has been many centuries, he can still recognize the hallmarks of a true vision.

My dreams have returned. The Legacy is even weaker than I imagined!

With a series of slow, powerful flaps of his great wings, he ascends toward the small opening in the domed ceiling thirty feet above him—the only way in or out of the circular room in his castle's tallest tower.

Breaching the arch of the dome, he continues to climb into the dull gray sky that marks every morning in his blasted realm. Far below his ever-growing army encircles the drab buildings of his capital, stretching out for miles in every direction: thousands upon thousands of monsters and mutants, twisted and deformed by generations of living in this Chaos-poisoned land.

His grotesque legions are eager for battle; even from on high he can sense their restless bloodlust. An army with no enemy to fight is dangerous; he knows there are many in the ranks who would throw themselves behind the rebels that seek to usurp him if given the chance. The longer they sit idle, the greater the risk of betrayal.

Fortunately, his dream has confirmed what he already suspected. Chaos is bleeding through the Legacy. It is time to begin deploying his troops, sending them in search of places where the Legacy is thinnest and most vulnerable. Massing there, they will strike the instant the barrier tears asunder, pouring through in an invasion the mortal world has no chance of stopping.

Tilting his head back, Daemron unleashes a piercing cry of exultation that echoes across the plains, causing the demonic soldiers below to cower and prostrate themselves on the ground.

His long exile is almost over. The time of his return draws near. And once again, the mortal world will be his.

Chapter 1

KEEGAN'S STOMACH WAS rumbling, but he did his best to ignore it. Instead, he focused only on putting one foot in front of the other, relentlessly marching west across the sparse scrubland that stretched ahead of him as far as his eyes could see. With Norr's death their numbers had dwindled to three: Jerrod, Scythe, and him—a trio of sorry figures trudging slowly across the tundra of the Frozen East.

He leaned heavily on Rexol's gorgon-headed staff, the powerful artifact reduced to a simple walking stick to help him on his way. Shifting the pack over his shoulder, he was reminded of how much lighter it had become. They had been rationing food ever since they left the icy peaks of the Guardian's territory over a week ago, hoping their supplies would last long enough to get them to the Southlands.

And then what? the young mage wondered.

From the Guardian, they had learned that Cassandra—the young woman who had unwillingly helped them escape from the Monastery—now carried Daemron's Crown. She had taken the Talisman and fled south once more, heading for the port city of Callastan, pursued by enemies even more dangerous than Raven, the bird-headed woman who had attacked them to try to get Daemron's Sword.

Even if we find her before they do, why would she want to help us?

In the wake of Raven's attack, Jerrod had once again revised his interpretation of the prophecy he claimed to serve. Seeing Scythe use the Sword had convinced him that there were actually three saviors, each bound to one of Daemron's three Talismans. When the Slayer returned, the monk had explained to them, Keegan, Scythe, and Cassandra would have to work together to defeat him, drawing on the respective powers of the Ring, the Sword, and the Crown.

Keegan wasn't certain he bought into the new theory, and he was almost certain Cassandra wouldn't, either. The Guardian had initially seen them as a threat; given what had happened at the Monastery, she was likely to do the same. Would Jerrod even have a chance to try to convince her he was right before she unleashed the power of the Crown against them?

He had no idea what the Crown did, exactly. But it had been powerful enough to destroy Rexol, Keegan's old master, when he tried to use it.

Will we be strong enough to defeat her? Or the enemies hunting her?

It wasn't just Jerrod's reinterpretation of the prophecy that worried Keegan. Though he wouldn't admit it, the monk was obviously still struggling with the strange double vision he'd been cursed with by Raven. Ironically, the Sword had protected him from the Minion's deadly spells when he'd fought her, but had done nothing to keep her from healing him of the mystical blindness that afflicted all the members of the Order. The gray veil that had once covered his pupils and irises had melted away, revealing a pair of very ordinary-looking brown eyes. Without his trademark feature, Jerrod no longer looked like one of the Order. Instead, he resembled a fit but otherwise unremarkable middle-aged man.

When they finally reached the Southlands, Keegan thought, the only thing people would find odd about them were their clothes. All three of them were still wearing the simple pants and shirts they'd taken from the Danaan patrol when they'd first met Vaaler, with an extra layer of furs thrown overtop in the style of the Eastern clans to help ward off the cold.

Jerrod hadn't spoken of what he was going through, but Keegan could imagine how difficult it must be. With his vision restored, his supernatural awareness was now under constant bombardment by a collage of light, shapes, and colors. Jerrod no longer moved with the sharp precision Keegan had grown used to; he seemed hesitant and cautious as his mind struggled to comprehend the overabundance of stimuli. He had survived his battle with Raven, but he had suffered a loss from which he might never fully recover.

And Scythe isn't herself anymore, either.

The young Islander followed close behind the monk, the weapon her lover had sacrificed himself for strapped across her back. Like the others, she carried a small pack slung over one shoulder.

At a glance, she appeared as she always did: a small, lithe young woman with olive skin, almond eyes, and straight, shoulder-length black hair. The blade seemed almost too large for her, but the weight didn't seem to encumber her. She still moved with a predator's grace, her muscles always taut and ready. Unlike Jerrod, Scythe's wounds were mental, not physical.

Raven's attack had snapped her out of her catatonic state of grief, but since her mind had returned, she hadn't mentioned Norr's death at all. She no longer seemed to blame Jerrod for her loss; she showed no signs of being interested in revenge or payback. In fact, she wasn't interested in much of anything. She was speaking again, but only when absolutely necessary. She didn't even question or challenge Jerrod's decisions anymore; she seemed to be willing to just follow along with whatever the monk suggested.

That's not like her. She used to oppose him just on principle.

Keegan had tried several times to draw her out of her shell, but she hadn't engaged him. Anytime he tried to start a conversation, she'd listen but wouldn't respond with more than one- or two-word answers.

In the past when she wanted to be left alone, she'd shut me down with quick, cutting words. It's like she just doesn't care anymore.

As much as he'd learned to fear her temper, it was far better than her newfound apathy. The only thing he hadn't tried yet was talking to her about what happened to Norr. If anything could stir up some emotion in her, that would be it.

But what could I even say to her?

He knew from experience that empty platitudes could offer no comfort. When his father had been killed, the last thing he wanted to hear was tired clichés about holding on to his memories.

That's just an excuse. The reality is, you're a pathetic coward. You're just afraid she'll see the truth!

Norr had been his friend, but a dark, twisted corner of Keegan's psyche was always jealous of the big man. *Part of me wanted Norr out of the way. Part of me wanted him gone so I'd have a chance with Scythe.*

He hadn't wished for Norr to die, of course. At most Keegan had hoped he might go back to his own people. And even that hope had been tempered by the understanding that it was just a foolish, selfish fantasy. The big man's heroic sacrifice had hammered home just how petty and shameful Keegan's feelings for Scythe really were . . . but that didn't make them go away.

Out of respect for Norr, Keegan had vowed to himself to never act on his feelings. But Scythe already knew he had a crush on her. What if she saw any effort to console her as a clumsy attempt at winning her heart now that his rival was gone? What if she saw him as a predator trying to take advantage of her vulnerable emotional state?

Right now she's cold and distant, but apathy is better than hate and contempt.

Ahead, Jerrod held up his hand and brought them to a halt.

"We stop here for lunch, then press on. We're getting close to the Southlands. If we're lucky, we should come across some of the outlying farms in the next few days."

To Keegan's dismay, Scythe didn't respond to his words. She didn't object, she didn't agree. She didn't even nod. She simply sat down, opened her pack, and took out a thin sliver of jerky—barely more than a few bites' worth.

With an inaudible sigh, Keegan took a seat on the cold ground beside her, using Rexol's staff to help lower himself. As he dug out his own rations, she didn't acknowledge his presence in any way.

Jerrod slung his pack off his shoulder and let it fall to the ground, then crouched and rummaged through it, digging his way past the blankets they used to ward off the cold whenever they made camp for the night. A few seconds later he produced his own piece of jerky, only to offer it to Keegan.

The young wizard shook his head and held up the stump of his left arm, waving the food away with a hand that was no longer there.

"I've got plenty," he lied.

"My body can sustain itself on the most meager of rations," Jerrod reminded him. "But you need to eat to keep your strength up."

"Give it to Scythe."

The monk turned slightly in her direction. She answered with a barely perceptible shake of her head.

"This is all I need," she said, holding up what was left of her scant meal.

"The Sword gives her strength," Jerrod surmised, turning his attention back to Keegan. "But the Ring is different. It seems to be draining you. You're wasting away."

"I'm sick of jerky," Keegan protested though he knew there was truth in what Jerrod said.

The Ring still dangled from a chain around his neck, tucked away beneath the cloth of his shirt. But though out of sight, it was never out of mind. He could always sense its power, calling to him, urging him to put the Talisman on his finger and unleash Chaos on the mortal world. Ignoring that call wasn't easy; it put a slow but constant strain on his mind . . . and possibly his body, too.

"Until we reach the farms, there is nothing else," Jerrod reminded him. "And if you don't eat to keep your strength up, one of us will end up having to carry you."

Realizing it was pointless to argue, Keegan took the jerky and grudgingly choked it down. The rest of the meal passed in silence and they were soon on their way again, but he couldn't stop himself from continuing to worry about Scythe.

If you're too much of a coward to speak with her about Norr, maybe you can convince Jerrod to try.

When darkness fell they bedded down for the night. As usual, Jerrod took the first watch. But instead of letting himself drift off to sleep, Keegan waited until he heard Scythe snoring softly. Then he quietly slipped out of the blankets he had wrapped himself in, stood up, and signaled for the monk to follow him a short way off from the camp.

Once they were out of earshot, the young mage said, "I'm worried about Scythe."

"Everyone copes with grief in their own way," Jerrod assured him, brushing aside his concern.

"I don't think she is coping," Keegan replied. "She's just blindly following along like some kind of pack mule. It's like part of her shut down."

"Perhaps Norr's sacrifice made her understand the true value of our mission," the monk offered. "Or maybe she felt something when she used the Sword to kill Raven, and she finally accepts the role she has to play. Maybe she no longer protests everything we do because she has decided to embrace her destiny as one of the three saviors."

I doubt that, Keegan thought. But maybe there was an opportunity to use Jerrod's beliefs to his advantage.

"What if she can't play that role in her current state?" Keegan wondered aloud. "After Raven's death, you said the flames of Chaos burn inside her. It's what makes Scythe who she is: spontaneous, argumentative, confrontational. But she's not like that anymore. What if that fire inside her has gone out?"

Jerrod hesitated, then shook his head. "Chaos cannot so easily be extinguished. It is part of her core, the very essence of her being. The Chaos in her blood defines her, just as it defines you." After a brief pause, he added, "And Cassandra, too, no doubt."

"I still think you should talk to Scythe," Keegan pressed. "If we can just get her to open up about what happened to Norr, maybe she'll go back to her old self."

"Such a conversation could have consequences we are not prepared to deal with," the monk replied carefully.

"What are you talking about?"

"Backlash," he said, his voice dropping into a low whisper. "You used the Ring to save us from the yeti horde. Maybe the backlash of the Chaos you unleashed is what caused Norr's death."

The idea wasn't new to Keegan; it's one he had struggled with himself. The thought that he might be indirectly responsible for what happened to Norr only intensified his guilt over his feelings for Scythe. But there was no way to be certain he was to blame, and he had already decided he wasn't going to take on the extra burden.

"If I hadn't done that, we'd all be dead," Keegan reminded him.

"I agree. But will Scythe see it that way? If we delve into this, she might decide you are to blame for Norr's death."

"Even if it was my fault," Keegan said, the words coming

grudgingly to his lips, "Scythe wouldn't blame me. She's smart enough to understand it was an accident."

"Was it?" Jerrod asked.

Keegan was too stunned by the accusation to answer.

"Your feelings for Scythe are obvious enough," the monk continued. "And your power is growing. Every time you've used the Ring, you've become stronger. More able to control and direct the Chaos it unleashes.

"What if your jealousy of Norr made you subconsciously direct the backlash in his direction?"

"That's . . . that's not even possible," Keegan stammered, shaking his head. "Nobody can control backlash. That's why it's so dangerous."

"Perhaps. But you have already done many things that no other has accomplished."

"I didn't cause Norr's death," Keegan declared. "Not on purpose, at least."

"It doesn't matter if you believe that," Jerrod reminded him. "Or even if I believe it. It only matters if Scythe believes it.

"If we ask her about Norr, she might start looking for reasons he is gone. She might stumble down this same road of thinking. She might decide you are to blame. And she might decide you must pay with your life."

"She wouldn't do that," Keegan said, though he didn't sound as confident as he'd hoped.

"It's a chance I'm not willing to take," Jerrod concluded. "Scythe is strong; I believe her spirit will return in time."

"Do we really have the luxury to just wait and see?" Keegan asked, still not willing to let it rest.

Jerrod considered the matter for several seconds before replying.

"You may be right," he conceded. "If Scythe has not shown any change or improvement in the next few days, I will speak to her."

Satisfied, Keegan nodded his thanks.

"Get some sleep," the monk said. "Tomorrow might be a long day."

It didn't take more than a few minutes from when Keegan bedded down before he was snoring soundly.

Scythe was careful to keep her breathing steady as Keegan got up and went to speak to Jerrod, maintaining the illusion that she was sleeping peacefully. She wasn't tired; since taking up the Sword, she only needed an hour of sleep each night. But she'd rather pretend to be unconscious than have to deal with her traveling companions right now.

On the few occasions when she did sleep, she dreamed of Norr. Her mind kept taking her back to a time when he was still alive, to their days in Praeton, mostly. Scythe had often found the small village mind-numbingly dull, but now she longed for its simple pleasures. Even the boredom would be bearable if Norr were with her.

But he's not. He's gone.

Every time she woke up, there was a brief moment when she expected to roll over and see Norr snoring beside her. And then reality would come crashing in, and the pain would hit her, hard and fresh. In some small way, it felt like he was dying over and over again.

Scythe had never given much thought to what happened to a person after death. Many of the new religions spoke of some other world where the deceased would be reunited with those they loved in some kind of never-ending paradise. A nice thought, but one she found far too convenient to be credible.

The Order preached that those who died would become one with the Chaos Sea, the essence that ignited the spark of life slipping away to rejoin the universal whole from which the Old Gods themselves had been born. There was something appealing in that theory—death as a release from everything, including your own sense of existence. And maybe someday she'd embrace such a fate. But for now she still welcomed the pain of Norr's memory. It was all she had left of him, and she wasn't about to give that up for eternal oblivion quite yet.

She continued to lie perfectly still as Keegan came back and lay down on the other side of the smoldering peat fire, maintaining the ruse until the young man started snoring softly. Despite their precautions, she'd overheard every word he and Jerrod had said about her; thanks to the Sword, all her senses had been unnaturally heightened.

The idea that Norr's death was due to backlash from Keegan's spell was nothing new to her. But she hadn't considered the possibility that Keegan had intentionally directed the backlash at her lover. Even if he had, though, it didn't change anything.

Norr had given his life because he truly believed Keegan was some kind of savior. Looking at him now, it was hard to see. He was thin to the point of being frail. His black hair and dark, sunken eyes contrasted with his skin to make it look white as the snow that surrounded them; his cheeks were so smooth and hairless that he looked more like a boy than a real man.

And he only has one hand!

Despite all this, however, Scythe couldn't allow herself to have any doubts about his destiny. Or hers. She'd seen Keegan's power, but that wasn't what sustained her faith. The only way Norr's death made any sense, the only way it had any meaning or purpose at all, was if Jerrod was right. For the sake of Norr's memory, Scythe was willing to buy into the mad monk's prophecy, no matter how many times he changed the details around. She was determined to see this through to the end, no matter what the cost.

I'll follow you to Callastan while you try to convince Cassandra to join us. If she refuses, I'll cut her down with the Sword and put the Crown on my own head if that's what it takes.

And in the end, if you decide the only way to save the world is for me and Keegan to sacrifice ourselves, then that's what's going to happen. And if Keegan isn't willing to pay that price, I'll be happy to send him on his way.

Norr had been the noblest, most generous, kindest man she had ever known, and now he was gone. He was a better person than she was; he was better than any of them. If he had to die for the cause, then why shouldn't she? Why shouldn't Keegan? Why shouldn't anybody—or everybody—else have to die, too?

She was no prophet; even armed with the Sword she hadn't started having cryptic dreams or visions. At night all she saw were memories of a time when Norr was still alive. But somehow she knew this already tragic quest wouldn't end without more blood-shed. And she was willing, even eager, to watch the crimson rivers flow.

Chapter 2

VAALER AND SHALANA were among the earliest to arrive for the scheduled meeting of the clan chiefs; only Roggen was there before them. Vaaler wasn't surprised; the newly acclaimed leader of the Sun Blades was usually the first one there.

The meeting hall was a temporary construction of hides stretched over a bone framework in the middle of the various tribal camps scattered around the Giant's Maw. There was no hearth to warm the interior; inside it was cold enough that Vaaler could see his breath. But at least the structure kept out the wind and provided shelter from the seemingly constant snowfall.

Roggen stood in the far corner of the tent, still and calm and apparently oblivious to the cold. He was clad in typical Eastern garb: high, heavy boots; a knee-length hide skirt; and a sleeveless vest that left his muscular arms bare. His thick black beard and long, wild hair gave him a brutish appearance, but Vaaler knew there was a refined intelligence behind his rough exterior.

Shalana and Vaaler were similarly dressed, though Vaaler had also thrown a cloak of sewn fur pelts over his shoulders to try to stay warm. Shalana's pale skin and auburn hair—bound in a long braid that hung over the front of her right shoulder—were common among the clans, but Vaaler would never have been mistaken for a native, even if he wasn't always wearing extra layers against the cold. Although as tall as Shalana, he was thin and wiry—a stark contrast to the burly, barrel-chested physique so common in the East. His skin, like all of the Danaan, had a faint greenish brown hue, and despite not shaving for weeks, his cheeks were still bare save for a wispy line of hair along the length of his jaw.

And yet, Vaaler felt more at home among these people than he ever had among his own kind. Roggen and the other chiefs accepted and respected him, and if anyone resented his relationship with Shalana, they were smart enough not to say anything around him . . . or her.

"Are you certain about this?" Roggen asked, coming over to clasp Shalana's forearm by way of greeting.

"You sound like you're expecting trouble," Vaaler noted.

"Not everyone will be pleased with what you have to say."

"It needs to be said," Shalana insisted, and Roggen nodded his agreement.

This was not the first meeting of the clan chiefs since the final battle against the Danaan, though Vaaler knew this one would not be like the others. In the week since the enemy had been routed, the leaders of all the clans had met every evening to share news and make plans for what should be done next. The newly formed alliances between former rivals were still strong, and so far they had been able to act with consensus in the aftermath of their costly victory.

There's still a common enemy that wants to wipe them out. Like the Danaan, the brutal winter has united the chiefs.

The massive casualties suffered during the campaign against Vaaler's former people had taken a harsh toll on every clan. Supplies were low, as was the number of able-bodied men and women capable of scouring the surrounding plains and nearby peaks for game. Even Terramon had agreed they should all work together and try to ride out the winter as a group here in the Giant's Maw.

It shows how desperate our situation is, Vaaler realized, *when even Shalana's father thinks cooperation is the only option.*

One by one the other clan chiefs and their advisers began to arrive, slowly filling the makeshift tent, the heat of their bodies in the enclosed space gradually bringing the temperature up. Vaaler studied them carefully, trying to gauge their respective moods as they entered.

Most still looked to Shalana as their unofficial leader, a role she had seized—with Vaaler's help—during the war against the Danaan. But as the focus of the chiefs switched from battle strategies and tactics to more mundane concerns, he'd begun to sense a subtle shift in their allegiance toward Roggen.

Shalana hadn't tried to fight it; in fact, she was more than happy to concede the role to him. For the past decade, Roggen had effectively been in charge of the Sun Blades, the largest and most powerful clan in the Frozen East. While he had deferred to the venerable Hadawas on larger decisions, he had been the one overseeing the day-to-day lives of his people.

At her core, Shalana was a warrior. She knew how to fight and how to rally her thanes to her cause. But Roggen was far better equipped than she was to handle the logistics of finding food, treating the sick and wounded, and making more permanent shelters that could withstand the inevitable blizzards that would threaten to bury them in ice and snow. And if any disputes did arise among the chiefs, he was far more experienced in the subtle politics of leadership than she was.

The clans will be in good hands when we leave, Vaaler assured himself. Knowing that helped calm him somewhat though he still felt anxious about what was to come.

Beside him, Shalana gave his hand a reassuring squeeze.

Is my nervousness so obvious? he wondered. *Or does she just know me that well already?*

"It's time," she whispered, releasing her grasp on his hand and stepping forward into the small circle that had naturally formed at the center of the crowd. Vaaler took a deep breath and silently wished his love luck in what was about to come.

Shalana let her eyes drift around the room before she spoke, taking in the twenty-odd faces. The assembled chiefs and a handful of their most trusted advisers—the recently united leaders of the Frozen East—waited patiently for her to begin. To her relief, she didn't see her father among the crowd. Before she could begin, however, one more figure slipped in through the meeting hall's entrance at the last second.

Terramon didn't offer her any apology for being late. Without a word or a glance at any of the others, he bumped and shuffled his way toward the front of the assemblage. Shalana noted Vaaler shooting him a sour glance, and she sighed inwardly.

Despite no longer having any official title, her father was still recognized and respected—though not necessarily trusted or liked—by virtually all the clans. His presence at the meetings of the clan chiefs was a nod to his reputation though he didn't always attend.

Of course he's here tonight. He always has to make things difficult.

She had been hoping Terramon would skip this meeting; she suspected things would go much easier if he weren't here. But there was no point in holding off; Vaaler was already worried they had waited too long.

"Welcome, my thane-chiefs," Shalana called out once the audience had settled back down after her father's late entrance. "I know you are all eager to hear the reports from the hunting parties we have sent out. Soon enough I will turn the floor over to Roggen, who has been coordinating their efforts.

"But first," she continued, "there is something we must tell you."

She paused, and cast a quick glance back toward Vaaler, who nodded his encouragement.

"As you all know, Vaaler was vital in our victory over the Danaan invaders. Without him, none of us would be here right now."

Her words elicited a spontaneous burst of cheers from the crowd, and she couldn't help but smile. Vaaler was no longer an Outlander; he had become a hero to her people. Which made what she was about to say all the more difficult.

"But Vaaler didn't come to the clans to warn us against the Treefolk. He, along with Norr and their companions, came to seek the aid of the Stone Spirits in something far greater.

"Long ago, a great evil rose up," Shalana explained, "a tyrant named Daemron the Slayer. He unleashed the horrors of the Chaos Spawn, and caused a Cataclysm that nearly destroyed the world.

"Now, after centuries of banishment, the Slayer threatens to return. That is why Norr and Vaaler first came to us: They seek a way to defeat him once and for all."

An awkward silence had fallen over the room as the thanes tried to wrap their heads around what she was telling them.

"The war against the Danaan is over," she continued, plunging forward. "But there is another war that must still be fought. And the clans must still be a part of it."

At first nobody spoke out though she could hear grumblings of confusion and discontent from the crowd. And then Terramon gave voice to what she knew many of the thanes were thinking.

"We have enough real problems to overcome without worrying about myths and legends," her father declared.

"How can you say that after what happened on the battlefield?" Shalana demanded, looking to quash her father's argument before others joined him. "You saw the Guardian give his life to save us! You know the legends are real. We've seen the proof."

There was a murmur of assent among the crowd. The image of

the magnificent, blue-skinned titan emerging from the mountains to grapple with the monstrous ogre was one none of them would soon forget.

"Even if some of the legends are real," Terramon argued, refusing to back down, "that does not change anything. Winter is here. The only enemies we must concern ourselves with are frostbite and starvation!"

"You cannot turn a blind eye to this," Vaaler warned, joining in the conversation. "The ogre slaughtered too many of your people to pretend the threat is not real."

"The ogre was born in the forests of the Treefolk," Terramon countered. "And the Guardian was a remnant from a forgotten age. They may have fought in our lands, but they had no place here. And now they are both gone—vanished like the ghosts of ancient history that they were."

"The ogre was not the first Chaos Spawn to rise," Vaaler warned. "And it won't be the last. Before I left my people, I saw a dragon awaken and level an entire city before it was slain."

"You only prove my point!" Terramon shouted. "The prophecy you and Norr follow came from the Order. You let your actions be guided by the blind monks who rule the Southlands, and you brought war to your people . . . and ours! How many more of us must die for their cause?

"We've already been drawn into someone else's war once," he reminded them. "Are we fools enough to let it happen again?"

"Hadawas understood the danger Shalana and Vaaler speak of," Roggen said, openly siding with them before any of the other thanes could speak. "He alone among us had the ability to see the future though his visions were faint and dim. Yet he knew a time of great upheaval was coming.

"That is why he called the Conclave. That is why he joined Norr and the others in their search for Daemron's Sword after learning of their quest. He understood that the Slayer's return will bring another Cataclysm upon the world, and the clans will suffer just as much as those in the North and the South."

"Even the bravest warriors can grow weary of battle," Shalana admitted, openly acknowledging what they all felt. "But a new threat is coming. If we ignore it with the excuse of trying to survive this winter, then none of us will live to see another."

Shalana paused, scanning the faces of the thanes in a desperate attempt to gauge their reactions. She feared she would see disbelief or scorn, but what she saw instead was concern and fear.

"What would you have us do?" a voice called out from somewhere in the back.

"The Guardian spoke to us before he died," Shalana told them. "He said he had given Daemron's Sword to Norr and the others. They are headed for Callastan now, in search of another who will join forces with them to defeat the Slayer. But they will not succeed without our help."

"What kind of help could we even give?" Terramon wondered bitterly. "The war with the Danaan has left us with nothing to spare."

"Vaaler has been part of this from the beginning," Shalana explained. "His fate is tied to those who will stop Daemron's return. We must escort him through the Southlands so that he may rejoin his friends."

"The journey will be dangerous," Vaaler admitted. "But I cannot make it alone. There are too many enemies between me and my friends. The Order is hunting them ... and possibly me as well."

"This is madness," Terramon mocked. "If we march into the Southlands, they will see it as an act of war! With our numbers so low, we wouldn't stand a chance against their united armies!"

"Sending an invading army would be suicide," Vaaler admitted. "But a small group moving quickly might be able to make it to Callastan with minimal resistance."

"All we are asking for is a dozen warriors to accompany us," Shalana said.

"You're going with him?" Terramon said, shaking his head in disbelief. "I thought my own flesh and blood would have more sense than to throw her life away."

His disapproving, disgusted tone was one Shalana was all too familiar with; she'd heard it all her life. But it no longer held any power over her, and she didn't even bother to respond.

"We can spare supplies for the first part of the journey," Roggen chimed in. "Enough for Shalana and her honor guard to reach the Southlands. After that, they will have to get by on what they can find for themselves."

"Roggen will stay behind to guide you through this winter," Shalana added. "Unless there is one among you who feels you can do better than he."

Not surprisingly, nobody came forward, though Terramon glared sullenly at the crowd as if he was trying to will one of them to step up.

"As Vaaler already told you," Shalana said, "the journey to Callastan will be dangerous. We are much more likely to find death than victory. But though the risk is great, we must make the attempt: The fate of the clans—of the entire world—hangs in the balance.

"We will leave tomorrow," Shalana continued. "After this meeting, go to your thanes and your clans and tell them what must be done. If any of your warriors wish to join our cause, they are welcome . . . though they must understand there is a good chance they will never return."

The morning of their departure was clear but bitterly cold. Shalana had expected their escort to be made up mostly of Stone Spirit warriors, but to her surprise nearly fifty men and women—

some from virtually every clan at the Giant's Maw—had volunteered to join them. Selecting only twelve from among them—seven men and five women—had been difficult, but fortunately the high turnout had allowed them to choose those with the courage and skill to give them the best chance of success.

Despite the cold and the early-morning hour, a massive crowd of men, women, and children had gathered to see them off, including Roggen and the other chiefs. Even Terramon was there, leaning on his cane and scowling at everyone.

Two small sleds had been loaded with supplies: hides and blankets to wrap themselves in when they camped each night; several bricks of peat they could burn to ward off the cold; and enough food to get them to the edge of the Southlands.

After that, the sleds won't be much use, Shalana thought. *We'll have to abandon them.*

The hope was that they'd be able to find enough supplies to keep going once they reached the more populated regions. Exactly how that was supposed to happen was something they hadn't yet figured out. Sort of like how they planned to get through hundreds of miles of hostile territory without being arrested or killed.

Vaaler was confident they would find a way to succeed. Shalana trusted him enough to believe the same thing despite all evidence to the contrary.

And everyone coming with us believes enough in me to follow my lead.

The honor guard were making the final preparations to the sleds; it was time to move out. From the crowd, Roggen stepped forward and held up a hand for silence.

"We are gathered here to wish good fortune on Shalana and Vaaler," he called out, his voice rising clearly in the cold, crisp air of the morning. "Together, they defied impossible odds and led us to victory when all seemed lost."

He paused, and a loud cheer rose from the crowd. Shalana

raised a hand to acknowledge their support though she couldn't help but notice Terramon standing motionless and silent at the front of the throng.

"Hadawas, Norr, and the others have forged ahead," Roggen continued. "Now these brave warriors must join them, for their destiny lies far to the South."

Roggen stepped forward to clasp first Vaaler, then Shalana by the forearm. When he spoke again, his voice was lower, his words meant not for the crowd but for them.

"Every winter must give way to spring. When the ice melts, we will be here, waiting for your return."

Neither Vaaler nor Shalana replied; everything that needed to be spoken had already been said. Roggen nodded, then turned away and retreated back into the crowd.

Before Shalana could give the signal for their escort to move out, Terramon stepped forward, his cane angrily stabbing into the snow-covered earth with every step.

"What does he want now?" she heard Vaaler hiss beside her ear, but she forced herself to remain calm.

The argument is over. We've won. Nothing he can say will change my mind.

Terramon kept coming forward, stopping only when he was directly in front of her. Then, leaning heavily on his cane, he reached out with his free hand and gripped her firmly by the shoulder.

"I still think this is madness," he told her. But he wasn't speaking loud enough to address the crowd; this wasn't some final political speech.

"Be careful among the Outlanders," he added, much to her surprise. "They are Barbarians with no honor."

"I will," she said, slightly taken aback.

"Look to Vaaler to guide you; he knows their ways. If anyone can keep you safe and bring you back, he can."

"We will look after each other," Vaaler promised, speaking up at her side.

Terramon nodded, but his hand kept its grip on her shoulder.

"You are my daughter," he added after a brief hesitation. "No matter what happens, never forget that."

And then he let his hand drop, pivoted on his cane, and quickly stomped off to disappear into the crowd. Stunned, Shalana watched him go in silence, trying to decide if she had caught a brief glimpse of a tear in his eye in the instant before he turned away.

"I guess that's his way of saying he's proud of you," Vaaler said softly once he was gone.

"I guess so," Shalana agreed.

With a final look over the faces of her people—faces she might never see again—she gave the signal and she, Vaaler, and their chosen dozen set out into the snow.

Chapter 3

"Pay attention, Cassandra."

Rexol's voice was low but firm. The Chaos mage loomed over her, a little blond girl with emerald-green eyes dwarfed by his tall, lean frame. His dark skin and cloak made him appear little more than a shadow in the flickering light of the lone candle that lit the small, circular room. His long black hair was tied in uneven braids that draped haphazardly over his forehead and shoulders. Only his bright white teeth—filed to points— and his wide, wild eyes stood out in the gloom.

"Look at the symbols on the floor," he instructed, and Cassandra cast her eyes downward. At her feet, a series of circles of varying sizes over-lapped each other. Inside each one was an unfamiliar rune.

"You must learn to read the words of power before you can bend Chaos to your will."

Though she was only a child, Cassandra knew he wasn't speaking the entire truth. The runes were only a mnemonic device; they helped create patterns of thought that allowed the mind to properly focus. But the true power to control Chaos came from within.

"Don't be so stubborn, child," Rexol told her even though she hadn't spoken her doubts aloud. "The Crown is too powerful to use without proper training. Let me help you."

"No!" Cassandra shouted, the sound of her own voice inside the dream snapping her awake.

Cassandra's blind eyes sprang open, an instinctive reflex that served no real purpose. The world of her dream quickly fell away as her supernatural awareness filled in the missing pieces of her surroundings. She was tucked under the covers of a small bed, her legs splinted and bandaged. A low fire burned in one corner of the room, a single desk and writing table stood in another. The Crown lay on the mattress beside her, hidden from view by the plain sack she had carried it in since fleeing the Monastery.

The only door to her chamber was closed, though in her mind's eye she could clearly see Methodis, the bookish healer who was caring for her, puttering around in the apothecary that stood on the other side. He moved with purposeful calm, checking the inventory of vials and jars that lined the many shelves.

He's going to steal the Crown! Rexol's voice warned her, speaking inside her head.

Cassandra ignored him. Had Methodis truly wanted the Talisman, he could have easily taken it when he first found her, unconscious in the rubble at the center of the earthquake Rexol had caused when the mad wizard had tried to possess her body to escape his imprisonment inside the Crown.

I saved you, Rexol protested. *I was the one who turned the Crawling Twins against each other. If not for me, they would have ripped you to shreds.*

"And then you almost wiped Callastan off the map when the Crown overwhelmed you," Cassandra whispered, abandoning her efforts to ignore him.

But you are stronger than me, Rexol countered. *I understand Chaos in ways the Order never could. I can teach you how to master your power. And the Crown.*

Instead of continuing the argument, Cassandra thought back on her dream. It wasn't a memory—not a real one, at least. The Order had saved her from Rexol when she was only six, but in the dream she had been older; nine or ten at least. And in the dream she still had her brilliant emerald eyes rather than the pure white orbs that signified Cassandra's willing sacrifice when she gave up her vision to gain the Order's mystical second sight.

I was showing you what could have been, Rexol insisted. *What should have been if you hadn't been stolen away from me.*

"Is this how you're going to try to control me now?" she demanded. "Through my dreams?"

Rexol didn't reply, and a second later there was a knock at the door. With her awareness, Cassandra clearly saw Methodis on the other side, waiting patiently for her to respond. In one hand he held a cup filled with a thick, cloudy liquid. Tucked under his opposite arm was a roll of cloth similar to the bandages binding the splints on her legs.

"Come in," she called out.

"I hope I'm not disturbing you," Methodis said as he opened the door and stepped into the room. "But I heard you talking, so I deduced you were awake."

He didn't bother asking her who she was talking to, despite there being no one else in the room.

Have I been speaking to Rexol often? she wondered. Though she felt clearheaded now, much of the last few days was still hazy. It was possible he'd heard her carry on her one-sided conversations many times. *He must think I'm mad. Or fevered from my injuries.*

Out loud she asked, "How long have I been here?"

"Nine days have passed since I found you in what was left of the jail," the healer replied as he crossed the room and set the cup down on the table beside her bed, just a few inches from the cloth sack containing the Crown.

He has a limp, Rexol pointed out, sounding almost jealous. *Faint, but noticeable. An old injury that never properly healed.*

If he's hiding that, the wizard pressed, *what else is he keeping from you? What other deceptions will he try?*

Cassandra recognized his paranoid ramblings for what they were and didn't acknowledge them.

The healer took a seat on the edge of her bed and set the bandages down beside him, being careful not to jostle or disturb his patient any more than was absolutely necessary.

"I can't believe I've been here nine days already," Cassandra remarked. Based on what she remembered, she would have guessed three or four at most.

"I gave you something to help dull the pain," Methodis explained, pointing at the mug of opaque liquid on the little table. "You spent much of that time asleep."

"You kept me here the entire time? Looked after me?"

He nodded.

"Does anyone else know I'm here?"

"Perhaps," he answered, "but not because of anything I have done. I took you from the jail wrapped in a sheet. I did the same with the remains of the guards. The people in the neighborhood think there were no survivors.

"But if the Order is looking for you," he continued, "you would know better than I if they could track you here."

The Order aren't the only ones looking for you, Rexol reminded her.

Though she didn't bother to answer, she knew it was true. The Crawling Twins weren't the only Minions of the Slayer that had crossed over to the mortal realm. The shadowy huntress that had stalked her through the Frozen East could still be looking for her. There might even be others.

"It isn't safe for me to stay," she said, struggling to rise despite the splints on her legs.

Methodis stopped her with a gentle hand on her arm.

"You are in no condition to go anywhere," he reminded her, nodding in the direction of her splints. "You need to lie still."

I will keep you hidden, Rexol assured her. *I've used the Crown to set up a maze of false trails throughout the city. If you let me, I can show you how to do the same.*

The trails didn't fool the Crawling Twins, Cassandra reminded him. *Sooner or later, one of the other Minions will come searching for me.*

I can teach you how to use the Crown to destroy them! Rexol reminded her.

"I'd like to check the injuries to your legs," Methodis said, breaking the silence of the room left by her inner monologue. "To make sure they are healing properly."

Cassandra nodded, and the little man smiled reassuringly.

"I'll try to be careful," Methodis warned her, "but this may hurt. Your injuries were severe."

Reaching out slowly, he began to unwrap the bandages that bound her left leg to its splint. His touch was gentle, but practiced and sure, and it didn't take him long to unwrap the dressing and expose the limb.

"This is . . . unexpected," he said once he was finished, clearly perplexed.

"Is something wrong?"

"Far from it. You are healing far better than I could have hoped for." From his tone, Cassandra knew there was more he wasn't saying.

"Isn't that a good thing?"

Methodis hesitated briefly before replying.

"Your injuries were extensive. Your skin was nothing but black-and-purple splotches. The bones of your legs weren't just broken; they had basically been shattered. The tendons and muscles were mangled and crushed, as if some great force had slammed into your legs over and over. I've never seen anything like it."

He knows you caused the earthquake! Rexol shouted in warning.

No, you caused it, Cassandra snapped back. *I stopped you.*

"I did my best to set and splint them," Methodis continued, unaware of the silent debate raging inside his patient's thoughts, "but I feared you would never walk properly again . . . if at all.

"But the bones are already mending, and the bruising is almost completely gone."

"Then my recovery is a tribute to your talents," Cassandra suggested.

The old doctor shook his head.

"This has nothing to do with me," he insisted. "I've heard tales of the Order's physical prowess. Rumors of unbelievable speed and strength. Incredible stamina. Remarkable healing powers. But I never imagined anything like this."

This is not just because of the Order's teachings, Rexol chimed in. *It's the Crown. You're instinctively drawing on its power.*

"How much longer until I can walk again?" Cassandra asked, ignoring the wizard.

"I really can't say," Methodis admitted. "If you continue to heal at this rate, another week or two, perhaps."

I don't have that much time, Cassandra thought, recalling something Methodis had told her the first time she had regained consciousness under his care. The Order was descending on the city. Even now, she suspected, Yasmin would have Inquisitors scouring the streets looking for her.

You could be fully healed in a few days if you embrace your full potential, Rexol reminded her. *All you have to do is let me teach you.*

"I can't stay here," Cassandra told him. "You've put yourself in great danger by taking me in. If the Order discovers what you've done, you will be burned at the stake as a heretic."

"If defying the Order makes one a heretic, the Pontiff will have to burn down the entire city," he replied with a shrug.

"What do you mean?"

"When the Pontiff declared her Purge, Callastan refused to bow down," he said, an unmistakable hint of pride in his voice. "Too many of us remember the last time. The senseless executions. The mindless fear that turned neighbors against each other.

"For all its failings, Callastan at least has the courage to defy the

Pontiff. When she declared the Purge, we responded by exiling all her followers."

"I thought the earthquake changed all that," Cassandra said. "When I woke up the first time, you told me the city was in ruins. You said there were riots in the streets. You told me the Order was coming to claim what was left of the city."

"I feared the worst," Methodis admitted. "Callastan is a mosaic of every sin and vice you could imagine. But despite this, or possibly because of it, there is a strength among its people. From the corrupt rulers to the ruthless crime lords all the way down to the cunning pickpockets who work the crowds at the market, all the citizens share one single trait: They do not bow down easily to authority.

"That is the reason the Enforcers police our streets. Yet even armed soldiers on every corner cannot fully keep the fiery spirit of Callastan's people in check."

"I thought the Enforcers used fear and violence to dominate the lower classes," Cassandra noted, recalling her lessons from the Monastery.

"There is some truth in that," Methodis admitted, "but in this city they are a necessary evil. Without them, the streets would run red with blood.

"And as unpopular as they are, the Order is even more so," he continued. "When word spread that the Pontiff's followers were coming, the ranks of the Enforcers tripled overnight as the nobles and the underworld set aside their differences and banded together against a common foe."

"An inspiring tale," Cassandra said grimly, "but in the end it won't matter. Even together, they are no match for the Pontiff and her Inquisitors. Not with the armies of the rest of the Southlands at her back."

"That may be true," the old man conceded. "But for now, the mere threat of resistance has kept the Order at bay. They are gathering outside the city; their numbers growing day by day. Yet so far they have not even dared to approach our walls."

Cassandra was puzzled by Yasmin's strategy. Callastan was a port city; laying siege to it was futile if the Order couldn't control the docks.

What is she waiting for?

You overestimate the Pontiff's power, Rexol told her. *Your mind is clouded by years of indoctrination inside the Monastery walls. The Order is not what it used to be.*

"Eventually their numbers will be enough that they will attack," Methodis said, as if he were privy to her and Rexol's private conversation. "But fortunately that day is not here yet."

"I have to leave before that day comes," Cassandra insisted.

"Then you need all the rest you can get right now," he said, handing her the cup.

Knowing he was right, Cassandra drank the murky liquid down as he began rewrapping her splints. It was bitter and so thick she felt it coating her tongue and throat, but there was no denying how effective it was: By the time the doctor was finished dressing her wounds, she was fast asleep.

"Pay attention," Rexol admonished her, *"it is the only way you will learn . . ."*

Chapter 4

LIKE ALL THE Pontiff's senses, her olfactory awareness was acutely heightened. Even camped a mile beyond the town walls, Yasmin could still smell the foul stench of Callastan on the night breeze blowing in from the sea. With each breath the stink of docks and sewers wafted up into her nostrils, mingling with the putrid stench of the vile city's moral corruption.

Sitting cross-legged in the middle of her otherwise empty tent, she couldn't help but think about how much she longed for another smell: the acrid aroma of smoke and fire as the Southlands' greatest abomination went up in flames. The city had long been a thorn in the Order's side, its defiance of their official proclamations teetering on the verge of open rebellion for decades.

Nazir should have wiped this place from the map long ago.

Now the task fell to her. Unlike her predecessor, however, the Order she ruled over was a tattered remnant of what it once had been. The attack on the Monastery had wiped out well over half their numbers. In the months since then, too many others had been lost or scattered in the hunt for the Crown and the other Talismans.

She no longer had the numbers simply to overrun the defenses of the city, not without help. The new Purge had brought others into the fold: soldiers and mercenaries under the command of nobles who were loyal to the cause. Many—but not nearly all—of these had joined her here on the plains just outside Callastan over the past week, their tents and campfires spreading in a long, thin line that ran parallel to the city walls. Each day more soldiers arrived from the Southlands, trickling in to slowly swell the ranks of her army. But she would gladly trade any fifty of them for a dozen more Inquisitors.

We must work with the tools we are given, she reminded herself.

Of the hundred-odd surviving members of the Order, fourscore had already answered her call to come to Callastan. A dozen of those had slipped secretly inside Callastan's walls, calling on their divine power to alter the appearance of their pure white eyes so they could blend in with the scum of the city. A few wandered the streets seeking out Cassandra and the Crown, but most—as per Yasmin's orders—were stationed by the docks in case the heretic tried to flee.

She has to know we are out here, gathering our forces.

The Pontiff had hoped the mere presence of her underwhelming army might be enough to flush Cassandra out of whatever hole she was hiding in. If she tried to escape the city by ship, her agents at the docks would be waiting. But the girl was cunning; so far she had the sense to simply wait them out, hiding behind the walls of the city and the might of the Enforcers.

If Carthin's troops were here, we wouldn't have to play this game.

As if on cue, she sensed Xadier approaching her tent, his second sight allowing him to cross the uneven ground smoothly in the black night. Over the past weeks the head of the Order's Seers had effectively come to serve as her administrative right hand, handling communications and logistics for the ever-growing army of loyal followers as the Purge spread across the Southlands.

There was something anxious and urgent about his gait, and Yasmin could already tell he was not coming to deliver good news.

He lacks proper discipline; he must learn to control his emotions. Or at least how to hide his true feelings from others.

Though capable enough at his job, Xadier was young and inexperienced. With the ranks of the Order so thin, Yasmin had been forced to promote him before he was ready.

We must work with the tools we are given, she reminded herself for a second time.

She rose to her feet as he reached the entrance to her tent, ushering him in with a subtle nod.

"You bring word from Lord Carthin?" she guessed.

"Yes, Pontiff. He sends his most sincere apologies for not answering sooner. He claims the first dispatches you sent did not reach him."

In the wake of the earthquake that had rocked Callastan, Xadier had sent several messenger falcons out with detailed instructions to all of Yasmin's Inquisitors and generals across the Southlands. Within three days she had received replies from everyone save Lord Carthin.

For centuries the Order had been using a network of trained birds and couriers on horseback to communicate quickly with their agents and followers in and around the Seven Capitals. And while there were occasions where the avian messengers ran afoul of some misfortune before reaching their destination, such incidents were extremely rare.

Still, she had been willing to give Carthin the benefit of the doubt; he was in the field of battle, and it was possible an enemy had intercepted the message. Hearing no response after three days, she had dispatched another bird. Only this one was sent to one of the Order's aeries close to where Carthin's army was stationed. From there, a courier had delivered her message in person. The process was slower, of course—no rider could travel as swiftly as the tireless falcons—but it was more reliable.

"But now that he knows my wishes, his army is on the way?" Yasmin asked.

"Hopefully within the next few days, Pontiff," Xadier replied.

"Hopefully?" she said, raising an eyebrow and tilting her bald head down and to the side, almost as if she was displaying the burns and scars of her scalp in a show of anger.

"Lord Carthin feels the rebels near Norem still pose a threat," Xadier hastily explained. "He claims they are hiding several practitioners of the Chaos arts around the city."

Lord Carthin of Brindomere had been the first noble of any real rank to take up the cause when she declared her Purge. Ruler of the largest of the Seven Capitals, his troops had been instrumental in quelling the first stages of resistance in the heart of the Southlands. For his loyalty, Yasmin had given him the title of Justice of the Order—a position he had pursued with zeal and vigor. Yet, like Xadier's, it was a title she had granted out of necessity rather than merit.

"I thought Norem surrendered to him weeks ago," Yasmin noted, recalling the message of the last falcon Carthin had sent her way.

"Officially, yes," Xadier agreed. "But Justice Carthin fears they will resume their heretical ways if he removes his troops from the city before hunting down those enemies still in hiding."

Yasmin was no fool. Carthin was a devout follower of the True Gods, but he was also a cold, calculating opportunist. He understood all too well that by the ancient laws, a portion of any lands and property he seized on behalf of the Order fell to him. Driven by the twin inspirations of religious duty and material greed, he had rooted out and ruthlessly crushed any and all he could find who were foolish enough to oppose the Purge. Fear of the new Justice's wrath had convinced a number of other powerful nobles to swear their loyalty—and their armies—to Yasmin.

Without Carthin's efforts, the Purge would have quickly lost much of its momentum. But at the same time, Carthin was quick to seize the coffers and take on the soldiers and mercenaries of his fallen rivals, increasing his own wealth and influence even as he spread the Pontiff's holy message.

"He knows I have declared that all of our secular forces must rally here in Callastan? Did I not make it clear in the message that this must be our top priority now?"

"Yes, Pontiff. And he has promised to send his troops the instant he feels they can be safely withdrawn from Norem."

Carthin wasn't fool enough to openly defy the Pontiff, but he was clearly stalling.

He could ignore the falcon I sent his way, but he couldn't ignore an actual courier.

"Do you think he is afraid to face the Enforcers?" Xadier asked.

Callastan's Enforcers were little more than brutish thugs, a police force that was nearly as bad as the criminals it kept in line. But the zeal for violence that allowed them to be so effective in maintaining some semblance of order in the chaotic streets of Callastan also made them a formidable obstacle to any enemies of the city. Carthin wouldn't be the first commander to hesitate before sending his army against such a foe.

"Perhaps he is afraid," Yasmin conceded, before silently adding, *I hope that is all that is keeping him away.*

The alternatives were much more unpleasant. It was possible Carthin had become so focused on material wealth that he was using every trick he could think of to ignore her orders while continuing to plunder the soft targets of the Southlands for as long as possible. He wouldn't be the first to lose his religious devotion under a mountain of gold.

Yet there was an even-more-troubling scenario. Carthin's army had swallowed up so many soldiers and mercenaries that it now dwarfed any other force in the Southlands. Had the Justice of the Order become so emboldened by his victories that he believed he was powerful enough simply to ignore the Pontiff's wishes?

Fear of the Enforcers or a faltering in his religious devotion were failings Yasmin could forgive. A possible threat to her authority was not.

I don't have time to wait and see how this plays out. Every day we waste with Carthin's games is another day Cassandra might slip through my fingers!

"Perhaps I must go see Justice Carthin in person for him to understand the urgency of our situation," she suggested aloud.

She expected Xadier to oppose her, but to her surprise the Seer answered, "Of course, Pontiff. Shall I assemble some of the Inquisitors to escort you?"

He understands the situation better than I thought.

"We lack the numbers to effectively keep Callastan under siege as it is," she reminded him. "If I draw even a handful of Inquisitors away, their spies might learn of it and the Enforcers might decide we are vulnerable to a counterattack."

"Surely you aren't planning to face Carthin alone!" Xadier protested.

"Send word to those Inquisitors still out in the field," Yasmin told him. "The ones out searching for Jerrod and his followers. Tell them to meet me at the aerie near Norem."

"There are already rumors that some of the mercenaries who have joined our cause are using the Purge as an excuse to terrorize innocent villages and farms," Xadier cautioned. "Especially along the borderlands of the Frozen East.

"The presence of the Inquisitors in that region might be all that is keeping those soldiers from rampaging completely out of control. If we recall them—"

"I do not enjoy leaving devout followers of the True Gods at the mercy of murdering swine," Yasmin interrupted, her voice cold and hard. "But the Crown is in Callastan! Cassandra already used it once; the Legacy barely survived.

"What if she uses it again?" she demanded. "If the Legacy falls, the Slayer will return. And his legions will unleash death and destruction a hundred times worse than the damage wrought by a few roving bands of corrupt soldiers."

"Of course, Pontiff," Xadier said, bowing low and clasping his hands in front of his chest by way of apology. "You are right. As always."

"Send a falcon to Lord Carthin to tell him I am coming," Yasmin commanded. "He has much to explain, but after all he has done for us it is only fair we give him time to prepare his defense."

Orath focused his energies inward, calling on the night to wrap itself around him like a black cloak, shielding him from the awareness of the Pontiff and her kin. But even with their sight obscured, he was careful to give the army encamped on the plains outside Callastan a wide berth as he crept toward the city walls. The Chaos storm unleashed by the Crown had restored much of his fading power, but not enough to take on an entire army of Inquisitors by himself.

In the aftermath of the storm he'd felt revitalized, his reserves of Chaos replenished enough that he had fled the battle between the Danaan and the Eastern Barbarians on a chariot of wind. But a few hours into his flight he'd felt the toll the spell was taking, so he'd abandoned it and continued his journey on foot.

He didn't know which side had won the battle at the Giant's Maw; he didn't know how many warriors on both sides fell to the ogre's fury once it broke free of his control. None of that mattered to him now that he'd felt the Crown calling to him.

Fighting the urge to use his magic to race to Callastan had been difficult, but he knew it was the wise choice. If the Crawling

Twins had succeeded in their mission to claim the Crown, they would have brought the Talisman to him by now. At the very least they would have used their power to make contact with their leader. But too many days had passed in silence, and he knew that they had failed. The Chaos storm unleashed by the Crown— a storm so powerful Orath had felt it hundreds of miles away— had destroyed them.

Raven failed, too, Orath recalled. Like the Crawling Twins, she had been hunting the young woman carrying the Crown. Now she, too, was gone.

Daemron's ritual had sent seven of them through the Legacy. He had chosen them to be his Minions in the mortal world because they were the strongest, the smartest, the most cunning and most ruthless of his followers. But for all their power, only the leader of the seven was still alive.

These are not ordinary mortals we face, Orath reminded himself, his batlike features twisting into a scowl. *These are the Children of Fire. Daemron's essence flows through them. They have been touched by a God.*

He reached the city walls unnoticed. At the base he pressed himself close against the stone face and dug in with the claws of his long, thin fingers. The rock cracked and crumbled into dust at his touch, making holds he could use to lift himself upward, one hand at a time. He scaled the twenty-foot wall in seconds, a slithering shadow, then dropped down over the other side and onto the empty street.

Torches set high into the wall every hundred feet illuminated the surroundings, but only barely. He paused just long enough to be sure no one had noticed his entrance, but there was no hue and cry. The city was as still and silent as death itself.

Tilting his head to the side, he breathed deeply, inhaling the intoxicating aroma. Almost ten days had passed since the Crown's power had been unleashed, but the scent was still thick in the air—just as it had been in Ferlhame in the aftermath of the battle with the dragon.

No, it's different here. Clean. Pure.

The dragon's essence had polluted the Danaan capital. And as powerful as the Chaos Spawn had been, the creature's might was merely a faint echo of what was trapped within each Talisman. Here in Callastan, he only sensed the Crown.

Chaos in its most elemental form. The very substance of creation.

The Talisman was still here; he could feel it calling to him. Thrumming vibrations ran through the earth beneath his feet and up through his bones, faint but impossible to ignore.

If I can feel it, I can find it. Track the call to its source.

Orath paused, and a question sprang unbidden to his mind.

Even if you find it, then what?

Whoever controlled the Crown now—most likely the same young woman Raven and the Crawling Twins had tracked across the width and breadth of the mortal world—clearly had the power to snuff out his existence. Using the Talisman to destroy him might be the final blow that brought the Legacy tumbling down, but Orath had no desire to be a martyr. What value was there in helping Daemron return if he wasn't around to reap the benefits of his loyal service?

Finding the Crown, he realized, was the least of his worries. Seizing it without being blasted into oblivion was a much greater challenge. Particularly now that he was the only one of his kind left.

In Ferlhame, he'd tried to recruit the Danaan Queen to his cause. But even with her army under his control, he'd failed to claim the Ring. He'd underestimated his opposition and been forced to sacrifice Drago and Gort. And in the end, he'd still been forced to flee, empty-handed. This time he needed another plan. A better plan.

What would Daemron do?

As calculating and cunning as Orath was, he knew his master was even more so.

The Legacy is thin and fading. It might be possible to contact him.

Such a ritual would be both dangerous and costly, but perhaps it was also necessary.

From a nearby street he heard the sound of voices drawing near, and he cut off his internal debate. Pressing himself up against a nearby wall, his form melted into the shadows and he stood completely still.

A few seconds later two figures emerged from around the corner, speaking softly. Even in the dim light of the torches, Orath's yellow eyes could clearly make them out. The larger of the two was a young man. He wore a padded leather vest and an ill-fitting helmet, and a short club dangled from his belt. The second was a young woman, her tight-fitting clothes clean but worn. Her blouse was cut low, exposing ample cleavage.

"That's more than I make in a week, darling," the soldier pleaded, his tone both teasing and desperate.

"I'm worth every coin," she answered, her husky voice trailing off into a suggestive laugh.

The pair passed only a few feet away from his hiding place, completely unaware of the Minion lurking in the darkness. Once they were by, he emerged silently from the shadows and fell into step close behind them.

"C'mon, darling. Don't you have a discount for Enforcers? We're working hard to keep the city safe."

"Every man and his brother's an Enforcer now," she purred. "I start giving you all discounts and I'll be out of business."

Orath had decided the necessity of trying to reach his liege was worth the risk. He needed Daemron's council. But to power the ritual he'd use to reach across the Chaos Sea and make contact, he'd need a sacrifice to draw on.

"What if I give you half now?" the man offered. "And the rest next week?"

"By next week I might have joined the Enforcers myself," the girl countered. "Won't need your money then."

Drawing on the Chaos flowing through his veins, Orath uttered a single word to focus his power. Hearing him, the girl spun around.

Her eyes went wide on seeing the inhuman creature stalking her, and her mouth opened wide to scream. But Orath reached out with a single clawed finger, his arm striking like a snake, and touched her shoulder. Her features froze in place, the scream dying in her throat as every muscle in her body was instantly paralyzed.

The man was slower to react; he had only half turned by the time Orath's touch left him immobile.

Orath took a moment to savor the helpless terror of his victims, the girl's dark brown eyes darting back and forth in confusion and fear. Extending his arms out at a forty-five-degree angle, Orath let his wrists go limp so his long fingers dangled loose and free. He twiddled the fingers of his right hand and the girl's body shuddered. Then she slowly lifted her right foot and pivoted on her left leg so that she was facing away from him, a barely audible whimper of pain escaping her lips as she did so.

Wiggling the digits of his left hand, Orath forced the soldier to also turn away from him. Though physically stronger, he offered less resistance to the unspoken command than his companion.

Fingers flickering and dancing, Orath marched his puppets quickly down a side street where the shadows swallowed all three of them up.

Chapter 5

JERROD GLANCED UP at the sky, studying the fading light as dusk approached. The farther west he, Keegan, and Scythe traveled, the stronger his supernatural awareness became. They had left the Frozen East behind and crossed over into the Southlands, where he could once again feel the faint echoes of Chaos in the firmament of the mortal world that fueled his abilities. Yet though his Sight had returned, it couldn't block out the light and color bombarding his functioning eyes, and the double vision was still disorienting enough to leave him feeling queasy and off-balance.

Closing his eyes did little to solve the problem. Keeping his lids shut wasn't natural; it was something he had to think about constantly, and it drew focus away from his other perception. And even closed, his eyes still registered changes in the intensity of the outside world's light, drawing even more focus away from his otherworldly perception.

Even so, he was able to reach out far enough ahead of their path to sense they weren't going to find any traces of Southern civilization before nightfall. He'd been hoping they would at least stumble across an isolated farmhouse today, but Keegan's strength was fading and Jerrod had been forced to slow their pace to keep the young wizard from overexerting himself.

"We'll make camp here," the monk declared.

Nobody spoke as they settled in and finished off the last of the rations. As they'd been doing for the past week, both Jerrod and Scythe gave most of their share to Keegan.

He's so frail, Jerrod noticed. *If we don't find a farm or village soon, he might starve to death.*

The idea that the destiny of one of the Children of Fire could be snuffed out by something so mundane as a lack of food was unsettling.

After all we've overcome, and all we've lost, is this how it ultimately ends?

Jerrod shook his head and tried to push his doubts to the back of his mind. Keegan could still last a few more days before things became desperate.

"I'll take the first watch," the monk said, eager to focus on something else.

Neither of the others replied aloud though Keegan gave him a weary nod. Exhausted by the day's travel, the frail young mage fell asleep within minutes of bedding down. Scythe lay beside him, still and quiet. But even though most of Jerrod's focus was on the dark perimeter of their camp, he sensed she was still awake.

Once more doubts began to creep into the monk's head. But this time it was Scythe he fixated on.

Keegan's right; she's not herself anymore. It's like the spark of Chaos has been extinguished.

It had taken him a long time to see the truth, but at last he understood how important Scythe was. Now he finally understood the true meaning of the prophecy of the Burning Savior.

Jerrod wasn't a true prophet; he had trained as an Inquisitor while still a loyal servant of the Pontiff. But the prophets weren't the only members of the Order who dreamed; they were just the most proficient at it. Jerrod's visions were rare, and they usually had little import. Yet, twenty years ago, there had been one image so powerful it had shaped the course of his life over the next two decades.

A horde of Chaos Spawn, stampeding across the plains of the mortal world. At their head, Daemron the Slayer, driving his army ever forward, slaughtering and burning everything in their path. And then a figure rises from the ground to stand against them—a mortal surrounded by the blue flames of Chaos, features completely hidden by the smoke and fire.

He wasn't the only one who dreamed of the Burning Savior. Ezra—his mentor—had seen it, too. And he had carefully gathered others who had supported their cause; heretics who realized the Order had been wrong. Daemron would not be stopped by the Pontiff's efforts to limit and control Chaos. The Legacy was fading, and the Slayer's return was inevitable. The only hope was to find someone strong enough to stand against their ancient foe, one powerful enough to use Daemron's own Talismans against him, just as he had used them against the Old Gods.

Or so we thought. If only we had known.

For a while, Jerrod had believed Keegan to be the Burning Savior. Now, however, he understood why the identity of the figure in his visions had been obscured. There wasn't one savior, but three— just as there were three Talismans. It made perfect sense now that he knew what he was looking for. Keegan and Scythe were both born beneath the Blood Moon. They were both touched by Chaos. They were bound by it, a force so powerful it had inexorably drawn them together from the distant corners of the mortal realm. Now that Jerrod knew the truth, it was impossible not to see it.

Cassandra was born under a Blood Moon, too. When I brought her to Rexol as a little girl, he'd said she had more potential than any apprentice he had ever known.

The Order had taken her from Rexol before the mage could train her. Looking back, Jerrod understood that wasn't a setback but rather another piece falling into place. If Cassandra hadn't been inducted into the Order, she never would have come into possession of the Crown. It was almost as if the Talisman had drawn her in.

Chaos calls to its own. Like calling to like.

Now all he had to do was bring the three of them together. His path was clear.

And then what? a small voice wondered in the back of his head. *Do they just sit and wait for the Legacy to crumble so they can face Daemron when he returns? Do they do something to bring the Legacy crashing down so they can destroy him? Or was the vision more symbolic? Are they really supposed to meet Daemron on the field of battle, or are they supposed to stop Daemron by restoring the Legacy?*

Jerrod ignored the contrarian voice. Ezra had once told him it was okay to have doubts. Faith didn't give you all the answers. Not all at once. But if you were true in your beliefs, it would eventually show you the way.

Keep to the path and it will eventually all become clear. Cassandra is in Callastan. All I need to do right now is make sure Keegan and Scythe get there, too.

But would that really be enough? He didn't know what the future held, but he was certain they'd need Scythe to be more like her old self before all this was over. They needed her to get past Norr's death. And even though he still felt it was dangerous to bring the subject up with the volatile Islander, the consequences of doing nothing could be far worse.

"Scythe," he whispered, though Keegan probably wouldn't wake even if he shouted. "I know you're awake. Come with me. We need to talk."

The young woman rolled out of her blankets and stood up, instinctively picking up the Sword. She carried it casually in her right hand, mutely following Jerrod until they were out of Keegan's earshot. Her complete lack of protest only added to his concerns about her state—in the past she would at least have demanded to know more before she bothered to accompany him.

Jerrod hesitated, uncertain how to broach the delicate subject of Norr's death and how she was—or wasn't—coping. In the end, he decided the best option was simply to be blunt.

"I'm worried about you, Scythe. So is Keegan."

He paused, but when she didn't respond or react he continued.

"Since Norr's death you don't seem like yourself."

"You want me to try and attack you again?" she asked, her voice a dull monotone. "Would you be happier if I was ranting and raving instead of going along with your plan?"

"You never seemed to believe in my visions before," Jerrod noted.

"Now I do. You finally made me understand that I'm a part of this. Congratulations."

Her voice was still flat and lifeless, but her bitterness was clear. It actually gave Jerrod a glimmer of hope.

"You're part of this because Chaos flows in your blood," he reminded her. "At least, it used to. Now you've become passive. Withdrawn. Apathetic."

"You think I've given up?"

For the first time, there was a hint of emotion in her words, and the hand carrying Daemron's blade twitched ever so slightly. Encouraged by her reaction, Jerrod pressed on.

"I'm worried you may be doing this for the wrong reasons."

"Do the reasons even matter?" she wondered. "As long as I do what needs to be done, right?"

"I've known martyrs before," Jerrod said. "In some cases they were so eager to throw their lives away for a cause that they did more harm than good."

"Don't worry," Scythe said with a rueful smile. "I won't throw my life away until the time is right."

"I'm hoping that time won't ever come," Jerrod said.

"Keegan might believe we can save the world and all live happily ever after," she replied, "but I think we both know better."

Jerrod hesitated before replying, choosing his next words very carefully.

"Keegan isn't the only one who believed you can both survive this. So did Norr. He wouldn't want you to throw your life away now."

In an instant Scythe's blade was at his throat, her muscles quivering with barely suppressed rage. She moved so fast Jerrod didn't even have a chance to react.

"Don't you dare!" she hissed. "Norr's gone! What he wanted doesn't matter anymore!"

She pressed the edge of Daemron's Sword up against his throat, drawing a tiny line of blood. Jerrod stood perfectly still, knowing there was nothing he could do to stop her.

"The next time you try to use Norr's death to manipulate me," she warned, "Keegan won't be the only one missing a hand."

She stepped away and let the Sword drop back to her side.

"I'm not the one you should be worrying about, anyway," she added, reverting back to her emotionless monotone. "I'm willing to do whatever it takes to stop the Slayer. Can you say the same thing about Keegan?"

"He has more courage than you suspect," Jerrod insisted. He could feel the thin line of blood welling up on his throat but didn't bother to wipe it away.

"If Keegan must sacrifice himself to save the world," the monk continued, "I believe he will do the right thing."

"What if the cost is even higher?" Scythe demanded. "What if he has to sacrifice me?"

Her question caught Jerrod off guard. Keegan's feelings for Scythe were obvious. If he had to choose between saving her or fulfilling his destiny, would he hesitate? Would he make the wrong choice?

"I won't have any problem sacrificing for the cause," Scythe continued when he didn't reply. "Me, you, Keegan—whatever it takes. You just make sure Keegan feels the same way."

Jerrod nodded once, acknowledging the truth of what she said.

"I'll take over the watch," Scythe told him. "I'm sure you've got a lot to think about."

Andar walked quickly through the streets of Ferlhame, making mental note of the state of repairs and reconstruction as he passed. It would be years—maybe even decades—before all of the buildings that had fallen during the dragon's attack were rebuilt, but though there was still a long way to go, it was heartening to see that progress was being made.

Though we would be much farther along if the Queen hadn't led us into a war with the Eastern clans.

The High Sorcerer frowned; though accurate, those kinds of thoughts were counterproductive now. The Danaan people were still reeling from their crushing defeat, and many were bitter and resentful over what had happened—too many lives had been lost, and they had nothing to show for it. Despite this, however, Andar knew they still believed in their monarch. They still wanted guidance; they still wanted to follow her down the proper path.

But will she lead them?

As he reached the gates of the Royal Manse, the guards stepped aside and bowed. It wasn't long ago that Andar had been a prisoner accused of treason. But in the aftermath of their retreat from the battle at the Giant's Maw, much had changed.

During most of the campaign against the Eastern Barbarians, Rianna had been under the spell of Orath—the vile creature that had raised the ogre from the Black Lake. But the Minion had fled the battlefield when the tide of battle turned, and with his disappearance his hold over the Queen had been broken . . . though at a great cost.

Rianna had been unconscious, her mind withdrawing into itself once Orath released his hold, unable to wake or respond. As a result, the war council—five of the Queen's most trusted advisers—had invoked a state of regency so they could serve in her stead. As their first acts they had pardoned Andar, restored his position as High Sorcerer, and elected him as their leader. Even Lormilar, the man who had been named High Sorcerer after Andar had been deposed, voted for him.

They're good people. They only want what is best for the Danaan.

Or maybe, a small part of Andar's mind whispered, the direness of their situation had simply forced them to put aside any thoughts of political advancement or self-interest. Far too many Danaan had died in the final battle, but many more had been in danger of perishing during the long journey back to their homeland. The Frozen East had lived up to its name, as winter had buried the plains under snow and ice. Supplies had been critically low, and many of the troops who had survived the battle were badly wounded. Even those who were healthy had been exhausted and demoralized.

A bad turn in the weather would have devastated their ranks. A fierce blizzard could have reduced their numbers from thousands to hundreds. But by some miracle the weather held, and they had reached the borders of the North Forest with far fewer casualties than any of them expected.

By then the Queen had regained consciousness though she could only remember small bits and pieces of the last few weeks. Once she learned all that had happened, she had fully supported the council's decisions and actions—proof enough for Andar that she was back in her right mind.

The rest of the council, however, were reluctant to surrender their powers back over to Rianna so soon. Given the Queen's recent erratic behavior, Andar understood their hesitation. Fortunately, the Queen was more than willing to let them continue to rule, claiming her weakened state made it impossible for her to resume her role as monarch in a time of crisis.

But she can't abdicate her responsibilities forever, Andar thought as he wound his way through the halls toward the Queen's private chambers. The royal family had ruled in an unbroken line for seven centuries. They were a powerful symbol of Danaan unity, strength, and perseverance. If Rianna stepped down now—without an heir to take the throne—her people would be devastated.

He paused at the door of the Queen's private chambers and knocked softly.

"Enter," she called from within.

Andar couldn't help but note how soft and frail she sounded— a sharp contrast to the confident, commanding voice she once possessed.

Inside, Rianna was sitting in her bed, propped up by several pillows behind her back.

"I bring news from the latest meeting of the Regent Council," Andar told her.

She nodded, though from her expression he could tell she didn't have much interest in what he had to say.

This is important! he wanted to shout, but he knew that wouldn't help.

"Pranya's spies in the Southlands are reporting that the Pontiff has begun another Purge."

To Andar's relief, the Queen's eyes momentarily widened with interest.

"Will we be able to mount a defense if they come for us?" Rianna asked.

"It doesn't appear it will come to that," Andar reassured her. "The Order is focusing their efforts on Callastan. They are gathering an army to lay siege to the city."

"Once Callastan falls, they may turn their attention to us," Rianna warned.

"The Free Cities will stand with us, just as they did in the last Purge," Andar insisted.

"Even after what happened in Torian?" Rianna asked. "Before he summoned the dragon that leveled Ferlhame, the Destroyer of Worlds rained Chaos fire down upon the entire city."

"There are some in Torian who support the Order," Andar admitted. "But many do not. The brutality of the Purge is not winning many converts to the Pontiff's cause."

Rianna nodded, and Andar wondered if she was recalling the tales from the last Purge, almost forty years ago. Seeing heretics burned alive at the stake in gruesome public executions could inspire obedience through fear, but it wouldn't earn loyalty.

"Pranya said there are rumors that many of the soldiers and mercenaries who claim to be working for the Order are pillaging the farms and smaller villages of the Southlands," Andar continued.

"There are always those who will use war as an excuse to unleash their worst instincts," Rianna noted with a heavy sigh.

"This time it seems worse than normal. The Pontiff has done little to rein them in; many of the soldiers are running wild.

"It has gotten so bad that Pranya's agents report that several of the Free Cities are considering sending out armed patrols to offer some protection to the surrounding villages."

Andar paused, hoping Rianna would ask for more details. Instead, she simply closed her eyes and lay back against her pillows, as if the news he'd brought had exhausted her.

The High Sorcerer waited for a few moments, then turned to leave so the Queen could rest.

As he reached the door, she called out, "Has there been any news of Vaaler? Do we know if he survived the final battle?"

Her eyes were still closed, and from the Queen's tone Andar couldn't tell why she was asking. Vaaler had betrayed his mother and his people when he allied himself with the human wizard who had nearly destroyed Ferlhame. That betrayal was a large part of what had driven the Queen into the rage and madness that had led the Danaan people into the disastrous war against the Eastern clans.

Yet he knew Rianna well enough to understand that she also felt guilt and regret over what had happened. She had forced Vaaler's hand by exiling him; she shared much of the blame for what had happened.

Do you want to hear that he's dead so you can finally put this all behind you? Or are you hoping your son is somehow still alive?

Whatever her motivations, Andar didn't have an answer.

"Once we realized the Barbarians weren't pursuing us, Hexiff pulled all his scouts back into the main ranks," the High Sorcerer told her. "We know the ogre eventually fell, but we know little else about what happened after we fled the battlefield."

Several seconds of awkward silence passed as Andar waited to see if she would ask anything else about her son.

"I'm tired," Rianna finally muttered. "I need to rest."

"Of course, my Queen," Andar replied, bowing his head slightly, then leaving the room and closing the door softly behind him.

Jerrod sensed the small farm in the distance before he saw it with his newly restored eyes, but just barely. His second sight was getting stronger, but it was still a shadow of what it had once been.

The distant farmhouse was a welcome sight; it gave him something to focus on besides the concerns Scythe had raised about Keegan. And it might give them a chance to restock their supplies. Water could be found easily enough; here on the borderlands there was still a thin layer of snow on the ground they could easily melt whenever they were thirsty. But food was scarce, and they had run out of their last rations yesterday.

Hopefully we can find something at the farm.

If the owners were generous, they might give them enough to continue on. If not, Jerrod had no reservations about taking what they needed. Hopefully this could be done without violence, but if it was necessary, blood would be spilled.

Our mission is too important. If some of the innocent must suffer for the greater good, it cannot be helped.

Ezra hadn't taught him that; it sounded more like something Rexol would have said. But that didn't make it any less true.

And maybe Ezra had always known it would come to this. He'd always warned Jerrod about the dangers of allying with a Chaos mage, but in the end he'd decided they had no other choice.

He knew that Scythe would support him if they had to take what they needed by force. With Keegan, however, he wasn't so sure. Hopefully the young wizard would understand.

We've come too far to falter now. All we need is a few supplies, and we'll be on our way.

As they drew closer to the farm, however, Jerrod realized that wasn't likely to happen.

Keegan's first reaction when he saw the distant farmhouse was one of relief: his empty stomach churned so hard in anticipation of a hot meal that it actually hurt. That emotion was quickly replaced by concern.

What if the farmer won't give us food? Will Jerrod just take it? What if he has a family? What if they try to stop us? Will Jerrod hurt them? Will Scythe?

Deciding it was better to try to head off any trouble with a discussion before things escalated, Keegan broke the traveling trio's silence.

"There's a farm up ahead. Maybe we can bargain with the owner for something to eat."

The sentiment was so blatantly obvious it sounded foolish even to his own ears, but the words were better than the eerie silence.

"We won't have to worry about that," Jerrod replied. "There is nobody living at the farm anymore."

"You can sense that even from here?" Scythe asked, showing her first spark of interest in anything since the battle with Raven.

"Most of my Sight has returned," the monk assured her.

"Good," she said matter-of-factly. "Sooner or later we're going to have to fight to keep moving forward. Nice to know you won't be a liability."

She didn't say anything further, and Jerrod didn't reply, leaving Keegan to bring the conversation back to the original topic.

"So the farm is abandoned?"

"Not by choice," was Jerrod's grim response.

Something in his tone prevented Keegan from asking any more questions. Scythe either sensed it, too, or she simply didn't care to press for more information. As they drew closer, however, the explanation became clear: Someone had razed the place to the ground.

The charred remnants of a crop field marked the outer edge of the property. A handful of animal corpses—a cow, two pigs, and several chickens—lay rotting slowly in the cool winter air, their throats slit. The burned-out frame of what had once been a small wooden barn in the corner looked ready to collapse at any moment. The farmhouse had fared better, but only barely: The stone walls were scorched completely black, and the thatch roof had been burned completely away.

"Bandits?" Keegan wondered aloud as they continued moving forward.

Jerrod shook his head and pointed to the farthest edge of the property, where five tall wooden stakes jutted up from the ground. Around each was a pile of ash and spent charcoal. Strapped to the stakes by twisted metal wire were shapes that had once been human. Now they were almost unrecognizable: black, shapeless lumps of flesh and bone twisted by the intense heat that had taken their lives.

"I've seen this before," the monk explained. "Yasmin has declared a Purge."

They had stopped on the edge of the farm, Jerrod bringing them to the very edge of the slaughter but not taking them any farther.

"Why would the Order execute people out here in the middle of nowhere?" Keegan asked, still not piecing it all together.

"Don't be so dense," Scythe answered, though there was no real venom in her voice. "The family must have been harboring a Chaos user. Probably trying to hide a relative from the Inquisitors."

"So the Order burned them alive?" Keegan exclaimed, his stomach rising.

"There is only one sentence for heresy," Jerrod reminded him. "Anyone here would be guilty by mere association."

Almost against his will, Keegan's eyes focused on the charred remains lashed to the stakes. It was difficult to say for sure, but some of the figures looked smaller than the others.

"Even the Order wouldn't execute children," the young wizard muttered, hoping it was true.

"The children would be spared," Jerrod agreed, much to Keegan's relief. "The young ones, at least. But any over the age of twelve would have to renounce their parents and watch them burn, or suffer the same fate."

"That's barbaric," Keegan muttered.

"It's no worse than what we've done," Scythe countered. "How many innocent victims have we left in our wake?"

Keegan didn't like to think about what had happened at Ferlhame. Hundreds had died the night he'd awakened the dragon; of course he felt some sense of responsibility and guilt for what had happened. But this wasn't the same thing.

"There's a difference between accidentally causing harm in the heat of the moment and cold-blooded murder."

"The victims are dead either way," Scythe said with an indifferent shrug.

"We are not like the Order!" Keegan insisted. "We're trying to save the world."

"So are they," Jerrod reminded him. "Though they walk the wrong path."

"They're the *enemy*!"

"No," the monk said. "Daemron is our enemy. Do not lose sight of that. The Order is merely an obstacle in the way of what must be done to stop the Slayer's return."

"They're trying to kill us!" Keegan reminded them both.

"They are merely following their beliefs with pure conviction," Jerrod offered. "And we do the same. In truth, there is little difference between us. In other circumstances, their efforts would be almost admirable."

Keegan couldn't think of an immediate response, so he looked over to Scythe for support. In the past, she'd always been the one to challenge Jerrod's fanaticism whenever he said something abhorrent. But she wasn't part of the conversation anymore. Instead, her attention was wholly focused on the burned bodies tied to the stakes.

"This is not admirable," Keegan finally spat out. "Whoever did this deserves to die!"

"A lot of people deserve to die," Scythe muttered, not bothering to turn toward them as she spoke. "But not all of them will. And many who deserve to live will not."

She didn't say anything else, and in the ensuing silence Keegan could barely hold himself back from screaming at her.

Snap out if it, Scythe! This isn't like you! This isn't who you are! This isn't who Norr wanted you to be!

Somehow, he held his tongue. Her lover's death had caused her to shut down, to close herself off from the world. But it was hard to believe she wasn't outraged by what had happened here, even if that outrage was buried beneath an ocean of numbing grief. Keegan had hoped this atrocity would trigger something in her— any kind of reaction would have been a welcome sign. But obviously she still needed more time. And shouting at her wasn't likely to help.

"How long ago did this happen?" Keegan wanted to know.

"A day or two at most," Jerrod guessed. "Judging by the decomposition of the livestock. But whoever was here is gone now."

"Any idea why they left?" Scythe wondered.

"Their work here was done," Jerrod simply replied. "It's almost sundown," the monk added. "I doubt we will find any provisions in the farmhouse, but the walls will give us some shelter from the wind and cold."

"We're not spending the night in this place," Keegan declared.

"The Order is unlikely to return," Jerrod assured him.

"I won't sit down and rest in the house of an innocent family while their bodies are still smoking only a few feet away!"

"We don't have time to bury them," Scythe chimed in.

"If we press on, we are unlikely to come across another farm before dark," Jerrod warned. "And the Order could still be patrolling the surrounding area. Finding another safe place to stop could be difficult."

"Then we keep walking through the night," Keegan insisted. "Right, Scythe?" he added, looking for support.

"It doesn't matter to me either way."

At least she answered me. A few days ago she would have just shrugged.

"Then we keep going," Keegan insisted.

After a brief hesitation, Jerrod nodded, and they set off again, heading west and giving the farm a wide berth.

Chapter 6

THE NIGHT SKY was clear and the moon was three-quarters full, giving the three of them just enough light to press onward.

Really it's only Keegan who needs to see, Scythe thought to herself. Jerrod was able to call on his otherworldly perception, and since she'd taken up Daemron's Sword, Scythe had found her own senses acutely heightened. Like some nocturnal predator, the faint light of the stars was all she needed to make out their surroundings.

The Sword was strapped diagonally across her back, held in place by a thin cloth binding around the blade just below the hilt and another near the tip. The bindings were secure enough to keep the weapon from slipping loose as she walked, but she knew if she needed to free it in a hurry, the Sword could slice through them with minimal effort.

Scythe honestly hadn't cared whether they stayed at the burned-out farmhouse for the night or if they kept going. But once the decision was made to press on, she realized she wouldn't be getting much sleep tonight, and for that she was grateful. The pain of dreaming she was with Norr, then waking to find it wasn't true, was something she didn't need.

"We can't keep going," Jerrod suddenly declared, drawing Scythe out of her introspective musings. "It's time to stop for the night. Gather our strength. We'll need it tomorrow if we run into the Inquisitors who burned down the farm."

This time, Keegan didn't offer any objection.

He's almost out on his feet, Scythe realized. He was slumped forward, his arms wrapped around Rexol's staff to keep himself upright.

The monk had obviously been paying more attention to Keegan than she had. For a brief moment she felt a pang of guilt, then pushed it away.

It's not my job to babysit him.

She couldn't really blame him for his weakness. Jerrod was sustained through the Order's ability to draw on their inner reserves of Chaos, and somehow the Sword was giving her extra reserves of energy. Apparently, the Ring he carried didn't offer the same benefit.

Jerrod was helping Keegan now, lowering the exhausted young mage gently down to the ground.

Maybe I could let him carry the Sword tomorrow, Scythe thought as she dug the blanket out of her pack and wrapped it around her shoulders.

But she discarded the idea as quickly as it had come to her. Letting Keegan carry the Talisman for a day or two probably wouldn't be much use. The physical augmentations Scythe now enjoyed hadn't taken effect immediately; they'd built up slowly as she'd carried the weapon, its heft on her back and shoulders becoming more comfortable and familiar with each passing day.

And if Jerrod is right, the Sword won't work as well for him as it does for me anyway. He said we all have Chaos in our blood, but it manifests itself in different ways. Maybe I'm the only one who can call on the full power of the Sword.

On some level Scythe knew she was rationalizing, coming up with reasons to hold on to the glorious weapon. But logically, there was no reason to give it to Keegan. If they ran into trouble on reaching the village, what good would it do for him to have it? She doubted Keegan even knew how to hold a sword properly. And if things got bad, he'd call on the power of the Ring, anyway.

Assuming he still can. He seems so frail right now. It's almost like every time he uses the Ring to unleash magic on the world, a piece of him burns away. Even carrying it seems to be slowly draining him.

Scythe suddenly felt like she was teetering on the edge of some great revelation or understanding—something profound and critically important. And then she sensed figures in the darkness, closing in on them from all sides, and the moment was gone.

"Inquisitors!" Jerrod hissed, his own awareness identifying the threat at virtually the same time as Scythe.

How did they get so close to us without his noticing? Scythe wondered, leaping to her feet and tossing her blanket aside, even as Jerrod did the same. Keegan reacted more slowly though he did manage to gain his feet.

"You are outnumbered," a voice called out from the darkness. "And surrounded. Surrender is your only option."

"How many?" Keegan asked, peering around helplessly in the darkness to try to get a glimpse of the enemy. Rexol's staff was clutched firmly in his good hand, but he wasn't leaning on it for support anymore. Now he held it like a weapon at the ready.

"Two Inquisitors," Jerrod said, laying out the odds. "And six ordinary soldiers. Mercenaries, probably."

The figures had drawn close enough for Scythe's keen eyes to make them out. The two Inquisitors stood in front of them, blocking their way forward. Two soldiers had circled behind them to cut off their retreat, with two more on the left and the last two on the right.

But they can't see any better than Keegan, Scythe realized. *They're basically just holding their positions. The Inquisitors are the only real threat!*

"Protect him," she said, grabbing Keegan by the shoulder and shoving him toward Jerrod as she sprang into action.

Reaching back over her shoulder she seized the Sword's hilt. A quick flick of her wrist severed the cloth bindings holding it in place, and she whipped the weapon up and around in front of her as she charged straight at the two Inquisitors.

Someone shouted at her to stop, but she wasn't even sure who it was. The warning was lost as a glorious burst of adrenaline surged through her body.

The Inquisitors were raising their staves to meet her charge, but their movements seemed awkward and slow, as if they were underwater. In contrast, Scythe felt herself moving with an easy, fluid grace.

In an instant she had closed the gap between them. She brought Daemron's Sword around in a wide, waist-high arc. The first Inquisitor managed to stumble back out of range, his retreat desperate and frantic. The other tried to parry the blow with his staff, but the Talisman sliced clean through the wood and opened a deep gash in his side. He grunted and doubled over, instinctively throwing himself down and to the side as he tried to roll clear of a second, potentially lethal blow. Before Scythe had a chance to finish him, however, his partner recovered enough to leap forward with a counterattack.

He jabbed the butt of his staff toward Scythe's face, but he still seemed to be moving at half speed. She calmly tilted her head to one side, allowing the staff to pass harmlessly by her head, mere inches away from her eye. At the same time, Scythe shifted her weight from one foot to the other and snapped her hand back in the opposite direction, bringing the Sword around in a backhanded slash meant to slice off her opponent's leg at the knee. At the last instant he spun out of the way, and instead of amputating his limb the weapon merely cut a long but superficial gash in his thigh.

He's faster than his partner, Scythe noted. *But not fast enough.*

The other Inquisitor was coming at her again now, his highly disciplined mind allowing him to block out the pain of the wound in his side. His staff twirled and spun in an attempt to disorient her, but instead of a constant blur of unpredictable motion Scythe saw the attack as a series of deliberate and laborious movements.

When he finally struck at her, she slapped the staff aside with an almost casual disdain. She could have finished him had she chosen to do so, but she wasn't worried about this one anymore: She barely even considered him a threat. Instead, her focus was on the soldiers in the darkness who were closing in on Keegan and Jerrod.

If the Inquisitors seemed slow to her heightened perceptions, then the soldiers appeared to be almost glacial: like statues struggling to come to life. The two closest to Keegan and Jerrod shambled forward, and Jerrod stepped up to meet them, dropping into a fighting crouch.

He's moving more slowly than the Inquisitors, Scythe noted.

Clearly he was still hampered by the strange double vision of his restored eyes. But he was still fast enough to send the two armed men stumbling backward with a pair of roundhouse kicks.

The more dangerous of the two men she was facing had launched another assault. There was a desperate fury in this pass, he was throwing everything he had at her. His staff whistled through the air in a series of quick slashes and strikes, interspersed with spinning, leaping kicks as he tried to overwhelm her. Scythe was forced to retreat for several steps, ducking, dodging, and parrying the blows as she picked up on the unconscious rhythm of her foe's movements.

And then she struck, a single forward stab of the blade so quick and precise that the monk never even had a chance to defend himself. The Sword plunged through his robes and into his chest, penetrating the flesh and slipping perfectly between his ribs to pierce his heart. A flick of her wrist withdrew the blade as easily as it had gone in and the Inquisitor collapsed at her feet.

The surviving Inquisitor was still coming at her, but Scythe ignored him. Behind her, the rest of the soldiers had finally joined the fray, and she spun around and raced in the opposite direction to help her companions.

The six mercenaries had formed a tight circle around Jerrod and Keegan, warily feinting and probing at their cornered foes as they tried to work up the courage to attack. Had they all charged at once, Scythe realized, they probably could have taken Jerrod down. But they were hesitant and unsure.

Is that just normal fear and respect for a dangerous foe? Or does Daemron's Sword undermine the confidence and morale of its enemies?

She didn't have time to ponder the question. Keegan had let Rexol's staff fall to the ground and was fumbling for the Ring on its chain around his neck, the young wizard preparing to unleash Chaos against his enemies. But she knew they didn't need magic to win this battle, and she didn't want to face the consequences of any backlash he might unwittingly cause.

Scythe fell on the soldiers like a savage wind, and the euphoria she'd felt earlier overwhelmed her. Surrendering herself to the power of the Talisman, she stopped trying to consciously control it and instead let it become an extension of her will. The blade seemed to move with a mind of its own, and she felt herself responding to it instead of the other way around. The padded vests and thin mail shirts offered little protection as Scythe carved the soldiers up; in a matter of seconds all six were down.

Keegan hadn't even had time to put the Ring on his finger. Hampered by his missing hand, he'd just barely managed to slip it off the chain hanging from his neck. He was holding it in his fist, staring dumbfounded at the carnage he'd just witnessed.

"The Inquisitor!" Jerrod called out, and Scythe snapped her attention back to the last remaining enemy.

He had given up any thoughts of victory; instead, he was trying to flee, hoping that the night could hide him from the she-devil who had slaughtered the others. Under ordinary circumstances, he might have been able to escape. But Scythe was no longer ordinary. Despite his head start, it took her less than thirty seconds to catch up and finish him off.

As she stood over his corpse, a crushing sense of emptiness fell on her. With the battle done, the euphoria vanished, leaving nothing to fill the void. The sense of loss was unlike anything she'd ever felt before—even worse than the instant she'd watched Norr buried beneath an avalanche of ice and stone.

It hit her so hard she rocked back and nearly lost her balance. For an instant the only emotion she felt was despair, then—as suddenly as it had come—the feeling disappeared, leaving her with the familiar, numb-stricken grief she'd carried ever since Norr's death.

Shaking her head, she turned and walked slowly back to Keegan and Jerrod. To her surprise, one of the soldiers was still alive. He lay on the ground, with Jerrod kneeling beside him, an expression of fear and pain etched on his hard, bearded features. His right arm was badly injured; the limb was bleeding profusely as the monk sought to staunch the flow of blood.

"Just let him die," Scythe muttered.

"We can't question him if he's dead!" Jerrod snapped without looking up from his patient.

With an annoyed sigh, Scythe stepped forward and gently lay the flat of the blade on the man's shoulder. He flinched away at the initial contact, his eyes wide and his teeth gritting against the pain of his wounds. And then he was bathed in a faint silver aura, and the fear and pain melted away. The arm stopped bleeding immediately, and a few seconds later the young man began to bend it at the elbow, staring in wonder at his own hand as he carefully flexed his fingers.

"Thank you," he whispered.

Scythe snorted and turned away, breaking the connection and snuffing out the silver light.

"You owe us your life," Jerrod said, taking over. "Do you understand that?"

"I do," he replied, though his tone was suspicious.

He's older. Midthirties. Probably been a blade for hire for at least a decade.

"Why were the Inquisitors waiting here for us?" Jerrod demanded. "How did you know we'd be coming this way?"

"They saw you earlier. Coming toward the farmhouse."

"Today?" Scythe asked.

The bearded man nodded. "Early this morning. One of them was standing watch, and he saw you. Or sensed you. They're not like normal people."

Jerrod's eyes aren't white anymore, Scythe recalled. The soldier didn't know he used to be with the Order.

"How come they could see you before you saw them?" she asked the monk.

"They could have posted a scout. If he was concentrating solely on keeping watch, his Sight would reach farther than normal. He would have sensed me before I sensed him."

A reasonable explanation, but Scythe wasn't wholly convinced. *Maybe your abilities have become weaker than you want to admit.*

Before she could press him further, however, Keegan took over the interrogation.

"You were with the Inquisitors at the farmhouse?" Keegan clarified. "You saw them murder that family?"

"That wasn't my idea!" the soldier blurted. "I was just following orders!"

"When did they die?" Jerrod asked.

"Yesterday. We were passing by when one of the Inquisitors suddenly stopped and said we had to investigate. They made us search the farm. Their daughter was hiding in the barn.

"I guess she was the one they wanted," the soldier said, his voice getting low. "After we found her, everything happened so fast. They made us tie them up, and they burned them alive."

"And you just sat there and watched?" Keegan demanded, disgusted.

"There wasn't anything I could have done to stop it," the man answered in a grim whisper. "I didn't help them, though. I didn't sign up for that."

"You serve the Order during a Purge," Jerrod countered. "What did you expect?"

"I'm just a soldier," the man insisted. "One of Lord Carthin's men."

"Carthin?" Scythe asked.

"The City Lord of Brindomere," Jerrod answered. "A generous contributor to the Order's coffers over the years."

"He's the Justice of the Order now," the soldier added.

"A poor choice," Jerrod mumbled. "His devotion is strongest only when it most benefits him."

"Brindomere's a big place," Scythe noted. "How many troops does he command?" she demanded, pointing the Sword at the prisoner.

"I don't know. I really don't," he said, before adding, "Thousands. Ten thousand, maybe. But they're spread out all over the Southlands right now. Looking for heretics and such."

"Looks like we'll have to fight our way through an entire army on our way to Callastan," Scythe said. She actually found the prospect exhilarating.

"That's where we were headed," the soldier admitted. "Before the Inquisitors made us stop at the farm."

"Why were you heading to Callastan?" Jerrod wanted to know.

"The Pontiff is laying siege to the city. She's gathering an army outside its walls."

"She must have felt the power of the Crown when it was unleashed," Jerrod said. "Getting to Cassandra might be more difficult than I thought."

Keegan glared at the monk and shook his head, clearly uncomfortable with his speaking so openly about their mission in front of the prisoner.

He thinks we're going to let the soldier live! Scythe realized.

"We'll need to find a way to sneak inside the city walls," Jerrod added, either ignoring or unaware of what Keegan was thinking.

"Callastan's still a long way from here," Scythe reminded him. "And we don't have any supplies."

"There's plenty of food at the camp," the soldier offered, trying to win the favor of his captors. "Horses, too. I can take you there."

"And how many more of you will be waiting there for us?" Scythe asked.

"None," he promised. "This is all of us. The whole patrol. The Inquisitors said we'd need everyone for the ambush to work. They were worried you'd try to make a run for it."

Scythe barked out a cruel laugh at the irony of their overconfidence.

"Take us to the camp," Jerrod said, roughly hauling the mercenary to his feet.

"Of course," the man said, his tone so ingratiating it made Scythe's skin crawl. "Whatever you say."

He has no idea what's going to happen when we reach the camp, she realized. *He may be older, but he's still just as foolish and naïve as Keegan.*

Keegan's mind was racing as they marched through the darkness, his exhaustion temporarily kept at bay by the adrenaline rush of the fight. Neither Scythe nor Jerrod had said anything about the prisoner, but he didn't think either one of them would suggest leaving him alive once they reached their destination.

And maybe he does deserve to die.

Try as he might, he couldn't stop picturing the atrocities of the burned-out farmhouse. Part of him screamed for justice for the unknown victims. But as much as he hated to admit it, Scythe had been right earlier—he'd unleashed a far greater slaughter on Ferlhame.

It's not the same! I acted on instinct. I was overwhelmed by the Ring. I barely even knew what I was doing.

The Inquisitors, on the other hand, had worked with cold, hard purpose.

Intention matters!

But if that was the case, then was it fair to blame the horrors of the Purge on a simple soldier? He claimed he couldn't have done anything to stop them, and he was probably right.

Is that really an excuse, though? Doesn't he still deserve to be punished?

It was a question Keegan honestly couldn't answer.

If Norr were here, he'd want to let him live.

The redheaded giant had been a fearsome warrior, but he had been no fan of unnecessary violence and killing.

Keegan had envied the relationship between Norr and Scythe. At first he'd assumed she loved him for his strength. Later he'd come to realize the trait Scythe admired most about him was his selfless compassion. And now that he was gone, Keegan was finally starting to understand how much Norr had done for the hot-tempered Islander.

He was the one who always tried to talk her out of doing something rash. Always the one trying to convince her to look beyond herself and think of others.

It had actually been Norr who convinced Scythe to join up with them in the first place, Keegan remembered.

He saw something in me. Something good. Something worthy. Something heroic.

Norr had truly believed Keegan to be some kind of savior. In the end, he'd believed so strongly that he'd given his life for their cause.

The more Keegan thought about it, the more he realized how important Norr had been; not just to Scythe, but to the entire group. He was their conscience, their moral compass. He'd pushed them to be better, more noble versions of themselves.

Norr saw us as saviors. Now that he's gone, what are we going to turn into?

If Scythe finally shook off her apathy, what would remain? Her anger? Her rage? And what about Jerrod? With a new interpretation of his prophecy fresh in his head, would his single-minded devotion slip into the realm of fanatical madness?

And what about me? What am I becoming?

"There," Jerrod said, interrupting his thoughts. "Just up ahead."

A few moments later they rounded a small rise and Keegan could make out a faint glow from the embers of a small fire, burning in a small pit dug in the underbrush. The silhouettes of three horses tied nearby were barely visible in the moonlight. When they got closer, Jerrod reached down and grabbed a nearby stick and stirred up the smoldering fire, illuminating their surroundings.

The three horses were short and wide, with thick, stubby legs—pack animals rather than mounts. The bags and packs they'd been carrying were piled beside them, and six bedrolls were scattered around the fire. Otherwise, the camp was empty—apparently the soldier had told them the truth about that, at least.

"First we eat," Jerrod said. "Then we rest until morning."

"What about the prisoner?" Keegan asked, though he knew what the answer would be.

"He'll slow us down," the monk explained. "And it's too dangerous to let him go free."

From the corner of his eye, Keegan saw the soldier tense up at the words. He wasn't armed, but he wasn't tied or restrained in any way.

If he tries to run for it, Scythe will cut him down.

Part of Keegan hoped he would do just that—it would make everything easier. But the man was too scared to make a break for it. Either that, or he simply knew there was no hope of escape.

"We can't just execute him," Keegan insisted.

"Why not?" Scythe asked, though there was no real concern in her voice. "We killed all his friends."

"You know that's not the same," Keegan snapped at her. "Killing an enemy in battle is one thing. Slaughtering a helpless prisoner is something else."

"When did you suddenly start following some warrior code?" Scythe snarled, showing a rare hint of real emotion.

"If Norr were still here," Keegan told her, daring to say the big man's name aloud, "you know he'd say the same thing."

"He's not here," Scythe hissed. "And you're not him!"

She raised Daemron's blade and held it poised above her head. To his credit, the prisoner didn't flinch or fall down and beg for mercy, though in the flickering light of the fire Keegan noticed his lower lip twitching.

"Please, Scythe," Keegan said, reaching out to her with his good hand. "Don't do this."

A new expression flickered across her face, vanishing before Keegan could read it. And then her features took on the familiar stone-faced apathy.

"Fine. It doesn't matter to me, anyway," the young woman said, lowering her weapon and turning away with an indifferent shrug.

She wandered off to where the packhorses were standing and began to dig through the bags, looking for rations.

"We can't just let him go," Jerrod said to Keegan, speaking calmly.

"I know," the young man replied. "But maybe there's another way. Just give me the night to think on it."

"I can watch him while you rest," Jerrod promised. "We will decide his fate tomorrow."

Jerrod motioned for the prisoner to sit down. As he did, the man gave Keegan a brief nod, though from the look in his eyes he clearly wasn't holding out much hope.

Neither am I, Keegan thought, turning away from the pitiful gaze. *Neither am I.*

Chapter 7

THE EARTHQUAKE THAT had rocked Callastan had caused widespread destruction. However, the extent of the damage varied wildly from one neighborhood to the next. The city walls were relatively unscathed though several of the small underground tunnels used by criminal gangs to secretly slip beneath them had collapsed. The docks had suffered only minor structural damage, as had the noble quarter, and repairs to those areas were already well under way.

In the poorer sections of town, closer to the epicenter of the quake, the situation was far worse. Most of the newer buildings had wooden frames, and when the foundations shifted many of the structures had been warped and twisted beyond their limits. Nearly one in three had collapsed in on themselves, and just as many were now so unstable they had to be abandoned. The older buildings made of brick, mortar, and stone had fared somewhat better: Most were in no danger of falling anytime soon, though ominous-looking cracks had appeared in many of the exterior walls.

The greatest damage, however, wasn't visible from the surface. Callastan was a city built atop a network of hidden cellars and secret basements connected by a labyrinth of sewers. Much of this hidden empire was now inaccessible, the hideouts cut off from each other or flooded by collapsing sewers. A few key thoroughfares—those most vital to the smugglers and various other criminal enterprises—had been cleared away and reopened. But it would be months—if not years—before everything was restored.

A radius of several blocks around what had once been a city jail was completely uninhabitable now—even the beggars and looters had abandoned it and pushed out to other, less damaged areas of the city. A scattering of bodies, buried beneath rubble or trapped in locations too difficult to reach, were slowly rotting, their foul stench and the scavenging vermin they attracted further dissuading any of the citizens from returning.

It was here that Orath had brought his two meat-puppets, looking for somewhere safe from prying eyes to conduct the ritual that would let him pierce the Legacy and reach across the Burning Sea to contact Daemron. The soldier and the harlot he had enslaved would serve as conduits, buffers to shield him from the unpredictable power of raw, elemental Chaos. But to prepare his sacrifices properly, he needed somewhere remote and isolated.

The entire city was thick with the almost overwhelming aura of Chaos magic—residue from when the Crown had killed the Crawling Twins. The essence of the Talisman was so pervasive it made it difficult for him to focus beyond what his eyes could see, especially while maintaining control of the courtesan and the soldier. By day, he and his toys would hide in the shadows—Orath in a meditative trance, his victims frozen in whatever position their master had left them in with his dancing, flickering fingers. At night, the three of them would wander the empty streets, Orath directing his prizes' every step even as his mind poked and prodded the ruins around them looking for a suitable location.

The Minion was becoming frustrated with his search. The humans he held in thrall wouldn't last much longer; without food or water their bodies would shut down completely in another day or two. The prospect of actually having to find sustenance for them was distasteful, but if he didn't come across what he was looking for soon, there wouldn't be any choice. They needed to be living— not healthy, but still imbued with some faint spark of life—to be of any use in the ritual he was planning.

And then he felt it: a large, empty cellar buried beneath the rubble of a collapsed building on the corner up ahead. In his mind's eye he could see the only entrance—a metal trapdoor in the floor, still locked and intact despite the damage on the surface.

Rescued from the indignity of having to scrounge up scraps for his slaves, Orath quickly directed them over to what had once been a small, single-story shop. Had he wanted to, the Minion could have easily cleared away the debris blocking the cellar's entrance. A simple spell could have blasted everything away, but he was loath to do anything that might announce his presence to the mortal who carried the Crown.

Even without calling on the power of Chaos magic, he was strong enough to have cleared a path to the trapdoor with minimal physical exertion. But such menial labor was beneath him. Instead, using a combination of mental commands and his twitching fingers, he set his slaves to the task.

Their fragile flesh-and-blood forms were ill suited to the grueling work. Their hands had quickly became scraped and cut from breaking up and carrying away the beams and bricks that covered the metal trapdoor. Their muscles were strained to their limits and beyond as they hoisted up massive wooden support beams and large chunks of what had once been the walls and ceiling.

Inevitably, their overstressed bodies were torn apart: Sinew ripped and muscles tore and tendons snapped beneath the skin. They were unable to scream—Orath had forever silenced their voices—but the twisted expressions of agony on their faces gave mute testament to their suffering.

Had it not been for the powerful spell keeping them animated, the humans would have collapsed into useless heaps. As it was, their bodies pressed onward, sustained only by the Chaos of the cruel master that commanded their every move. Unmoved by their plight, Orath pushed them even harder, knowing this torture was nothing compared to what would befall them later.

They finished just before sunup, their hours of brutal labor finally exposing the trapdoor. The ordeal had left their limbs mangled and useless, their bodies and spirits broken. In their eyes, Orath could see they yearned for death. But they still had one more purpose to serve before he would grant them that release.

Knowing even their Chaos-augmented strength wouldn't be enough to snap the lock that held the trapdoor closed, Orath stepped forward and wrenched it open. Then he turned to his victims and marched them down the cellar stairs, their broken bodies staggering and stumbling grotesquely with every step. Halfway down, the woman's already damaged kneecap dislocated completely and she toppled forward into the soldier ahead of her. The pair tumbled down the stone steps in a tangle, bones snapping and cracking until they ended up in a heap of quivering flesh at the bottom.

For an instant Orath feared they might have snapped their necks, and he cursed his carelessness—he needed them alive! But as he scrambled down to check on them, he found fortune was on his side. Gruesome as their injuries were, none of them had proved fatal.

They couldn't walk anymore; even Orath's spell had its limits. But he didn't need them to go anywhere else.

"Soon this will all be over," he assured them, though he doubted they could hear him through the shrieking agony of their abused bodies.

It would take many hours to make the necessary preparations for the spell to reach across the Burning Sea and contact his liege. Though the Legacy was fading, the power of the Old Gods was still strong enough to keep Daemron banished. But piercing the

Legacy was the least of Orath's worries. Once he reached beyond the mortal world his consciousness would have to cross the Burning Sea, an ocean of Chaos in its purest and most powerful form. If he wasn't careful, he would be consumed by the fires.

In theory, it was possible to reach across the Burning Sea to send a message to Daemron through sheer force of will. But doing so would push Orath's strength to its limits, and leave his reserves of Chaos drained. Instead, he would call upon the rituals he had learned at the feet of the Slayer himself. He would use the life energy of his victims to summon Chaos into the mortal world, controlling it with runes and arcane symbols traced in their still-warm blood. When the spell was over the mortals at his feet would be gone—their bodies, minds, and spirits completely consumed by the power of Chaos.

But their sacrifice will keep me safe. Shield me from the backlash of the spell and protect me from the Chaos flames of the Burning Sea.

Or so he hoped.

He took a deep, cleansing breath, focusing his will for what was to come. Then he climbed the stairs and pulled the trapdoor closed again, sealing the three of them inside the suddenly pitch-black cellar.

"It is time to begin."

"Remarkable," Methodis said, shaking his head as he finished re-wrapping the splints and bandages around Cassandra's legs. "If there were some way to share these incredible healing powers with the masses, maybe the Order wouldn't be viewed with such suspicion and fear."

Cassandra didn't say anything. Rexol had claimed that much of her amazing recovery could be attributed to her drawing on the power of the Crown; despite her mistrust of most of what the wizard said, she thought in this case he was right. But so far Methodis hadn't asked her about the Talisman, and she didn't want to be the one to bring it up.

"I suppose it takes years of intense training," the healer continued. "Though I imagine there are some who would be willing if given the chance to learn the Order's secrets."

"Training alone wouldn't be enough," Cassandra said. "Those of us brought into the Order have been touched by Chaos. It gives us abilities beyond those of ordinary men and women."

"Like the film over the eyes," he said, nodding in understanding. "According to all medical knowledge, you should be completely blind. Yet you clearly see the world better than I."

He's fishing for information! Rexol hissed. *He's up to something!*

It did seem as if the doctor wanted to know more, but Cassandra didn't sense anything sinister in his words.

"My Sight is far superior to ordinary vision," she admitted. "Yet it also serves as a powerful reminder of the twisted nature of Chaos. Only by becoming blind can we truly learn to see."

"Did it hurt?" Methodis asked. Then he drew in his breath sharply. "I'm sorry. I have no right to pry into your personal life. Sometimes my curiosity gets the better of my manners."

"It burns for a few seconds," Cassandra said, speaking slowly as she thought back to the memory of the ritual that forever marked her. "But the pain passes quickly. A small price to pay for what I have gained."

"How old were you when they did this to you?"

"This was not done to me," Cassandra said, a sudden urge to defend the Order she was no longer even a part of. "It was my choice!"

"A poor choice of words on my part," Methodis apologized. "Please forgive a foolish old man. We don't have to talk about this."

"I was thirteen," Cassandra said after a brief pause. She wasn't sure why she was opening up to him, but she suddenly wanted to get the words out.

"That seems quite young to make such an important decision," he said. But his tone was mild, and Cassandra didn't see his comment as a challenge.

"I understood the consequences of my choice," she said. "I had already been living and studying at the Monastery for many years before that."

"I've never understood that," Methodis continued. "Why must the Order take children from their parents at such a young age?"

They didn't take you from your parents! Rexol shouted inside her head. *They stole you from me!*

"The training must begin early in life," Cassandra explained, ignoring the wizard. "If the Order waited until we were older, we could never learn to control the Chaos that rages inside us."

"They took you in as a child and set you on this path," Methodis pressed. "Don't you ever feel like your future was stolen from you?"

It was, Rexol chimed in. *You should have been the greatest Chaos mage since the Cataclysm.*

"Life and fortune pushes us all down certain paths," Cassandra answered. "This was mine. I have no regrets."

"Yet now the Order is hunting you," Methodis reminded her. "Something clearly happened that was not part of the plan."

Don't tell him anything else! Rexol snapped. *You've said too much already.*

This time Cassandra decided to heed the wizard's advice. She wasn't worried about Methodis betraying her, but she wasn't eager to confess her betrayal of her brothers and sisters at the Monastery, or the terrible burden Nazir had put on her before his death.

"I'm feeling a bit tired," she said. "I think I need to rest."

"Of course," Methodis said, clearly sensing he had gone too far. "I will get you something to help you sleep."

A few minutes later he returned with the familiar elixir. Knowing rest would help her body heal more quickly, she drank it without protest. Within seconds she felt herself slipping away into unconsciousness. Yet even as her muscles relaxed and her Sight faded into blackness, she kept her mind focused and alert, knowing what was to come. It was time to resume her battle with Rexol.

Each time she drifted off to sleep now she would find herself as a child once again, remembering lessons at the mage's feet that never actually happened. And though she tried to resist his efforts to teach her, the mage was crafty and cunning. He would constantly change her surroundings, altering the trappings of the dream each time to disorient her. He would craft elaborately detailed scenarios to trick her into believing she was still a child. Sometimes she would be studying incantations and words of power from an arcane tome. Other times she would be practicing strange gestures or reciting mystic chants under Rexol's watchful eye, a student dutifully performing her daily exercises.

Sometimes she would be very young—six or maybe seven. Still of an age when adult authority was accepted without question. Other times she would be older; on the cusp of womanhood, her mind filled with the questions and insecurities every teenager faced. In every case, however, the wizard's goal was the same: to convince Cassandra's subconscious that she was his apprentice and he her mentor.

Typically, it would take some time before Cassandra was able to remember her true identity and shake off the ruse—time the wizard used to force his knowledge into her mind, bit by bit. And each time she rejected him, he would threaten, cajole, or tempt her in a futile but relentless effort to win her over.

I can teach you to control the power of the Crown so that it won't harm anybody else.

If you don't learn these lessons, you will be defenseless the next time the Slayer's Minions find you.

Listen to me and you can become a God!

Ultimately, however, Rexol's desperate ploys held no sway over her. The Order had trained her too well; her mind was too disciplined to ever embrace what he was trying to tell her.

You know that's not true. Like it or not, you're beginning to understand the true nature of Chaos rather than the myths and lies taught to you by the Order.

This time there was something different about the dream. Rexol wasn't projecting an image of her younger self. He didn't seem to be projecting any kind of image at all—it felt as if she were standing in a completely dark room.

This dream is not of my doing.

She could still feel the wizard's presence, but she sensed him only as the incorporeal voice inside her head rather than the stern and commanding authority figure he typically portrayed himself as.

The room is dark, but you have the ability to see what is in here . . . if you dare.

Cassandra concentrated, and details came into focus as her Sight pierced the blackness. As the picture emerged, a shudder of revulsion ran down her spine.

She was in a cellar, empty save for three figures. Two were human, or had been once—a man and a woman. Their bodies were twisted and mangled, their bones broken and their flesh ripped and torn. They had been positioned on either side of the room, their figures prone on the earthen floor, their broken limbs splayed out at forty-five-degree angles.

Their stomachs were split open, exposing their entrails. The blood from their wounds had been used to trace a wet circle around them, and from the circle extended five sharply pointed triangles, one each aligned with their arms, legs, and head.

They're still alive, Rexol noted.

To her horror, Cassandra saw he was right. Though motionless and silent, the eyes of both figures still flickered from side to side and the muscles of their faces twitched and shuddered.

Blood magic, Rexol explained. *An ancient practice even I found too abhorrent to study in detail.*

Repulsed, Cassandra wrenched her focus from the helpless suffering of the victims and focused on the other figure. It was pacing back and forth anxiously between the man and the woman, making a final check on the preparations of his spell. She sensed it wasn't human, but Cassandra's Sight couldn't make out any specific details. It was as if the being was shrouded in a veil of blue-green mist that kept it hidden.

It's using Chaos to mask its true form, Rexol noted. *It is a monster that does not wish to be seen.*

Cassandra concentrated, trying to peer through the fog. For a moment the vapors seemed to thin, and the figure suddenly stopped. Its head snapped quickly from side to side, scanning the room.

It senses your presence.

The figure let loose a low, angry hiss, then clenched its hands into fists and thrust them toward the ground. The image around Cassandra began to fade, the walls and bodies of the cellar slipping away as the monster tried to push her away.

It's fighting you! Rexol told her. *Remember your lessons! Fight back! Draw upon the Crown!*

She was loath to embrace Rexol's teachings, but she knew the gruesome spectacle was too important not to see. Ignoring her reservations, Cassandra did as she was told, reaching out with her mind to the Talisman that lay on the nightstand beside her bed in the world outside this vision.

The room came into focus again. But this time Cassandra took care to mask her presence from the fog-shrouded figure.

Clever, Rexol said. *Let it think it's won.*

She wasn't exactly certain how she made herself vanish. In some ways she was mimicking what she sensed in the mists of the creature she was spying on though she had instinctively altered aspects of the spell to render herself completely invisible.

This is what you've learned from all my lessons and exercises, Rexol crowed. *A true mage has an instinctive understanding of how to manipulate Chaos to his or her will.*

Cassandra was too focused on the scene before her to protest that she wasn't, and never would be, any kind of wizard.

Working carefully, she called upon the power of the nearby Crown to enhance her vision once again. This time the figure didn't react as the concealing mists were peeled away.

The monster revealed was clearly not of the mortal world, though in dim light and at a distance it might have been able to pass itself off as one of the Danaan. It was tall and thin. Its fingers were disproportionately long, and they were tipped by hard, pointed yellow nails that looked as deadly as any tiger's claws. Its too-narrow skull was hairless, and its ears and nose were nothing but small, sunken pits in its head. Its slitted eyes glowed faintly with power, and its small mouth was filled with fangs, giving its features an overall batlike appearance.

But it wasn't just the physical appearance that came into focus. She also got a brief glimpse into its mind—a dark cesspool of hate, cruelty, and contempt. This creature lived only to make others suffer. Utterly selfish, it preyed on the weak and vulnerable while bowing down to the strong even as it schemed betrayal.

It calls itself Orath, Rexol said, and Cassandra realized that whatever she saw, the wizard did, too. *Another of the Slayer's Minions.*

Orath was no longer pacing. Now it stood between the two helpless humans, arms raised above its head. Its face and hands were streaked with fresh blood from its still-living victims. Its voice was whispering a low, sibilant chant, and Cassandra could feel it gathering Chaos—somehow drawing it out of the man and woman on either side of him.

Chaos is the source of all things: life, death, creation, and destruction, Rexol reminded her. *Even those who have no ability to call on magic still possess a fundamental spark of power.*

Cassandra had no guess as to what the purpose of the ritual might be, but she knew she had to stop it. She reached out to the Talisman again, drawing Chaos into her. She let it build for several seconds, until the power became too much for her to contain. And then she released it in a sudden burst, directing it at Orath.

Nothing happened.

You are only an observer of this scene, Rexol told her. *You cannot stop it. Did the Order teach its Prophets nothing?*

The monster's chant became louder, and Cassandra could see thin wisps of green smoke curling up from the gaping wounds in the victims' stomachs. If they hadn't been paralyzed by Chaos, their screams would have echoed off the cellar walls. As it was, Cassandra could still sense their suffering as Chaos poured into them, burning them alive from the inside out.

Is this really so different from what the Order does to heretics? Rexol demanded.

Cassandra ignored him, her attention focused entirely on the spell before her. Maybe Rexol was right; maybe she couldn't stop it. But she had to watch. At the very least, she might learn what the creature was doing.

More green smoke curled up from the bellies of the humans, thick enough to coalesce into a large cloud in the center of the room.

Orath slowly lowered its arms, then brought its hands together in front of its chest, extending its arms. Its long fingers pressed together, forming a triangle with its thumbs as the base.

Through the gap, Cassandra caught a glimpse of the Burning

Sea for the first time—an infinite, untamed ocean of blue fire. A deafening roar erupted from the tiny portal Orath had opened, the sound shaking the cellar so hard that bits of dirt began to shake loose from the walls. Heat poured through, so intense it made the Minion gasp and stagger back. Its victims began to buck and thrash, the spell keeping them frozen, unable to withstand the raw power rushing through them.

Bright blue flames leapt from Orath's hands and began to dance about the room, bouncing off the walls and ceiling. Protected by the sacrificial offerings, the Minion seemed unharmed by the fire, though the skin of its victims began to blister and bubble.

The noise had become so loud it was difficult for Cassandra to think. Even though she wasn't really there, Cassandra felt the Chaos fire searing her skin and singeing her hair. The unbridled fury of the Burning Sea pummeled her awareness with heat and sound, overwhelming her.

Pull back! Rexol shouted, his voice nearly lost in the swirling madness. *Pull back now!*

Cassandra snapped her head to the side and let loose a primal scream, severing the clairvoyant connection with Orath's ritual. Her eyes snapped open and her Sight came crashing in to reveal she was still in her bed at the back of Methodis's shop.

An instant later the little doctor came rushing in, drawn by her cry. He stopped and his eyes went wide, and Cassandra realized her skin was covered with burns and blisters from the heat.

How are you going to explain this? Rexol wondered, his tone almost mocking.

Fortunately, she didn't have to. At least not yet.

"I have a salve that will help those burns," the doctor said, regaining his composure. When he turned to leave, however, it seemed to Cassandra he was moving a little more quickly than normal.

"Daemron and his Minions have to be stopped," she whispered

aloud, still partially in shock as her memory replayed all the horrors of what she had witnessed.

You can stop them, Rexol promised. *If you let me teach you.*

Cassandra hesitated. Her entire life she'd been warned about the dangers of Chaos. She had dedicated herself to defending the mortal world against it. Embracing Rexol's teachings would be a rejection of everything she believed in. And she'd already betrayed the Order once.

You were only a child when they stole you from me, Rexol reminded her. *They indoctrinated you into their cult but now they have cast you out!*

"I've seen the harm Chaos causes," she whispered. "I've seen the damage someone like you can do."

And what of the damage that creature you saw in your visions will do? Let me help you, Cassandra. Set aside the life the Order thrust upon you and embrace the destiny that is rightfully yours.

The gruesome images of the ritual Cassandra had witnessed in her vision were still burned in her brain. The enemy they faced was brutal, bestial, and utterly without mercy. She couldn't count on the Order to save her; Yasmin had led them down the wrong path.

And the Minions were still hunting her; eventually they would find her and take the Crown. She couldn't let that happen. But she wasn't strong enough to keep them at bay.

You are strong enough, Rexol cooed. *I can show you how to unlock your true potential.*

"Teach me. I'm ready to learn."

Orath knelt on the cellar floor, the packed dirt cool beneath him. His head was bowed, his breathing shallow. He was alone now, his sacrifices reduced to small piles of ash by the fury of Chaos he'd unleashed.

They served their purpose.

He was mentally and physically exhausted but otherwise unharmed. He had pierced the Legacy, sent a message across the Burning Sea, and survived. But he couldn't exult in his success. Instead, his mind was troubled.

Just before the ritual began, he'd felt an intruding presence—someone watching him from a great distance. It wasn't hard to imagine who the unwelcome observer might be.

The Crown gave Daemron the gift of omniscience.

The young woman who carried it was drawing on the Talisman's power more freely than he'd ever imagined. Yet another reminder of how dangerous she was.

He'd managed to drive her away. At least, that's what he'd believed at first. But during the ritual he'd sensed something strange: the distant echo of a powerful blast of Chaos being unleashed.

It had been so faint he couldn't even be certain it had been real. Perhaps in the struggle of his spell, he'd imagined it.

Or maybe she was still here, watching me. Trying to disrupt my spell from afar.

If so, she had failed . . . though Orath couldn't help but wonder what kind of backlash her ill-advised attempt might bring. There were always repercussions to using Chaos.

It doesn't matter now. The ritual is over.

She had only found him because of the ritual—gathering so much Chaos for a single spell was like setting out a beacon. Now that Orath knew she was searching for him, he would be more careful. He would stay hidden—at least until he received guidance from his master.

Daemron will know how to defeat her.

Orath had sent out his call. Now he only had to wait for the Slayer to answer.

Chapter 8

KEEGAN WAS DEEP in a dreamless sleep when a wave of Chaos rolled over him. He didn't wake, but his subconscious mind was instantly roused by the unmistakable—though distant—sensation of blue heat.

Rexol, his former master, has taken on a new apprentice—a young blond girl with emerald-green eyes. The Chaos mage looms over her as she sits on the floor, studying a large open book in her lap.

Even asleep, Keegan recognized he was experiencing some kind of vision—the details were more sharp and precise than an ordinary dream.

At first the girl appears to be no more than six or seven, but as she recites her lessons she seems to change, morphing from a child into a teenager, then a young woman.

Rexol was dead; Keegan had watched as he'd been consumed by the Crown. So was this a glimpse of the past?

The woman closes the book and sets it aside, then stands up to face the Chaos mage. Her green eyes shimmer briefly before transforming to pure white.

He recognizes her now—Cassandra. The one who helped them escape from the Order's prisons back in the Monastery.

Rexol extends his hand to the young woman, his face grim and determined. She scowls and shakes her head at first, then slowly reaches out.

As their fingers interlock a pillar of blue flame erupts from the ground, swallowing them both up with a terrible roar.

Keegan's eyes snapped open, wide and alert. His head whipped about as he struggled to kick off the blanket that had somehow tangled about his arms and legs. His heart was pounding, his body reacting with an instinctive fear to the sudden explosion of Chaos he'd just witnessed.

"What's the matter?" a voice whispered in his ear. "What's wrong?"

It took a second for the young man's mind to register who was speaking, though once he did it didn't come as any surprise. Jerrod—watchful and protective as ever—was kneeling at his side.

Daybreak was still an hour away, but the sky had already changed from black to gray. In the early twilight, Keegan could just barely make out the details of the Inquisitor camp. The horses were off to one side, sleeping on their feet. Scythe sat on the ground near them, her back resting against the supply packs for support. Daemron's Sword lay across her lap. Her gaze shifted over to Keegan briefly, then back to the dwindling fire in the middle of the camp and the sleeping soldier lying next to it.

So he didn't try to escape in the night, Keegan thought. *If he had, Scythe or Jerrod would have killed him.*

"Keegan," Jerrod snapped, clutching at his shoulder. "Are you okay? Answer me!"

"I'm fine," Keegan said, reaching up with his good hand to brush the monk away. "It was just a dream."

"A dream? Or a vision?"

"A vision," he admitted. "But it didn't make any sense."

"They never do," Scythe called out from where she sat.

"Interpreting them can be a challenge," Jerrod conceded. "But there is always truth hidden within them."

"I saw Rexol," Keegan told him. "He was with Cassandra."

"This may have been a glimpse into the past," the monk suggested. "She was his apprentice for a time before the Order took her away."

Keegan shook his head. "She wasn't a girl in this vision. Well, she was at first. But by the end she was an adult."

Scythe snorted and shook her head. Keegan welcomed her derision—she was starting to act more like her old self. *Ever since the fight with the Inquisitors. Maybe using the Sword helped her somehow.*

"Tell me more," Jerrod urged, drawing Keegan's attention away from her.

"I think Rexol was teaching her. Or trying to. It seemed like she didn't want to work with him."

"That could be symbolic of her time with the Order," Jerrod explained. "They would have indoctrinated her to reject his teachings."

"He reached out to her, and eventually she took his hand," Keegan continued. "And then they were both swallowed up in an explosion of Chaos."

"She helped us escape the prisons," Jerrod reminded him. "But she didn't do so willingly. She was compelled. Rexol had bound her loyalty through some kind of spell."

"And after we were free," Keegan added, nodding his agreement, "Rexol was consumed by the Crown. It makes sense."

Scythe laughed. "A vision isn't much good if it only shows you something you already know happened."

"There must be a reason Keegan witnessed this vision tonight," Jerrod explained. "A catalyst that will give further meaning to what we already know."

"Give me a minute to think," Keegan said, feeling like some important revelation was lurking in the corner of his mind, just waiting to be revealed.

He recalled the strange sensation of Chaos rolling over him at the start of the vision. It almost felt as if someone had tried to cast a spell without any understanding of how to direct or control the power he summoned, only to have the Chaos break free and run wild through the mortal world.

Maybe it was backlash from Scythe's using the Sword.

But that explanation made no sense; as far as they knew, the blade suppressed Chaos. Swallowed it up and trapped it within itself.

That's why it was so hard to use the Ring in the Guardian's cave. And that's why the Frozen East has no wizards. The Sword dulls the power of Chaos.

Maybe it had only been his imagination. Or maybe the Chaos he'd felt had just been part of the vision. But if that was the case, then what had been the catalyst? Why had he suddenly had a vision of Rexol and Cassandra?

His eyes dropped to their prisoner as he rummaged through his thoughts. The soldier was awake now though he lay motionless on the ground, his eyes following their conversation with apprehension and confusion.

"Him," Keegan said, pointing at the mercenary as it all fell into place. "He's the catalyst."

"You saying he has Chaos in his blood?" Scythe asked, suddenly on her feet with her blade at the ready.

"No," Keegan said quickly. "But maybe my vision was meant to show me what we should do with him."

"I already know," Scythe said. "We all do."

Keegan ignored her and turned his attention to the mercenary on the ground.

"Maybe she's right," he said, still trying to work his way through the details of his sudden revelation. "You served the Order. Why shouldn't we kill you?"

"I didn't know they were going to kill those farmers," he said. "Not like that. Not all of them."

"You're not some naïve raw recruit," Keegan countered. "You're a mercenary. A hired blade. Why should what happened at the farm even bother you?"

"I'm not like that," he protested. "I've seen my share of battles. Even killed a man once. But that was in a fair fight! I'm no murderer!"

"Is there some point to this?" Scythe wanted to know.

There was, but Keegan didn't want to explain himself yet. He had an idea, but it wasn't something he was willing to try unless he believed the man was worth saving.

"When Carthin started taking orders from the Pontiff, I didn't know it was going to be like this," the soldier continued. "I was always taught that the Order protected us. The Purge was supposed to keep us safe from dangerous witches and wizards. And then everything got out of control."

"What do you mean?" Keegan asked.

"Once Carthin was named Justice, every noble who wasn't in his pocket suddenly became a heretic. If they bowed down to him and swore allegiance, they'd escape the worst punishments. If not, he'd butcher them and take their holdings for his own."

"You were actually surprised by this?" Scythe sneered.

"His army doubled in size as guards and men-at-arms from fallen houses swore allegiance to him. And the more troops he got, the worse the Purge became. Half the soldiers who joined were just bandits lured in by the promise of good pay for easy work.

"There were rumors. Nasty stuff. Innocent villages terrorized by bands of armed men claiming to serve the Justice. Homes looted and razed. Men killed and women violated.

"I thought the Order was trying to keep them in check. Until I saw what the Inquisitors did at the farm."

"You're a little old to just be figuring out that there are no good guys in the world," Scythe mocked.

"No!" Keegan snapped. "That's not true. Evil exists, but there are those who stand against it. Heroes. Like us!"

She raised an incredulous eyebrow, then simply shook her head and turned away.

"Heroes don't kill unarmed prisoners," Keegan added, this time speaking to Jerrod.

"A noble sentiment," the monk admitted. "But our cause is too important simply to let this man loose. Especially with all he knows about us."

"I won't tell anyone," he swore, struggling to his knees. "I don't want anything more to do with the Order!"

"If we release you," Keegan asked, "what will you do?"

The man blinked quickly and wet his lips with his tongue, his mind frantically searching for the right answer.

"The Free Cities," he finally said. "I'll go there. Torian has sworn allegiance to the Order, but none of the others have."

"Good," Keegan said with a nod. "If the Order lays siege to Callastan, we may need allies to help us break through their ranks. Go to the Free Cities and tell them what happened here. If enough people hear of the atrocities of the Purge, maybe they will do something about it."

"I doubt one common soldier can convince the Free Cities to wage war against the Order," Jerrod said.

"But it can't hurt," Keegan countered.

The soldier was nodding vigorously now. "Yes. Of course. I'll tell them what happened. I'll tell them anything you want!"

"I believe you," Keegan said. "Because I am going to use Chaos magic to bind you to my will."

Insanity, many in the Order believed, was an inevitable side effect of summoning Chaos; every mage, every wizard, every witch and conjurer would eventually succumb to madness.

Jerrod had never accepted this doctrine. He believed in the

prophecy of the Burning Savior. He believed that mortals touched by Chaos could learn to control the fires of creation, harnessing the power to defeat Daemron upon his return.

He'd seen madness in Rexol, but he'd chalked it up to the mage's own ambition and arrogance. When Rexol had placed the Crown atop his head, Jerrod had blamed hubris—not insanity—for his death.

Even so, he'd studied Keegan carefully ever since the young man had claimed the Ring, watching for some hint that he was becoming unhinged. The Talisman had taken a toll on him, but so far the effects had seemed primarily physical. But the decision to bind the soldier to his will was not that of a sound and rational mind.

"Keegan," he said, choosing his words carefully so as not to upset him, "that would be a very bad idea."

"No," the wizard replied, his tone calm. "It makes perfect sense. Think about the vision I just had. Rexol bound Cassandra to his will. I can do the same with this man."

"Did Rexol teach you this ritual?" Jerrod asked, hoping he could use logic to help Keegan see how dangerous and foolish his idea was. "Directing and controlling Chaos in such a specific way would be incredibly complicated."

"I understand the principles well enough," Keegan assured him. "And this would be much simpler than what Rexol did. He had to let his spell lie dormant for years, and the magic had to be powerful enough to make Cassandra betray her own kind."

The young man's voice was strong, his bearing supremely confident.

I've never seen him act like this. What's gotten into him?

"All I have to do is place a mark on this soldier that will keep him from running to the Order the moment he leaves our sight. Something he has no intention of doing anyway. It will be an easy task."

"Please," the man said, crawling forward and groveling at Keegan's feet. "You don't have to put some kind of hex on me!"

"No harm will come to you," the wizard assured him, though there was more threat than comfort in his tone. "As long as you keep your promise and go to the Free Cities."

Jerrod glanced over at Scythe for support, but she seemed to have lost all interest in the conversation.

The monk grabbed Keegan's good hand by the wrist, his grip hard enough to make Keegan wince.

Maybe the pain can snap him out of this!

"I know you do not want us to kill the prisoner, but this is not the answer! Chaos is not something to be trifled with!"

Keegan gave Jerrod a withering stare, and the older man loosened his grip, allowing the younger to shake his arm free.

"I am the savior of the mortal world," Keegan proclaimed, his voice dripping with contempt. "Do you really doubt that I can do this?"

What's wrong with him? Jerrod wondered. *He's haughty. Arrogant. Just like Rexol.*

"I used my power to help Norr defeat Shalana in the duel ring," he added.

"That was different," Jerrod protested.

"No. Not if you think about it," Keegan insisted. "I used my power and turned him into a champion to lead his people!"

No you didn't! You plotted with Scythe and Vaaler to sabotage Shalana. You cheated her out of her victory. It was all just a trick!

Suddenly Jerrod understood what Keegan was actually trying to tell him. And he realized why the young man was acting so much like his mentor.

It's a performance! He's trying to scare and intimidate the prisoner!

"I am a Chaos mage!" Keegan declared. "Do you really doubt that I have the power to compel an ordinary soldier to obey me?"

"Forgive me," Jerrod said, bowing and taking a step back. Now that he knew the game, he understood how to play his own role. "I would never doubt you, Keegan of the Gorgon Staff."

The young man's eyebrow twitched upward at the unexpected title, but fortunately the soldier at his feet didn't notice.

"But I beg you to be careful," the monk added. "If you summon too much Chaos, the mark you place on the prisoner will be unstable. If something goes wrong, it will explode and we will all be turned into ash."

The soldier's wide eyes were fixed on Jerrod as the monk slowly retreated, leaving him and Keegan alone beside the fire. Then his gaze snapped back to Keegan looming over him.

"You don't have to do this," the man begged. "I won't tell the Order about you. I promise! I'll go to the Free Cities just like you said! I'll tell them what happened here!"

Keegan slapped the man's check with his good hand, though not particularly hard.

"There is no other way. I bind you to my will, or we execute you. This is your choice."

The soldier swallowed, then nodded slowly.

Keegan began a soft chant. Jerrod had no idea if he was speaking actual words of power or pure gibberish. Then he reached into the fire pit and pulled out a small stick—charred, but still intact. To Jerrod's surprise, the stick flickered with blue light and thin wisps of smoke curled up from the tip.

"Hold still," Keegan commanded, slowly bringing the stick toward the still-kneeling prisoner.

The soldier clenched his eyes shut as Keegan touched the tip of the stick to his forehead. He let out a low moan and gritted his teeth as the mage made a few quick strokes, tracing out a simple circle with several diagonal slashes. Outlined in ash, the mark glowed faintly with a blue aura for several seconds.

"It burns," the soldier whimpered though Jerrod suspected he was more scared than in pain.

Keegan's voice rose higher, the strange words coming more quickly now. He spat them out, harsh and bitter, then cast the glowing stick aside.

The soldier opened his eyes, then closed them as Keegan reached out with the stump of his left hand and pressed it against the mark on the soldier's brow. There was a brief but intense blue flash. Knocked off-balance, the soldier let out a yelp of surprise as he fell over backward.

"It is done!" Keegan declared, drawing his stump in a quick horizontal slash in front of his chest. "On your feet!"

The soldier scrambled to get up, then stood at attention before the young man.

"What's your name?" Keegan demanded.

"Darm. Darmmid, I mean. But everyone calls me Darm."

"You are bound to me now, Darmmid," Keegan told him. "Do you understand what this means?"

The soldier nodded but didn't speak.

"My mark is working its way inside you. It's in your brain. Your guts. Can you feel it? Churning in your stomach? Making you sweat and tremble?"

"Yes," the terrified soldier whispered, the power of suggestion making perspiration break out on his forehead. "I feel it."

"This sickness will soon pass. But it will return if you even think about betraying me. It will grow stronger with each passing second. The Chaos will burn away your organs, melting them insider your body. You will die writhing in agony, and no one will be able to save you!"

The soldier moaned but didn't speak.

"You are mine now, Darmmid," Keegan pressed. "I own you. I am your master, and you will obey me!"

The soldier nodded.

"Say it!" Keegan barked.

"I will obey you, master! I promise!"

Satisfied, Keegan stepped back.

"Grab enough food for a week and go. The Free Cities are waiting for you."

Scythe watched the terrified mercenary fumbling with the supply packs, his hands shaking so badly he could barely loosen the knots at the top. He glanced up once and saw her staring, then quickly averted his eyes.

A few minutes later he had somehow managed to gather what he needed, and he set off in the early-morning light. He was heading northwest, toward the Free Cities, but she wondered how long he would keep that path. Once he was out of earshot she made her way over to where Keegan and Jerrod were standing together, watching the prisoner's rapid departure.

"Quite the performance," Scythe remarked. "But sooner or later he's going to realize it was all just a trick."

"Maybe not," Jerrod said. "The power of suggestion can be very powerful. His own mind will be working to maintain the illusion.

"Every time he feels anxious or nervous or even just sick to his stomach, he will blame it on Keegan, which will only reinforce his belief that he has been bound to the will of a Chaos mage."

"You seem to know a lot about tricking people into believing things that aren't real," Scythe remarked. "Must be a religious thing."

Jerrod didn't rise to the bait.

"I'm more concerned about the Chaos you unleashed during this charade," he said to Keegan. "It seemed an unnecessary risk."

"I had to do something to make him believe the ritual was real," the young man objected.

Scythe noticed that the arrogant tone he'd been using was gone from his voice; now that the performance was over he had returned to his typical self.

"Don't worry," Keegan assured the monk. "I was careful. But I thought it was worth the risk."

"It wasn't," Scythe said. When Keegan looked at her in confusion, she continued, "This entire thing was pointless."

"We spared a man his life," Keegan reminded her.

"Did we? How far do you think he'll get on his own? If the bandits don't get him, the Order will. I'm guessing they treat deserters about the same as they treat heretics.

"And they'll probably torture him first. Your fake spell won't keep him quiet once they bring out the molten iron. He'll break and tell them everything he knows about us."

"At least I gave the man a chance!" Keegan snapped. "At least I tried to help him!"

"The only person you helped was yourself," Scythe countered. "This whole thing was just a way to make you feel less guilty about doing what we all know was the right thing."

"He might make it," Jerrod chimed in, throwing his support behind Keegan now that the task was done. "Stranger things have happened."

"We couldn't just kill him," Keegan said. "If we truly are destined to save the world, we have to start with one person."

That sounds like something Norr would say, she thought. Maybe she was being too hard on Keegan. Maybe he really was trying to do the right thing.

Or maybe he thinks acting more like Norr will win me over.

Scythe felt a wave of disgust wash over her. Keegan wasn't trying to keep Norr's memory alive—he was trying to replace him!

"You're not Norr," she spat out. "And you never will be, so stop trying to act like him!"

"Scythe," Keegan said, reaching out toward her. "That's not what I meant—"

"Norr was a good man," she said, cutting him off. "It was in his nature. We're not like that. There's Chaos in our blood. We are bringers of death and destruction!"

"Maybe we don't have to be," Keegan said. "Maybe we can change. Maybe we really can become the kind of heroes who will stop Daemron."

"Daemron was a hero once, too," Scythe reminded him. "And look what he became. In a thousand years, will the Order be looking for someone to save the world from us?"

"Daemron was corrupted by the darkness inside his own heart," Jerrod said. "His pride and arrogance led him to betray the True Gods!"

"Or maybe his true nature finally showed through," Scythe argued. "You can't change who you are, Keegan. You're not Norr. You're not a hero and you never will be. Just accept it."

"You're upset," the young man said. "You don't mean that."

"Do I look upset?" she asked, her voice calm. "I'm not saying this out of anger or spite. I'm saying it because it's true."

She waited for Keegan to reply, but he didn't have anything left to say. He stared at her for a few seconds, then turned away, shaking his head.

Scythe looked over at Jerrod, who was staring at her intently. Even without the white veil obscuring his eyes, however, she still couldn't tell what he was thinking.

When he finally spoke, all he said was, "We should eat, then move out. Callastan is still a long way off."

"Exactly," Scythe agreed. "We've already wasted more than enough time this morning."

Chapter 9

YASMIN ARRIVED AT the Order's aerie in the early afternoon. It had taken her three days to make the journey from the siege camp outside Callastan, resting only a few hours each evening in deep meditation to maintain her strength.

Ermorr, the elderly Keeper of the aerie, was waiting at the gates to meet her.

"Welcome, Pontiff," he said, tilting his head slightly in a sign of respect. "I am honored that you have chosen to grace our humble outpost with your presence."

Yasmin waved aside his comments with an impatient hand— this was not the time for formalities.

"I trust my message was received," she replied.

"Of course, Pontiff. Nearly a dozen of your loyal followers have gathered here as per your instructions."

Yasmin scowled. She'd been hoping for more, but the Order's numbers were not what they once were. And many of her supporters were already either at Callastan, or too far away from Norem to answer her call in time.

We must work with the tools we are given, she reminded herself.

"Send word to Lord Carthin," she said aloud. "Tell him to prepare for our arrival tonight."

"Tonight?" Ermorr said, mildly surprised. "You do not wish to rest from your journey?"

"My business with the Justice cannot wait," she explained. "I will leave within the hour."

The sun was just beginning to set as Yasmin entered the Norem city gates, flanked by her eleven followers. She could have added Ermorr to their numbers, but she thought it best to leave him back at the aerie in case any urgent messages needed to be sent.

A blare of trumpets announced the Pontiff's arrival, their call echoing across the rooftops. As she and her entourage made their way down the city streets, people flocked from the buildings to see them, crowds forming along their route like a parade. But though the people clapped and cheered, the expressions on their faces wasn't joy or excitement, and the Pontiff suspected the enthusiastic welcome had been staged by Lord Carthin.

He knows I'm displeased with him. Does he really think he can get on my good side with such an obvious ploy?

Norem was by far the smallest of the Seven Capitals though what it lacked in size and population it made up for in arts and culture. Sculptors, painters, architects, and musicians flocked to the city en masse, eager to make their reputation and secure the patronage of one of the city's wealthy nobles. Lord Unferth, the current City Lord, was rumored to be particularly generous when it came to rewarding those with artistic talent.

Yet even though Lord Unferth had always been a supporter of the Order, the same could not be said of many of his subjects. Unlike other City Lords, he was notoriously lax in persecuting those who spoke out against the Pontiff and her decrees. In his efforts to cultivate an atmosphere of creative freedom, he had turned a blind eye to blasphemers who hid their criticisms of the Order in their art. As a result, Norem had become a haven for heretics and nonbelievers, and when Yasmin had declared another Purge, it proved to be a focal point of resistance and rebellion.

Unferth had tried to quell the unrest in his city, but he lacked the stomach for the harsh measures. It was said he had the soul of an artist though Yasmin understood this was merely a polite way of saying he was a weak ruler.

As Justice of the Order, Lord Carthin had been right to focus his efforts on Norem. Lord Unferth had welcomed his arrival, quickly turning over control of the city to the Pontiff's duly appointed representative.

But that was weeks ago, Yasmin reminded herself. *More than enough time for Carthin to crush the small pockets of rebellion and bring the city into line.*

Norem was laid out in a series of ever-widening circles, with the wealthiest residents living in the neighborhoods closer to the center. In the very middle of the city was a sprawling castle—the Unferth ancestral home.

Yasmin had never had reason to visit Norem before, but she had heard tales of the incredible beauty of castle Unferth. When she finally laid eyes on it, however, she was struck more by its impracticality than its majesty. There was no exterior wall to blunt the charge of an attacking army. The grounds were covered by lush gardens and hundreds of massive statues carved from marble—perfect spots for an enemy to take cover against archers inside the main building. The castle itself was long and narrow, with six spires rising along the length of its structure, each spaced far enough away from the others that defenders at one location would be unable to offer support or reinforcements to another. Worst of all, hundreds of massive stained-glass windows covered the entire building, many on ground level.

No wonder Unferth was loath to use force against his subjects, Yasmin thought. *If they turned against him, his castle would be overrun in minutes!*

As the Pontiff and her followers neared the main entrance of the castle, a small honor guard emerged: six mounted soldiers in full armor carrying red-and-gold banners surrounding a single rider wearing the city colors. To Yasmin's surprise, however, it wasn't Lord Carthin who had come to greet her.

"Welcome to Norem, your Eminence," Lord Unferth said, dismounting so he could grace the Pontiff with a low bow. He was an older man, well into his fifties. At barely over five feet tall, his head barely reached up to Yasmin's chin. His face was round and puffy, his nose red and veined from years of enjoying too much good wine. His suit was well tailored, but it couldn't completely hide the small paunch that overhung his belt.

"My city is honored by your visit," he added, puffing slightly from the exertion of climbing down from his horse.

"Is it still your city?" Yasmin asked.

Unferth blushed as he stammered out a reply. "I am the official ruler of Norem though I have given Lord Carthin temporary control of my soldiers so that he may deal with the rebels in our midst."

So Carthin has added Norem's forces to his ever-growing army.

"A noble cause," Yasmin replied, "but not the one he is supposed to be pursuing. Were my instructions to gather our forces at Callastan not received?"

Lord Unferth looked even more uncomfortable than before. He licked his lips before saying, "I dare not speak for Justice Carthin, Pontiff."

"Perhaps it is just as well that he speaks for himself," Yasmin said with a nod. "I trust he is expecting us?"

"News of your arrival came this afternoon," Unferth assured her. "Lord Carthin has prepared a special feast in your honor.

"However," he added unexpectedly, speaking far more quickly than before, "if you are tired from the journey, I can escort you to the guest rooms so you can refresh yourself before the meeting."

"That will not be necessary," Yasmin assured him.

"Of course," he said, sounding disappointed. "Lord Carthin is ready for you, then. I will take you there now."

That was odd, Yasmin thought. She focused the full attention of her Sight on Lord Unferth, sensing something wasn't right. The night wasn't particularly warm, but he was sweating profusely. And his eyes kept darting from side to side, as if wary of the soldiers escorting him.

Maybe his surrender of the city wasn't as willing as he makes it seem. Maybe he's a prisoner in his own castle. Maybe he was hoping to get some time alone with me to plead his case.

It wouldn't be out of character for Carthin simply to seize control of Norem's forces without asking. He could easily justify it as a necessary first step in restoring the Order's authority over the city. Technically he wouldn't be overstepping the boundaries of his office as Justice of the Order, though he would be pushing the limits.

Even more reason to have this meeting. Carthin needs to be put in his place. He needs to remember that he serves at my discretion.

Unferth took them to the main entrance of the castle on foot, leading his horse by its bridle. The six soldiers escorting him remained mounted and followed close behind.

"This is where I must leave you, Pontiff," he said once they reached the door. "A steward will lead you to the banquet hall where Lord Carthin awaits."

He bowed deeply once more. As he did so, he whispered in a voice so low even the Pontiff's superior senses could barely hear him, "Don't drink the wine!"

The door opened and Unferth stood up and turned away quickly, relinquishing Yasmin to the steward waiting on the other side before the Pontiff had a chance to even react to his cryptic warning.

"Justice Carthin is expecting you, Pontiff," the steward said with a small tilt of his head.

He led the way into the castle, through winding halls and past countless rooms. Though she appeared outwardly calm on the journey, Yasmin's mind was spinning.

Don't drink the wine!

She had hoped this visit would bring Carthin back into line— a face-to-face meeting to reassert her authority. But if he was planning to betray her, there was only one way to deal with his treachery.

But is he really planning to betray me? Or is Unferth trying to use me for his own game?

If Unferth had been forced to step down, the older man would be resentful. Was he cunning enough to try to trick Yasmin into turning against Carthin with a carefully placed lie?

She glanced back over her shoulder at her Inquisitors.

There are twelve of us, all armed with quarterstaffs. We could fight our way out of here right now, and Carthin's men couldn't stop us all.

But if Unferth was lying, they would end up slaughtering dozens of innocent soldiers. More importantly, the relationship between her and Carthin would be destroyed, and she still had need of his troops.

None of the others had heard Unferth's warning; only she had been close enough to pick up the faint whisper. But there was no need to warn them; if the time for action came, they would follow her lead without question or hesitation.

I just have to be certain that time has come.

The steward led them into a large banquet hall. The cavernous room could easily seat a hundred diners, but only a few tables in the center of the hall had actually been set—just enough for the Pontiff and her retinue.

But though it appeared they would be dining alone, they were not the only people in the room. Standing at attention along either side of the hall were twoscore soldiers, all fully armored and carrying long spears.

Eighty of them against twelve of us, Yasmin noted. *Close to even odds.*

At the front of the banquet hall was a raised stone platform. Typically this would have been used as a stage for whatever entertainment would be on hand to amuse the nobles during their feast. On this particular evening, however, the stone stage was occupied by a single large, ornate chair. Seated in it, and flanked by a half dozen guards on either side, was Lord Carthin himself.

It was possible the setup was meant only to feed Carthin's ego, allowing him to look down on the Pontiff and her Inquisitors like a King lording over his subjects.

Or maybe he wants a clear view of the slaughter when he betrays us.

The soldiers along the walls seemed tense and wary. But that alone wasn't proof of anything: Ordinary men and women were often nervous and unsettled in the presence of those who served the Order, particularly when they saw the Pontiff and the prominent burns and scarring on her bald scalp.

Along the back wall was a balcony, twenty feet above the main floor. Merchants and other tradesmen could purchase seats there to watch the entertainment while the nobles dined below, but tonight the balcony was empty.

If he was setting a trap for the Pontiff, Carthin could have placed archers on the balcony to rain arrows down on them from above. The Inquisitors could duck, dodge, or deflect some of them, but even they couldn't survive a coordinated volley.

But if he tried to hide archers up there, he knows I would have sensed them the second we entered the banquet hall.

The steward guided Yasmin and the others to their tables, then scuttled away. Yasmin didn't take a seat but instead leaned on her staff and looked up at Carthin, who at least had the decency to rise in her presence.

"Welcome to you and yours, Pontiff," he called out, his voice booming and cheerful. "Please, partake of this feast we have prepared in honor of your arrival!"

The Justice of the Order was smiling—the broad grin of an overeager servant desperately seeking approval from his master.

If he's planning betrayal, he's doing a good job of hiding it.

Yasmin's eyes skimmed the table, noting the extravagant feast that had been laid out. In particular, she noted that a full cup of dark red wine, already poured, had been placed at each setting.

"Are you not going to join us while we eat, Justice?" she asked.

"I am your humble servant, Pontiff," Carthin replied. "I am not worthy to dine with you and your revered companions."

His tone was as ingratiating as ever, and once again Yasmin could detect no hint of malice or duplicity in him.

Is Unferth the one I should be doubting?

"We have urgent business," the Pontiff insisted, trying to push him into revealing something. "Perhaps it would be better if we save the meal until after we speak."

"If that is your wish, then it shall be so," he readily agreed. "Though it seems a shame to let such a succulent feast go cold.

"Shall we adjourn to my private chambers?" he asked. "I can have my servants take the meal back to the kitchens to try to keep it warm until our meeting is over."

If this is a trap, Yasmin thought, *then he seems content not to spring it.*

"That would be preferable," she said.

Carthin nodded and held up a hand. But as he opened his mouth to call for the servants he suddenly stopped and tilted his head to the side, as if he just had a sudden inspiration.

"Perhaps while we are in our discussions," he suggested, "the rest of your companions can enjoy the feast. Unless you require them to be part of our conversation?"

Yasmin glanced quickly from side to side. Her Inquisitors were standing calm and still by their respective dinner chairs, their staves held casually at their sides. If they sensed anything unusual about the exchange, they were careful not to let it show in their bearing.

She was still wary, but so far there had been nothing to indicate Carthin was guilty of plotting against her. True, he was a nobleman who had pushed a little too hard in his efforts to add to his own power and influence. But that was to be expected, and his only real transgression was making up excuses to delay sending his troops to support the siege at Callastan. To suddenly go from loyal, if reluctant, servant to traitor was a great leap, even for a man as ambitious as Lord Carthin.

Don't drink the wine!

There really was only one way to discover the truth.

"The others can stay and eat," Yasmin agreed. "There is no need for them to be privy to our discussions.

"But allow me a moment to slake my thirst before we speak," she added, picking up the wine goblet in front of her.

She brought it slowly to her lips, focusing her Sight on the rich, ruby liquid. She sensed nothing unusual about it, though she knew there were poisons so subtle even she wouldn't be able to detect them until it was too late.

Tipping the glass back, she let the wine brush against her lips, though she was careful not to let any slip into her mouth. Most toxins would take time to have any effect, and she doubted a single swallow of anything would be enough to incapacitate her. But there was no point in taking an unnecessary risk.

As she set the goblet down on the table she let her awareness drift back across the room toward Carthin. His face was still plastered with the same ingratiating grin he'd worn since she entered, but for an instant she saw something flicker in his eyes—a smug glint of cruel satisfaction. It came and went in an instant, but the Pontiff had no doubt about what she'd seen.

Fourscore against a dozen.

There was no time to accuse, no time to explain. Not if she wanted to get to Carthin before he could escape.

Yasmin leapt forward, her long legs propelling her onto the top of the table with a single step as she rushed toward the raised stage. At her back the Inquisitors instantly sprang into action, responding to her charge by fanning out in all directions, their staves spinning furiously through the air.

She had already covered half the distance between her and Carthin by the time he realized what was happening.

"Nightfall! Nightfall!" he shouted, yanking out a black kerchief and waving it above his head.

In response to his signal, the guards aligned along the wall lowered their weapons and rushed forward, trying to mow down the Inquisitors in the center of the room with a wave of spears crashing in from either side.

Yasmin ignored the battle behind her, gaining speed and momentum as she threw herself from the floor and up onto the stage. The dozen guards surrounding Lord Carthin barely had time to ready their spears before she landed among them.

The stone stage was large, but with nearly a dozen armed combatants battling on it there wasn't much room to spare. The Pontiff was a blur of motion, spinning, leaping, and ducking to avoid the clumsy thrusts and stabs of the soldier's spears in the close quarters. She lashed out with her staff, catching one of the guards across the helm. The force of the blow dented the side of his helmet and made his eyes roll back into his head, but it also caused Yasmin's staff to snap in two.

Carthin had scrambled out of his seat, knocking his makeshift throne onto its side as he desperately tried to stay out of the melee. Yasmin took a step to follow him, only to be cut off by several of the guards.

Dropping to the floor, Yasmin rolled clear of three soldiers who tried to tackle her to the ground, then sprang to her feet and hurled the splintered remains of her weapon at the nearest opponent. She threw it with such force that the jagged end of the staff ripped through the guard's chain-mail shirt and buried itself deep in his chest. He clutched at the protruding shaft and staggered back before disappearing off the edge of the stage.

Several soldiers closed in on Yasmin from all sides, forcing her to leap off the stage and back onto the floor below. On an instinctive level, she was aware that her Inquisitors were wreaking havoc among the guards on the floor—at least twenty soldiers were already down. But two of her brethren had already fallen, and the others would soon begin to tire and slow. Eventually they would be overwhelmed by the sheer numbers against them.

I have to get to Carthin—force him to surrender!

The remaining guards atop the stage were too disciplined to follow her down to the floor. Instead, they had formed a protective wall between her and the Justice. Fortunately, the rest of the soldiers were too preoccupied with the Inquisitors to come to Carthin's immediate aid, giving Yasmin enough time and space to try another tactic.

A quick backflip took her from the floor and up onto the table where the feast had been prepared. Her lips were burning from where the wine had brushed against them; whatever poison Carthin had chosen was incredibly potent. In a single fluid motion, the Pontiff crouched, scooped up one of the still-full wine goblets and hurled it at the soldiers. They cried out in surprise, then ducked away and covered their eyes and mouths with the crook of their arms as it sprayed over them.

In rapid succession she whipped the remaining goblets at the guards, causing their ranks to break and scatter. Three fell to the ground, writhing in agony as the vile liquid splashed into their eyes, blinding them almost instantly.

With the wine gone, Yasmin simply switched to the silverware on the table. The knives were dull and ill balanced, and the three-pronged forks were blunted from years of use. But they were heavy and metal, and thrown with enough force they could still be deadly.

Yasmin unleashed a barrage of the unorthodox missiles, each one thrown with extreme velocity and devastating accuracy. She scored a direct hit to the face on three of the soldiers, shattering noses, teeth, and jaws. Several others managed to throw their arms up to shield themselves, only to have wrists, elbows, and forearms cracked and snapped by the deadly projectiles. Within seconds, the stage was littered with the prone bodies of grown men, groaning and whimpering in pain . . . or lying deathly silent.

Carthin stared in dumbfounded disbelief at the carnage around him, then dropped to his knees in supplication as Yasmin bounded up onto the stage.

"Call them off!" she barked.

He nodded emphatically and whipped out a white handker-chief, then shouted "Daybreak! Daybreak! Daybreak!" while waving it above his head.

It took a few moments for his command to make its way across the battlefield, but soon all of the soldiers had set down their weapons and retreated back to the edges of the banquet hall.

Yasmin looked out at the carnage, taking quick stock of the casualties. Four Inquisitors were dead, along with nearly thirty of Carthin's men, not including the dozen she had dispatched up on the stage.

The now-unarmed soldiers were huddled together against the side walls of the banquet hall, watching her with fear and trepidation.

"Go spread the word through the castle," she told them. "Carthin is my prisoner, and Lord Unferth is once again in charge!"

Relieved to be spared their lives, the soldiers rushed off to fulfill her commands.

"Go with them," she told her Inquisitors. "See that my orders are followed."

As her loyal followers disappeared, she turned her attention back to her prisoner.

"Did you really think you could overthrow the Order?" she asked him. "We have stood for seven hundred years!"

"Your power is far less than you know," Carthin answered.

His insolence surprised her. She'd expected him to grovel and beg for mercy though it would have been to no avail.

"Your Purge would have ended before it ever started if it wasn't for me," Carthin continued, his face twisting into a sneer. "Nobody cares for your religion anymore. My coin is what brought swords to your cause!

"If you execute me, how many of my mercenaries do you think will follow you to Callastan?"

He laughed, his eyes wild and crazed. "You still need me, Pontiff. If you want my armies, then we still have to work out some kind of deal!"

"You might be right," Yasmin admitted after a moment's thought. "Most of these soldiers care more for coin than for what is right.

"But," she added, even as a faint glimmer of hope appeared in Carthin's eyes, "it doesn't matter to any of them where the coin comes from.

"You are expendable," she whispered, leaning in close to his ear. "And tomorrow, I will watch you burn!"

The smell of burning flesh was abhorrent to many, but the Pontiff understood it for what it was. Like the putrid scent of a gangrenous limb being amputated, it represented a necessary measure to save a greater whole. And so she welcomed the oily stench, for she knew the fire cleansed and purified.

Beside her, Lord Unferth struggled not to gag as the wind shifted and the black smoke rolled over them. His position had been restored, but she sensed he was still disturbed by the scene of Carthin's execution.

In a perfect world, the former Justice would not have been the only one put to the flame. Each and every soldier who had raised a weapon against her Inquisitors deserved a similar fate. But at Unferth's urging, she had decided to show them clemency.

"They were only following orders," he had pleaded. "And if you show them mercy, they will owe you their lives. What better way to secure their loyalty before we march on Callastan?"

His words made sense, but they rankled nonetheless. It stank of weakness.

They say he has the soul of an artist. In the end, though, she was forced to accept his logic: They needed all the troops they could muster.

"Have you sent orders to the other garrisons Carthin controlled?" the Pontiff asked.

Unferth coughed and cleared his throat several times before speaking, struggling to spit out the taste of the bitter smoke.

"Birds and messengers have been dispatched. But I cannot say how many will respond.

"Even Carthin was having trouble keeping control of his troops, especially the mercenaries patrolling the borderlands. Now that he is gone, things will only get worse."

Yasmin nodded. Unferth had filled her in on the situation. The reports of soldiers going rogue—looting and pillaging defenseless villages—were more widespread than she had first imagined.

"Surely there are still some out there who are loyal to the Order," she mused.

"Some will answer your call, Pontiff," Unferth agreed. "But many will not.

"At least you can count on the support of me and my people," the old man added. "I may not be the warrior Carthin was, but I promise my devotion will not waver."

Perhaps the soul of an artist has more mettle than I thought.

"We will leave in three days," Yasmin told him. "And I will personally lead your troops as we march on Callastan."

Chapter 10

DARMMID WOKE FEELING nauseous. He peeled off the damp blanket he wrapped himself in and sat up from the small ditch at the side of the road where he'd spent the night.

The motion made his head spin, and he coughed and choked, spitting up globs of mucus and sour bile. He took a quick swig from his wineskin to wash the taste away, but it did little to settle his stomach.

The sun was barely up, but he knew better than to try to get back to sleep. The hex the one-handed mage had cast on him was powerful magic: He didn't feel sick just when he thought about disobeying his orders; he even felt ill if he stayed too long in one place.

Damn wizard got his hooks into you good, Darm. Nothing you can do but keep moving.

He got to his feet, rolled up his blanket, and stuffed it inside his pack of dwindling supplies. A few minutes later he was on the move again, pack slung over his shoulder, moving at an easy but steady pace down the narrow dirt road. With every step he felt the sickness slipping away, and within an hour he was back to feeling normal.

For a while, at least. Enjoy it while you can, Darm.

Ever since leaving the wizard and his strange companions, Darm had been marching steadily northwest toward the Free Cities. He avoided the main roads—too much chance of running into Inquisitors or Carthin's men. He hadn't survived this long just to be executed as a deserter.

Whenever he came across a village or small town, he took a wide detour around it—too many of those had been overrun by rogue mercenaries, and he didn't want to run afoul of them, either. But he was always quick to get headed back in the right direction as soon as possible. The one time he'd dared to try and actually change his course he'd been racked by stomach spasms and a vomiting fit so severe he thought he was going to die; since then he hadn't even thought about disobeying the wizard's instructions.

Of course, he had no idea what he was supposed to do once he got to the Free Cities or what the hex would do to him if he failed to convince them to come to Callastan's aid.

Don't have to worry about that yet, Darm. At this rate, it'll take you another week at least to get there.

"Things would go faster if I snuck into the next village and stole a horse," he muttered aloud.

He paused after the words were out of his mouth, waiting to see if they brought on another wave of nausea or some other physical ailment. Fortunately, he felt nothing. Apparently the curse he was under didn't care if he stole somebody's mount.

Just as long as you get where you're going, Darm. That's the only thing that matters. Just get where you're going.

"I think there's a small village a few miles over the next hill," Vaaler said.

"How could you possibly know that?" Shalana wondered.

Almost two weeks had passed since they'd left the clan camp at the Giant's Maw, heading out with the dozen warriors chosen to be in their honor guard. The winter snow and winds that had slowed their progress in the first days had been left far behind, the weather getting steadily warmer the farther west and south they went.

Two nights ago they had finally abandoned the supply sleds; now that they were in the border regions of the Southlands there wasn't enough snow on the ground to make them worthwhile. They had now traveled farther west than Shalana had ever been in her life, where the flat, snow-covered plains gave way to gently rolling hills of yellow-green grass and copses of small trees, their branches bare as they waited patiently for spring to return.

"The Danaan cartographers made detailed maps of the areas around the Free Cities," Vaaler explained in answer to her question. "I used to study them when I was a child."

"And you still remember them?" Shalana asked, raising one eyebrow.

"I don't forget things very often," he said with a self-effacing shrug. "The village is called Othlen, I think."

"You continue to surprise me," Shalana told him, leaning over to give him a quick peck on the cheek.

A few of the warriors in the honor guard chuckled, and the faint green hue of Vaaler's skin deepened with embarrassment.

"We should make camp here," he said, all business after flashing her a brief, shy smile. "If we crest the hill, someone in the village might see us."

Shalana nodded, and the others began to set up camp. The Stone Spirits had never attacked any of the settlements in the Southlands; their territory was farther east. But the same could not be said of other clans. Here they were still close enough to the Frozen East for the locals to be wary of raiding parties, and the sight of fourteen armed warriors descending on their town might send the people into a panic.

"In a few days we're going to run short of food," Shalana noted as she set down the pack she'd been carrying. "We might be able to hunt for what we need, but it will slow us down."

"Maybe I can go into town and bargain for what we need," Vaaler suggested.

"How?" she asked with a laugh. "We have no money. Nothing to trade but our weapons. And I think we'll need those once we reach Callastan."

"It's worth a try," Vaaler insisted. "I can be very persuasive when I have to."

"I won't deny that," she admitted with a smile. After a moment's consideration, she added, "You're right. We should go into town."

"Things will probably go better if I'm by myself," Vaaler noted.

"I didn't mean all of us," Shalana said, exasperated. "Just you and me. The others can stay here out of sight."

"Barbarians aren't very popular in these parts," Vaaler warned.

"Barbarians? Really?" She wasn't so much offended as surprised; she'd never heard Vaaler refer to her people in that way before.

"That's how folks around here see you."

"You're one of us now," Shalana reminded him. "Just look at how you're dressed."

Vaaler shook his head.

"People see me and the only thing they notice is the color of my skin. They think Danaan, not Barbarian. They'll see you as a threat. They'll see me as a curiosity, no matter how I'm dressed."

"You still shouldn't go alone," she insisted. "It's dangerous. Besides, I speak Allrish. I can blend in."

"Your accent would give you away. And besides," he added, reaching out to brush her cheek, "you are far too striking ever to just blend in anywhere."

Shalana didn't smile at the compliment; she was still worried about the idea of his going on alone. The journey so far had been easy and without incident, but she knew it was only a matter of time until trouble found them.

"I know you don't like this, but we don't have a lot of other options."

Gritting her teeth, Shalana finally nodded. *He's always so calm and logical. It makes it that much more frustrating when he's right!*

"I'll probably have to spend the night there," he said. "So try to at least wait until tomorrow afternoon before you panic and come charging in to save me."

"I'd rather you were careful enough that you don't need saving."

"I can't promise that," he said with a wink. Then he gave her a kiss and set off.

She watched until her love disappeared over the hill, then turned back to the others. "Sill and Genny, take the first watch. The rest of you try to get some sleep. I want to move out as soon as Vaaler gets back."

Village was too grand a word for the handful of small, nondescript buildings that greeted Vaaler. Othlen was really just a hamlet; nothing more than a small tavern and a few shops to service the surrounding farms.

It would have been strange to find the streets bustling with activity, but Vaaler was surprised to see them completely deserted. At the very least he would have expected some wagons or a few horses to be lashed to the hitching post outside the tavern; during the winter months farmers had little else to do but come into town to drink and share stories with each other.

Something feels off about this place. Like there's a pall in the air.

His first thought was plague. But if Othlen had been abandoned because of some kind of disease, there would have been quarantine markers along the road warning travelers away.

Maybe you're overreacting. Maybe it's just a slow night in a quiet little town.

Wary, he entered the village and made his way slowly down the middle of the dirt path that served as the only through road. In the evening's dusk, he caught a glimpse of light from under the tavern door as he passed by, and he felt some of his tension slip away.

At least someone's still here. Putting on a smile, he approached the door, pushed it open, and stepped inside.

The interior looked much as he'd expected: several small tables, a dozen chairs, and a simple bar against the far wall. A man of about forty stood behind the bar, a woman of about the same age hovered in the shadows of a back corner. Two men sat at one of the tables; based on the matching uniforms they wore and the short, broad swords dangling from the hilts slung over the back of their respective chairs, Vaaler guessed they were soldiers of some kind.

Everyone had turned to look at the new arrival, their eyes going wide on registering the stranger in their midst. One of the soldiers smiled and chuckled softly, shaking his head before giving his companion a knowing look. Vaaler waited for someone to speak, but nobody said anything else.

"Good evening," Vaaler offered, addressing the barkeep while trying to make his voice light and breezy. "I was wandering by and noticed a light from under the door. I trust you are open?"

The barkeep glanced at his other two customers, then back at Vaaler, his expression anxious.

"We're open," he finally said though the words sounded like a confession.

"I'm on a bit of a journey," Vaaler said, approaching the bar, "and I seem to be running short on supplies."

He tried to keep his manner casual, but he was careful not to lose sight of the two soldiers. He noticed they were watching him with keen interest.

"We don't have much in stock," the barkeep warned him. His

eyes kept jumping from Vaaler to the pair at the table. "Maybe you should just move on."

"Don't be so hasty, Gred," one of the soldiers called out, pushing his chair back and rising to his feet. "I'm guessing this Treefolk feller has something worth trading for."

The barkeep's face paled, and Vaaler's mind began to review his options. He was carrying his long, thin rapier at his side, but the last thing he wanted was for this to come to bloodshed.

"I'm afraid I don't have any coin," Vaaler admitted. "I was hoping I could maybe trade some interesting tales or maybe a song for a small bit of food."

"We don't have much use for stories or songs here," the second soldier said, also standing up now. "But those boots you have are mighty fine. Wouldn't mind a closer look at them."

"And maybe that pretty little blade, too," the first one added. "Not much use in a fight, but it would look good up on the wall."

"My blade is better in a fight than you might think," Vaaler said, his voice no longer light and charming. "Pray you don't find that out the hard way."

The first soldier held up his hands and took a half step back, laughing. "No harm meant. Just poking a little fun. Nobody's looking for trouble here."

That's an obvious lie, Vaaler thought.

"I'm sorry to bother you," he said to the barkeep. "I should go. My people will start to worry if I'm not back before sunset."

"Your people?" the second soldier said, his voice high and mocking. "And just how many people do you have? Ten? Twenty? A hundred?"

"I'm leaving now," Vaaler said, cold and hard. "You two step over to the wall. Leave your swords on the chairs!"

The first soldier shook his head and drew his blade. "We don't take orders around here. We give them."

His partner drew his own weapon and winked at Vaaler. Then they both charged.

Shalana had just finished eating when Sill came into the camp, breathing hard.

"What's wrong?" she asked him. "Where's Genny?"

"She's still keeping watch. We were patrolling the perimeter when she noticed smoke. A lot of it."

"From the village?" Shalana asked, instantly concerned about Vaaler.

"No. Farther south. We went to investigate. Saw some soldiers setting fire to a stable on a small farm."

"Were you spotted?"

Sill shook his head. "Genny stayed to keep an eye on them. Sent me back to get you."

Shalana whistled twice. In response, the entire camp sprang to their feet and grabbed their weapons.

"Show me."

The soldiers came at Vaaler from either side, spreading out as they rushed forward to try to flank him. A simple tactic, but one that killed his hope they were inexperienced or untrained.

He scampered back quickly, circling around so that they were both still in front of him. As they turned to cut off his escape, his eyes flicked down to their boots. You could learn a lot about an opponent simply from their footwork and balance. The men coming at him had the basics down, but they didn't pivot, slide, or turn with any kind of grace—their footfalls were heavy and deliberate.

They've been trained for field combat but not for dueling.

His theory was further supported by their weapons. Their short blades were durable and effective when hacking and slashing indiscriminately at enemies in the chaos of the battlefield, but they lacked precision and their weight made it difficult to thrust and parry. Vaaler's rapier, on the other hand, was light and quick—an ideal weapon for taking on one or two opponents.

Breaking off his retreat, he sprang forward and to his left, moving nimbly on the balls of his feet. The soldiers were caught off guard; clearly they'd expected him to keep giving ground. The closest tried a clumsy swipe of his blade, but his momentum was still moving in the wrong direction and he never came close to his target.

Vaaler's aim was much better, as he stabbed the tip of his blade into the meaty flesh of the soldier's right bicep.

Just like you taught me, Drake—always try to draw first blood.

The wound was far from lethal, but it was painful enough to make the soldier cry out and pull back . . . sending him right into the path of his companion. The two became momentarily tangled up with each other, preventing either one from attempting any kind of counterattack as Vaaler darted in close and circled around behind them, slicing open the cheek of the already wounded soldier with the rapier's fine edge.

The wound sent his opponent into a rage. He shoved his partner aside, using his weight for leverage to change his own direction so he could charge at Vaaler again. But the Danaan was ready for him as the soldier cocked his arm back and snapped it forward with all the force he could muster, and he easily spun out of the way of his wild, overextended swipe.

The missed blow sent the soldier stumbling off-balance, and Vaaler stepped forward as if to finish him off. The second soldier fell for the feint. Thinking he had a clear shot, he moved in hard, making no effort to protect himself. Vaaler seized the opportunity by swiveling his wrist and completely changing the orientation of his rapier—an impossible move for a heavier blade.

He delivered a quick thrust toward the face of the onrushing soldier, taking out one of his eyes. The injured man screamed and dropped to the floor, his free hand coming up to clutch at the ruptured, oozing orb.

By this time the first soldier had recovered enough to launch a counterattack. He moved more cautiously, jabbing and prodding with the point of his sword in small, quick strokes. But this wasn't some new tactic; the initial wound to his bicep simply made it painful to extend his arm fully.

Vaaler easily rocked back just enough to get clear of his limited range, then retaliated with a series of diagonal cuts that shredded the exposed knuckles and fingers wrapped around the blade's hilt. The soldier gasped and reflexively snatched his hand back, his sword falling from his gashed and bleeding digits.

Drake had taught Vaaler a hundred ways to finish off a disarmed opponent; Vaaler chose one and ended the soldier's life with a single stab through the heart.

The second soldier had struggled gamely back to his feet though he was still clutching at what was left of his eye with one hand. He lumbered forward, flailing desperately. Vaaler picked up the ponderous rhythm of his broad, sweeping strokes, then timed a quick thrust to the throat to put an end to the battle.

Throughout the brief altercation, the barkeep and his wife had stood still as statues. As Vaaler turned his attention away from his defeated foes, however, they both threw their hands up and began to speak at the same time.

"What have you—going to kill—back soon—get out."

Their words ran over and into each other, obscuring whatever message they were trying to get across. Then they both fell silent, their faces frozen in masks of utter horror.

"I won't harm you," Vaaler assured them. "These men forced my hand, but you have nothing to fear."

The man shook his head and let his gaze drop to the floor. The woman stepped from the shadows and approached Vaaler cautiously.

"You have to go," she said as she came forward. "Now. Get out of here before Skrill and the others get back!"

"Who's Skrill? Another soldier?"

"You have no idea what you've done to us," the man said, his voice mournful.

"Stay off the road," the woman continued. "Get as far away as you can, as fast as you can. If they find you, they'll kill you."

Vaaler's next question died on his lips as they heard the pounding of hooves and the neighing of horses coming from the street.

"You have no idea what you've done to us," the man repeated, still staring at the floor.

The woman grabbed Vaaler's arm and pulled him along toward a door in the wall beside the bar.

"Tell them he left," she snapped at her husband as she led Vaaler into the back room, closing the door behind her.

A small kitchen greeted them. A long counter cluttered with pots, pans, and cutlery filled up most of the room, and a tiny stove was stuffed into the corner. In the rear was a narrow hall that led farther into the building; glancing down it, Vaaler saw a large storeroom and another hall branching off to one side.

Even as Vaaler's mind was processing what was happening, they heard loud, laughing voices coming from the other room as the riders outside entered the tavern. These quickly changed to curses and exclamations of surprise and anger.

The woman crouched down and rapped her hand hard on the wooden floor. There was a soft click, then a virtually invisible trapdoor opened to reveal a narrow staircase. A shadowy figure with a dim lantern looked up at him from below.

"Down there. Quickly."

Vaaler didn't argue. The shadowy figure—a young woman—

pressed herself to the side, and there was just enough room for him to squeeze past. Then she pulled the trapdoor shut, sealing them in the hidden cellar.

She motioned for him to continue down the stairs. It didn't take Vaaler long to reach the bottom; the cellar was at most ten feet deep. Above them he heard more angry shouts, and heavy boots thumping on the floor as several large men stamped and stomped around in all directions, no doubt searching the premises for him.

The young woman reached the bottom of the staircase and motioned for him to follow her. Vaaler realized that the cellar was actually a long, narrow passage that led back out under the main tavern.

Smuggler's tunnels, Vaaler realized.

"Who are you?" he whispered, leaning in close to the young woman.

She flinched away momentarily, then leaned back in close to answer. When she spoke, her words were so soft Vaaler could just barely hear her.

"I'm Milliss. My parents hid me down here when the soldiers came."

"How long have you been down here?"

"Two weeks."

"You've been living in this tunnel for two weeks?"

"Better than being found," Milliss answered. "The soldiers take whatever they want."

Vaaler's stomach rolled as he caught the true meaning of her words.

"Is there a peephole or something?" Vaaler asked. "I want to see what's happening up there."

Milliss nodded. She walked forward, then snuffed out the lamp, leaving them in total darkness. Vaaler's ears pricked up at the faintest sound of a bolt being drawn, then a narrow beam of light streamed in from above.

The young woman stepped aside, and Vaaler moved forward. He found himself looking up through a small hole in the floor, but it was angled so that he could see the bar and a good portion of the tavern's main room.

A crowd of six or seven soldiers filled the room, dressed in the same uniforms as the men Vaaler had killed. The soldiers had dragged the barkeep and his wife into the center of the room, where the bodies still lay on the floor where they had fallen. One of the soldiers—a tall man with a dark beard, probably the leader— was shouting at the cowering couple.

"Where is he?"

"He ran off," the barkeep answered. "We don't know in which direction!"

"He was Danaan," the wife added. "Probably headed north, back to the forest."

"Why would a tree hugger show up in a crap heap of a town like this?" the soldier demanded.

"We don't know!" the barkeep protested. "He didn't say much. Just exchanged dirty looks with your men, then the fight broke out."

The soldier slapped the barkeep across the cheek with the back of his hand, his expression never changing. The older man's head snapped back and he grunted; his wife let out a single, sharp cry of distress.

In the tunnel beneath the floor, the young woman gasped softly, her hand going up to her mouth in horror. Vaaler didn't react physically, but he felt a righteous rage bubbling up inside him.

"I don't think you're telling me the truth," he said.

"Please, Captain Hirk, why would we make up a story like

that?" the wife begged, as her husband shook his head to try to clear the cobwebs.

"How long ago did he leave?" Hirk asked.

"Twenty minutes, maybe," the barkeep mumbled.

Hirk casually reached out and slapped him again, this time hard enough to make him stumble backward. Another soldier caught him and held him up as the captain stepped forward and delivered a hard punch to the gut. The barkeep doubled over and sagged to his knees as his wife tried to hold back her sobs.

"So you just let my men lay in their own blood for twenty minutes?" Hirk asked, dropping down to a knee so he could get face-to-face with the barkeep.

Vaaler turned away—he could see where this was headed. The soldiers wanted someone to suffer for what had happened. He briefly considered rushing back up the stairs and through the trapdoor, then quickly dismissed the idea. For one thing, it would reveal the secret hiding place and could expose the young woman beside him. For another, he'd be trapped in the bar with no way out, facing a half dozen armed and angry men.

"Is there a way out to the street?" he whispered, knowing most smuggler's tunnels had multiple exits.

The woman nodded, an expression of hopeless resignation on her face as she realized he was going to abandon them. She pointed to a small passage leading off to the side.

There wasn't time to justify or explain what he was doing, so Vaaler simply darted off in the direction she pointed, leaving her all alone in the small, dark tunnel.

Chapter 11

CROUCHED WITH HER warriors in a small grove of trees less than fifty yards from the farm, Shalana had a clear view of everything that was happening. Five armed soldiers had dragged a young couple out into the field, forcing them to kneel and watch as their stable was consumed by flames. From inside the burning building came the sound of squealing pigs, the helpless animals trapped by the flames while the soldiers stood by, laughing.

Is this some kind of punishment for something the couple did? Shalana wondered. *Or are the soldiers just sadists?*

"I do love the smell of roast pig!" one of the soldiers joked, his voice rising up above the crackling flames.

The young man kneeling on the ground turned his head and said something to the soldier, but Shalana couldn't hear him.

"Should have thought of that earlier," the soldier snapped back. Then he slammed his boot into the side of the man's ribs.

The woman jumped to her feet and tried to rush to his aid, but two of the soldiers grabbed her, one seizing each arm.

"I like a woman with some spirit!" one of them barked, and they began dragging the struggling, screaming woman in the direction of the small farmhouse.

Shalana had seen enough.

"Don't hurt the farmers!" she called out to her followers as she leapt from her hiding place and raced toward the farm.

The war cries of her honor guard rose up from behind her, and she felt the familiar rush of adrenaline that preceded every battle.

The sound drew the attention of the soldiers. The pair holding the young woman let her go, fumbling for their weapons. The other three took one look at the horde descending on them and simply turned and fled, making a run for the horses tied up to the hitching gate twenty yards away.

Shalana cocked her arm back and hurled her heavy spear, the missile slicing through the air and burying itself in between the shoulder blades of one of the fleeing soldiers. Four more spears launched a second later, and the other two dropped as well.

Without breaking stride, Shalana pulled the long knife from her belt as she bore down on the last two. One threw down his blade and held up his hands, while the other stepped forward to meet her charge.

Gripping the hilt with both hands, he brought the blade down in a diagonal chop. But Shalana was already leaping forward, her right leg kicking out. The hard leather of her knee-high boots caught the flat of the blade and knocked it away, sending it flying from the soldier's grasp. The momentum of her jump brought her crashing into her opponent, knocking them both to the ground. They rolled twice in a heap, then Shalana stood up, her blade dripping from where she'd plunged it into his heart.

The other man was still standing with his arms raised, watching the slaughter with wide eyes. Shalana watched as Genny came rushing toward him, the twin axes she carried raised high.

Only those warriors who are worthy are allowed to surrender, Shalana thought, making no move to intervene.

Genny's axes chopped down hard, coming into the soldier's neck at a forty-five-degree angle from either side and cleanly severing his head.

Shalana cast her head from side to side, looking for others they might have missed. The only people left alive were hers and the young couple. The man still lay on the ground clutching his side; the kick had obviously injured his ribs. The woman had rushed over to him during the fight. She stood above him protectively, awkwardly brandishing the sword from one of the fallen soldiers.

"Try to get the pigs out of the barn," Shalana called out to her people. Then she addressed the woman in Allrish. "We won't hurt you."

She turned her back on the couple and went to retrieve her spear. When she returned the woman had dropped her sword and helped the man to his feet. He was leaning heavily on her for support.

At the burning stable, her warriors had smashed open a locked gate on one of the walls that wasn't completely ablaze yet. As it swung open, five hogs came barreling out, running wildly around the farm in a panic. Recognizing they just needed to run themselves out, Shalana turned back to the couple.

"Who were those men?" she asked.

"They work for Hirk," the man replied. "Him and his group showed up a couple weeks ago. Just kind of took over the town."

"How many others?" Shalana asked, a new fear clutching at her insides.

"I think eight or ten, maybe," the man told her.

"Where are they?"

"They usually gather at the tavern each night. In Othlen."

Vaaler!

"Which way?" she shouted. "Show me!"

The cramped tunnel was longer than Vaaler expected. When he finally reached the end and climbed the rickety stairs back to the surface, he found himself emerging from an abandoned well almost a hundred yards away from the back of the tavern.

He covered the distance back to the tavern's front door with long, quick strides, his rapier clutched tightly in his hand. He threw himself through the door, causing it to crash loudly against the wall as it flew open.

The soldiers in the tavern spun around in surprise. The barkeep was still conscious, though his face was bloody and one eye was shut. His wife was on her knees, her hands clasped in front of her as tears streamed down her cheeks.

"What kind of coward beats an unarmed man?" Vaaler spat.

"Kill him!" Hirk shouted, and the soldiers all rushed forward.

Vaaler sprang backward and slammed the door behind him, then turned and took off running down the road, hoping to lead them away from the tavern. Most Danaan were fleet of foot, and he was confident he could outrun them.

Glancing back over his shoulder, he suddenly realized the obvious flaw in his plan as Hirk and his men threw themselves onto the backs of their horses. Realizing it was time for a new plan, Vaaler veered off the dirt road running through the center of town and made for the surrounding hills and trees, hoping to shake off his pursuers.

But the soldiers knew the area better than he did, and he heard Hirk barking out orders for his men to cut him off. Vaaler spared another glance back and saw several soldiers wheeling their mounts in different directions, circling around wide to make sure he couldn't escape.

Vaaler changed direction again, heading back to the town.

Maybe I can find shelter in one of the other buildings. Hide out or at least find somewhere to try to hold them off.

Unfortunately, Hirk had already anticipated this move, and Vaaler saw that his path back to Othlen was already cut off by the captain and two of his soldiers.

"Over here!" Hirk called out. "We got him!"

Knowing escape was hopeless, Vaaler dropped into a fighting crouch.

Maybe they'll come down off their horses to fight me on the ground. At least then I might take one or two of them with me.

Now that he had his prey cornered, however, the captain suddenly became cautious. He didn't order his men to charge recklessly forward; instead, they slowed and came to a stop about twenty feet away. A few seconds later Vaaler heard more horses closing in from either side, until he was surrounded by a circle of seven armed riders.

"Throw down your weapon!" Hirk ordered.

"I've seen what you do to unarmed men," Vaaler reminded him.

"I can do a lot worse if you make me angry," Hirk warned. "But get on my good side and maybe we'll let you go with just a beating."

"We both know that's not true," Vaaler answered.

"You can't get out of this."

"True. But I can take at least one of you with me."

Vaaler could tell some of the soldiers were shaken by his confidence; they had obviously gotten used to bullying defenseless townspeople.

"The others may take me down," he continued, "but the first man to come near me dies. So . . . any volunteers?"

Silence hung in the air for several seconds before Hirk said, "Someone go into town and find me a bow so I can shoot this tree hugger in the face."

Before any of the riders could react, a familiar voice rang out from the shadows outside the ring of horses.

"How about a spear?" Shalana shouted.

Hirk half turned in his seat to see who was speaking, so instead of piercing him through the back, Shalana's weapon buried itself in his right side just below his armpit with a heavy thud. The force of the blow knocked him from his saddle and he fell hard to the ground.

For a second the sight of their leader going down seemed to

stun the others. And then as one they broke ranks and turned to flee. But the honor guard of Eastern warriors fell on them like a divine wind of retribution.

Vaaler simply watched as the soldiers were slaughtered in brief and brutal fashion. Shalana marched out of the shadows and pulled her spear from Hirk's side, then rolled him over with her foot to see if he was still alive. Satisfied that he was gone, she left him lying in the dirt, his frozen face staring up at the night sky in an expression of utter disbelief.

"You were supposed to stay out of trouble," Shalana said, coming over to check on Vaaler.

"I told you I couldn't promise that," he reminded her, as they embraced.

For a few seconds he simply held her, reveling in the warm feel and familiar scent of the woman he loved. *I almost died tonight, and she knows it.*

His heart was pounding even faster now that the threat was gone, his mind conjuring up all the horrible things that could have happened.

But they didn't. And there's no point imagining the worst when it didn't happen. Shalana understands that.

Of course, that didn't mean they shouldn't take proper precautions.

"This might not be over yet," Vaaler said, reluctantly breaking their embrace. "There could still be other soldiers nearby."

"I think we found them all," Shalana reassured him. "Took out a handful at a nearby farm earlier tonight."

"I still need to go back into town," Vaaler said. "We need supplies, and I want to check on some people who helped me."

"Okay," Shalana agreed. "But this time, we're all coming with you."

As they marched back to town, Shalana was well aware that the people of Othlen might not welcome their arrival; a dozen armed Easterners descending on a town that had been terrorized by soldiers had the potential to cause a panic. But she wasn't willing to let Vaaler go off alone again.

Until we know for sure there are no more mercenaries in the area, we aren't splitting up.

The dark streets were empty as they approached, guided by the light of the moon above. But as Vaaler led them to the tavern in the center of town, she caught glimpses of light shining through shuttered windows.

They're watching us from inside, too scared to come out.

She felt pity for these people. Among her culture, the stronger clans demanded tribute from the weak. But they also provided protection and stability; they wouldn't commit atrocities against helpless victims.

Mercenaries have no honor. They're animals.

"This is it," Vaaler said, stopping at the tavern's closed door. "Let me go in alone first."

Shalana shook her head. "What if there's an ambush inside?"

Vaaler sighed, then nodded.

He knocked on the door, waited a few seconds then gently pushed it open.

The tavern was empty save for the bodies of two soldiers in the middle of the floor.

"I ran into some trouble when I first got here," Vaaler explained in response to her raised eyebrow.

"Hello?" Vaaler called out as the rest of the warriors made their way into the building. "We don't mean you any harm."

In response to his call a young woman emerged from the back room.

"Milliss," Vaaler said. "Where's your father? Is he hurt?"

"Mother's looking after him in the back," she said.

"May we see him?" Vaaler asked. "I'm not a healer, but I know something about treating injuries."

The young woman nodded, and Vaaler signaled for the others to wait where they were. Shalana ignored him and fell into step at his side.

They passed through a door in the rear of the tavern and into a small kitchen, where a middle-aged man was resting on the floor as his wife pressed a damp cloth against his temple. His face was badly bruised and swollen, and his shirt was stained with blood from his nose. But his eyes were clear and focused, and when he saw his new guests enter he gently pushed his wife away and gingerly rose to his feet.

"Thank you," he said, extending his hand in Vaaler's direction. "I fear they would have killed me."

"What happened to Hirk and his men?" the wife asked as Vaaler shook the man's hand. "Are they coming back?"

"No," Vaaler told them. "They're dead."

The hint of a smile touched the woman's lips, then vanished as she turned back to her husband's swollen face.

"Bastards deserve no better," she muttered.

"Do you know how many men Hirk had working for him?" Vaaler asked. "We need to know if some got away."

The husband closed his eyes and did a run-through of the names, his lips moving silently as he counted them off on his fingers. "Fourteen, I think. Including Hirk."

"We killed five at the farm," Shalana said. "And seven riders when we caught up with you in the woods."

"And two more here in the tavern," Vaaler added. "I think that's all of them."

Milliss, the young woman, put her hands up to her face, her eyes brimming with tears. Then she stepped over and wrapped her arms around Vaaler in a fierce hug.

"Thank you," she whispered. "You've saved us all."

Looking awkwardly over at Shalana, Vaaler untangled himself from the girl's gratitude.

"We don't have much to repay you," the father said. "Hirk and his crew took almost everything of value. But whatever we can spare is yours."

"We need supplies," Vaaler said. "And a place to rest for the night." Then he added, "There are fourteen of us in all."

"You're welcome to stay here in the tavern," the barkeep told them.

"We can feed you tonight, but we don't have enough food in stock to get you very far," his wife warned.

"What about the rest of the town?" Milliss said. "They've been storing up for winter. Hiding and rationing food since the soldiers came. Maybe they have enough to spare?"

Her father hesitated, then nodded his agreement.

"The people here will want to show their gratitude," he told Vaaler. "If you're willing, I'd like them to come here tomorrow to meet you."

Vaaler looked over at Shalana. "I think we can spare one day," she said. "It'll give us time to recover from the battle."

"Go across to Irven's shop," the barkeep told his daughter. "Tell him what's happened. Have him send his sons out to the surrounding farms to share the news."

Milliss turned and vanished through the kitchen door the instant he was finished speaking.

"She's been cooped up in those smuggler's tunnels for too long," Vaaler noted. "Probably dying to go outside."

Shalana didn't follow what he meant but the words weren't meant for her anyway.

"I only have enough beds for four," the barkeep apologized. "The rest of you will have to sleep here in the tavern."

"I'm so used to sleeping on the ground that I doubt a bed would do me much good anyway," Vaaler said.

"I'll send Genny and Sill back to the camp to get our stuff and bring it here," Shalana added. "They'll welcome spending a night with a roof over our heads and a warm meal in our bellies, even if we all sleep here on the floor."

Vaaler was roused from his slumber the next morning by the smell of freshly baked bread. He stood up and stretched, amazed at how rested and refreshed he felt. He'd gotten used to sleeping on the road, wrapped tightly in blankets to ward off the chill. Even so, it was nice to have a night where the wind wasn't whistling by his ears or the damp morning dew seeping through his bedclothes.

Shalana and the others were already up. They were gathered at the bar, laughing and chatting among themselves in Verlsung as they feasted on eggs, bacon, and buns. Vaaler made his way over to the bar to find a plate had been set aside for him. In addition to what everyone else had been served, there was a small bowl of wild berries.

"Milliss picked those just for you," Shalana said, grinning. If she was jealous of the young woman, she didn't show it.

She knows she's got nothing to worry about.

"It would be rude not to eat them," he said, giving his love a wink as he popped one into his mouth.

The berry was so tart it made his mouth pucker and his eyes water.

"Those aren't really in season yet," the barkeep said as he emerged from the kitchen. "But Milliss wanted to get you something special."

"Very kind of her," Shalana said, trying not to laugh. "It would be rude not to eat them," she reminded Vaaler.

Somehow, he managed to finish off the bowl, hiding the bitter taste with generous mouthfuls of egg and bread.

"The townsfolk have gathered outside," the barkeep told him once he was finished. "They're waiting to meet you."

"We're ready if you are," Shalana said.

"No sense keeping them waiting," Vaaler replied.

The crowd outside was far larger than he'd expected: nearly sixty men, women, and children had gathered in the middle of the dusty road going through town.

They must have come from every farm in a ten-mile radius, Vaaler thought.

As soon as he and Shalana emerged from the tavern, a smattering of applause broke out. As their honor guard came out to join them, the applause spread until the entire crowd was cheering enthusiastically.

It continued for nearly twenty seconds before an older, portly man stepped forward and held up his hand, calling for silence. Based on his age and the way he carried himself, Vaaler guessed he was the mayor or some other kind of elected official.

"My name is Lember," the man said, his voice carrying to the farthest edges of the crowd. "Reeve of Othlen. On behalf of our village, we offer you great thanks for liberating us from the monsters who terrorized our homes!"

Again, the crowd broke into cheers. The reeve let them continue for a few seconds, then motioned for quiet.

"We have gathered here today not only to thank you," he continued. "But to offer our support for your cause. Whatever you need—food, weapons, horses—we will give you."

"Thank you," Vaaler said, staring out at the crowd. "The food is welcome, but we have weapons of our own. A packhorse or two might be useful, but most of us aren't used to riding—we will travel better on foot."

"Make a list of what you need, and we will have it for you by nightfall," the reeve promised.

A short, stocky man of about forty stepped forward from the crowd. His leather smock was black with scorch marks, and the muscles in his neck and shoulders were so thick they seemed ready to burst from his shirt.

Must be the local blacksmith.

"I'm Irven," he said, executing a clumsy bow in Vaaler's direction. "My sons and I want to volunteer to join your army."

He pointed a beefy thumb back over his shoulder at three young men, short but as thick across the chest as their father.

"You want to come with us to Callastan?" Vaaler said, confused by the unexpected offer.

"Callastan?" the reeve said. "We thought you were heading to Shelder next."

Vaaler quickly consulted the image of the childhood map still lodged in his memory: Shelder was the next town over, roughly two days ride from Othlen.

"My sister lives in Shelder," the smith said. "They've had trouble with soldiers, too."

"Hirk's group aren't the only mercenaries in the area," the reeve explained. "Several of the other nearby towns are suffering just as we were."

"I'm sorry," Shalana chimed in. "But I think there's been some confusion. We didn't come here to liberate your town. What happened was just a fortunate accident. We need to get to Callastan."

There was some grumbling from the crowd, but it stopped when the reeve held up his hand.

"Have the Free Cities decided to try to break the siege, then?" he asked.

"What siege?" Vaaler asked.

"The Pontiff's army has surrounded Callastan. I would have thought that news would have reached the Free Cities by now."

"What do the Free Cities have to do with us?" Shalana asked.

"Aren't you one of the patrols from the Free Cities?" the reeve asked.

"Do we look like we're from the Free Cities?" Vaaler replied.

"I . . . I don't know," the reeve answered. "I've never been there. None of us has."

Vaaler wasn't surprised by the admission—the Free Cities were at least a week farther north and west. It was doubtful anyone in a small town like Othlen would ever need to go there. All they would know about the Free Cities were tales told by travelers and merchants passing through; to them they would seem like wild, exotic locations populated by strange people wearing even stranger clothes.

Can't really blame them for assuming that's where we came from. Makes a lot more sense than the truth.

"We heard a rumor the Free Cities were sending out patrols to protect the nearby villages from the Order's mercenaries," the reeve explained. "We thought we were too far away to get help, then you showed up."

"We were just passing through," Shalana said. "We can't stay."

"If you leave," the barkeep said, stepping out from where he stood behind Vaaler near the door of his tavern, "it won't be long before another group of soldiers comes to claim this town for their own."

"Please," the smith said, "Hirk and his crew were bad, but I heard the ones in Shelder are even worse."

"You won't have to do this alone," the reeve promised. "Irven and his sons aren't the only ones who will join you."

"He's right," a young man said, stepping forward from the crowd. "You saved my farm last night," he said, nodding at Shalana. "I won't be a helpless victim again! If you give me a weapon, I'll fight with you when you go to Shelder."

"So will I!" a voice called out from the crowd.

"Me, too!" another chimed in.

"We can't waste our time clearing out every band of rogue mercenaries and deserters wandering the countryside," Shalana whispered in Vaaler's ear. "Not if you want to get to Callastan anytime soon."

She was right, of course. But even if they got to Callastan, what would they do next? He'd been hoping they could find Keegan and the others while they were looking for Cassandra. But if the Order had an army camped outside the city walls, what help could his small group of warriors be? They'd never even get close to the city.

The fate of the mortal world is at stake, Vaaler thought. *But do I really have any part in that anymore? I already abandoned Jerrod's cause to help Shalana and the clans. How is this any different?*

"If Callastan is under siege, then going there would be suicide," Vaaler said, speaking softly to Shalana. "We'd be throwing our lives away for no reason.

"And these people need us," he continued. "We can make a real difference here. I don't know if I can just turn my back on them."

Shalana smiled and reached out to grasp Vaaler's shoulder, turning him slightly so they were staring directly into each other's eyes.

"We are not here because of the blind monk's prophecy," she told him. "We are here because of you. We trust your judgment. And so should you.

"If you feel your destiny has led you here to help these people, then that is what we must do. Whatever you decide, we will stand with you."

Her words crystallized and clarified what had moments ago seemed so confusing. *Keegan and Scythe don't need me—they have the Talismans. Whatever part I had to play in their destiny has come and gone; the fate of the mortal world is in their hands now, not mine.*

The fate of the villagers before him, however, was another matter. These people were suffering. They needed help.

I can't turn my back on these people. This is where I belong.

Turning to the crowd, he called out in a loud voice, "Tomorrow we march on Shelder, and we welcome anyone who will march with us!"

Chapter 12

CASSANDRA NO LONGER fought against Rexol's presence in her dreams. After witnessing the gruesome ritual of the Slayer's Minion, she had finally embraced the necessity of becoming his student. Yet at the same time she wasn't ready simply to cast aside everything she had learned in the Monastery, and she remained guarded even as she began her apprenticeship.

Each night in her dreams she would find herself studying at his feet. And in the surreal realm of her subconscious, her studies were progressing at an astonishing rate. In a single night she could grasp what might take months to fully understand in the real world, the knowledge passing from Rexol directly into her eager, hungry mind.

She didn't have a use for everything he taught her; many of the lessons were focused on the ways a wizard could summon and control the power of Chaos. And though she couldn't help but learn something of the mage's art, she made no real effort to memorize the spells and incantations Rexol shared with her. Without Chaos root to open her mind, she reasoned, even the simplest spell would be far too taxing.

The underlying theory of his lessons, however, was immensely valuable. It had helped her understand the fundamental nature of Chaos. In many ways it was like a living thing though its existence was awash in paradoxes. It could be incredibly malleable and pliant, yet at the same time it was stubbornly resistant to a mage's will.

The teachings of the Order were rigid and dogmatic; they had given her will great strength, but at the cost of flexibility. With Rexol's help, her mind was becoming more adaptable and versatile—a key component in mastering and manipulating Chaos.

Most important, Rexol was teaching her how to draw on the Crown. The Talisman had seemingly limitless reserves of power she could tap into, as long as she was careful.

Your caution is a by-product of what you learned in the Monastery, Rexol told her. *It is holding you back.*

Cassandra knew there was no point in arguing with him. The wizard was far too rash; even the destruction of his physical form hadn't quelled his recklessness. And for all the wisdom he had shared with her, his imprisonment inside the Crown had clearly driven him insane.

Each time she drew from the Crown, she felt Rexol lurking. Watching and waiting for her to drop her guard so he could swoop in and seize control of her body, as he'd done when she placed the Talisman atop her head during the battle with the Crawling Twins. But Cassandra wasn't about to let the mad wizard escape again. Instead of wearing the Crown, she would only reach out to it with her mind, barely brushing up against the edges of its power.

Even that was enough for her. The injuries to her legs were almost completely healed; she was able to stand and walk without pain. In another day or two her limbs would be fully restored.

Why wait another day? Do it now! You know you can if you just dare to wear the Crown!

She was grateful to Methodis for all he had done for her, but soon she would be ready to leave his care. The army of Inquisitors outside Callastan only added to her urgency to leave, but she had to be careful. Methodis had warned her there were rumors that the Pontiff had agents inside the city looking for her. But that wasn't the only problem she faced. Even if she could slip past the Order and leave Callastan, she still had no idea where to go.

Daemron feels it in the back of his horned skull—a faint but relentless thrumming, like the waves beating endlessly against the shore. At first he tries to ignore it; he has other troubles on his mind. His armies grow restless, impatiently waiting for the Legacy to fall. Centuries of pent-up anger and frustration simmer and bubble, and his generals are not strong enough to keep it from boiling over in skirmishes among the troops.

Sometimes his soldiers argue over who must take next watch. Other times, one is caught stealing rations from another. The fights typically end in bloodshed. The losers that survive these confrontations are immediately culled: crucified to serve as an example for the rest. Supplies are scarce, and weakness will not be tolerated.

Daemron does nothing to quell the sporadic outbursts of violence. It means the troops are primed for battle. The war they are about to fight will not be won with discipline and tactics; fury and rage are the hallmarks of his forces. Yet he also understands the precariousness of his position. If the Legacy does not fall soon, his troops will tear each other apart.

Or finally turn against me.

If the generals feel he is waiting too long—if they start to believe his promises that the Legacy will fall are nothing but a trick to hold on to power—they will betray him. He is still far stronger than they can imagine, but together they have the numbers to overwhelm him.

For now, they are scattered—each leading a portion of his forces deployed in search of locations where the Legacy is most fragile. When the barrier finally collapses, it will not come down all at once. Chunks will crumble and fall away, exposing portals that connect to the mortal world. He can use these portals to send his army through and begin the invasion . . . but first they must be found.

A dozen military camps dot the barren landscape of his kingdom, separated by many leagues. He visits each one every two or three days, soaring above the troops so they see him, watching from above—a constant reminder of who they serve.

But today he must cut his rounds short. The pounding in the back of his head has become too insistent to ignore. At first he dismissed it as the distant rumblings of Chaos, seeping through the fraying Legacy. Now, however, he recognizes it for what it truly is: a call from his Minions in the mortal world.

He is loath to abandon his army, even for a day—their leash must be kept taut. But he must heed the call, and so he returns from the camps to his now-abandoned capital city. With powerful beats, his wings take him high above the spires of his castle, to the dome above his inner sanctum. Then he folds his wings and drops like a stone, plummeting through the hole in the roof and hurtling headfirst toward the floor.

At the last second he unfurls his wings and flips around, landing on his feet hard enough to send a reverberating crash echoing off the walls of his sanctum. The stone floor beneath his hooves cracks from the force of the impact, sending up a small cloud of dust, but he cares nothing for the damage. He has turned his focus back to the mortal world, and now he realizes everything here—the city, the castle, even his inner sanctum—is worthless and wretched.

The pounding in his head continues, like an angry, urgent fist hammering on a door. He takes a deep breath, forcing a calm to fall over him. He closes his eyes and pushes away thoughts of the approaching invasion and his fears of betrayal, leaving only a vast emptiness inside his mind.

Instantly images from the mortal world rush in to fill it: the fall of the Monastery at his Minion's hands; the splintering of his followers; a dragon, slaughtered by the power of his Ring; the rise of the ogre; armies marching into battle; the return of the Guardian; and, finally, Chaos unleashed by the Crown and a city under siege.

His eyes snap open as the scattered images assemble into a message from Orath—a warning and a cry for help. The Children of Fire—the four mortals touched by his spell from long ago—are far stronger than even he imagined. They haven't just found his Talismans—they are actually learning to control them. Of the Minions, only Orath still lives; one lone survivor from seven of his most powerful followers. And despite the destruction of the Monastery, the Order still survives . . . and they are close to recovering the Crown.

Daemron tilts his head back and bellows his rage to the sky. Orath has failed. His mission was to find the Talismans and bring down the Legacy. Instead, the mortals now have the weapons they need to stand against his army. Perhaps they even have the power to kill an Immortal.

He takes deep, angry breaths, snorting like a bull until he regains his composure.

All is not lost. The Children of Fire are using the Talismans, but they still do not understand their true nature. And they have not all joined forces yet. There is still hope.

A plan begins to form in his mind, a way to hasten the fall of the Legacy. He recalls his recent dream: the Old Gods, gathered at the Keystone to enact the ritual that banished him. He didn't understand at the time, but now he knows the purpose of the vision. He realizes there is a way to make sure he knows exactly where the first breach will happen.

Sending a reply to Orath will be difficult, but he has reached across the Burning Sea to touch the mortal world before. This time will be easier than the last; the Legacy is fading, and instead of having to navigate the vastness of the Burning Sea he can simply retrace the path of Orath's message back to the source.

For a few days he will be drained: exhausted and vulnerable. But the generals will be too busy to plot against him during that time. He will send out orders that the scattered camps must be struck; the generals must rally his entire army at a single location. The Legacy is still strong at the Keystone, but that is where the invasion will begin. And, if his plan works, the Children of Fire will be the ones who open the way.

Orath hadn't left the cellar since performing the ritual that sent the call out to his master. For three days he'd waited patiently for the inevitable response, so when it finally came he was eager to receive it.

Like his own message, it arrived in the form of disconnected images, one rolling into another in a rapid-fire stream. But Daemron's call was far more powerful than the one Orath had sent out. When the Minion opened his mind, it was nearly overwhelmed by the raw power of an Immortal's will flooding in.

His head snapped back and he hissed in pain, the images searing his thoughts as they burned themselves indelibly into his consciousness. But with the suffering came knowledge, and as the pain slowly faded away Orath understood the trap his master had set.

He was not the only one who would be affected by Daemron's call. There were some among the mortals—prophets and Seers with Chaos in their blood—who would pick up echoes and reflections of what Orath had seen. But they would only see what Daemron wanted them to see: carefully crafted visions to lure them into the trap.

Orath still had to play his part, of course. So far he had failed in his mission; Daemron was clearly displeased. Yet there was still a chance to redeem himself. The growing army of monks and soldiers just outside the city walls was not part of his master's plan; he could not allow the Crown to fall back into the Order's hands.

The Crown must be brought to the Keystone.

The Children of Fire had found the Talismans. They had called upon their ancient power and unleashed Chaos into the mortal world. But now that power was about to be turned against them.

Cassandra stands on a beach of white sand, the waves of the Western Sea lapping against the shore at her back. A massive obelisk of black obsidian stands before her, reaching up fifty feet into the sky.

She takes a slow step forward, inexorably drawn to the smooth, dark stone. As she draws closer she sees runes carved into the sides, and she can sense something moving beneath the surface of the rock.

It reminds her of the Monastery. The spirits of devoted monks who passed from the mortal realm lived on inside the stone walls, watching over their brethren in the Order. Like the True Gods, they sacrificed themselves so that their essence could help protect the Monastery and keep its enemies at bay.

"But the Monastery has fallen," Rexol reminded her.

In her vision, the wizard wasn't speaking from inside her head; he was standing beside her, his body whole once more.

Ignoring him, Cassandra reaches out and lays her left palm against the obelisk. The stone surface is warm from the sun, and she can feel it tingling beneath her touch.

The sky above them explodes in a panoply of colors—millions of bright beams of red, blue, yellow, and green shoot back and forth, interweaving to form a massive dome of brilliant white light.

"The Legacy!" Cassandra gasps, awestruck at the beauty of the final gift the True Gods bestowed upon the mortal world.

She had never heard of the Keystone before—if the Pontiff or any in the Order knew of its existence, they had never shared their knowledge

*with her. Yet as she stared up in amazement at the brightness in the sky,
she instinctively knew what the obelisk was and what it was called. This
was where the True Gods had sacrificed themselves to banish the Slayer.
This was where the Legacy had been born.*

"It's fading," Rexol notes.

*To her dismay, Cassandra sees that he speaks the truth. Now that her
initial wonder has passed, she notices that the glowing magnificence of the
Legacy is marred by small, scattered patches where it has turned dull and
gray.*

*As she watches, the gray patches begin to multiply. They begin to grow
and spread, joining together to swallow up the pristine whiteness. And as
the Legacy fades, Cassandra is able to sense what waits on the other side:
Daemron the Slayer and his monstrous hordes.*

*"There isn't much time," Rexol warns her. "You must use the Crown
to defeat Daemron when he returns!"*

*For the first time in the vision, Cassandra realizes she has been clutch-
ing the Talisman in her right hand. She knows that the wizard is right;
Daemron has to be stopped.*

She brings the Crown up and places it on her head . . .

Cassandra's mind snapped her back to consciousness. Even in a
dream, she wasn't ready to wear the Talisman again. Not yet.

With her Sight, she could see it was dark outside; night had
fallen over Callastan. A full moon hung above the city—but instead of its normal color, it was dark red.

Cassandra knew the Blood Moon as a portent of impending
disaster, an ill omen that hadn't been seen in nearly twenty years.

You were born under the Blood Moon, Rexol reminded her. *It
means Chaos has been unleashed upon the mortal world.*

The crimson orb in the sky only confirmed what her vision
had already shown her. The Legacy was about to fall. Daemron
was about to return.

Despite what Rexol had said in her dream, however, she knew
she didn't have to fight Daemron. A battle with the Slayer and his

army would not save the mortal world—it would only bring death and destruction.

The Legacy must be restored. If I go to the Keystone, I can use the Crown to repair it!

She expected Rexol to make some snide comment, but the wizard only asked, *How are you going to get there?*

"My vision will guide me," Cassandra said aloud. "The island sits at the farthest edge of the Western Sea. All I need is a captain and a ship willing to take me."

Outside her room, Methodis was puttering around his apothecary. The kindly doctor had already done so much for her she hated to ask anything else of him. But she was a stranger in Callastan, and he knew the city and its people.

You're a fool, Rexol declared. *The only sailors he knows will be pirates! You can't trust them!*

"You don't trust anybody," she muttered.

Rolling from her bed, she took a few seconds to test her legs. The muscles felt strong, her balance was good, and she felt no pain of any kind.

Every day that she stayed hidden in the back room put Methodis at greater risk. Eventually, the Pontiff's army outside Callastan's walls would attack. A number of Inquisitors had probably already infiltrated the city, searching for her and gathering information in preparation for the inevitable assault.

Even if they find you, Rexol reassured her, *you can use the Crown to defeat them and get away!*

The wizard was probably right but Cassandra would only use the Talisman as a last resort. She had accepted the need subtly to draw on it to heal herself, but she still wasn't willing to take the risk of unleashing its full power by actually placing it atop her head.

More importantly, if the Inquisitors found her, Methodis would be the one to suffer if she escaped. If the venerable healer somehow survived the Pontiff's brutal methods of interrogation, he would still end up being burned as a heretic for daring to help her.

She had stayed hidden long enough. She was healthy and strong again. It was time to ask her host to help plan her escape from Callastan.

Chapter 13

THE CLOUDS ABOVE their makeshift camp were too thick to see the night sky, but Jerrod's Sight—weakened as it was—allowed him to pierce the veil and sense the Blood Moon hovering above them. He didn't know what it meant, not exactly, but its presence filled him with dread.

The last Blood Moon heralded the birth of the Children of Fire. Does this one foretell the final fulfillment of the prophecy of the Burning Savior, or does it warn of their death and defeat?

Scythe and Keegan were sleeping, wrapped up in blankets against the dampness of the grassy hollow where the three of them had bedded down. They were only a few days away from Callastan now. A few days away from reaching Cassandra and the Crown . . . assuming they could find a way to get past the Order's siege.

And then what happens? Jerrod wondered. *Will she believe me if I say she has to join us? What if she refuses?*

The Blood Moon didn't augur well for how such a confrontation might end.

Jerrod pulled his focus away from the sky and down to his two young traveling companions. Scythe's eyes were closed and her breathing was slow and rhythmic, but he didn't actually know if she was asleep. Now that she carried Daemron's Sword, she only needed one or two hours of rest each night. And even when she drifted off, part of her senses were always on high alert, ready to spring into action.

Keegan, on the other hand, was in a deep slumber. His soft snores were interrupted by quiet moans and momentary shudders as his mind wrestled with its nightmares, a common occurrence ever since he'd first used Daemron's Ring.

Three children born under the Blood Moon, each carrying one of Daemron's Talismans, on the verge of meeting beneath another Blood Moon. Jerrod knew it had to be more than coincidence.

Cassandra has to join us. I have to make her understand that she is part of the prophecy of the Burning Savior!

And yet, a small part of Jerrod's mind couldn't help but wonder if his interpretation of the prophecy was wrong.

He wasn't a Seer. As a young child, he'd seen visions in his dreams—frequent enough that his devout parents had willingly given him to the Monastery when he was only five. But after joining the Order, his visions had faded. He was trained to be an Inquisitor, and as a young man he'd served zealously in his role.

Like most Inquisitors, he rarely had dreams of any real significance. But one night, almost twenty-five years ago, he'd had a vision that changed his life forever. He could still remember the dream: a figure bathed in fire; a champion taking up the ancient Talismans created by the True Gods to stand against Daemron the Slayer and thwart his return. For three straight nights the dream had come to him: an image so vivid, so intense, that even while awake he had thought of nothing else.

When he spoke of it to Nazir—Yasmin's predecessor—the Pontiff had confirmed that others had recently shared a similar dream. He also told Jerrod that the figure bathed in flames wasn't actually a champion or savior. The Seers, the Pontiff explained, had already interpreted the true meaning of the vision, cobbling together all the details from several different accounts.

"The Legacy is crumbling, Jerrod. Daemron is dying; our ancient enemy grows desperate to escape his prison. But the burning figure you see is actually symbolic of Chaos itself; it represents all the torment and suffering it will cause if allowed to run free in the mortal world.

"The vision is a warning that we must be ever vigilant in our duty. As the Legacy grows weaker, the influence of Chaos on our world grows stronger. Now more than ever, we must seek out those touched by Chaos—the Children of Fire—and bring them into the fold of the Order before they unleash terrible destruction upon the world."

Jerrod had accepted the words of the Pontiff though even then some part of him had not been able to fully embrace the official interpretation of the dream. Yet he kept his doubts silent lest he be accused of lacking faith.

It was only when Ezra—one of the Order's most revered Seers—approached him that he learned there were others who shared his misgivings. Ezra drew him into the circle of those who rejected the official interpretation of his vision and Jerrod was quick to embrace their cause. Unlike the Pontiff, they did not believe Daemron would perish before the Legacy fell. Ezra and the followers of the Burning Savior believed a mortal champion was destined to arise and turn the Slayer's own weapons against him in order to save the mortal world.

For twenty years Jerrod had devoted himself to this new belief—first, as a secret follower working within the Order to find and recruit others to the cause, including Rexol, the most powerful Chaos mage in the Southlands. Later, when Ezra died, Jerrod became the leader of the old Seer's small but loyal group of followers. Eventually Rexol exposed him and he was forced to flee, but he never lost his faith.

His belief was so strong that when he had a vision of Rexol and his young apprentice being imprisoned beneath the Monastery, Jerrod had arranged for himself to be captured so he might help them escape. And when Rexol was destroyed by the power of the Crown, Jerrod had been quick to take Keegan under his wing. After all, who better than he himself to protect the prophesied savior of the mortal world?

Throughout it all he had remained confident in his convictions. The exact details of the prophecy were unclear, and over the past few months he had refined and clarified the specifics of what he believed. At his core, however, one fundamental truth remained unchanged: The Children of Fire were saviors who would destroy Daemron the Slayer.

Yet ever since Norr's death, the first seeds of doubt had taken root in the corners of his mind. For the first time in over twenty years, his confidence had wavered.

Part of it had to do with his normal vision's being restored. With the white veil across his eyes removed, he struggled to use his Sight. But the effects were even more far-reaching; he'd felt it when he faced the Inquisitors in the ambush a few nights ago. With his focus split between combat and allowing his Sight to pierce the images of his normal, human visions, he was much slower than he had once been. If not for Scythe, the Inquisitors would have won that battle.

You're letting your lack of faith in yourself weaken your faith in the prophecy.

But he knew it was more than just that. Something Scythe had said when they set the soldier free kept gnawing at him.

"There's Chaos in our blood. We are bringers of death and destruction! Daemron was a hero once, too—and look what he became. In a thousand years, will the Order be looking for someone to save the world from us?"

Keegan had power—he'd seen ample evidence of that. And Scythe had an incredible, almost indomitable, will. But was that enough to save the world?

He'd watched Keegan struggling to do the right thing, trying to use his power for good. He'd helped Norr win his duel with Shalana even though he clearly had feelings for Scythe. He'd re-

fused to let them execute a prisoner, making every effort he could
to spare the soldier's life.

He's still just a kid, but at least he's trying to be a good man.

Still, Jerrod had his doubts. Keegan still showed flashes of the
selfishness and arrogance Rexol had taught him. What if defeating
Daemron required him to make the ultimate sacrifice? Did he
have it in him to give up his life—or his power—for the sake of
others? Or, like Scythe had said, what if he had to sacrifice her?
Would he be willing to pay that cost?

And what about Scythe herself? Despite her insistence that she
was ready to do whatever was necessary to fulfill her destiny, Jerrod still had his doubts about her.

Norr's death had changed the young woman. She no longer
fought Jerrod at every step. She even seemed to embrace her role
as one of the Children of Fire. But what was really driving her?
A hunger for vengeance? Nihilistic rage and hatred? Could she
really be a savior if her motives weren't pure?

Jerrod had chosen his path long ago; he wasn't about to change
it now. But as they marched inevitably toward the end of this long
journey, he was no longer certain they were doing the right thing.

He'd tried to recall the vision that had inspired him so long
ago. But he was no longer able to recapture the vivid intensity of
the dream. The details were blurred and half-forgotten, faded over
the years just like the certainty of his youth.

This is the danger of letting dreams and prophecies guide us, he
thought. *When the visions stop, what are we left to cling to?*

*Keegan stands on the shores of a white sand beach. He recognized his
surroundings; he'd seen this place in other visions. This time, however,
something was different.*

*Previously, there had been another with him—a woman lying on the
sand at his feet. A figure of fire had loomed above him, and he'd seen the*

enemy hordes rushing through the breach in the Legacy. This time, however, he was completely alone.

Yet though the island was deserted, it wasn't empty. Farther inland, a massive black obelisk rises from the earth before him. Curious, Keegan begins to walk toward it.

The obelisk pulses with power, simultaneously compelling yet repulsive. Reaching the base, he reaches out with his good hand and places it on the surface. Instantly, a collage of images floods his mind: the Old Gods, the Keystone, the creation of the Legacy, the banishment of Daemron the Slayer.

He staggers back and drops to his knees, overwhelmed. Yet on some level, he knew what he'd seen wasn't real. Unlike his previous visions of the island, this one felt unnatural. Manufactured. Artificial.

"Something's not right," he mutters.

And then the Keystone explodes, swallowing him up in a pillar of searing blue Chaos fire.

Keegan woke with a start, his heart pounding. He didn't know if he'd cried out, but Jerrod was at his side in an instant.

"What's wrong?" the monk demanded.

"A vision," Keegan said, breathing slowly to calm his racing heart.

"Great," Scythe said from close behind him. "These are always so useful."

Jerrod shot her a sour look, then turned his attention back to Keegan. "What did you see?"

"An island," he said. "A place I've dreamed of before. I think it's where we will battle Daemron when the Legacy falls."

"Let me guess," Scythe interjected. "You have no idea where this island is, do you?" When Keegan shook his head, she added, "Perfect."

"What else did you see?" Jerrod urged.

"There was an obelisk made of dark stone. Like the walls of the Monastery. It's called the Keystone."

From the blank look on Jerrod's face he clearly had no idea what Keegan was talking about.

"It's where the Old Gods created the Legacy," Keegan said. "The Order doesn't know anything about this?"

"Perhaps the Pontiffs knew of such a place," he explained, "but if so, it was a secret kept from the rank and file."

"I thought the Order was supposed to defend the Legacy," Scythe noted. "Why would they keep this from you?"

"The existence of the Crown was a secret known only to a few," Jerrod reminded them. "Perhaps the Keystone is dangerous. If it was used to create the Legacy, maybe it can also be used to bring it down.

"What else did you see?" the monk asked.

"Nothing, really," Keegan said. "But there was something odd about this vision. It felt off."

"What do you mean?"

The young mage shook his head. "It's hard to put into words. The vision felt artificial. As if it almost wasn't real."

"It wasn't real," Scythe said. "It was just a dream."

"Visions feel different from dreams," Jerrod insisted. "They are projections born from the Sea of Fire, manifestations of raw Chaos seeping into the mortal world. There is an intensity—an insistence—about them that is unmistakable. If anything, they feel almost too real."

Keegan nodded. "Right. But this vision didn't feel like that. It almost felt . . . staged.

"I probably wouldn't have noticed, but I've seen this place in other visions. It's familiar enough to me that I sensed something wasn't right."

"Maybe someone is trying to trick us," Scythe said. "Is it possible to send out a false vision?"

Keegan shrugged and looked over to Jerrod, who shrugged in return.

"I suppose such a thing is possible," the monk admitted. "Though I have never heard of it. It would require incredible power."

"Maybe it's Cassandra," Keegan suggested. "She could be using the Crown to reach out to us!"

"Or maybe it's the Slayer setting some kind of trap," Scythe countered.

"Daemron cannot touch the mortal world," Jerrod insisted. "The Legacy keeps him at bay. That is why he sent his Minions to be his agents."

"Then maybe it's one of the Minions," Scythe said. "Or maybe the Legacy is weaker than you think.

"You keep talking about Daemron's return, but it seems like you haven't really thought it through," she added. "If he's out there waiting for the Legacy to fall, do you really believe he's just sitting around doing nothing all this time?"

"You speak about things you cannot possibly understand," Jerrod told her.

"Don't pretend you're some all-knowing oracle," Scythe shot back. "It's obvious you're stumbling around as blind as the rest of us!"

Keegan was glad to see some of the fight had come back to Scythe, but he didn't want his companions to keep arguing.

"If the vision returns, I can explore it more thoroughly," Keegan offered. "Maybe even track it back to its source and find out what felt so strange about it."

"No!" Jerrod barked, surprising them both with the sharpness of his outburst.

"The history of the Order recounts several such attempts in our past," he explained. "A number of powerful Seers—many of them among the greatest prophets ever to dwell within the Mon-astery walls—have tried to seek out the source of their visions.

"Through meditation and mental exercises, they learned to induce their dreams on purpose, then tried to strip away the projected images to reveal what lay beneath.

"None were ever successful. They all became lost forever in the Burning Sea, their identity swallowed up by the flaming ocean of Chaos. What remained was nothing but an empty shell of flesh and blood—a mindless husk that lived on for days until it withered away from hunger and thirst."

"Of course," Scythe said, throwing her hands up in exasperation. "Why did I think anything about dreams or visions could actually be useful?"

"Promise me, Keegan," Jerrod said, grabbing the young mage by his shoulders. "If the vision returns, do not do anything foolish."

"I'm not going to throw my life away," he answered.

Jerrod stared into his eyes for several seconds, then nodded.

"A Blood Moon hangs in the sky above us," the monk added. "There are difficult and dangerous times ahead. Whatever your vision means—whether it is a call from Cassandra, a trick from Daemron, or something else entirely—will be revealed soon enough."

"There are still a few hours until morning," Scythe grumbled. "You two get some sleep and I'll take the next watch."

When Jerrod hesitated, she added, "You still need to rest, even if it's only a few hours a night. Maybe it'll help get back some of that special Sight you've lost."

Keegan braced himself for an angry retort, but the monk only nodded. He hadn't realized how much Jerrod was still struggling since the return of his normal vision, but it clearly hadn't escaped Scythe's notice.

Maybe she's right. Maybe sleep will help him.

The two men bedded down while Scythe got up and began to walk the camp's perimeter, Daemron's blade clutched firmly in her grasp.

Scythe circled the camp with quick, forceful steps. The calm she'd felt in the aftermath of her fight with the Inquisitors was gone, replaced by a restless frustration she couldn't seem to shake.

She was angry at herself for arguing with Jerrod. She'd vowed to honor Norr's memory by following the monk and his prophecy without question. She'd promised herself she would see it through to the end, no matter what. And for a while, she'd been able to hold her tongue.

But lately she'd been snapping at him more and more. The cold, emotionless calm she'd worn like a shield ever since Norr had fallen was getting harder to keep up, and she couldn't stop challenging Jerrod every time he said something that sounded foolish or even insane.

You can't honor my memory by becoming something you're not.

The voice in her head was Norr's, but she knew it wasn't real. Her mind was just calling up memories of him to try to cope with his absence.

That doesn't mean I'm wrong. You can't shut yourself off to emotion, Scythe. That's not who you are.

That was becoming clearer with each passing day. Unfortunately, as the numbing, single-minded resolve fell away other emotions rushed in to fill the void. The pain of losing Norr was still fresh, and if she thought about him too long, unwelcome tears would well up.

You don't have to go through this alone.

She knew Keegan was also struggling with Norr's death; Norr had been his friend.

It's not just that. He's also struggling with how to help you cope with my loss.

Once again, Norr's voice was right. She could see it in the awkward, uncertain glances the young wizard gave her. He wanted to comfort her, but he didn't know how. Not that there was anything he could do or say to make her feel better anyway.

You don't know that. You haven't given him much of a chance.

Maybe I don't want to, Scythe thought, arguing with her own subconscious. *It will just make everything more complicated.*

The young wizard's feelings for her had been obvious enough though he'd never done anything to act on them while Norr was around. And, to be honest, Scythe had felt a similar attraction to him, too. As Jerrod had said: They were both touched by Chaos. They shared something others couldn't possibly understand.

She would never have acted on it, of course—she loved Norr with all her being. And now that he was gone, the spark between her and Keegan had been snuffed out by her grief. Her near-catatonic state had been a way for her to try to avoid dealing with Norr's loss. But it wasn't just that—it had also helped push Keegan away. The last thing she wanted right now was for him to think she was interested in him in that way.

But he still cares about you as a friend. Quit shutting him out.

She brushed Norr's words aside; there was a reason she was shutting him out. Jerrod had warned them of a Blood Moon hidden in the night clouds. As far as Scythe was concerned, there was only one explanation: Their quest was going to end soon, one way or another. And she had a strong feeling it would end with blood and death. She knew she was ready to face whatever was to come. But she wasn't so sure about Keegan. Any feelings he might have for her could make it even more difficult for him.

Or maybe the opposite is true, Norr's voice chimed in. *He's not as strong as you. He'll need your help and support before this is all over.*

"Maybe you're right," Scythe whispered. "You were usually right about this kind of thing. But I'm not ready yet."

Much to her dismay, the voice in her head didn't answer. Norr wasn't really there; it was just some small part of her—the part that wanted to make her into a better person—drawing on his memory.

"I miss you," she whispered as she continued to stalk the perimeter of the camp, wiping a tear away from her eye. "I always will."

Keegan had no trouble falling back to sleep again—his body was still recovering from the toll of the many miles they'd traveled that day. He knew he was holding Jerrod and Scythe back on their journey to Callastan, so he tried not to complain or show his fatigue. And though Jerrod always seemed to be watching him, by the time they stopped each night he was utterly exhausted.

Even so, once the conscious world slipped away he was surprised to find himself back on the deserted island, standing by the Keystone.

This has never happened before. I've had recurring visions, but they come to me night after night. I've never had the same vision on the same night!

He could hear the water lapping at the shore in the distance behind him, but his attention was focused on the black obelisk.

Why am I seeing this again? And why doesn't this vision feel like the others?

He approached the Keystone, as he had before. But instead of reaching out to it, he simply stared. Strange shapes seemed to dance beneath the obsidian surface. Slowly, Keegan circled the obelisk, carefully studying the twisting, writhing shadows.

There's something deeper here. Something beneath what I can see.

He hadn't forgotten Jerrod's warning: Some of the most powerful Seers in the Order's history had perished trying to find the true source of their visions.

But were any of them touched by Chaos and born under the Blood

Moon? Were any of them prophesied as saviors of the entire world? Were any of them able to call upon the power of Daemron's Ring?

In his dream, the Talisman hung from a thin chain around his neck—just as it did in the real world.

Scythe is right. What good are dreams and visions if they're nothing but images and scenes we don't really understand?

Still staring at the Keystone, he reached up and wrapped the fingers of his good hand around the Ring. On a subconscious level, he sensed his sleeping body respond the same way in the real world.

I didn't notice the Keystone in my other visions. It has to be the key.

Wearing the Ring in real life was dangerous; the Chaos that flooded into him was always nearly impossible to control. But doing so now, in a dream, might let him draw power from the Talisman without the risk of backlash.

He let go of the Ring and fumbled with the clasp of his chain until it came free. Then he placed the Talisman on his finger.

The Keystone suddenly changed from black obsidian to translucent glass, revealing the shifting shapes to be the churning blue flames of the Chaos Sea.

Keegan shuddered, remembering the time Scythe had nearly killed him with an overdose of Chaos root. His mind had been lost in the fires of creation for many days.

But eventually I found my way back. Why can't I do it again?

Taking a deep breath, he stepped forward, letting his body fall toward the Keystone. The glass surface shimmered and fell away as he toppled downward, falling through the window and into the swirling Chaos below.

Heat enveloped him, the flames wrapping themselves around his body as he plunged into the depths of the Burning Sea. But his mind remained tethered to the Keystone in his dream—a lifeline he could use to find his way back.

For an instant he teetered on the edge of panic as the flames dragged him down deeper and deeper, but he fought it back with the mental discipline of a true Chaos mage. He'd used the Ring several times; the surge of power when he opened himself up to the infinite ocean of Chaos no longer overwhelmed him.

I am in control. Tethered to the Keystone. My lifeline keeps me safe.

He lost all sense of time as he continued to sink. Around him the heat grew more intense, but he felt no pain. And then the blue flames fell away and disappeared.

He found himself standing on a barren, gray plain beneath an ashen sky, staring at an army of disfigured Chaos Spawn, his tail twitching slightly.

This isn't my body!

He was no longer a too-thin young man with a missing hand. He stood eight feet tall, on thick legs atop a pair of hooves. The red, scaly skin of his massive arms and chest rippled with muscle, and he felt the weight of giant horns on his head. A pair of enormous wings sprouted from his back, thick and leathery.

He sensed another consciousness brush up against him, something so alien and ancient it caused his mind momentarily to recoil in horror.

Daemron senses the intruder; like an insect crawling along the skin at the base of his skull—a mortal mind, reaching across the Burning Sea to touch his realm.

How is that possible?

Then he senses the spark of the divine, a tiny ember inside the mortal shell, and he knows this particular mortal is one of his Children, born from the ritual two decades ago.

Orath was right; they've grown far stronger than I thought possible.

Looking out over his assembled armies, he is careful not to

react to the unwelcome visitor. There are rebel spies among his legions, watching him for signs of weakness and vulnerability. He does not want them to know how powerful their enemies have become.

And he does not want the mortal to escape.

Keegan had recovered from his initial shock though he was still awed by what had happened.

I'm inside the mind of a God!

He could feel the unfathomable strength and power flowing through the Slayer—a deep reserve of pure Chaos far greater than anything he'd felt even when using the Ring.

How can we defeat an enemy like this? Keegan wondered.

A sudden terror gripped him, and he knew it was too dangerous to stay. Reaching for the invisible tether linking him to the Keystone in his vision, he frantically began to pull himself back before he was discovered.

Daemron senses the invader's flight, and a low growl rises from his throat. He lashes out at the retreating mind with his own, trying to snatch it in his mental grasp. But the trap is sprung an instant too late.

He can feel the mortal's panicked retreat, fleeing into the obscuring flames of the Burning Sea.

You are not free yet, he thinks, quickly gathering Chaos.

He lets the power build for several seconds, then lashes out with a single burst, sending his rage shooting into the depths of the Burning Sea and along the path left by a mortal foolish enough to think he could escape the vengeance of a God.

The image of Daemron and his army vanished, swallowed up by the blue flames of the Burning Sea as he climbed back up toward the Keystone.

Across the gulf of time and space he heard a bestial scream, deafening in its fury despite the distance. In response, he felt a ripple in the Chaos that surrounded him. Then the ripple became a wave that picked him up and spun him around.

Another wave hit him a second later, and then another, battering him and tossing him about. Disoriented, it was all he could do to cling to his lifeline as the Burning Sea was racked with a Chaos storm unleashed by the anger of a God.

Above him, he could sense the Keystone drawing closer as he continued to climb.

Almost there! Almost there!

The waves continued to hammer away at him, and he cried out in fear and pain. A second later he breached the surface of the Burning Sea, dangling from his tether above the raging maelstrom of Chaos, the Keystone just above him.

One final wave surged up from the fiery depths, reaching for him like a grasping claw. It hit him with enough force to snap his mental lifeline, and his mind plunged back down into the abyss.

Daemron hears the mortal's psychic scream as his essence is swallowed up by the blue flames, and a thin smile of satisfaction parts his scaled lips.

Now there is one less to oppose me.

Chapter 14

DESPITE THE LATENESS of the hour, there was a bounce in Andar's step as he made his way through the castle halls to meet his Queen. As leader of the Regent Council, he spoke to her almost every day, but the meetings were always at his request. This was the first time since they'd returned from the East that she had asked him to come to her.

Maybe she's starting to feel like her old self. Maybe she's thinking about retaking her throne.

The Council had governed effectively enough in her stead, focusing mostly on rebuilding Ferlhame, ensuring food supplies were available, and restoring the patrols guarding the borders of the North Forest. But though the Council could manage the day-to-day affairs of the kingdom, it couldn't inspire the Danaan people. Not the way a single strong, confident ruler could.

The royal line is part of who we are. We need our Queen.

The appearance of the Blood Moon had only made things worse; it was generally seen as an ill omen. There were persistent rumors in the city that the Queen was dying—or that she was already dead. The Council had issued an official proclamation attesting to her health and insisting she would soon resume her monarchial duties, but Andar knew only a public appearance by Rianna herself would end the speculation.

The guards ushered him in when he reached Rianna's private

chambers. To his relief, the Queen wasn't lying in her bed even though it was past midnight. Instead, she was seated at a small table that had been set for two. A collection of bread, cheese, and wine rested on a tray atop a cart in the corner. A single valet stood by the cart, ready and eager to be of service to her monarch.

He waited patiently at the threshold of the room for Rianna to acknowledge him. The Queen was wearing a simple—almost plain—dress, but the fact that it was embroidered with the royal seal further fanned the flames of Andar's hope.

"Thank you for coming," she said, extending a still-frail-looking arm toward the seat opposite her own. "Please join me."

Andar did as instructed, and the valet brought over two small plates of food, poured them each a glass of wine, then smoothly returned to her station by the cart.

"It's good to see your appetite returning," Andar said, as the Queen popped a small cube of cheese into her mouth.

"With each day I am feeling better," she told him. "Though I fear it will be some time before my full strength returns."

"The Council would welcome a visit from you when you are feeling up to it," Andar reminded her, as he did every time he came to see her.

"Soon, I hope," she replied—the same answer she'd given every other time.

The Queen finished off what was on her plate, but to Andar's dismay she didn't signal the valet to bring her more.

Hopefully she already ate a full dinner earlier in the evening.

She waited patiently for the High Sorcerer to finish his own helping. Once he was done the valet swooped in and whisked their plates and cups away. She piled everything onto the cart and disappeared with it through the door, closing it softly behind her and leaving the two of them alone.

"I had a dream last night," the Queen told him. "A vision. The first one since the Ring was taken from me."

Andar's heart skipped a beat with excitement. This was what the kingdom needed! The prophetic abilities of the royal line had guided the Danaan for hundreds of years. Knowing their Queen's powers had returned would ignite the flames of patriotism in her people.

"This is excellent news!" he exclaimed. "We must tell the rest of the Council right away!"

"No," Rianna said. "Not yet."

"What's wrong?" Andar asked.

"The vision makes no sense," the Queen said. "I cannot understand its meaning or purpose."

"That is not so strange," Andar assured her. "Throughout history our monarchs often turn to their advisers to help interpret their visions.

"What matters is that your visions have returned. Eventually they will guide us down the proper path."

"Will they?" Rianna countered. "My husband saw a vision of a Chaos Spawn prowling the depths of the forest. He went to destroy it, and lost his life."

"But the beast was defeated," Andar reminded her. "The kingdom was saved."

"My visions led me to banish my son," she continued as if she hadn't heard him. "They turned him against us and led us into a war from which it will take generations to recover."

"It was Orath that led us into war," Andar said. "Not your visions."

"But my visions were the catalyst," she insisted. "And they did nothing to spare Ferlhame from the destruction wrought by the dragon."

Andar couldn't think of an appropriate response, so he simply stayed silent.

"We thought less of Vaaler because he didn't have the Sight," she continued. "But maybe what seemed a weakness was really a strength.

"Instead of relying on obscure dreams to rule us, he would have used logic and reason. Maybe he would have been the greatest Danaan King of all."

"Vaaler was a good man," Andar said. "And maybe you were wrong to banish him. But he is no longer one of us."

"Have you heard anything more about him?" she asked.

The High Sorcerer shook his head.

"Pranya's spies have been focusing on the Free Cities and the Southlands, watching for signs the Purge might turn its focus in our direction.

"For now the Free Cities remain strong in their resolve to resist the Order, and the Pontiff seems to be concentrating on Callastan. There was some dissent among her followers, and even rumors of a failed assassination attempt. But the Order has reasserted its authority.

"Most of the monks and Inquisitors are already gathered at Callastan, and the Pontiff is leading an army of ordinary soldiers toward the city. If the Free Cities don't intervene, Callastan will fall within a fortnight."

Partway through his report, he realized Rianna was only half listening to him though he had dutifully continued to the end.

She really only wanted to know about Vaaler.

"I would like you to tell me about your vision," Andar said, trying another tactic to engage her. "Despite all that has happened, I cannot believe that the incredible gift of your Sight is a curse. I still believe your visions will do more good than harm.

"If you share it with me," he continued, "perhaps together we can understand what it means—and why it came to you."

She didn't answer right away, and Andar thought she might refuse. But in the end a lifetime of believing in the importance

of her visions overcame her recent lack of faith, and she re-
lented.

"I saw an island, deserted and remote. A large obelisk of black
stone rose from the center. The Destroyer of Worlds—the one
who woke the dragon—was there.

"But this time he did not appear as a figure bathed in the
flames of Chaos. He looked like an ordinary mortal man. Young
and scared."

"Was he alone?" Andar asked.

"I don't believe so," she said. "The vision wasn't clear. Much of
it was faint and blurred. I was only able to pick out a few details."

That doesn't sound like the kind of visions you used to have, Andar
thought. *Their meaning might have been unclear, but you always described them with incredible clarity and precision.*

"Perhaps this wasn't even a vision," the Queen said with a sigh,
possibly picking up on Andar's feelings. "Maybe it was only a foolish dream."

"Do you believe it was just a dream?" Andar asked.

"No," she admitted. "But as I said before, I have no idea what it
means."

"Let me search the Royal Archives," Andar suggested, hit by a
sudden inspiration. "Maybe in the ancient texts I can find some
mention of this obelisk that will help us find the proper interpretation."

"There are thousands of volumes in the archives," the Queen
noted. "It would take months—maybe years—to look through
them all."

"With your leave, I could recruit others to aid me in the task.
Lormilar is more familiar with the ancient texts than I am, and
I'm certain he knows several other capable scholars who would
be eager to help."

"That would mean telling him that my visions have returned,"
Rianna noted.

"Yes," Andar said, not bothering to dance around the issue. "And Lormilar still serves on the Regent Council. He will probably want to share this knowledge with the rest of them, as well."

Please, my Queen, he silently added, *do not be afraid. Letting the Regent Council know your Sight has returned is the first step toward restoring you as the ruler of the Danaan.*

"Very well," Rianna said. "Tell Lormilar and the rest of the Council what I have seen. With luck, you will find something in the archives that will help me lead my kingdom down the proper path."

My kingdom. It was an offhand comment, one probably delivered out of habit more than anything else. Yet those two little words were enough for Andar to hope that Rianna would soon reclaim her throne.

Jerrod woke early, his body instinctively rousing itself as the first rays of sunlight began to peek over the horizon. The clouds from the night before had turned to a gray haze that would probably burn off by noon.

Scythe was awake, of course—she had taken the final watch to let Jerrod rest. And he actually felt the extra sleep had helped wash away some of his mental fatigue.

But will it be enough to help my Sight return to full strength?

He turned his attention to Keegan, who was still sleeping.

No, not sleeping—something's wrong!

The young man's eyes were closed, but his body was tense and his breathing was too rapid and shallow. His hand was clutching the Ring at his neck, the grip so tight the thin metal chain had actually cut the skin.

"Keegan!" he called out, dropping to a knee at the young man's side. "Keegan—can you hear me?"

"Let him sleep," Scythe said. "He's exhausted."

"He's not asleep," Jerrod said, reaching out to place a palm on his forehead.

An instant later Scythe was crouched beside him, her features wrinkled up with concern.

"No fever," Jerrod said, taking his hand away.

He reached out gently and lifted one of Keegan's eyelids. The eye beneath had rolled so far back into his head he could barely see the pupil.

"What's wrong with him?" Scythe demanded.

"His mind is lost in the Burning Sea," Jerrod said, adding a silent curse. "I told him not to do anything foolish!"

"He tried to find the source of his vision," Scythe muttered, as she stood up and stepped away from the catatonic young man. "We should have known he would try this."

She was right, but Jerrod knew there was no point in blaming themselves now.

"What can we do?" Scythe asked.

"Nothing," Jerrod said. "He will have to find his own way back."

"Step aside!" Scythe snapped.

Jerrod did as he was told, and the young woman stepped forward and laid the blade of Daemron's Sword across Keegan's chest. The Talisman glowed softly, and Keegan's body shuddered and seemed to relax. His hand fell away from the Ring, and his breathing became soft and even.

"Keegan," she said, dropping to a knee and gently shaking his shoulder. "Keegan, wake up!"

When there was no response, she lifted his eyelid as Jerrod had done. The white orb of his rolled-back eye stared out at her.

"The Sword can heal his physical wounds, but it cannot guide his mind back to us," Jerrod said. "There is nothing we can do but wait."

"Well we're not just going to sit here on the side of the road!" Scythe snapped. "Help me carry him!"

"This hollow is hidden from any travelers passing by," Jerrod argued. "And moving him might make it harder for his mind to retrace its path to our world."

"Do you know that, or are you just guessing?" Scythe demanded.

"A guess," Jerrod admitted. "But even if moving him does no harm, it won't help."

Scythe glared at him, then gave a curt nod.

"How long until he comes back?" she asked.

"He may not come back at all," Jerrod said.

"How long until we know, one way or the other?" Scythe pressed.

Unfortunately, her question was one Jerrod couldn't possibly answer.

I'm still alive, Keegan thought.

He was floating in the Burning Sea, but he wasn't drowning. The Chaos flames swirled around him, searing him with their intense heat. But though he felt the pain, he wasn't being devoured. Not yet.

I'm strong enough to keep the Chaos at bay. But for how long?

The storm that had ripped away his connection to his vision—and the mortal world—had passed. But the Chaos still boiled and churned, tossing him back and forth until he had no sense of where he was.

The Burning Sea is infinite. It has no edge, no bottom. How am I going to find my way back without something to guide me?

Although he had no physical form, he felt as if his flesh were being melted off his bones. Yet somehow he was able to keep the agonizing pain at a distance, keeping it from overwhelming his mind and driving him mad. It was hard to focus through his suffering, but he tried to remember how he had returned to the mortal world after Scythe had given him the massive overdose of Chaos root.

The Ring. I could sense its power, shining like a beacon. It brought me back.

Casting out with his awareness, he sought out the unmistakable signature of the Talisman, peering far into the depths of the blue flames surrounding him in all directions. But he saw nothing.

Am I too far away? Or has carrying the Ring for so long made its call too familiar—too mundane—for me to sense it now?

With nothing to guide him back, he would be lost forever. As if sensing his despair, the heat from the flames flared up and he cried out.

How much longer can I last? How soon until my strength gives out?

When he became too weak to hold back the Chaos the flames would devour him, his essence consumed by the fires of creation from which all things were born.

His situation was hopeless; instead of fighting to prolong his suffering, it would be easier just to surrender and let the Chaos take him. A quick and merciful end.

No! Scythe wouldn't give up. She'd fight to the end even if she couldn't win. And so will I!

Gathering his will, he pushed back against the Chaos. The heat from the flames abated, though it was still hot enough to make it feel like his nonexistent skin was blistering.

Jerrod and Scythe will help me. They'll find a way to bring me back!

Chapter 15

YASMIN PASSED THROUGH her army's camp like a specter in the night, illuminated by the orange light of a small fire one moment, then vanishing into the shadows the next. Few of the soldiers noticed the Pontiff's passing; those that did quickly looked away, as if afraid of drawing her notice.

Their fear was understandable; the public execution of Lord Carthin and several of his inner circle had sent a clear message through the ranks. As she'd expected, most of the troops had fallen into line once word spread of the former Justice of the Order's grisly end. Officers formerly under Carthin's command had quickly assembled their men and marched double time to Norem to swear their allegiance to the Pontiff in person lest they suffer a similar fate.

There had been some who chose a different path, of course: deserters and mercenaries who set off on their own rather than join the force preparing to march on Callastan. Yasmin had sent patrols to make examples of a few of these traitors, but her wrath could only reach those within a few days' march of Norem.

She could do little to stop the bands of armed men wreaking havoc on the farthest borders of the Southlands—not until after Callastan had fallen and the Crown was safely back in her hands, at least. But eventually there would be a reckoning for all those who refused to answer her call.

As she walked among the soldiers, she could sense their fatigue. She had pushed them hard, driving them toward Callastan to join up with the army already encamped outside the city walls. Were it not for Carthin's betrayal, the battle would have been over weeks ago. But now the end was near. In a few more days they would reach their destination though she knew she'd need to give the troops time to recover from the march before she ordered the final attack on the city.

However, fatigue was not all she sensed from her troops. She could hear them speaking in tense whispers; she saw the concern on their faces. Some were mercenaries or trained soldiers drawn from the ranks of guards, but most were ordinary civilians initially recruited through their faith in the Order or the promise of coins from Carthin's coffers. The prospect of charging the heavily defended walls of Callastan made them anxious, a natural reaction about which Yasmin could do little.

The presence of the Blood Moon had only added to their apprehension though Yasmin saw the red orb that filled the night sky as a portent of victory. In a few days there would indeed be death and suffering, but it would be her army that unleashed it upon a city of infidels and heretics that had defied the Order for too long.

She expected Callastan to offer minimal resistance. If her scouts were accurate, the Order had an almost three-to-one advantage over the makeshift army opposing them. And though many in her ranks were inexperienced, they were bolstered by trained mercenaries and her Inquisitors.

Apart from the city's Enforcers, the enemy ranks would be filled with thugs and criminals from Callastan's underbelly. Once the tide began to turn against them, Yasmin knew, their true nature would show through. At the first sign of trouble, they would abandon their efforts to hold the walls and scuttle back into their tunnels and sewers to save their own wretched skins.

But the city is not our true goal, she reminded herself. In the confusion of the attack, Cassandra would try to escape with the Crown.

She'll make for the docks. And my Inquisitors will be waiting for her.

"Remember, Cassandra," Methodis warned as they wound their way through the dark back alleys of the docks district, "these are dangerous men. They are not to be trusted."

The old healer had found someone who claimed to know the location of the island Cassandra had seen in her dreams . . . someone who might also be willing to smuggle her out of the city. But his contact wanted to meet her in person before agreeing to any kind of deal.

"If the honorable cannot help me," Cassandra told him, "then I must deal with those who have no honor."

She was wearing a heavy robe, with the hood pulled up to hide her features as they wound their way through the dark back alleys of the docks district. The Crown was tucked away in a thick leather satchel, the leather straps slung over both shoulders so she could wear it like a backpack.

These streets are crawling with pickpockets and thieves, Rexol complained. *It isn't safe to be carrying the Crown in this part of town!*

Safer than leaving it back in Methodis's shop, she countered, shutting the wizard up.

"Saying these brutes have no honor undersells the point," Methodis chided. "They are pirates, pure and simple. They attacked my ship, killed my crewmates, and took me prisoner. For several years they forced me to serve as their healer, keeping me shackled and bound below the decks."

"How did you win your freedom?" she asked.

"Bo-Shing, their captain, contracted a prolonged case of what sailors call 'root rot,'" Methodis explained. "Rarely fatal, but a particularly frustrating and humiliating condition—particularly when the sufferer visits the brothels in a port of call."

Though she had been raised in the Monastery, Cassandra knew enough about the world to understand what the healer was implying.

"I offered Bo-Shing a cure on the condition that he set me free."

"And he honored this agreement?" Cassandra asked, with mild surprise.

"A pirate who cannot fornicate is barely a man in the eyes of the others," he told her. "I promised never to mention his ailment to any of the crew, and he thought it wiser to let me go than keep me around and risk having his shameful secret exposed."

"His ailment was a fortunate occurrence for you," Cassandra noted.

The old doctor gave her a sly wink. "Fortune often favors those who take pains to make it happen."

The pirates underestimated him, Cassandra realized. *Methodis seems harmless, but there is much more to him than meets the eye.*

"It would be wise not to mention any of this at the meeting," he said, as they rounded another corner. "Though I rather doubt he will bring it up."

The pair found themselves in a dead-end alley. In the rear wall was a heavy wooden door reinforced with steel bars. A small rectangle had been carved out at eye level and shuttered on the other side.

"How exactly did you get these men to agree to this?" she asked.

"They are no friends of the Order," he told her. "And I appealed to Bo-Shing's ego. He takes immense pride in his ship. He claims *The Chaos Runner* was built from trees harvested from the North Forest by a great wizard many centuries ago, giving the vessel powerful mystical properties."

"Do you believe these tales?"

"*The Chaos Runner* is easily twice as fast as any other ship I've seen, and Bo-Shing has guided it unharmed through fierce storms that would sink an entire fleet. No matter how skilled his crew, that wouldn't be possible without some kind of magic.

"And despite his moral failings, Bo-Shing's ability as a captain makes him worthy of such a ship. He is one of the few sailors skilled enough—or mad enough—to travel into the uncharted waters beyond the Western Isles. I think he welcomes the challenge."

"And this was enough to convince him?"

"I may also have hinted that the Keystone was erected to mark the location of a vast treasure buried somewhere on the island."

"And what will happen when they discover this is not true?" Cassandra asked.

"Hopefully we will have come up with a plan for that event when the time comes."

"You're coming with me?" Cassandra asked, surprised.

"Of course. I wouldn't leave you alone with these men—they'll betray you the first chance they get. You'll need someone to watch your back."

He just wants to stay close to the Crown! Rexol warned, paranoid as ever.

Cassandra had her own reservations about Methodis's coming with her, though it had nothing to do with trusting him. Now that her legs had healed, she was far more capable of taking care of herself than the old healer was. His presence would just mean she'd have to watch out for him, too. But she was still touched by the gesture, and she didn't see any point in arguing with him about it right now. Especially since the pirates hadn't yet agreed to take her.

If you use the Crown, you can make them do anything you want, Rexol reminded her.

Cassandra had no intention of unleashing the Talisman's power unless she had no other choice, so she simply ignored his suggestion.

"Are you ready to meet some of the most vile, cruel, and evil men Callastan has to offer?" Methodis asked.

When she nodded her assent, he reached out and knocked twice on the barred door. The panel slid open and a pair of eyes peered out at them through the slit. Then the panel slid shut, and she heard the sound of metal grating on metal from the other side. A few seconds later, the heavy door slid slowly open and they stepped inside, Methodis leading the way.

The room beyond the door was smaller than she expected— barely twenty feet on each side. The walls were bare and the furnishings plain: a large, circular table sat in the center, with ten chairs around it. A small corridor in the opposite wall led to another door similar to the one they had entered: heavy wood reinforced with metal bars, with a small viewing window carved into it.

With her Sight, Cassandra knew the scene beyond that door was what one would typically expect in a busy tavern near the docks: a boisterous crowd of sailors, whores, and petty criminals drinking, fighting, and carousing as buxom barmaids moved among the tables dropping off drinks and slapping away unwanted hands grabbing and groping at them as they made their rounds.

The scene in this small room at the back, however, was far tamer. Five men had gathered to meet them. His olive skin, colorful and flamboyant clothes, and wild tattoos marked the one who'd let them in as a native of the Western Isles, as were two of the others sitting at the table. Standing guard near the door to the main tavern was a tall, muscular Southlander wearing the local garb. Another Southlander—at least twenty years older than any of the others in the group but dressed in the same style as the Islanders—was also seated at the table.

"Wasn't sure you'd show," one of the Islanders at the table said in a thick accent.

"You know I always keep my promises, Bo-Shing," Methodis replied.

Now that she knew who the leader was, Cassandra gave him a more careful evaluation. She guessed his age to be somewhere in his midthirties. He was heavyset and powerfully built, though a layer of fat now covered his muscles. His skin was naturally dark, but years of exposure to the sun while sailing the seas had turned it from olive to a burnished bronze. He had a long black beard and hair that hung down to his shoulders, both of which were bound in numerous tight braids by gold and silver ties. He wore a thin, tight-fitting red shirt with short sleeves and a low, plunging neck, exposing the tattoos on his arms and chest. One cheek was marred by a long, uneven scar.

"Tell your friend to remove her hood," he said. "I like to look a woman in the eye when I talk to her."

There was something in his gaze that set Cassandra on edge—an intensity and hunger, like those of a predator stalking its next meal.

You could crush him like an insect, Rexol told her.

I need these men to help me, she reminded him.

She pulled the cowl back to reveal her pure white eyes.

"Did you sell us out to the Order?" Bo-Shing hissed.

"I do not serve the Pontiff," Cassandra assured him. "Not anymore."

Though she was facing Bo-Shing, her awareness encompassed the entire room. When the Islander who had let them in pulled a knife from his belt and rushed at her from behind, she had plenty of time to think about her reaction.

You don't even need the Crown for this, Rexol snorted with disdain.

He was right, of course. It was common knowledge that the

Inquisitors spent years honing their fighting skills and transforming themselves into deadly warriors. But they were not the only
members of the Order trained in the martial arts. Every monk
within the Monastery was taught the basics of self-defense, and
from a young age Cassandra had learned how to channel the
power of Chaos that flowed through her into physical action. A
Seer might not be able to take on a half dozen trained soldiers at
once, but a single pirate posed no real threat.

She didn't even bother to turn to face her attacker. Instead, she
lashed out behind her with her right arm in a diagonal strike that
caught him on his wrist. She could easily have broken the bone,
but she was worried the others might not help her if she inflicted
too much damage. Instead, she struck with just enough force to
stun so that the blade went flying from his grip.

In the same motion, she redirected the momentum of her arm
upward and cocked her elbow, catching him in the throat just
beneath his chin. Again, she only struck hard enough to leave him
choking and gasping for air rather than crush his windpipe.

As her arm was incapacitating her opponent, her feet took a
single step to the left so that the charging man's momentum
wouldn't send him crashing into her as he collapsed. Instead, he
slammed into the edge of the heavy table with a loud thud. The
table rocked slightly but didn't give way. The pirate, on the other
hand, ricocheted off and hit the floor hard.

The fight was over before any of the others even realized it was
happening. Bo-Shing's eyes went wide a second later once his
mind caught up and processed what had just happened. Then he
threw back his head and laughed as his man writhed on the floor,
coughing, wheezing, and turning purple as he struggled for air
from the blow to the throat.

"Shoji never was a smart one," Methodis remarked, even as he
bent down to check on the fallen man's injuries.

"He'll live," Cassandra assured the others. "But the next person who attacks me won't be so lucky."

"I like you, girl," Bo-Shing said, flashing a wide grin that exposed several missing teeth. "I think we can do business."

"I'm looking for an island," Cassandra said, jumping straight to the heart of the matter. "One with a large black obelisk on it."

"I've seen it," the old man sitting at the table said, his voice thin and reedy. "Through my looking glass."

"Tork," Bo-Shing said by way of introduction. "My navigator."

"And you can take me there?" Cassandra asked.

"The island you seek lies on the edge of the world," Tork said. "Beyond the Kraken's Eye."

He didn't look at Cassandra as he spoke; he seemed focused on something above and behind her—something too far away for even her Sight to detect. And there was something disconcerting about the way he spoke; the inflection and pacing of his words were more than a bit unusual.

"Is he drunk?" Cassandra asked.

"Tork was always a little off," Methodis said as he helped the still-wheezing pirate up to a sitting position.

"He has the far-sight," Bo-Shing explained, though Cassandra had no idea what that meant. "If he says he's seen your island beyond the Kraken's Eye, then that's where we'll find it."

"What's the Kraken's Eye?"

"A stretch of ocean filled with titanic waves and massive whirlpools large enough to swallow a ship whole. Some say it marks the edge of the world—that no ship can pass."

"But you've been through it?"

"Tork has. Twenty years ago. But if another ship can survive the journey, then so can *The Chaos Runner.*"

"Aye," the old man said, still staring off into space. "I can guide you safely through."

"Does this mean you're agreeing to take me?" Cassandra asked.

"First tell me why you want to go there," Bo-Shing said.

"That is something I cannot reveal," Cassandra replied. "But I assure you it has nothing to do with the treasure hidden on the island," she added, building on the foundation of the lie Methodis had laid down earlier.

"Is there really a treasure there?" the pirate asked, cocking his head and squinting one skeptical eye at her.

"For centuries the Order has been manipulating and controlling the rulers of the Southlands," she answered. "With all the gold and coin that has gone into their coffers, do you really think it would all be kept at the Monastery?"

"And you'd just let us take it?"

"I am not interested in material wealth. I serve a higher purpose."

Bo-Shing laughed again. "I should have guessed."

"Methodis says there is no other sailor skilled and daring enough to take me there," she said, hoping the pirate was susceptible to flattery.

"This isn't going to be easy," Bo-Shing warned. "Getting supplies for the voyage is difficult. Nobody knows how long this siege will last. Food is going to be expensive."

"I have enough to fund the expedition," Methodis volunteered.

Bo-Shing raised an eyebrow. "The medicine man has done well for himself, has he?"

"Not all my clients live on the streets," the old man said. "Nobles pay very well for my discretion."

"Getting onto the ship and casting off from port is another problem," the pirate continued. "I've heard the Order has spies watching the docks. Probably looking for you, right?"

"If this were going to be simple, I wouldn't have come to you," Methodis reminded him. "You'll figure something out."

Bo-Shing crossed his arms and sat back in his chair, staring intently at Cassandra as he mulled the offer over.

This is a mistake, Rexol warned. *The instant you're out at sea they'll try to take the Crown from you!*

They don't even know about the Crown, she reminded the ever-paranoid mage. *And if they try, I can stop them.*

She could sense that Bo-Shing was intrigued, but he still needed one final push to get him to accept.

"I feel I must be honest with you," she said. "The treasure on the island will make you rich beyond your wildest dreams, but the Pontiff will not be pleased. The Order will forever curse your name. Inquisitors will search high and low for the outlaw Bo-Shing, and you will always be remembered as one of history's greatest villains."

"Fabulous wealth, infamy, and the chance to piss off the Order?" Bo-Shing said, uncrossing his arms and clapping his hands together. "How could I possibly refuse?"

Chapter 16

VAALER AND SHALANA walked side by side down the corridor of cheering men and women lining the street. Their honor guard marched close behind them, followed by a long, irregular column of their ragtag army.

"Another hero's welcome," Shalana whispered." And more mouths to feed in your ever-growing legions of followers, no doubt," she added.

Vaaler was too busy smiling at and waving to the exuberant crowd who had come to greet the liberators of their town to reply, though he knew she was right.

Since slaying Hirk and his band in the tiny hamlet of Othlen, they had been steadily gathering more and more volunteers eager to strike back at their oppressors. The people in Othlen had pleaded with him to drive out the mercenaries occupying the nearby village of Shelder, and a half dozen men and women had aided in the attack.

Their victory in Shelder had been quick and decisive, just as it had been in Othlen. Not only did they have the element of surprise on their side, but a small company of deserters bullying helpless townsfolk were no match for the battle-hardened clan warriors who made up the honor guard he and Shalana had brought with them from the Frozen East.

After Shelder, they moved on to nearby Pilkin and Howellend, striking fast before the scattered mercenary bands could unite and form some kind of coordinated resistance. And at each town, Vaaler's tiny army grew. People were tired of being terrorized. His arrival ignited the smoldering hatred the people had for the soldiers exploiting the political turmoil to set themselves up as petty warlords and dictators.

Vaaler had welcomed them into the ranks, though not out of any real need on his part. In the last few towns they'd come to, they hadn't even encountered any resistance. News of the avenging band of Easterners was spreading quickly, and the mercenaries who were happy to bully and harass helpless victims weren't nearly as willing to stay and fight to protect the territory they had previously claimed.

Just the rumor that we're coming their way is enough to send the cowards running, Vaaler noted, and he couldn't help but feel a swell of pride at what they'd accomplished in such a short time.

But even when their victories came without fighting or bloodshed, the people of the town still hailed them as heroes. And many of them still wanted to join the fight. They numbered over a hundred now, and Vaaler and Shalana spent as much time worrying about the logistics of keeping their soldiers fed and clothed as they did planning tactics and picking targets.

"Sill said our supplies are running low, even with the rationing," Shalana reminded him as their victory parade wound through the town's main street. "Tell this mayor we don't need more farmers to march with us. We'd rather have them give us some of their winter food stores than their loyalty."

Vaaler nodded, though he didn't hold out much hope. The towns they saved were quick to offer what they could, but these were not rich people. They had little to spare, and any surplus from their harvests had been sold and shipped off to the Free Cities at the beginning of the winter.

That's one of the reasons so many of them are so eager to join us.

They're tired of living in rural poverty, tired of living a hand-to-mouth existence.

The crowd was funneling them toward the town square, where a matronly woman was standing along with several middle-aged men, patiently awaiting their arrival.

"How come these welcoming committees always seem so puffed up by their own importance?" Shalana grumbled. "If I was a leader of one of these towns, I'd be ashamed that I needed outsiders to come in and protect my people."

"Things are different here in the Southlands," Vaaler reminded her. "They rely on government and the rule of law to keep them safe."

"And when all that breaks down, what are they left with?" Shalana wondered.

"It doesn't usually break down," Vaaler reminded her. "These are strange times."

The Blood Moon still hung in the sky each night, waxing and waning, but its color never changed.

Another reason we have so many volunteers. They're scared. They don't feel safe unless they're part of an army.

Few of the volunteers understood the true horrors of war. A handful were retired veterans who had served as guards in some of the Free Cities, but even these had never seen any real battles.

Not like what we went through at the Giant's Maw.

Apart from the Easterners, his followers still clung to an idealized, romanticized notion of war. The easy victories against overmatched opponents had only strengthened their misconceptions.

"Remember," Shalana whispered, as they finally reached the dignitaries waiting for them in the town square. "We need food, not volunteers!"

"I am Mayor Thelna," the matronly woman said, stepping forward to clasp Vaaler's outstretched hand.

"On behalf of the entire city, I wish to thank you for driving off the brutes and cretins who terrorized us for far too long!"

Her voice was surprisingly loud for her size, and it carried well into the crowd. Predictably, her words elicited another round of cheering and applause. Vaaler turned and acknowledged the adulation with a wave. Shalana did the same, he could tell she was weary of these public performances.

The townsfolk who had joined their army along the way were basking in the moment, smiling and shaking hands with people in the crowd. In contrast, the members of their honor guard stood straight and tall, with stoic expressions on their faces, looking every inch the Southland stereotype of the noble savage.

They're playing to the crowd, Vaaler realized. *They like being seen as emotionless warriors who only live for battle.*

"Anything we can provide is yours for the asking," Thelna said. "We owe you our lives."

"And many of our people are ready to swear allegiance to you and join your ranks," one of the men behind her added.

Beside him, Shalana groaned. Fortunately, Vaaler doubted anyone else was close enough to hear it over the buzz of the crowd.

"Your generosity is much appreciated," Vaaler told them. "And we have need of any food you can spare."

"They say an army travels on its stomach," Thelna agreed. "Our winter provisions are low, but I will give you whatever we can spare."

Shalana groaned again. This time it was loud enough to cause the mayor to give her a funny look. Then she turned her attention back to Vaaler.

"We have a special gift for you," she said, holding up her hand and motioning to someone hidden in the crowd.

The people parted and two burly men came forward, each holding the arm of a bearded soldier. His hands were tied in front of him, and his face was swollen and bruised.

Vaaler felt his heart sink. The last thing he wanted to deal with was a prisoner.

Given everything that's happened, they'll probably want some kind of public execution to satisfy their hunger for vengeance.

"My brother and I caught him trying to steal a horse at my farm!" one of the men holding his arm said. "Put up quite the fight!"

"I can't stay here!" the prisoner shouted. "I have to go to the Free Cities or the curse will kill me!"

The man's eyes were wild, his voice high and shrill. His hair was tangled and filled with leaves and small twigs, and his clothes were dirty and rank.

"Clearly this man isn't in his right mind," Vaaler said. "Is he really one of the men who terrorized your town?"

"No," the mayor admitted. "He wasn't with those scum. But look at his uniform. He's a mercenary, just like the others!"

"I'm not!" the man shrieked. "You have to let me go. I have to get to the Free Cities. I have to tell them to help Callastan! The wizard said so!"

Vaaler let out an inward sigh. The mayor and the others were looking at him expectantly, no doubt waiting for him to pronounce some kind of judgment.

"I don't know what crimes this man has committed," Vaaler said. "And neither do you. Clearly he is unbalanced, and he may be a danger to himself or others. But I do not think we can punish him for what was done to your town. That would not be justice"

The mayor's expression changed from expectation to disappointment, then to one of resignation.

"Of course," she said, chagrined. "You're right." Addressing the men holding the prisoner, she said, "Take him away but be gentle with him."

"No!" the soldier squealed, bucking and thrashing against the men holding him. "I have to go to the Free Cities!"

His knees suddenly gave out, catching the men holding him off guard as he slid from their grasp and collapsed on the ground. Hands still bound, he scurried across the earth to grovel at Vaaler's feet.

"You have to let me go to the Free Cities," he whimpered. "If you don't, the wizard's hex will kill me. I must obey the will of Keegan of the Gorgon Staff."

"Wait!" Vaaler shouted, holding up a hand to stop the men who were rushing forward to haul the prisoner back to his feet.

He dropped down to one knee so that he was eye to eye with the man.

"What was that name?"

"Keegan of the Gorgon Staff," the man whispered. "The wizard cursed me. Bound me to his will. Told me I had to go to the Free Cities."

"Describe this wizard."

"Tall. Thin. Young. And he has only one hand!"

"I need to speak with this man in private," Vaaler said. "Right now!"

Shalana's head was spinning as she and Vaaler followed the mayor to one of the nearby buildings, the two farmers dragging the struggling prisoner along with them.

"You have to let me go!" he wailed. "The wizard will kill you all if you interfere with my mission!"

The chances that the mad soldier had actually come across Keegan were small. The odds that he would then run into Vaaler were so infinitesimal they defied believability.

This is no coincidence. The forces of Chaos are at play.

When Vaaler first told her he had to leave the East and return to the Southlands, she had been reluctant. But her love had explained that he and Keegan shared something deeper than their time together studying under Rexol. He said he was bound to the young wizard's destiny to save the world. Though Shalana wasn't certain if she believed in such things, Vaaler clearly did, and so she had agreed to go with him.

"Our town is too small to have an actual jail," the mayor explained as she walked. "So we converted one of the stalls in the stable into a cell for emergencies."

Vaaler nodded, but Shalana could tell he wasn't listening.

This must be as shocking for him as it is for me.

Faced with the suffering of the townsfolk in Othlen, Vaaler had undergone a dramatic change of heart. He chose to help those who needed it most, rather than pressing on toward Callastan to try to play some unknown role in Jerrod's prophecy.

Shalana had actually been relieved when he asked her to abandon their original quest. She was a warrior, plain and simple. She knew nothing about Chaos and magic and the fate of the world. She preferred what she could see and touch and feel. She understood the plight of the villagers they helped, even if their inability—or unwillingness—to fight to protect themselves frustrated her at times.

My role in Keegan's destiny is finished, Vaaler had whispered to her that night.

Apparently, he'd been wrong.

"Almost there," the mayor said, turning sharply to the left and heading down a small side street. A simple wooden structure stood at the end. From the smell it was obviously the stable the mayor had mentioned, though Shalana guessed it was only large enough to hold three or four horses at any one time.

Or one prisoner.

Inside the animals had been removed, and a stall in the corner had been lined with sharp, twisted wire along each wall. The wire extended out above the stall and was wired together at the top to form a rudimentary cage.

"Don't put me back in there!" the soldier shouted, renewing his struggles to break free of the men holding him. "I must serve the wizard's will!"

"You are," Vaaler assured him. "I am Keegan's ally. We studied together for many years."

The soldier froze in place, his head tilting to one side.

"You don't look like a wizard," he mumbled.

"I'm Danaan," Vaaler said. "We are all wizards."

The man nodded slowly, obviously accepting his words as fact.

"Leave us alone with him," Keegan said to the mayor.

"Do you think we can't protect ourselves from one man?" Shalana asked when she hesitated.

"No, of course not," she replied. A few seconds later she and her entourage were gone, leaving Shalana and Vaaler alone with the prisoner.

"What's your name?" Vaaler asked him.

"Darmmid. But they call me Darm."

"Good, Darm. My name is Vaaler. Keegan is my friend."

Darm shook his head vigorously from side to side.

"No! It's a trick! You're lying!"

"I know Keegan and his companions," Vaaler assured him. "A giant with red hair. A man with pure white eyes like the monks of the Order. And a young Islander woman."

"No!" the soldier spat out. "You're lying! There was no man with white eyes! No redheaded giant!"

Shalana's stomach knotted up. Even someone as mad as Darm would remember Norr. And after all that had happened, she knew he would never leave Scythe's side. Not willingly.

"The Islander woman," Vaaler said, still trying to win the man's trust. "She was there, yes? Small. Pretty. Angry."

"She wanted to kill me," the soldier whispered. "With that silver sword she carried. She wanted to kill me, but Keegan of the Gorgon Staff saved me!"

"Tell me what happened," Vaaler said, his voice calm but firm. "Tell me everything."

"The Inquisitors said we had to attack them. I didn't want to, but the Inquisitors made us."

Inquisitors! Shalana thought. *Is that what happened to Norr? Is that why he wasn't there?*

"You attacked them," Vaaler said. "I understand. Then what happened?"

"They killed everyone. The Inquisitors. My friends. They would have killed me, too!"

"But Keegan helped you," Vaaler interjected, still speaking in a soft, soothing tone. "You said he saved you."

"He cursed me!" the man said. "He put a hex on me so that if I disobey him, I'll die!"

"Could Keegan really do that?" Shalana asked.

"Possibly. It wouldn't be the first time he cursed someone."

"He cursed me!" Darm insisted. "I feel it in my gut, eating away at me from the inside. It'll kill me if I don't get to the Free Cities!"

"Why did Keegan send you to the Free Cities?" Vaaler asked.

"Callastan. The Order laid siege to the city. The wizard wants me to ask the Free Cities to break the siege."

Despite his obvious insanity, Shalana thought his story made sense. The Guardian had told them that Cassandra had gone to Callastan with the Crown and that Keegan and the others had gone there to find her. If they found the city surrounded by the armies of the Order, they'd want reinforcements to break through the lines.

But why would he think one mad soldier would be enough to convince the leaders of the Free Cities to help?

Vaaler hadn't said anything for several seconds. She recognized the expression on his face; his mind was lost in deep thought as he struggled to make sense of all the pieces. Shalana knew the best thing she could do was let him work it out.

"I know what kind of hex Keegan placed on you, Darm," he finally said, "and I know how to remove it."

Shalana did her best to hide her surprise. She knew Vaaler well enough to tell that he wasn't being completely honest with the prisoner but wasn't exactly certain why he was lying. Still, she trusted him enough not to say anything.

Her lover had a gift for deduction, an uncanny ability to analyze almost any situation and understand it better than most. Whatever he was up to would probably turn out to be the right move.

"Listen to me, Darm," Vaaler continued. "Listen closely. I am a wizard, too. Remember? I understand Keegan's power. I know how to break the curse. I can free you if you let me."

"I want to be free," Darm said with a soft sob. "Please help me."

"Close your eyes," Vaaler told him. "Open your mind to mine and I will reach in and break the bonds that tie you to Keegan."

Darm did as he was told and closed his eyes. Then he dropped to his knees in front of Vaaler, his bound hands clasped tightly together as if he was praying.

Vaaler glanced over at her and shrugged, then he reached out to place his hands atop the kneeling man's head.

"Take a deep breath, Darm. Good. Now another. Nice and slow. Stay calm as I search your mind."

Vaaler's fingers began to gently massage the man's scalp through his matted hair.

"I can feel the chains Keegan used to bind you," Vaaler continued. "I see where he has tied your will to his."

Darm let out a soft sob, but his eyes remained shut.

"I'm going to count backward from five, Darm," Vaaler said. "And when I'm done, I'm going to break the bonds and free you from the curse. Do you understand?"

"Yes," Darm whimpered. "Please help me."

"I will, Darm. Take a deep breath. Good. Don't be afraid; this won't hurt. Five . . . four . . . Take another deep breath."

Vaaler's voice was getting softer and softer, like a parent trying to lull a child to sleep.

"Three . . . Breathe, Darm. Stay calm. Two . . . don't worry, this won't hurt. Just relax. One . . . BE FREE!"

He shouted the last words so loudly that Shalana actually jumped. Darm let out a cry and his head snapped back as if he'd been struck though Vaaler's hand on his head had never moved.

The soldier's eyes snapped open, and a broad grin spread across his face.

"I'm free!" he called out. "I'm free!"

"You're free," Vaaler agreed. "Now . . . sleep."

Darm's eyes snapped shut and his body went limp. Vaaler caught him before he fell, then gently lowered him to the stable floor.

"What was all that?" Shalana asked.

"The power of suggestion," he replied. "I don't think Keegan actually cursed him. They just made him think he was cursed, and his own mind did the rest."

"Why would they do that? Did they really think he'd be able to convince the Free Cities to help them against the Order?"

"I think sending him on that mission was just a way to keep him busy. They wanted to make sure he didn't do something to betray them if they let him go."

"It might have been kinder just to kill him," she noted.

"Darm might disagree with you," Vaaler noted. "Especially if his sanity returns."

"So you think you cured him of his madness? Just like that?"

"I don't know. He's suffering from dehydration and malnutrition; he's probably been having hallucinations for days. And he was emotionally traumatized by his meeting with Keegan. If he gets food and water and no longer believes he's under some wizard's curse, then hopefully his mind will start to see the world more rationally again."

"You know if that happens, your new followers are going to

start proclaiming you have mystical healing powers," Shalana warned.

From the way his eyebrows arched up she realized he hadn't actually considered that.

It's good to know you're not always two steps ahead of me.

"So what happens now?" she asked.

"I don't think running into him like this was an accident," Vaaler said.

"I was thinking the same thing. It looks like you're still part of Keegan's destiny after all. And that means so am I. So what do we do next?"

"We know the Order is laying siege to Callastan," Vaaler said, speaking slowly as he tried to work it all out. "If Cassandra's in the city, Keegan and the others might need help to break through their lines to find her."

"You haven't got that many followers yet," Shalana warned. "Unless you plan to hit every town between here and Callastan."

"That would take far too lo—" he cut himself off when he realized she'd been making a joke. "I was thinking we should march to the Free Cities."

For a moment, Shalana thought he was now joking with her. Then she realized he was completely serious.

"Why would we do that?"

"Like you said, one soldier isn't going to convince the Free Cities to march against the Order. But an army of refugees show-ing up at their gates telling tales of the horrors they've suffered because of the Order's Purge might have more luck."

"Not everyone has as soft a heart as you do," she reminded him.

"It's worth a try," Vaaler said. "And don't forget—I can be very convincing when I have to."

Chapter 17

SCYTHE AND JERROD took turns watching over Keegan through the night, though neither one slept at all. By the time morning broke, though, nothing had changed; he hadn't even moved from the position they'd left him in.

"We have to do something," Scythe said, picking up Daemron's Sword and pacing angrily back and forth. "Instead of just sitting here wasting our time!"

"There's nothing we can do," Jerrod insisted. "It is up to him to find his way back to us."

"No, I don't believe that," Scythe replied. "How did he find his way back the last time?"

"He felt the Ring calling to him. After he woke, we took it from the Danaan Queen."

"So why can't he sense the Ring now?"

"The ways of Chaos are unpredictable," Jerrod answered.

Scythe still wasn't satisfied. She had accepted that she and Keegan were both touched by Chaos. She could accept that they shared a bond that also connected them to the prophecy Jerrod followed. But she couldn't accept the idea that they were all just being swept along by events beyond their control.

There are rules that control Chaos, even if we don't understand them.

She wished that Vaaler were here; the Danaan understood these things better than she did. He'd studied the ways of Chaos.

But he has never used one of the Talismans, Norr's voice chimed in. *That is something you and Keegan have in common.*

Scythe realized she was casually twirling Daemron's blade in her hand as she thought. The Sword was so light, and it felt so natural in her grip that she sometimes forgot she was holding it.

"That's it!" she cried out as inspiration struck.

Jerrod turned his head toward her, his expression confused.

"The Sword is a counter to the Ring," she said, speaking quickly as the idea took shape in her head. "It absorbs Chaos. Blunts its power. Remember when Keegan tried to use magic against the Guardian?"

"That is why the Frozen East has no wizards or prophets," Jerrod agreed.

"That's why Keegan can't sense the Ring this time. It's hidden by the power of the Sword."

"Even if you are right," Jerrod said. "Where does that leave us?"

Scythe chewed on her lower lip, looking for an answer.

"He can't sense the Ring hanging on the chain around his neck, but what if we placed it on his finger?"

"No," Jerrod said. "He can barely control the Ring's power when he's conscious. In his current state the rush of Chaos would destroy him, and the backlash would be devastating."

"What if I use the Sword to help him?" Scythe pressed. "Its power would balance out the Ring, allowing Keegan to control the Chaos and the backlash!"

"You are not a mage," Jerrod reminded her. "You don't understand how Chaos works. This plan is madness."

"You're no wizard, either," Scythe shot back. "And you keep saying how Keegan and I share a bond. If that's true, then maybe this will work."

"Or maybe it will kill you both!" Jerrod snapped. "Keegan foolishly put himself in danger. I won't allow you to do the same."

"Allow me?" Scythe snarled. "You can't stop me!"

Jerrod stiffened, then relaxed and bowed his head. "You speak the truth. With Daemron's Sword you are far stronger than I.

"But I'm asking you not to do this. Remember what you told me. You said Keegan's feelings for you might compromise his ability to fulfill his destiny. Maybe you were right."

"What does that have to do with anything?"

"I'm worried your feelings for Keegan are the reason behind your insistence on doing this."

"I don't have any feelings for Keegan," Scythe snapped.

"Is that true? You said Keegan might not be willing to sacrifice you for our cause," Jerrod continued. "But now you are the one who cannot let him go."

"That has nothing to do with my feelings for him," Scythe insisted. "I told you I'd do whatever it takes to make your prophecy come true. How can that happen if Keegan's stuck like this?"

"Maybe Keegan will find his way back on his own," Jerrod whispered.

"I don't think you believe that," she said. "I think you've given up on him."

When Jerrod didn't reply, she knew she was onto something.

"You believed he was some kind of savior," she continued, "but you've seen too many of his flaws and failings. You're starting to wonder if he can ever be the hero you need him to be."

"He has so much power," Jerrod said. "So much potential. And yet he seems so frail and weak.

"If his mind cannot even find its way back from the Burning Sea, maybe he was not meant to save us."

"Or maybe he's not meant to save us alone," Scythe argued. "Maybe he needs me to help him."

Jerrod was silent, his brow furrowed as he thought about what she was saying.

"You're right," he finally admitted. "My faith in the prophecy has wavered, but that is my failing, not Keegan's. You must try to help him."

Scythe nodded, then went over and crouched beside Keegan's nonresponsive body. She gently rolled him over onto his back, then lay down beside him. In her right hand she clutched Daemron's Sword, her left she wrapped around Keegan's own.

She'd managed to convince Jerrod that they had to try something but she still really had no idea what she was doing. All she was doing was acting on instinct, trusting her gut.

It's what you're best at, Norr's voice told her.

"I'm ready," she said, closing her eyes and trying to ready her mind for whatever was about to happen.

She heard Jerrod fumbling with the chain, then she felt the monk's hands as he slid the Talisman onto Keegan's finger, being careful not to disentangle their grip.

As he stepped away, Scythe clenched Keegan's hand tightly with her own. For a few seconds she felt nothing, then she heard something: a low rumble coming from a great distance. A sudden heat sprang up around her, and her eyes snapped open.

She was no longer lying on the ground beside Keegan. She was alone, floating in an ocean of blue fire, with Daemron's Sword still clutched in her hand.

The Burning Sea!

The roar of the heaving ocean waves was so loud she could barely think, and she began to panic. The flames seemed to respond to her fear, wrapping themselves around her body and limbs like serpents coiling around their prey. She cried out as she felt them tighten, and they began to drag her down deep below the surface.

Her panic disappeared, replaced by the familiar rage and fury. She slashed at the flames with the Sword, hacking and chopping until the tendrils finally fell away. Then she thrust the Sword straight up above her, kicked her feet once, and shot back toward the surface.

A wave picked her up and tossed her, sending her spinning out of control. Scythe let out a scream and stabbed at the waves with her blade, using it like an anchor to slow and stop her momentum.

Another massive wave rose to tower above her, then came crashing down with enough force to crush her. She brought the Sword up and held it above her head with both hands like a shield. The blade struck the wall of Chaos fire, carving through it and slicing the wave perfectly in half, leaving her unharmed.

Around her, the ocean suddenly grew calm, and she bobbed gently on the surface. She cast her head from side to side, but all she could see in every direction was the blue fire stretching out to infinity.

The Sword could protect her from the fury of the Burning Sea, she realized, but it couldn't help her find her way back to the mortal world. To do that, she'd need Keegan's help.

"Keegan!" she called out. "Keegan, can you hear me?"

In the far depths of the Burning Sea, the heat of the Chaos fire was relentless. Keegan's mind had retreated into a tiny cocoon, drawing itself in tighter and tighter as he struggled to keep the flames from turning him into ash. Yet though he was alive, he still felt the searing pain as it crawled over his skin—a never-ending torment.

Why am I still fighting? Why suffer like this? Just let go and it will be over in an instant.

Before he could surrender himself to the flames, he felt a sudden rush of power. In the alternate reality of the Burning Sea, Daemron's Ring suddenly appeared on his finger.

All thoughts of giving up were swept away as he began to draw on the Talisman. He still felt the heat of the Chaos fire, but it was no longer unbearable torture. Instead, he welcomed the heat—drawing it in and shaping it to his will.

The flames around him began to swirl quickly, creating a vortex that propelled Keegan back to the surface of the Burning Sea. As he breached, he heard someone calling his name—the voice barely audible above the roar of the waves, but one he recognized immediately.

Scythe!

Gazing out across the boundless ocean of blue fire, he saw a flickering point of silver light. Focusing his will, he summoned a wave of Chaos to carry him in that direction.

As he drew closer, he saw Scythe floating in a tiny pocket of calm tranquility.

The Sword is holding the Chaos at bay, he realized.

At the same time, he felt the wave beneath him surge, growing to gargantuan size and accelerating out of control.

"Scythe!" he screamed, hoping she could hear him above the deafening thunder. "Look out!"

Scythe heard Keegan's voice, and her head snapped around to see the titanic swell bearing down on her—twice the size of the one she'd beaten back earlier. Riding the crest was Keegan, though he was clearly not in control.

She brought the Sword up again, hoping to blunt the force of its impact. This time, however, the Chaos overwhelmed her and she was buried beneath a wall of scorching blue fire.

The wave swallowed her up and dragged her down far below the surface. The fire flooded her nose and throat, making her choke and cough. She flailed about with the Sword, beating the wave back until she could breathe again.

Then she saw Keegan floating beside her, his eyes closed. She screamed his name, but her voice was smothered by the flames that enveloped them both. She reached out with her free hand and seized his ankle, pulling him in close enough for her to grab his hand.

"Keegan!" she screamed again, and this time his eyes fluttered open in response though they were glazed and unfocused.

"You have to get us out of here!" she shouted. "You have to bring us back!"

The young wizard didn't respond; he still seemed disoriented and confused. From far below Scythe could feel another enormous wave building, rising to swallow them both.

"Keegan—you have to do it now! You have to save us!"

His eyes suddenly snapped into focus and his jaw clenched. He pulled Scythe in close and wrapped both his arms around her just as the massive wave hit them. There was a sound Scythe could only describe as reality itself being ripped apart, then suddenly everything went dark.

Jerrod sat on the ground, his legs crossed and his hands resting lightly on his thighs. He was taking slow, deep breaths; his eyes were closed but his Sight focused intently on the motionless forms of Keegan and Scythe.

Despite his efforts to induce a state of meditative calm, he felt a painful knot in his stomach and his neck and shoulders were so tense the muscles were starting to ache.

What if they don't come back? Then only Cassandra is left to fulfill the prophecy . . . assuming I can even find her.

Several hours had passed since Scythe's desperate ploy to save Keegan. In that time, neither one had shown any movement or any kind of sign that their bodies were anything but empty shells.

Even if this doesn't work, Scythe was right to make the attempt.

The young Islander truly believed in Keegan, a belief he had momentarily lost. The strength of her conviction made him ashamed when he thought back on how he had let his personal doubts undermine his faith.

The path of the Burning Savior has never been an easy one to walk. The way will only become more difficult now that we are near the end.

Keegan and Scythe needed his help; they needed his support.

I will not doubt either of you again, he vowed. *Just please come back to me.*

As if in response to his wish, their bodies began to twitch and shiver.

Jerrod leapt to his feet, then stopped himself before he touched them. He did not know what was happening, but he feared his interference would only make things worse.

Keegan cried out, his back arching so severely Jerrod feared his spine would snap. Then Scythe moaned softly and began to convulse.

They're on the threshold of the mortal world! Now they just need to burst through!

At the same instant, both their eyes popped open and consciousness violently slammed back into their bodies.

"Keegan! Scythe! Are you okay?"

Neither gave any indication they could hear him. Disoriented and confused, they each rolled to the side, breaking the grip they had on each other's hand. A second later, Jerrod felt the unmistakable sensation of Chaos building.

"The Ring, Keegan!" he shouted. "You have to remove the Ring!"

The young wizard still didn't acknowledge him. Instead of removing the Ring, he clenched his fist and instinctively clutched the Talisman closer to his body.

Jerrod glanced over at Scythe, who lay in the fetal position, clutching at the Sword with both hands. Realizing neither one was in a state to react to what was happening, Jerrod threw himself on top of Keegan.

The young man tried to fight him off, but though the terrible power of Chaos was rapidly building up inside him, physically he was still much weaker than Jerrod. The monk seized his wrist and twisted, forcing him to expose his hand. Wrapping his legs around Keegan's arm and shoulder to lock the limb in place, Jerrod clawed at his still-clenched fingers, peeling them back so he could get at the Ring.

A second later he had his prize, and he yanked the Talisman free. In response, the still-semiconscious wizard released the gathering Chaos in a single burst of raw power. The burst sent Jerrod flying twenty feet through the air, still clutching the Ring.

He hit the ground hard, momentarily dazing him. By the time he got back to his feet, the worst was over; the wave of Chaos had dispersed into the mortal world.

And what consequences will the backlash bring?

By this time Scythe was back on her feet, swaying slightly as she fought to keep her balance. She staggered over to Keegan and collapsed on top of him.

"You did it," she said, her voice trembling. "You brought us back!"

Keegan reached up with his good hand to caress the back of her head as she lay across his chest.

"No, you did it. I was lost, and you came for me."

For an instant they stared into each other's eyes. Jerrod saw Keegan's head tilt forward slightly, even as Scythe pulled back and rolled off of him, then sprang to her feet.

He was going to kiss her. And she knew it!

Scythe had insisted she had no feelings for Keegan; she'd even tried to convince Jerrod that Keegan's feelings for her could be a bad thing. Now, however, the monk wasn't so sure.

You risked yourself to save him because you care—and it worked!

Scythe reached down and offered Keegan her hand. After a brief hesitation, the mage took it and she hauled him to his feet. Then she turned to Jerrod.

"What are you staring at, White-eyes?" she asked.

White-eyes?

Jerrod had gotten so used to struggling with the strange double vision of his restored sight that it took him a moment to realize it was gone.

"I don't understand," Keegan said, staring at the monk in utter amazement. "Is your Sight back?"

"It never left," Jerrod said, speaking slowly as he pushed out with his awareness, testing its limits. "But having my normal vision restored interfered with my ability to use it."

He walked toward them and extended his hand, offering the Ring back to Keegan.

"Backlash," Scythe said. "That has to be it, right? I felt the burst of Chaos when you yanked the Ring off Keegan's finger."

"Backlash is a destructive power," Jerrod told her. "It does not heal."

"Technically you're not healed," she reminded him. "Raven used the Sword to heal you when she restored your sight. The backlash just undid her spell. Basically, it made you blind."

She's right, Jerrod thought. *I'm blind, and now I can finally see again!*

Keegan wolfed down his food, not caring that he was devouring three days' worth of their rations in a single sitting. His ordeal had left him physically and emotionally drained, and he needed to eat to restore his strength.

"How are you feeling?" Scythe asked, kneeling beside him to catch some of the heat from the small fire.

"Better with every passing second. I think I'll be ready to head out for Callastan tomorrow morning."

"I'd rather we wait another day," Jerrod said, striding over to join them.

The milky veil covering the monk's eyes had only returned a few hours ago, yet already Keegan sensed a difference in Jerrod. He stood up straighter; he moved with more purpose and confidence.

"I agree," Scythe said. "Even I wouldn't mind another day to recover, and I wasn't trapped in there nearly as long as you were."

But I've been there before, Keegan thought. *And I'm a mage. The training Rexol gave me helped me survive.*

He didn't bother to argue, however. If Scythe and Jerrod were united on the issue, he knew it would be almost impossible to change their minds.

"If you're up to it," Jerrod said, "I would like to speak about what you saw."

Keegan froze, his hand halfway to stuffing another piece of hard cheese into his open mouth. Then he slowly set it down and nodded.

"I . . . I think I'm ready."

"Are you sure this is a good idea?" Scythe asked. "I can barely remember what happened when I was trapped on the other side. I don't *want* to remember."

"Keegan became lost because he tried to find the source of his vision," Jerrod said. "Given all that happened because of this, I hope he at least discovered something valuable."

"Hey," Scythe snapped. "Don't sound so high-and-mighty. If he hadn't done this, you'd still be stumbling around half-blind. Or double-sighted. Or whatever."

"I am grateful my true Sight has been restored," Jerrod admitted. "But it doesn't change the fact that what he did was foolish and rash."

Their bickering had a comfortable, familiar feel, and Keegan couldn't help but smile.

For the first time since Norr's death, they finally seem like their old selves.

Unfortunately, thinking of Norr brought on a fresh wave of guilt as he recalled how close he had come to kissing Scythe only a few hours ago, and his smile slipped away.

She came to save me—she still cares about me. But when I tried to kiss her she recoiled in disgust. And why wouldn't she? Norr's only been gone a few weeks.

Yet Keegan couldn't help but feel there had been an instant when she'd almost kissed him back.

We still share a connection; I felt it. Without it she couldn't have pulled me from the Chaos Sea.

"Come on, Keegan," Scythe encouraged. "Tell White-eyes that this wasn't just a waste of time."

"I did see something," Keegan admitted, grateful to have something else to focus on. "Before I became lost."

Both Scythe and Jerrod hunched forward, eager to hear what he had to say.

"The vision wasn't spawned in the Burning Sea. That's why it felt so strange to me."

"Where did it come from?" Jerrod asked.

"Daemron sent it."

"Why?" Scythe demanded.

"It's a trap," Keegan said. "I think he's trying to lure us to the Keystone. I think if we go there, the Legacy will fall."

"Simple solution," Scythe said. "We just don't go there."

"Keegan may not be the only one who saw this vision," Jerrod reminded her. "Cassandra is also a prophet and one of the Children of Fire.

"The Order teaches us that our most sacred duty is to preserve and protect the Legacy," he continued. "If Cassandra saw a vision of the Keystone, she might think her destiny is to take the Crown there to repair the Legacy."

"But instead she'll bring it crashing down," Keegan said. "And Daemron will return."

"We must get to Callastan and stop her," Jerrod said.

"Like I said before," Keegan told them, "I think I'll be ready to head out in the morning."

This time nobody objected.

Chapter 18

"WELCOME BACK, PONTIFF," Xadier said, gracing Yasmin with a deep bow. "The troops have been eagerly awaiting your return."

Yasmin very much doubted that was true, but she saw no point in correcting the Seer.

"See to it that my reinforcements are well fed and stationed somewhere they can sleep well when night comes," she instructed. "They need to rest before we launch our attack."

"Of course, Pontiff."

A stiff wind was blowing in from the sea, carrying the smell of salt mingling with Callastan's putrid stench.

"After you've seen to the troops, come to my quarters and deliver a status report," she commanded.

Xadier bowed and scampered off to carry out her orders while Yasmin made straight for her tent.

The bare interior offered little comfort, but once inside she was able to pull the flap closed to keep out the worst of the stench.

Soon that smell will be swallowed up by smoke from the fires of the Purge, she thought, and a smile crossed her lips.

By the time Xadier arrived to make his report, Yasmin had already taken water and bread to refresh herself from the long journey. Yet even with her superlative physical prowess, she still felt the weariness of the long march from Norem deep in her bones as she sat cross-legged on the ground. Her fatigue didn't bode well for the state of the ordinary soldiers.

I pushed them too hard. I am overeager to see this end. I must be careful lest I make a mistake.

Yet she couldn't wait forever. The Crown was still in Callastan —or so she hoped—and the longer she waited the greater the chance Cassandra would slip through her fingers.

"Join me," Yasmin offered, motioning to the bare earth in the middle of her tent.

Xadier lowered himself and mimicked her cross-legged position. Even with both of them seated on the ground, Yasmin towered over him, her scarred scalp a full head higher than his.

"Status reports," she said.

"Our troops are tense, but discipline still holds," the Seer assured her. "We have plenty of supplies and the weather has been mild.

"Word of what happened to Carthin when he betrayed you has also helped keep potential agitators in line," he added.

"What about Callastan?"

"The weather has been a boon for our enemy as well," Xadier admitted. "Our spies within the city report that their morale is still high despite our presence beyond their walls.

"The numbers of armed defenders is greater than we expected; the Enforcers have opened their ranks to anyone able to swing a club. Despite this, we should still have the numbers to overwhelm them quickly thanks to the reinforcements you have brought us."

"What about passage into and out of the city?"

"We have been able to secure most routes by land," he told her, "though it was more difficult than we first imagined."

"This is a smuggler's city," Yasmin reminded him. "There will always be tunnels for the rats to flee. As long as Cassandra and the Crown do not escape."

"That has not happened," Xadier promised. "Inquisitors patrol the perimeter on a regular basis. They would sense the Talisman if she passed anywhere near them."

"What about those who come and go by sea?"

"As you instructed, we have teams of Inquisitors watching the docks in case Cassandra attempts to flee by ship.

"They patrol the water's edge, boarding any vessels that try to launch. But given our limited numbers, I have instructed them to focus only on those trying to leave. They have done little to stop the arrival of the small skiffs and rafts bringing food into the city."

"We never intended to starve them out," Yasmin reminded him. "Making sure the Crown does not leave by ship was always our primary goal."

Xadier bowed his head respectfully at her implied approval before continuing on with his report.

"We have agents spreading information and rumors within the city walls," he added. "We are offering a bounty for Cassandra though there are no reports of anyone fitting her description yet.

"And we have made it known that when the attack comes, any who wish to switch sides and join our ranks will be welcomed without judgment."

Yasmin nodded. Normally she wouldn't approve of such a decree: Righteous punishment of the sinful was a sacred duty. In a perfect world, every inhabitant of Callastan would suffer for defying her and the entire city would be turned into a smoking ruin.

But this was not a perfect world, and breaking the city's spirit wasn't her true goal. Nothing mattered but capturing the Crown.

Everything Xadier said was as she expected; he had done well in her absence. Yet despite his assurances, she needed to know for certain that he had not failed her.

Yasmin took a deep, cleansing breath then reached out with her Sight, pushing her awareness to its farthest limits. Thousands of images assailed her: the soldiers in her camps, biding time until the battle; the inhabitants of Callastan going about their daily business even as the threat of attack loomed over them. Ignoring these, she let her mind drift rapidly back and forth until she sensed it: the familiar pulse of the Crown.

It was clearly emanating from somewhere inside the city, though when Yasmin tried to focus her Sight, the Crown suddenly seemed to move and jump around erratically.

She has learned how to lay false trails to mislead us. No wonder the Inquisitors searching for her have failed.

But though she could hide the exact location of the Crown from the Pontiff, Cassandra couldn't fully mask its presence. The Talisman was still there, waiting for Yasmin to claim it.

To this point, Cassandra had been more patient than she imagined. Given the girl's youth and inexperience, the Pontiff had expected her to try to flee Callastan long ago.

She's more clever than I thought. She's going to wait for the battle to begin before she makes her move. But I still have some tricks up my sleeve.

"The only way to flush the heretic out is to attack the city," she told Xadier. "Spread the word among the troops that we will storm the walls in five days."

"Is it wise to announce our plans so far in advance?" Xadier asked. "There could be enemy spies among our ranks. They will alert those inside the city to our plans."

"That's exactly what I'm counting on," Yasmin said with a smile.

Rianna's health was returning. She was eating again and had gained back much of the weight she had lost in the dark days before Vaaler stole the Ring from her. But though she had made great progress physically, there were still deep mental scars.

Sometimes she still imagined she could hear Orath whispering inside her head—compelling her and controlling her like some kind of puppet made of flesh and bone. The sensation never lasted more than a fleeting second—their connection had been severed when the Minion fled. But each time it happened, she remembered the horror and violation of having a demon crawling inside her thoughts, and it was all she could do not simply to curl up into a ball on the floor, weeping with terror.

Yet not all her scars had come from Orath. There were emotional wounds as well. She'd exiled her only son; she'd driven him away and turned him into a traitor against the people he was supposed to rule. And then, when her kingdom was in crisis, she'd put her own desire for vengeance over the needs of her people.

I don't deserve to rule them anymore. When Andar arrives, I will tell him that the Regent Council must choose a new monarch.

She had struggled with this decision for many nights, never quite having the courage to take the final step. But tonight, when Andar came to share the decisions the Regent Council had made that day, she would finally tell him.

The High Sorcerer arrived soon after, prompt as always. When his face appeared at the open door to her chambers, she ushered him in with a brief wave. As he always did, he closed the door behind them so her guards wouldn't be privy to their conversation.

"I have important news," he said.

She noticed he was slightly out of breath, as if he'd run over from the nearby council chambers. He joined her at the table where they shared a small bite each night. For convenience, she no longer had the serving staff on hand as they ate only to be dismissed once their discussions began. Instead, everything was set out beforehand.

Normally they would dine before they discussed the events of the day, but obviously Andar was excited enough about something to break form.

"I also have important news," she said. "I've reached a crucial decision."

Andar's face momentarily lit up, but his joy quickly faded as he picked up on her somber tone.

He so badly wants me to return to my throne, she thought. *He clings to some idealized notion of what I used to be. He doesn't see what I've become.*

"Before you tell me anything," he said, an unexpected urgency in his voice, "you must listen to what I have to say!"

His words were mildly inappropriate; even though he was head of the Regent Council, it wasn't proper to tell the Queen she *must* do anything. However, considering she was about to abdicate, Rianna didn't see any point in correcting him.

"Very well," she said. "Tell me your news."

"Two things," he said. "First, Vaaler is alive!"

Rianna felt herself swaying in her chair, and she grabbed on to the table to steady herself.

"My son is alive?" she whispered, her brain still reeling from the shock. "He survived the battle with the ogre?"

"He's been seen in the Southlands," Andar confirmed. "They say he's gathering an army of peasants and farmers."

"An army? For what?"

"They say he's liberating villages in the borderlands from the tyranny of soldiers and mercenaries left behind by the Order," he told her. "His reputation is spreading far and wide. They've even heard of him in the Free Cities."

"It sounds as if these may be nothing more than rumors and tall tales," she said, some of her hope fading.

"There are too many accounts to dismiss them," Andar assured her. "They all speak of a Danaan named Vaaler and his honor guard of Eastern Barbarians."

"This makes no sense," Rianna said. "First, he leads the armies of the clans when we attack them, and now he's gathering another army in the Southlands?"

"It sounds like madness, I know," Andar conceded. "But perhaps it has something to do with the wizard he befriended."

"The Destroyer of Worlds," Rianna muttered.

"Do you remember why you banished Vaaler?" Andar asked her.

"He was bringing outsiders into our land. To our capital! He violated one of our oldest laws."

"Do you recall why he was bringing them to us? Do you remember what the messenger he sent to you said?"

So much had happened since then that it was hard for her to recall the exact details. And at the time, her mind had been consumed by her terrifying visions of the Destroyer of Worlds.

"I'm sorry," she said. "I don't remember."

"Vaaler claimed the wizard—a young man named Keegan— was destined to save the mortal world. He said he was destined to stop the return of Daemron the Slayer and restore the Legacy."

Rianna nodded; she remembered now. At the time, she'd thought he'd been corrupted by his time among the foreigners. The Danaan honored the Old Gods in their fashion, but they understood that they had passed from the mortal world centuries ago. Vaaler, however, seemed eager to embrace the Southlands' irrational belief in prophecies and legends.

"What does this have to do with Vaaler gathering an army of peasants and farmers?" she asked.

"There are some who believe he plans to take his army to Callastan and do battle with the Pontiff's forces there. If that is true, it could have something to do with whatever he believes Keegan's destiny to be."

"I am ashamed for what I did to my son," the Queen said, speaking slowly. "And I thank you for telling me this. I am grateful to learn he is still alive even if he is still taken by this mad belief in some Southern prophecy."

"It might not be madness after all," Andar told her.

"Please don't tell me you believe that my son and this wizard are destined to save the world and restore the Legacy," she said, already exhausted by the preposterousness of their conversation.

"That is the second thing I came to tell you," the High Sorcerer answered. "Lormilar and the other scholars have found mention of the obelisk you described. The one from your dream.

"It's called the Keystone, and according to a passage Lormilar himself translated, that is where the Old Gods created the Legacy."

Impossible!

"He must have made some mistake with the translation. The ancient tongues have been lost for many generations; it is easy to misinterpret them."

"There is no mistake," Andar told her. "The Keystone is where the Legacy was born. And the text gives the exact location of the island on which it stands."

I saw the wizard there on the island, standing before the obelisk. Rianna's thoughts were spinning out of control, coming at her from all directions. *Does this mean Vaaler was right all along? Is this vision proof that Keegan must restore the Legacy?*

"Vaaler tried to tell me, but I wouldn't listen," she muttered.

No! My visions were strongest when I still had the Ring. They showed me the wizard bathed in fire and flame, bringing devastation to our city!

"None of this makes any sense," she said aloud. "In one vision he is the savior, but in another he is the Destroyer of Worlds?"

"That is the essence of Chaos," Andar reminded her.

"He unleashed the dragon that nearly wiped Ferlhame off the map," the Queen said. "What if everything he touches will turn to death and destruction? What if my dream of the obelisk was a portent of disaster?"

"Then we must warn Vaaler that he is going down the wrong path," Andar said.

"But what if he is on the right path?" Rianna countered. "What if the wizard is meant to go to the Keystone?"

"Then we must do whatever we can to help Vaaler get him there."

"I don't know what to do, Andar," Rianna confessed. "Take this to the Regent Council. Let them decide what must be done."

"I already have. They decreed that this must be your decision, my Queen."

"No," she said. "What if I'm wrong? I've already done so much harm."

"You have made mistakes," Andar agreed. "And, as Queen, the consequences of your mistakes can be devastating. But you cannot hide from your responsibilities because of that.

"You must try to atone for the transgressions of your past. Your people still look to you for guidance. Even though you are scared, you must give it to them.

"Whatever you decide, the Regent Council will support you."

Rianna didn't say anything. She was afraid to speak, terrified that whatever came out of her mouth would be the wrong choice.

What would Vaaler do? she asked herself, and in that question she knew she had her answer.

"Each time I've opposed Vaaler," she declared, "it has brought ruin upon the Danaan people. Perhaps it is time I try to help him instead."

"Well said, my Queen," Andar told her. "I will tell Lormilar to prepare a delegation to go meet your son."

"No," Rianna said, holding up her hand. "This is too important, and Lormilar has never traveled to the Southlands or the Free Cities.

"But you have. You must be the one to go to Vaaler."

"I am the leader of the Regent Council," Andar reminded her. "If I go, who will rule the kingdom?"

"I will," she said, and the High Sorcerer's face broke into a broad grin. "Tell the Regent Council their Queen has returned."

Chapter 19

CASSANDRA FELT GUILTY about going to see Bo-Shing behind Methodis's back, but she needed to speak with the pirate captain alone.

Since their first and only meeting so far, the Pontiff and thousands of reinforcements had arrived to swell the numbers of the army camped outside Callastan's walls. It wouldn't be long before they attacked the city, and Cassandra needed to be certain Bo-Shing actually had a plan to help them escape the city.

It was dangerous wandering the streets during the day; Methodis had warned her that the Order had put out a bounty asking for any information on someone fitting her description. She kept her hood up to obscure her blond hair and white eyes, hoping not to draw unwanted attention.

It's still dangerous, Rexol warned her. *You're carrying the Crown. What if you cross paths with one of the Inquisitors?*

The wizard had a point; she knew some of Yasmin's people had infiltrated the city and were searching for her. If she ran into them, they'd be able to sense the Crown tucked away in her backpack.

You'll have to kill them, Rexol told her.

Cassandra had easily handled the pirate who attacked her, but she was no match for an Inquisitor. Not unless she called on the Crown's power to aid her in the fight ... and that might alert every member of the Order within the city.

And then you'll have to kill them all! Rexol cackled.

She didn't bother to reply but she wasn't certain she would win such a confrontation. At least, not without putting the Crown atop her head and unleashing its full power. And after what happened last time, that was something she would only do as a last resort.

Am I doing the right thing? she wondered as she marched quickly down the twisting streets of the dock district.

It seemed as if her life had been spinning out of control ever since the night she'd freed Keegan, Jerrod, and Rexol from their cells beneath the Monastery. Her failure and weakness had set in motion a series of events that had unleashed the Minions on the mortal world and left the Monastery in ruins and Nazir dead.

Yet despite her betrayal, Nazir had given her the Crown and warned her to keep it safe.

He saw something in me. He believed this was my fate. My destiny.

But what if he was wrong? Yasmin—the new Pontiff—had declared her a heretic. As far as the Order was concerned, Cassandra was an agent of Chaos. A bringer of death and destruction and a threat to the preservation of the Legacy.

Given how close the Legacy had come to falling when Rexol had temporarily seized control of her body and used the Crown, it wasn't hard to see what they were afraid of.

The Order fears Chaos because they are ignorant of its true nature, Rexol reminded her. *You've grown beyond their simplistic dogma. You've accepted your true destiny.*

But had she? Rexol's teachings had given her a much better understanding of Chaos, but it was still her vision of the Keystone on a tiny island on the edge of the world that was guiding her now.

What am I now? A fallen prophet of the Order? An apprentice to a mad wizard? What path do I walk now? And is it the right one?

For once, Rexol didn't seem to have anything to offer to her inner debate. Not that he would have added anything constructive.

He'd just tell me to use the Crown. Embrace my power and ignore the consequences. He doesn't care if the Legacy comes crashing down.

That was the key. At least, she hoped it was. Get to the Keystone and use the Crown to restore the Legacy. Why else would she have seen it in her visions? Whatever doubts she might have, at least this was one thing she could cling to.

She turned down the dead-end alley leading to the pirates' lair and knocked on the barred door. The panel slid open, and the pair of eyes looking out at her opened wide in surprise.

"I need to speak with Bo-Shing," she said.

The panel slid shut, then the door opened. Cassandra stepped inside the small room. This time there were only two men there: the large man standing guard near the door at the back leading out to the tavern, and Shoji—the pirate who had attacked her during the first meeting.

Shoji closed the door behind her and called out to the other man. "Get Bo-Shing. Tell him the client is here."

The other man slid back the panel on the door he was guarding and whispered to someone on the other side, then snapped the panel shut again.

Reaching out with her Sight, Cassandra saw that even though it was the middle of the afternoon, the tavern was still packed with drunken customers.

"Bo-Shing is with his women," Shoji told her, his lips stretched wide in a creepy smile. His accent was thick, and Cassandra wasn't sure if he'd actually meant to use the plural or not, but she decided not to ask.

"Where is doctor man?" the leering pirate asked.

He was standing closer to her than she liked, but if he tried anything, she'd be ready.

"Methodis doesn't know I'm here," she said. "He's busy calling in outstanding debts from some of his wealthy clients. Bo-Shing is going through money much faster than we expected."

Shoji shrugged. "A long voyage to the Kraken's Eye. Many supplies needed. Food is expensive."

They stood in uncomfortable silence for a short while until a knock came at the far door. The guard peeked through the viewing panel, then opened it so Bo-Shing could enter. He was shirtless, exposing the tattoos on his chest and back, and his leather breeches weren't tied at the top. Two other pirates—both fully dressed and armed with curved cutlasses—followed close behind him.

"Am I interrupting something?" Cassandra asked archly.

"They'll wait," Bo-Shing replied. "Why are you here?"

"I want to talk business."

"Have a seat," he said, pointing to the table.

"I prefer to stand."

The pirate shrugged and slumped down into a chair facing her.

"Tell your man to step away and stop grinning at me like a fool," Cassandra warned, "or I'll punch him in the throat again."

"Shoji might like that," Bo-Shing warned. "He pays extra to have the whores get rough with him."

"I'm not one of your whores," Cassandra snapped.

She turned and gave Shoji a dark stare, and his smile vanished as he backed away.

"You want to talk business," Bo-Shing said, "then talk."

"The Pontiff has arrived with reinforcements. I need to know you'll be ready if she attacks the city."

"Word is out," the pirate said, waving his hand dismissively. "Her soldiers need time to recover from their march. The attack is still three days away."

"I want to know the plan," Cassandra said.

"We've been sneaking to the docks and slowly loading supplies at night," Bo-Shing told her.

"The Pontiff will have Inquisitors watching the docks," Cassandra warned him.

"We've seen them. And they've seen us. We've made sure they take a special interest in what we're doing."

"It's a decoy," Cassandra said. "That's why you need so many supplies. You're stocking two ships!"

"Very good," Bo-Shing said. "But the second batch of supplies is actually being loaded into a wagon in a warehouse a few blocks away from the docks.

"We know when the Pontiff is planning her attack. Once the battle begins, people are going to try to flee the city by the hundreds. It will be impossible for the Inquisitors to stop every ship heading out to sea. They'll need to focus on a few—like the decoy we've set up.

"We all meet at the warehouse, and while they're chasing after the other ship, we roll the supply wagons onto *The Chaos Runner* and cast off."

"Why are you so certain they'll stay focused on the wrong ship?" Cassandra asked.

"*The Chaos Runner* isn't just fast; she tends to go unnoticed while she's in port," he bragged. "Another of her special talents. Plus I'm doing everything I can to draw attention to the other ship.

"I've hired a special crew to load it and sail it. They have orders to cast off as soon as the Order attacks the city. And I've told them you're going to be hidden on the boat.

"The Pontiff is offering a large reward for any information about you," Bo-Shing continued. "I know the kind of men I've hired. At least one of them is sure to betray the rest of the crew for that kind of coin.

"One of the Pontiff's agents has probably already gotten word that you'll be on board. The Inquisitors think they know exactly what ship you'll be on. They're going to focus all their efforts on stopping it from leaving."

It wasn't a perfect plan, but Cassandra thought it could work. In the confusion of the battle, things would happen quickly. With the decoy drawing most of the Inquisitors' attention, *The Chaos Runner* really might be able to slip out of the city with the rest of the fleeing vessels unnoticed. But one thing about the plan troubled her.

"Do you realize what will happen to the crew on the decoy when the Inquisitors discover they've been tricked?" Cassandra asked.

"I'm sure they'll be captured, interrogated, and eventually executed," Bo-Shing said with a shrug. "But these are the kind of men who don't deserve to live."

"Many might say the same thing about you," Cassandra noted.

"This is why I didn't tell you about the plan," he explained with a sigh. "When the attack comes, people are going to die. A lot of people. Many more than just the crew of my decoy vessel.

"If you want to get out of Callastan, you have to accept that lives will be sacrificed to make it happen. If that's a problem for you, just turn yourself over to the Pontiff and maybe she won't attack the city at all. Thousands will be spared."

"It's not the same," Cassandra replied though she felt guilt gnawing at her.

The city is under siege because of me. He's actually right about that.

"These are not innocent victims," Bo-Shing insisted. "They've all committed crimes so horrible that no captain will even take them on again. That's why they're all available for this crew.

"If anyone deserves to suffer at the hands of the Order, they do."

"You of all people are not fit to judge them," Cassandra said. "Methodis told me of the things you've done."

"Then you judge them," Bo-Shing said, flashing her a sly grin. "You're the client. Just give the word and I'll call the whole plan off. You and Methodis can try to find some other way to slip out of the city.

"Or tell me you want to go ahead. Tell me you don't mind if a ship full of savage killers and brutal deviants falls into the Order's hands while you make your escape."

Sick bastard is enjoying this. He likes watching me squirm.

Methodis had warned her about Bo-Shing, and now she understood what a completely vile and amoral monster he was. Yet there was some truth in what he said.

She couldn't save the city—not if she wanted to save the entire world. She was willing to let innocent men, women, and even children die rather than hand the Crown over to the Pontiff. So why should she care that she couldn't save a boatful of criminals?

"Stick to the plan," she said.

There is one person I can save, though. Someone who deserves it.

"I don't want Methodis to come with us," she declared.

"Really? And how are you going to stop him?"

"Methodis doesn't know I'm here. Give me the address of the warehouse. But I want you to give him a false location of where to meet. I'll find some excuse for him and me to split up as we come to meet you."

"Betraying the man who took you in?" Bo-Shing chuckled. "The more I get to know you, the more I like you!"

It's not a betrayal, Cassandra thought. *I don't know exactly what will happen when I reach the Keystone, but I doubt any of us will be coming back from that island. If Methodis gets left behind, at least he has a chance to survive.*

She didn't say any of this to Bo-Shing, however. She didn't owe the pirate any explanations.

"Give me the address of the warehouse," she said. "I need to be back before Methodis realizes I'm gone."

It was time for Orath to leave the dank cellar he'd been hiding in ever since the dark ritual to reach across the Burning Sea and contact his master. The Pontiff's armies were gathered outside the city and a Blood Moon had hung in the sky for weeks—war was coming, and the Crown would soon be on the move.

Daemron had sent a vision into the mortal world. By now the one who carried the Talisman had seen it in her dreams; she would be trying to get to the Keystone. And the only way to reach it was by ship.

Before leaving his sanctum, though, Orath needed to cast another spell. One that would keep him hidden from the Sight of the Inquisitors he'd sensed wandering the streets, searching the city for the Crown. One that would keep him hidden from the woman who carried the Crown lest he suffer the same fate as the Crawling Twins.

They tried to take it from her by force. They underestimated her power.

Fortunately, Orath had no need to try to seize the Talisman. He only had to ensure she brought it to the Keystone.

Little remained of the victims who had fueled the ritual to contact Daemron. What had not been consumed by the spell had rotted and decayed into putrescent puddles on the cellar floor. A sacrifice was always strongest when it was still alive or freshly killed. But the spell he needed now was not one of raw power. It was an enchantment of subtlety and stealth; he needed something to help him blend in with the shadows and the darkness.

He began to chant, the invocation tumbling in a soft whisper from his lips. As he did so, he crawled over to where the first victim had died. Chaos began to gather, wrapping itself around him in response to his words. He dipped a clawed finger into the liquefied remains, then scooped up the dark, sticky fluids with a cupped palm and smeared them over his head and face.

Still reciting the mystic chant, he scuttled over to where the second victim had died and did the same, painting himself with the gore. As Chaos enveloped him his features blurred. By the time the ritual was done, even his body seemed to flicker slowly in and out of phase.

The illusion wouldn't make him invisible, not completely. But it would allow him to become one with the darkness. Like an image glimpsed out of the corner of the eye, he would be ephemeral and amorphous unless someone focused directly on him. And if he stayed in the shadows, he wouldn't be seen at all, not even by the mystical awareness of the Order.

Cloaked in his veil, he climbed the steps and wrenched open the door above. He made his way quickly but carefully through Callastan's streets, the red light of a quarter-crescent Blood Moon providing him ample darkness to mask his passing.

As he neared the docks he moved more slowly, taking extra care to stay in the blackest corners, where he wouldn't be seen. He could sense agents of the Pontiff patrolling the area. He sensed them instinctively: The unmistakable spark of Chaos burned within them, though not nearly as strongly as in the Talismans or the Children of Fire.

They're watching in case the Crown is smuggled out of the city by boat.

Orath knew that eventually the mortal bearing the Talisman would have to come here. He also knew that he must not let it fall into the Order's hands.

She must reach the Keystone. That is all Daemron wants of me now.

He closed his eyes so he could better focus on the burning essence deep within them. He sensed a dozen Inquisitors in the area, but they were scattered and separated, each one acting alone.

He opened his eyes and crept down another street, bringing him closer to the waterfront. He found a dark corner and settled in to wait, remaining completely motionless for over an hour.

One of the Inquisitors passed only a few yards from where Orath stood. The Minion braced himself as she approached, paused, then continued onward. He studied her as she walked away. There were two others close by, the Chaos in them shining like beacons to show him exactly where they were.

From the safety of the shadows, he studied his three targets. They seemed to be moving randomly, turning left or right at the corner of each street on a whim. Sometimes they doubled back down an alley they had just traversed, other times they unexpectedly broke into a brief sprint before falling back into a brisk walk.

They're patrolling the area, but they don't want anyone to be able to pick up a pattern that might let them slip through unnoticed.

But their efforts to remain unpredictable meant there were times when the three were inadvertently patrolling areas almost too close together. More importantly, it meant there were times when they were much farther apart.

The first Inquisitor passed by him two more times that night. In the second instance, Orath sensed one of her brethren only two streets over—close enough to notice and react if anything happened to her. But the third time the others were many blocks away, lingering on the fringes of Orath's awareness . . . and safely beyond the limits of their own.

He took the moment of vulnerability to strike, lashing out from the shadows with his razorlike fingernails to rip out the Inquisitor's throat before she even had a chance to scream. He caught her body as it fell, his thin lips pressing themselves to the gushing wound on her neck to feed.

There was Chaos in her blood; the power was faint but it helped restore some of what he'd lost in casting his most recent spell. And gorging himself on her blood would keep any evidence of her death from being left behind.

Her body went into convulsions as Orath sucked her dry. After thirty seconds the convulsions stopped, and a minute later it was done.

Tossing her drained corpse over one shoulder with a strength that belied his tall, thin stature, Orath retreated before the others returned. He carried her body away from the docks and stuffed her under a pile of refuse behind an abandoned building in the next district over.

One more tonight, he thought. *But this time from another part of the docks.*

He had no doubt his victim would be missed, but he doubted there would be much of a search. They couldn't abandon their posts to look for their missing comrade. Eventually another would be sent to replace her, but it would take time for word to reach the Pontiff that she had vanished.

For the next few nights, the remaining Inquisitors would have to divide up the area she was patrolling. They would each have to cover more ground, giving him more opportunities to pick them off one by one.

The Crown will not fall into the Order's hands, he vowed, his long tongue licking the last few spatters of warm, sticky blood from his chin. *It will reach the Keystone!*

There was still almost two hours before the first rays of dawn chased away the night, Orath realized. If he was lucky, there might be enough time for him to take another victim tonight.

He turned away from the refuse pile and the corpse beneath it, his recent feast whetting his appetite rather than sating it. Blending artfully into the shadows, he made his way eagerly back to the docks.

Chapter 20

TWO DAYS AFTER his ordeal, Keegan still wasn't feeling completely recovered. But he was anxious to get to Callastan as quickly as possible, so he'd insisted they set out that morning.

Jerrod was up ahead, but he was setting an easy pace. Keegan followed a few feet behind the monk, and Scythe brought up the rear. As they marched in silence, Keegan kept replaying the almost kiss over and over in his head.

Whatever your feelings for Scythe, it was wrong. Norr deserves better. So does she.

Thinking of Norr brought a familiar wave of guilt. But it wasn't just his inappropriate feelings toward Scythe that brought it on. Jerrod had suggested that some small part of Keegan had actually wanted to get rid of Norr, that maybe subconsciously he'd directed the backlash of his spell so that it brought about the big man's death.

What if he's right? Scythe risked herself to save me—would she have done that if she knew I was to blame for Norr's death?

Keegan didn't know what they'd find when they reached Callastan, but whatever happened he wanted to face it with a clear conscience.

Slowing his pace, he fell farther behind Jerrod until he was walking beside Scythe. He knew the monk's keen ears would pick up everything he said but didn't care. He had to tell Scythe the truth.

"What's wrong?" she asked. "Is White-eyes going too fast for you?"

"No," Keegan said. "I just . . . I have to tell you something."

The young woman's sharp features tensed up but she nodded for him to continue.

"It's about Norr."

"I don't want to talk about him," Scythe said.

"Please," Keegan whispered. "This is important."

When she nodded again, he continued.

"You know I have feelings for you. I care about you. And not just as a friend."

"I thought this was about Norr." Scythe delivered her words through a clenched jaw.

"It is. His death . . . it might have been my fault."

"I think I know a bit about how backlash works now," Scythe said. "Even if it did cause Norr's death, you couldn't help it."

"Maybe," Keegan admitted. "But it's possible . . ." He hesitated, the words sticking in his throat. He took a deep breath and just blurted them out in a rush.

"Maybe I somehow directed the backlash at Norr. Maybe some part of me was jealous. Maybe I wanted him out of the way."

Scythe was quiet for a few seconds, then shook her head.

"No. That's not what happened."

"It's possible," Keegan insisted.

"No, it's not." Her tone was adamant.

"How can you be so sure?"

"Norr was your friend. You wouldn't hurt him on purpose. You wouldn't hurt me on purpose."

"Not on purpose," Keegan agreed. "But what if—"

Scythe stopped and turned, grabbing Keegan by the shoulders and spinning him to face her.

"What happened to Norr wasn't anyone's fault. It just happened. Understand?"

Keegan nodded slowly, trying not to wince at Scythe's viselike grip on his shoulders.

Sensing his discomfort, she let go.

"Norr made his own choices, Keegan," she continued. "He chose to follow you. And he chose to sacrifice himself to save you. Do you know why?

"Because you're a good person. Not perfect, but who is? Norr could see what kind of man you are. He didn't give his friendship lightly, but he considered you his friend.

"And so do I," she added.

Keegan wanted to say something but couldn't think of anything. Instead, he just nodded again.

"It's okay to grieve for Norr," Scythe said, wiping away a tear from her eye. "It's okay to feel pain and sadness that he's gone.

"But he'd want us to keep going. He'd want us to stay strong. He'd want us to see this through to the end. Most of all, he'd want us to do it together.

"Can you do that, Keegan?" she asked. "Can you promise me that much?"

"We'll see this through to the end," Keegan said. "You and me. I promise."

Scythe pulled him close and gave him a short but fierce hug. As she let him go, Keegan turned to see that Jerrod had stopped up ahead and turned back toward them. The monk didn't say anything, he just stood there, silently watching.

"Let's keep going," Scythe said. "Hate to keep White-eyes waiting."

That night, after they had made camp and Keegan was snoring away, Jerrod came over and stood beside Scythe while she was on watch.

"What?" she said, not turning her head to look at him.

"That was an interesting conversation you had with Keegan."

"One you weren't supposed to be part of."

"You know this affects all of us," he reminded her. "And you were the one who warned me that Keegan's feelings for you could make things more difficult."

Scythe shrugged. "Maybe I was wrong."

To her surprise, Jerrod said, "I'm starting to think that as well.

"You and Keegan share not only a destiny but a deep and powerful bond," he continued. "Whatever happens, I think it will be better if we all accept that.

"Together you have accomplished far more than either of you could have alone."

"Who knows," Scythe answered. "Maybe all of us will get out of this alive."

But though she spoke the words, in her heart Scythe still didn't believe they were true.

For several days, Vaaler and his motley army of followers had marched steadily northwest. The closest of the Free Cities was Torian but he doubted he would find support there: Before joining with him, Keegan and the others had narrowly avoided execution within its walls. And during their escape, Keegan had rained fire down upon the city, nearly burning it to the ground.

Torian chose to side with the Order, Vaaler reminded himself. *They got what they deserved.*

The next closest city was Cheville. During his history lessons growing up, Vaaler had learned that Cheville was one of the most outspoken opponents of the last Purge—anti-Order sentiment ran deep within its people.

At least it used to.

Lord Bonchamps, the most recently elected ruler, had only taken office two years ago and Vaaler knew little about him or his policies. But Cheville was the largest and most influential of the five Free Cities; if he could convince them to take action against the Order, it was very likely the others would fall in line.

The road ahead twisted and turned, winding its way through the rolling hills that marked the territory just south of the city. Their journey would have been quicker on horseback, but Shalana and her honor guard had never learned to ride—horses weren't a luxury the Frozen East could afford.

We never would have found enough horses for everyone anyway, Vaaler reminded himself.

He no longer had any idea of the exact numbers in his band though they had swelled to several hundred. In addition to those who had volunteered to fight with him, they had been picking up entire families during their march toward Cheville. A rumor had flown ahead of them, claiming that Lord Bonchamps was taking in refugees. Faced with the prospect of staying in their undefended homes, many had chosen to join Vaaler's retinue as it passed by their towns.

His force was so large now that he had to pick a dozen or so of the more experienced among them to serve as his lieutenants. He would have preferred to assign the task to his honor guard, but they only spoke Verlsung, making it impossible for them to communicate with the bulk of his army.

It wasn't just horses they lacked, either. The families who'd joined him had brought many of their treasured household possessions with them, carrying their lives on their backs. But encumbered with their material wealth, they hadn't thought to bring provisions. Food was running short, and it was getting difficult to find enough freshwater on the journey despite the rivers and streams that wound their way throughout the fertile Southlands.

Vaaler couldn't blame the refugees; he'd seen what they were fleeing in Othlen and the towns around it. These were simple folk who just wanted to find somewhere they could be safe. But he was worried about what would happen if Lord Bonchamps refused to take them in.

We'll have our answer soon enough, he thought, as they crested a small hill and the city came into view.

The walls of Cheville were thirty feet tall and made from marble that had a distinct pinkish hue. The reflected color made it look as if the rising sun was shining on the city even though it was midday.

A handful of spires and domes on the city's largest buildings peeked over the pink walls, but Vaaler was more interested in the massive city gates. In a few miles the road they were following would bring them to Cheville's main entrance, and Vaaler had expected to see a steady line of visitors coming and going into the bustling metropolis.

The gates, however, were closed. He glanced over at Shalana and saw she had noticed it, too.

"Not the welcome we were hoping for," she said.

"It's probably just a precaution," Vaaler said. "By now they must have gotten word that we're coming. The City Lord probably just thought it was safer to seal the gates until they meet with us and learn our intentions."

"Maybe we should stop here and send a small delegation ahead to parley with them," she suggested. "To make us seem less threatening."

It was a good idea, so Vaaler raised his hand and called a halt. His order was repeated and relayed through the ranks by his newly appointed lieutenants. Then he waved his hand and called Darmmid over.

The ranting lunatic Vaaler had encountered when they first met was gone, exorcised when Keegan's imaginary curse had been dispelled. No doubt there were lingering emotional scars from what he had suffered, but he no longer seemed like a dangerous madman.

Still, Vaaler wasn't about to simply turn him loose. But instead of keeping him as a prisoner, he'd decided to name Darm as one of his honor guard. The appointment was purely ceremonial as he wasn't given any kind of weapon. Yet it seemed appropriate, given his strange connection to Keegan.

And it seems to be helping, Vaaler noted. Responsibility, duty, and a designated chain of command seemed to be exactly what the recovering soldier needed.

Darm hustled over in response to Vaaler's wave, snapping off a brisk salute and standing at attention as he awaited his orders—the model of a perfect soldier.

"Tell the lieutenants to make camp," he said. "Shalana and I are going on ahead to meet with the city officials."

"Yes, sir!" he barked before rushing off to fulfill his duties.

"I can't believe the change that's come over him," Shalana noted. "Was his madness really just a creation of his own imagination?"

"That, plus a lack of food and water and the stress of seeing his entire company slaughtered," Vaaler suggested.

"I'd like to bring our honor guard with us," Shalana said.

"I can think of no one better to be at my side during a battle," Vaaler objected, "but even they won't be able to save us from an entire city if things go wrong."

"Appearances are important," Shalana reminded him. "Your words will carry a lot more weight if you meet the City Lord flanked by a dozen fiercely loyal warriors.

"And there's no point leaving them here to watch over the troops. Not when none of them speak the language."

"Good point," Vaaler conceded. "I guess they'll be coming with us, then."

It didn't take long for them to get ready. Once Vaaler was confident the rest of his army was secure, he, Shalana and his Eastern honor guard headed off alone toward the imposing gates set into the pink walls.

When they were still half a mile away, they heard a loud blare of trumpets coming from the city. The massive gates began to grind and slowly swung wide, revealing a score of armed cavalry. Behind them were at least fifty foot soldiers, each wearing a doublet bearing Cheville's official crest: the morning sun rising over a walled city.

At the head of the company was a dour-looking man of at least seventy, with a long white moustache that hung down an inch below his chin.

"Jendarme Lamette," Vaaler whispered to Shalana. "He was appointed head of the city guard forty years ago when his brother became City Lord."

"Is his brother still in charge?"

"City Lords are only elected to ten-year terms," Vaaler told her. "And by law anyone who has served cannot run again. But every incoming ruler since then has kept Jendarme on as Captain of the Guard. He's a legend in the Free Cities."

The old man raised a hand and the cavalry charged forth from the gate.

"I'm starting to have second thoughts about this plan," Shalana muttered.

"Hold your ground but keep your weapons lowered," Vaaler called out, knowing the clan warriors could react violently to even the slightest provocation.

The riders continued to bear down on them, breaking off less than ten yards away to encircle them in an impressive display of horsemanship.

Jendarme had stayed back during the charge, but now he spurred his steed forward. Two of the riders in the circle nudged their horses, who stepped smartly aside to make room for the captain to pass.

He stopped only a few feet in front of Vaaler and Shalana, close enough for them to see the deep wrinkles that lined his face and the gray cataracts that completely blinded one eye. Despite these signs of age, he carried himself straight in his saddle, his stature and movements those of a much younger man.

"Why have you brought this army to our gates?" he asked, peering down from atop his horse at the strange interlopers. Like his movements, his voice was forceful and strong.

"I request an audience with Lord Bonchamps," Vaaler said. "About an urgent matter that affects us all."

"Lord Bonchamps is not in the habit of meeting with Barbarians," he said, giving Shalana and the others a disparaging look.

Shalana stiffened beside him, but she had enough control to hold her tongue. As for the rest of the honor guard, Vaaler was just glad they didn't understand what the captain was saying.

In Torian, the city still paid a bounty for any Easterners killed or captured within twenty miles of the city. But Cheville was far enough west that the surrounding settlements didn't have to worry about raiders from the Frozen East.

He's probably just testing us, Vaaler thought, recalling the captain's reputation. *Pushing us to see how we'll react.*

"The clans are not your enemy," Vaaler said aloud, his voice calm and confident. "And we both know the Order are the true Barbarians."

"Is that why you've brought these refugees to our gate?" Jendarme asked. "Has the Pontiff turned her Purge away from Callastan and against her own people?"

"These are things we should discuss in private with Lord Bonchamps," Vaaler insisted. "Not standing in a field with our weapons at our sides."

"Escort them into the city," the captain said, wheeling his horse around.

The riders closed in tightly around them, almost as if they feared Vaaler and the others might try to flee, and marched them into the city.

At least he let us keep our weapons, Vaaler thought as the heavy gates slammed shut behind him.

Shalana had never seen a city the size of Cheville. Most of the clans lived a nomadic existence, and even the strongest—like the Stone Spirits—only had settlements that were little more than permanent camps.

The people they'd liberated had all lived in small towns and villages; at most they'd have two or three main streets and a few dozen buildings surrounding the town square. In all of them, it was possible to see clearly from one side to the other, the view broken up only by a smattering of two-story structures.

In contrast, Cheville was a labyrinth of massive buildings and cramped, busy streets crisscrossing back and forth and extending in every direction farther than Shalana could see.

She was awed by the sheer crush of people on all sides. Even with their armed escort keeping the crowds at bay, she felt as if the sweat and stink of so many bodies crammed together made it hard to breathe.

There was a constant buzz in the air, the indistinct echoes of voices and footsteps and slamming doors emanating from every side street they passed. As news of their arrival spread, people began to line the way as they passed, their whispered comments a constant murmur adding to the general din.

Jendarme's men led them farther and farther into the city, taking so many twists and turns that Shalana's normally infallible sense of direction deserted her entirely.

It was all too much to process. Her mind began to spin, and her breath became quick and shallow. Her eyes darted from side to side, overwhelmed by the never-ending blur of faces and buildings on all sides.

She jumped as Vaaler's hand wrapped around hers, then felt the momentary panic fade as he gave her a reassuring squeeze.

Glancing back over her shoulder, she saw the rest of the honor guard were faring better than she had. None of them seemed overwhelmed or alarmed, though several of them were staring with slack-jawed amazement at the wonders around them.

After what seemed like hours they finally reached their destination. She, Vaaler, and the others were shuffled into a long, wooden, single-story building. At first she assumed they'd been led to Cheville's Long Hall to meet the City Lord, but she quickly realized that wasn't the case: The building was too plain and simple to be used for any kind of important meetings.

The furnishings were sparse—some cots, along with a few tables and chairs. There were several small windows, and doors led out both the front and the back.

"Are we prisoners?" Shalana asked.

"I don't think so," Vaaler said. "There are no bars on the windows or doors, and they didn't disarm us. I think this is an old guard barracks."

Shalana wandered over to the window and peered out. The entire building was encircled by armored soldiers carrying long pikes.

"If this isn't a prison, then why the guards?"

"Just a precaution, I'm sure," he said though she could tell even he was starting to have doubts.

"So what do we do now?"

"I guess we wait for Bonchamps to come see us."

Several long, slow hours slid by. Inside the city walls darkness came quickly as the sun set, and they eventually found themselves sitting in a room full of shadows as time dragged on.

Their forced vigil was eventually broken by a knock on the front door. A second later it swung open and Jendarme strode in. Behind him came a half dozen guards, each carrying a softly glowing lantern.

"I'm sorry to keep you waiting in the dark," he said, though his brusque tone didn't sound apologetic.

While the first guards hung the lanterns on small hooks protruding from the walls around the barracks, several more came in carrying wooden trays of food. As they set them down on the nearest table, Shalana's stomach growled loudly. It had been many hours since their last meal, but in all the strangeness of the city she hadn't realized how hungry she'd become.

Jendarme jerked his head toward the door and the guards left, leaving the captain alone with them.

He trusts us, Shalana thought. *That's a good sign.*

"Where is Lord Bonchamps?" Vaaler asked. "Is he on his way?"

"Our City Lord is a vain, pompous, craven, selfish little man," Jendarme said, his voice dripping with venom. "And he sees no reason why he should meet with you."

"We share a common enemy in the Order," Vaaler said. "An enemy that may soon turn its attention to the Free Cities once they've finished with Callastan."

"Lord Bonchamps's simpering advisers believe we should remain neutral in this affair for as long as possible," Jendarme explained. "They seem to think if they ignore this problem, it will go away on its own."

"You don't believe that, though," Shalana said.

"Why would anyone listen to me?" Jendarme snarled. "I'm just a doddering old fool too far past his prime."

"Please," Vaaler said. "If Lord Bonchamps will just meet with me for one hour, I think he will see that an alliance will benefit us all."

"Our vainglorious and self-serving ruler would rather spend

that time currying favor with the merchants guild, or cozying up with the city nobility, or taking bribes from those rich and powerful enough to dream of being his successor.

"To clarify," Jendarme concluded, "Bonchamps only meets with those who can further his political influence or line his coffers. And, sadly, you have nothing to offer him."

The captain's barely contained rage obviously wasn't directed at them but Shalana couldn't help but feed off his anger.

"Cheville is enormous!" she blurted out. "There must be ten thousand people inside these walls! How did such a pathetic excuse for a leader gain control over the fate of so many?"

"I didn't vote for him," Jendarme spat. "But for the next eight years I must follow this sniveling sack of excrement's orders. Unless the Old Gods take pity on me and finally send me to my grave."

"So what will happen to us?" Vaaler asked.

"Tomorrow morning I am to escort you back outside the city walls, and you and your followers will return to your homes.

"If you refuse to disperse," he continued somberly, "Bonchamps will turn his soldiers loose on you."

Shalana could only shake her head in helpless frustration, unable to find the words to articulate the anger she was feeling.

"Many of my followers are refugees," Vaaler said. "Women and children. The elderly. Would Bonchamps really order his soldiers to slaughter them?"

Jendarme turned away and didn't answer.

"I will see if I can find food for you to take with you," he said as he walked slowly toward the door. "I know some merchants— good people—who might be able to donate a cart or two filled with provisions."

That won't last a single day, Shalana thought. *Not when we have so many mouths to feed.*

The old captain opened the door, then turned back to them one last time.

"I'm sorry," were his parting words. "There is nothing more I can do."

Vaaler barely slept that night. The cots in the barracks were comfortable enough; he'd gotten so used to sleeping on the ground they almost felt luxurious. But he couldn't stop his mind from racing.

When the guards arrived at the morning's first light to bring them breakfast, part of him wanted simply to refuse to get up from his bed. But there were too many people counting on him for him to surrender.

There has to be some way to get Bonchamps to hear me out! he thought, silently chewing his food.

"There is still hope," Shalana said, reaching across the table to take his hand. "We can go to the other City Lords. Maybe one of them will help us."

Vaaler appreciated her efforts to lift his spirits even though he knew it wasn't true. It would take them at least three days to travel to Accul—the next closest of the Free Cities—and his followers were already running out of food.

Even if Jendarme somehow finds enough supplies to keep us going, we're running out of time. Callastan will fall any day, and the Order will reclaim the Crown.

"Cheville was our best chance to help Keegan," he said. "And I failed."

"Failure is not a word you easily accept," Shalana reminded him. "We will find another way."

She said it with such earnest belief that Vaaler could almost believe it was true. Swallowing the food in his mouth, he reached across the table and drew her in close so he could plant a long kiss on her lips, oblivious to the stares and coy smiles of their honor guard.

Their embrace was interrupted by a sharp knock on the door. Vaaler turned just in time to see it swing open and Jendarme stride through. Though it was hard to tell beneath his long, flowing moustache, the old captain appeared to be smiling.

He was followed in by several more guards, then a tall, dark-haired, blue-eyed man in his early forties.

"I am Lord Bonchamps," he said, tilting at the waist just barely enough for the action to be considered a bow. "Ruler of Cheville."

His voice was deep and rich, and his eyes almost seemed to sparkle as he spoke.

This man refused to help you, Vaaler reminded himself. *Just because he's charming doesn't mean he's your ally.*

"Please accept my most sincere apologies for what happened yesterday," Bonchamps continued. "There was a breakdown in our lines of communications. Isn't that right, Captain?"

"Exactly, my lord," Jendarme agreed, with no hint in his voice of the animosity Vaaler suspected he truly felt. "A breakdown in our communications."

"I would never have kept you waiting so long," Bonchamps apologized, "had I known you were next in line for the Danaan throne!"

It was all Vaaler could do to keep the shock from showing on his features. Beside him, Shalana arched an eyebrow in surprise but otherwise maintained her composure.

"I never gave you my name," Vaaler said. "How do you know who I am?"

"I understand the need for secrecy," Bonchamps assured him. "Someone as important as you must keep a low profile. I myself know this all too well.

"But now that the rest of your delegation has arrived, the truth can come out."

Vaaler had no idea what Bonchamps was talking about but

decided to play along. Whatever was going on, at least it had convinced Bonchamps to come meet them.

"As you can guess," Vaaler said, putting on his most noble airs, "I would not have come here unless I needed to speak with you on a matter of great importance."

Bonchamps nodded vigorously. "Of course, Your Majesty. Of course. And I am eager to hear what you have to say. But wouldn't we be more comfortable if we continued this discussion in my offices?"

"As long as we go there immediately," Vaaler pressed. "Time is of the essence."

"Excellent," Bonchamps said with a decisive clap of his hands. "The rest of your people are already there waiting for us."

Shalana flashed Vaaler a quick look. Even though she didn't speak, he knew her well enough to know what she was thinking.

Your people? Who is he talking about?

He answered with the faintest shrug of his shoulders. *I have no idea.*

Bonchamps spun on his heel and vanished through the door, followed closely by a pair of guards. Jendarme stepped forward but paused before following.

"I could have done more to help you yesterday if you'd just told me who you were," he whispered to Vaaler though not angrily.

Before Vaaler could ask any questions, Jendarme was off.

"What's going on?" Genny asked in Verlsung.

"We're not sure yet," Shalana replied in the same tongue. "But it could be good news."

Or very, very bad news, Vaaler thought as they followed the captain out of the barracks.

Once again a squadron of guards escorted them through the city, but this time Vaaler didn't feel like they were prisoners. The soldiers around them had the hyperawareness and puffed-up importance of a King's personal guard. Not surprising if they believed he was one day going to take over the Danaan throne.

But what happened to make them think that?

The Danaan had always had a mutually beneficial relationship with the Free Cities. There was regular trade between the North Forest and Cheville, and a handful of adventurous Danaan would sometimes even travel to the human settlements if they sought out an exotic, but relatively safe, vacation.

Despite this, the Danaan had always kept the Free Cities at arm's length. Human visitors were barred from the North Forest, and they shared as little information about their kingdom as possible.

The Free Cities were probably aware that a Danaan army had invaded the Frozen East, though Vaaler doubted they knew how spectacularly the campaign had failed. And he was almost certain they wouldn't know that the Queen had exiled her only son.

They shouldn't even know who I am at all, he thought as they wound their way toward the heart of the city.

He was still struggling to make sense of it all when they reached the City Lord's offices. Bonchamps led them inside, with Jendarme following a step behind. They passed through a number of architecturally stunning and opulently furnished rooms until they reached a set of bronze double doors.

A ceremonial guard stood on either side, a scene that reminded Vaaler of his childhood in the Danaan palace. The guards pulled the doors open to reveal a large conference hall dominated by a massive table carved from the same pink stone used to construct Cheville's walls.

Seated around the table were several Danaan, including a man Vaaler recognized immediately: Andar, the Queen's High Sorcerer.

It's a trap! Vaaler realized.

Somehow, the Danaan had discovered he was in the Southlands, and they'd sent Andar and the others to find him.

Was this Bonchamps's plan? Turn me over to the Danaan so they can drag me back to Ferlhame and try me as a traitor?

Even as all of this was running through Vaaler's head, he couldn't help but notice that Bonchamps, Jendarme, and everyone else still seemed calm and relaxed. If a trap was being sprung, they seemed to be unaware of its existence.

Andar pushed his chair back from the table, popped to his feet, and rushed forward, speaking quickly. The other Danaan remained seated, trying to appear calm, though Vaaler could see the nervous way they regarded his honor guard.

Behind him, he sensed Shalana and the others tense up as well—the only other time any of them had ever been face-to-face with the Danaan was on the field of battle. To their credit, however, they remained calm as the High Sorcerer approached.

"It is good to see you again, Your Highness," he said in Allrish. Switching smoothly to Danaan, he added, "I'm here to help. Play along."

The High Sorcerer dropped to one knee a few feet in front of Vaaler, bowing his head and waiting for permission to rise.

"What's going on?" Vaaler asked in their native tongue.

Andar stood up, acting as if the words had been the acknowledgment he was looking for.

"Lord Bonchamps," he said, addressing their hosts in a language the humans could understand, "before we begin our discussions, might I have a private moment with the prince? I bring a personal message from his mother."

"Of course," the City Lord replied.

A few seconds later, he and his guards were gone. Jendarme was the last to leave, carefully closing the doors behind him as he did so.

"A brilliant performance," Andar said, once more speaking Danaan. "I would have given you more warning if I could, but I trusted you would be quick enough to get through the first meeting without any prompting.

"I suggest we avoid speaking Allrish for the moment," he added. "Bonchamps probably has spies listening in."

"Everything's okay," Vaaler said in Verlsung to reassure Shalana and the others. "At least, I think it is."

Turning back to Andar, he said, "Tell me why you're here."

"We've been heading to intercept you and your army for several days," the wizard explained. "But by the time we caught up with you this morning, we heard you'd been taken prisoner by Lord Bonchamps. I thought he might rethink his position if he thought he had a chance to win the favor of the future Danaan King."

"I'm not the future Danaan King," Vaaler spat back. "I'm an exile."

"He doesn't know that."

"Why did you come looking for me in the first place?"

"Your mother sent me. She had a vision."

"You know what I think of the Queen's visions," Vaaler told him.

"She was wrong, Vaaler," Andar said. "We all were. She understands that now."

"If she sent you to ask my forgiveness, then you wasted your time," Vaaler said, his voice rising as he fought to control his anger. "Too many lives have been lost. Too much damage has been done."

"That's not why I'm here," Andar said. The High Sorcerer took a deep breath, collecting himself before he continued.

"There are great forces at play. You know this better than I. The fate of the mortal world hangs in the balance.

"You tried to warn us, but we wouldn't listen. And we have all suffered for it.

"But now the Queen is ready to accept the truth. Now she knows you were right and she sent me to help you in your quest."

"She did all this because of another dream?" Vaaler asked, shaking his head in disgust.

"Her visions are part of who she is," Andar said. "But that is not what drives her now. You are her son. Even after all that has happened, all the blood that is spilled, that will never change.

"If she could change what happened, she would. But even the great mages before the Cataclysm could not roll back time.

"She has made mistakes, Vaaler," Andar said. "We all have. Even you. Dwelling on them now will only bring further harm."

Vaaler knew he was right but didn't see how he could just accept Andar's aid as if nothing had ever happened.

"What's he saying?" Shalana asked in Verlsung.

"He said the Danaan want to help us now," he answered.

"Then let them," she said, much to Vaaler's surprise. "We need all the help we can get."

Chapter 21

YASMIN WOKE BEFORE the sun, as she always did. The Blood Moon was setting, but she took comfort that it was still there. Never before in the history of the Southlands had a Blood Moon lasted as long as this manifestation: a clear sign that events of historic significance were about to unfold.

She stepped from her tent and surveyed her troops. Despite the early hour, the camp was a bustle of activity. From the very beginning of the siege, she'd put her followers on a strict schedule of early nights and even earlier mornings. She wanted her troops to be able to strike with the rising sun, while their opponents were still sluggish from drinking and fornicating deep into the night.

As he always did, Xadier arrived at her side mere moments after she emerged from her tent to deliver the daily status reports. Today, however, she cut him off before he could begin.

"Tell the generals to ready the troops," she said. "We hit the city in three hours."

"Based on your previous orders, everyone has been making preparations for an attack tomorrow," he reminded her.

"That is why we must strike a day early. The enemy spies have all of Callastan thinking this is their final day of freedom. Half the city will have spent last night in one last drunken revelry. Our own troops may not be expecting this, but the defenders will be at a much greater disadvantage if we strike now."

"Of course, Pontiff," Xadier said. "Forgive me for doubting you. I will inform the generals right away."

Behind her, Yasmin could just make out the first rays of the sun peeking up over the horizon. By the time it set below the edge of the Western Sea, Callastan—and the Crown—would be hers.

The light of the early-morning sun shone in through the apothecary window, casting a warm, comfortable glow over the shop and the two figures diligently working within.

"Each of the vials on the top shelf must be individually wrapped in cloth and tightly tied before you place them in the sack," Methodis said. "But don't bother with anything on the shelves below. Bo-Shing said we must travel light."

Cassandra nodded but didn't speak as she helped Methodis pack the most important of his medicines in preparation for their journey.

A journey he will not be making, Rexol reminded her. *Are you going to let him take everything he packs to the false meeting point, or will you bring some of this medicine with you onto the ship?*

Cassandra had no intention of stealing any of the healer's wares. She already felt guilty enough about leaving him behind.

And how do you intend to do that? Rexol asked. *You don't even have a plan yet.*

As she so often did, she simply ignored the wizard's voice even though in this instance he was correct.

"How much have you spent helping Bo-Shing prepare for this journey?" she asked aloud.

It seemed the pirate captain had sent someone around each day saying they needed more money to purchase essential supplies, and she was worried the old doctor would be left penniless when she was gone.

"Don't fret over my finances, child," Methodis said, reaching over to give her a reassuring pat on the hand. "A good healer never wants for anything.

"And I'm one of the best," he added with a sly wink.

Despite her forebodings over what was to come, Cassandra couldn't help but smile.

Please stay safe after I'm gone, she thought.

She valued her time with Methodis, brief though it had been. He was one of the kindest, gentlest souls she had ever met. Yet he also possessed a quiet, inner strength she found inspiring.

This day was likely to be their last together. It was an open secret around the city that the Pontiff was planning her attack for tomorrow.

Bo-Shing and his men aren't the only ones making preparations to leave, she thought. From what Methodis had told her, it seemed that virtually all of his wealthier clients were going to try to flee the battle rather than stay and submit to the Order's rule.

She couldn't blame them for running; that was all she had done since Nazir had given her the Crown.

The nobles knew that the city had no chance of winning the coming battle. Even those who were going to stay and fight felt that way; they'd just rather die fighting than give up or run away. Cassandra admired their courage.

Maybe they could win if you helped them, Rexol said. *You still haven't pushed the Crown to its limits. You still have no idea of how truly powerful you can be.*

Cassandra had actually considered doing exactly that, though she wasn't certain if it was her own idea or if Rexol had somehow slipped it into her thoughts. But as powerful as the Talismans were, she didn't think the Crown alone would be enough to take on an entire army.

And even if she could somehow defeat all the soldiers, the Inquisitors and even the Pontiff herself, unleashing that much Chaos was sure to bring the Legacy crashing down.

My path is clear now. I must restore the Legacy. My destiny awaits me at the Keystone.

"What about the bottles on the table?" Cassandra asked, looking to take her mind off the future. "Are we bringing any of those?"

Before Methodis could answer, the city bells began to clang, the sound reverberating throughout the city.

Methodis uttered a curse completely out of the old man's character. "Should have guessed the Pontiff would strike a day early!"

You really should have guessed that, too, Rexol chided her.

Cassandra didn't bother to reply, her mind racing as it tried to grasp the reality of what was happening. The inevitable attack had finally come; it was time for her to leave Callastan.

The Pontiff sent her Inquisitors in as the first wave. They rushed the eastern wall, knifing back and forth in wild, unpredictable patterns to disorient the archers atop the walls. The defenders panicked and fired haphazardly, desperately unleashing arrow after arrow in a futile attempt to thwart the charge. The Inquisitors dodged and weaved through the incoming missiles, rapidly closing the space between them and their objective.

Instead of concentrating on the main gates, the Inquisitors fanned out all along the east wall, forcing the defenders to spread their lines too thin. The monks hit the wall at full speed, leaping up so their momentum threw them high into the air before latching on to the tiny cracks and crevices in the rough-hewn stone surface.

Scuttling up the wall like a swarm of spiders, the Inquisitors took only seconds to reach the battlements on top. Callastan's defenders rushed to engage them, trying to overwhelm the deadly whirling dervishes tearing through their ranks.

Bells were ringing through the city, calling reinforcements to man their posts. Atop the wall, however, the only sounds to be heard were those of combat and the screams of the dying.

The Inquisitors spun, kicked, and flipped their enemies off the wall. Bodies sailed through the air before plummeting down to the earth twenty feet below. Many were dead before their fall, a neck snapped or a skull crushed. Others were dashed upon the hard ground, their bones broken and their bodies smashed by the impact.

Within minutes, the ground on either side of the east wall was littered with the mangled corpses of Callastan's defenders, along with a smattering of robed Inquisitors who were felled by a lucky blow.

The massacre ended quickly, and with the top of the wall secured, the Inquisitors focused on opening the gates. Inside the city, bleary-eyed reinforcements stumbled from taverns and private homes into the streets, squinting against the early-morning sun as they raced to help hold the wall. They didn't even come close to arriving in time.

The Inquisitors swept through the soldiers guarding the gates, slaughtering them by the dozens. In short order they had wiped out all opposition, and they opened the gates as the Pontiff's second wave arrived.

Thousands of ordinary soldiers under the Pontiff's command rushed through the breach as the gates swung wide, pouring into the city like a wave. As they spread out into the streets, they were met with fierce resistance by the reinforcements as they finally arrived, and brutal hand-to-hand combat ensued.

Inside the city, panic reigned. Those who hadn't sworn to help fight off the attackers—and many who had—fled toward the docks, only to discover the enemy waiting for them. While the assault on the east wall had drawn the defenders' attention, hundreds of soldiers had come up on the city's western edge on small rafts launched before the attack began.

The unexpected invasion by sea was supposed to cut off all hope of escape, but the rafts they floated on were slow and unsteady, making it difficult for the soldiers to land. And the denizens of the docks were not helpless prey. Their numbers were bolstered by pirates, mercenaries, and private guards assigned to protect the ships and holdings of wealthy masters. Seeing the enemy trying to come ashore, they launched a vicious counterattack.

Heavy barrels and anchors were thrown from the piers and the decks of tall ships at the tiny rafts on the water below. Each direct hit sent one of the rafts—and the armored soldiers atop it—to a watery grave.

But the sheer numbers of the invasion ensured that some of the vessels made it through the barrage of ballast, and the soldiers scrambled out onto the docks to engage the enemy. The attackers hacked and slashed wildly at anyone within reach, trying to force them to retreat into the city. But the defenders refused to give ground, knowing the ships were the only hope of escape. Southern short swords clashed with the curved blades of the Western Isles, and the brackish water of Callastan's port began to run thick with the blood of the fallen.

Outside the gates on the east wall, Yasmin regarded the scene from afar. She had wanted to be at the head of the assault, but as the Pontiff she had to stay in the rear to coordinate the efforts of her army.

The east wall had fallen even more quickly than she'd hoped; as she'd planned, the early-morning assault had caught the defenders completely off guard. But now that her troops were inside the city they were meeting staunch resistance. The defenders were poorly organized, but they didn't lack for courage and fighting spirit.

Reaching out with her awareness, she sensed that the reinforcements she'd sent to help secure the docks had failed.

But my Inquisitors are still there, she reminded herself.

It had been many days since their last report to Xadier, but she wasn't concerned. They had no reason to check in with him or the Pontiff. Their mission was simple: secretly patrol the docks at night, keeping watch in case Cassandra tried to slip out of the city.

If they joined the assault, Yasmin realized, they could probably turn the tide of the battle at the docks. But she had given them strict instructions not to help the soldiers when she first sent them into the city. If they were to take part in the battle, the Crown might slip through their fingers in the confusion.

The Talisman is the real goal here. And soon Cassandra will bring it right to them!

"We have to go!" Methodis said, shouting to be heard over the clanging bells. "Bo-Shing won't wait for us! We have to get to the warehouse!"

"You go on ahead," Cassandra told him. "Let me finish packing this shelf!"

"I'm not going to leave you behind!"

"You don't want to leave these vials behind, either!" she shouted. "They're too valuable to let them fall into the Order's hands!

"And I can move much faster than you," she reminded him. "I will catch up!"

She could see him struggling with the dilemma. He wanted to watch over her, but he also didn't want to abandon the most useful medicines. Like all great craftsmen, the healer had a strong attachment to his tools.

"You will only slow me down once we're out on the streets," she insisted. "It will actually be easier for me if you go on ahead!"

To Cassandra's immense relief, the healer nodded.

"Do you remember how to find the warehouse?"

"I will be there," she told him.

Lies come easy to you, Rexol noted. *Is this something you learned in the Monastery?*

It's for his own good, she shot back.

"Be careful," Methodis told her before slipping out the door with a half-full sack slung over his shoulder.

Cassandra watched him through the window, his limp more pronounced as he tried to hurry down the street. When he finally disappeared around the corner, she turned her attention back to his workshop. She rummaged around for a few seconds until she found a small piece of chalk and a slate he used to write down orders and notes.

I'm sorry, she scribbled. *But I know you will understand why it had to be done. I can never repay the kindness you showed me. Thank you for everything, and I will pray to the True Gods to keep you safe.*

Then she left the shop carrying nothing but the Crown in the sack strapped across her back, leaving the precious medicines behind.

That's a mistake, Rexol insisted.

I won't need them, she answered. *Not when I can call upon the Crown to heal me. And Bo-Shing and his men don't deserve them.*

Out in the street the ringing bells were so loud they were almost deafening. People were running madly in all directions—some toward the east wall, some toward the docks, and others heading off in search of loved ones or to simply hide in their homes until the fighting was done. But the soldiers hadn't reached this neighborhood yet—the battle was still confined to the outskirts of the city.

Cassandra broke into an easy run, the hood of her robe pulled up to hide her features. She could have moved much faster, but she worried a robed figure racing by at superhuman speed might draw too much attention. As it was, she was already traveling at a pace few ordinary people could match.

She wound her way through the streets and arrived at Bo-Shing's warehouse. Three wagons overflowing with provisions were already out in the street. Each wagon had a towrope manned by four burly pirates. The rest of Bo-Shing's crew, nearly two dozen in all, had formed an armed wall around their convoy.

"Wasn't sure you'd make it," the pirate captain called out as she arrived.

"How far to your ship?" she asked.

"Only a few blocks," he told her. "But soldiers have hit the docks. We might have to fight our way through."

"Put me with the vanguard and we can clear a path," she said.

He nodded, and barked out commands in an Island dialect she couldn't follow. Six of his men, including Shoji, stepped forward.

"Stay close," Shoji told her with his familiar lecherous grin. "I want you to make sure I get out of this alive."

Bo-Shing called out a command, the men on the ropes grunted and pulled, and the wagons began to roll. Cassandra and the vanguard took up a position about thirty feet ahead of the convoy, Shoji leading the way to the ship. It wasn't until they rounded the second corner that they ran into the fleeing crowds.

Shoji and the other pirates began shouting loudly for people to clear a path, punctuating their words with swears and angry swipes of their cutlasses through the air. Despite the madness and confusion, the crowd parted quickly; even in their haste to flee, nobody wanted to get cut down by a horde of angry pirates.

"Soldiers around the next corner!" Cassandra shouted, her Sight giving her advance warning.

She rushed ahead to meet the enemy, Shoji and the vanguard close on her heels.

Eight soldiers had fanned out in a line across the street, forming a roadblock between them and the now-visible docks. Despite being outnumbered, the pirate vanguard threw itself at the enemy. Cassandra was quick to join them, knowing they needed to end this before more soldiers—or even some Inquisitors—arrived.

The pirates attacked with wild abandon, relying on speed and fury instead of tactics, strategy, or technique. They screamed like gibbering monkeys as they charged, an unnerving, high-pitched squeal that rose and fell in quick, staccato bursts.

The soldiers held their ground, drawing their ranks in to meet the charge. Cassandra reached out with her mind and gently tapped into the Crown on her back, drawing its power into her muscles and limbs before exploding into action.

In three quick, bounding steps she closed the gap between her and the soldiers, easily outpacing Shoji and the others. She dropped into a roll and came in low, sweeping out the legs of the two closest to her. She heard the sound of a blade whistling past as one of the others took a clumsy swipe in her direction, but she knew it wouldn't make contact and she didn't even bother to move out of the way as it passed over her shoulder. Instead, she threw her left elbow into the chin of one of the fallen soldiers, then twisted and drove the heel of her right palm into the side of the other's helmet, rendering them both unconscious. She didn't want to kill anyone unless she had to.

She sprang back to her feet just as Shoji and the others joined the fray. With her heightened reflexes and awareness, everyone and everything around her seemed to be moving in slow motion. She took down two more soldiers with a leaping split kick, her boots connecting simultaneously with each man's helmet. The pair dropped instantly, incapacitated but still alive.

Unfortunately, the other four were taken down by the pirates, and they did not share Cassandra's qualms about killing their foes. Steel flashed and blood flew, and within seconds the fight was over.

Bo-Shing and the wagons came rolling up behind them, and Shoji and his crew scrambled to move the fallen bodies out of the road so the convoy wouldn't have to stop and lose its momentum.

With the way ahead cleared, the men on the towropes picked up their pace, the wagons bouncing and clattering over the rough cobblestone street until they reached *The Chaos Runner.*

To Cassandra's eye, the ship looked unremarkable. But when she concentrated on it carefully, she could sense the faintest aura of Chaos emanating from deep inside the hull.

It really is an enchanted ship, she thought, though she wondered how strong the magic could actually be. If she hadn't already known it was there, she would never have noticed the faint spark of Chaos.

"Lower the gangplank and get these wagons on board!" Bo-Shing shouted.

Several of the pirates sprang into action, leaping from the pier onto cargo nets hanging from the ship's side and scrambling up onto the top deck. The sails unfurled and a large wooden plank slammed down on the dock beside them, just wide enough for the wagons to cross.

Several of the pirates got behind the first wagon and began to push. Others, including Bo-Shing, seized the towrope and pulled. Together they managed to get it up and onto the ship.

Cassandra let her awareness drift outward, taking in her surroundings. Skirmishes between the soldiers and those trying to get to the ships were still being fought on several of the nearby piers, but it was clear the Order's troops were overwhelmed. Already, several ships had cast off and many more would soon join them.

What about Bo-Shing's decoy? she wondered, casting out in vain for a ship under attack by a team of Inquisitors.

"Care to help?" Bo-Shing asked, as they came down the gangplank to load the second wagon.

"I'm keeping watch," Cassandra said. "In case the Inquisitors weren't fooled by your plan."

"Do you sense them?" he asked, making no effort to mask his fear.

"No. Not yet. That's what worries me."

Turning to his men, Bo-Shing shouted, "Get these other wagons on board—NOW!"

Orath flitted from pier to pier, using his long fingernails to crawl along the underside of the docks. The water below was littered with bits of broken rafts, a random assortment of boots, gloves, and capes, and the occasional bloated corpse. Above him the Pontiff's soldiers were slowly being overrun by the crush of Callastan's citizens determined to escape by sea.

He scuttled along, searching for the Crown, and it didn't take him long to find it.

The Talisman wasn't actually visible; the mortal who carried it wasn't foolish enough to leave it out in the open. But as he drew close, he could feel its power calling to him.

Knowing his own presence would be masked by the spell he'd used to hide himself from the Inquisitors' Sight, he slowly worked his way along the underbelly of the piers until he sat directly beneath his target.

The slight woman stood on the wooden slats above him, completely oblivious to his presence even though he was mere inches away. Part of him wanted to tear through the boards, drag her down into the cold water, and rip the Crown from her drowning grasp. But another part of him—the part that had kept him alive and helped him climb the ranks until he was one of Daemron's favorites—knew better.

She thwarted Raven and killed the Crawling Twins. She is far more dangerous than she appears.

Why take the risk of striking now and failing when she was already doing exactly what Daemron desired? Why had he gone to the trouble of killing off all the Inquisitors on the docks over the past few nights if he wasn't going to let her escape the city?

Watch and wait. See that she reaches the Keystone.

Above him, the humans were loading several wagons onto their ship.

"Let's go!" one of them shouted. "Come on!"

"I don't understand," the woman carrying the Crown answered. "Even if the Inquisitors fell for your trick, I still should be able to sense them."

"This is a good thing!" the other replied. "Now get on board so we can cast off!"

Shaking her head, she scurried up the gangplank and onto the ship. Orath let go and plunged straight down into the cold water below with barely a ripple. With quick, powerful strokes he swam to the vessel as it pushed off from the pier, holding his breath and staying below the surface.

He latched on to the hull, his nails carving long furrows into the wood as he crawled up the stern. Unnoticed in the commotion of setting out to sea, he dragged himself upward until he reached a small porthole, then wrenched it open. The opening was a tight fit, but Orath's body was thin and sinewy, and he was just barely able to slither through and into the dank cargo hold on the other side.

Manacles and chains lined the walls, but the pirates weren't carrying slaves today. To his surprise, he felt the familiar tingle of Chaos magic in the hold's stuffy air. The power was strong but dormant—as if the magic slept while the ship was in port.

Satisfied the vessel would be able to deliver Cassandra to the Keystone without his help, Orath crawled into a back corner of the empty cargo hold. Pressing himself into the shadows, he became one with the darkness.

Cassandra stared back at Callastan as they slowly pulled out, hardly daring to believe they'd made it.

It almost seemed too easy, Rexol said. *Like this is all part of some elaborate trap.*

You're paranoid, she reminded him as she gazed back at the city.

Several tendrils of smoke curled up from various parts of the city, though whether the fires were set by the attackers or defenders she couldn't say. The battle still raged inside the city walls; with her Sight she sensed that the fighting had intensified and spread throughout the entire city.

She reached out to the Crown, pushing her awareness as far as she could in the hopes of finding Methodis. But even with the aid of the Talisman, she couldn't locate a single man inside an entire city.

May the True Gods watch over you, she thought.

The True Gods are dead, Rexol reminded her.

"Shut up," she whispered, turning her back on the slowly receding city.

Chapter 22

VAALER HAD FORGOTTEN how much easier it was to ride rather than walk; they had traveled over ten miles already today and he wasn't even tired.

But most of the soldiers are traveling by foot, he reminded himself. *It's important not to push them too hard.*

He glanced down from his mount at Shalana, walking close beside him, her long strides matching the easy pace of his steed. She and the rest of his honor guard—who were also marching along on foot—could easily travel thirty miles in a day. But that kind of pace would be far too much to handle for the bulk of his troops.

"I think we should make camp in a couple hours," he said.

"Are the royal buttocks become sore from sitting in a saddle all day, Your Highness?" she teased.

"I keep telling you we can find you a horse if you want one," Vaaler objected. "I can teach you how to ride."

Shalana gave the beast beneath him a suspicious, sidelong glance.

"I think I'll walk . . . like the rest of your soldiers."

"The horse is a gift from Lord Bonchamps," Vaaler said in his defense. "It would be rude not to make use of it."

Thanks to Andar's ruse, Cheville's City Lord had completely changed his attitude. Once he believed Vaaler was the heir to the

Danaan throne—and a potentially valuable political ally—he'd offered soldiers, supplies, refuge for the civilians following Vaaler,
and the promise that messenger birds would be dispatched to the
other Free Cities asking for them to send reinforcements to march
with them.

Unfortunately, the numbers were far lower than what Vaaler
had hoped for. Cheville could have raised an army of a thousand
on short notice, but Bonchamps had given them only five hundred. Still, he couldn't blame him for being reluctant to turn over
his entire fighting force to their cause: It would have been
irresponsible—and politically foolish—to leave his city completely undefended.

And he did give me a very nice horse, Vaaler reminded himself.

"The least you can do," Shalana told him, "is to watch where
you're going. If you keep riding with your nose buried in those
pages the Danaan brought you, that animal is going to step in a
hole and you're going to fall off and break your neck."

"My horse is a lot smarter than you give him credit for," Vaaler
assured her. "And these pages are important," he added, holding
up the sheaves of paper he carried with him as he rode. "They
could hold the key to helping Keegan fulfill his destiny."

Andar and the rest of the Danaan delegation had joined them
on their journey to Callastan, though Vaaler was careful to make
sure they were always positioned well away from his honor guard
whenever they made camp. They had brought with them a number of transcribed passages from the Danaan archives, all of them
making references to something called the Keystone and the birth
of the Legacy. According to Andar, the Queen had seen the Keystone in her dreams, and she believed it would play a crucial role
in Keegan's—and the entire world's—fate.

Vaaler didn't have much use for his mother's visions, but he
knew there was a wealth of valuable but long-forgotten information buried in the Danaan archives. Since leaving Cheville three

days ago, he'd spent several hours each day studying the transcriptions. And each night, he would meet with Andar and the other Danaan scholars to analyze and discuss what he'd read. No single passage explicitly described the exact purpose or location of the Keystone, but Vaaler knew if they could properly assemble all the various bits and pieces, they could build a complete picture.

But will we be able to finish it in time?

At their current pace, they would reach Callastan in a few more days.

And then what?

In addition to the soldiers from Cheville, several hundred more from Accul had caught up with them last night. But he suspected they were still not even close to matching the size of the force the Order had assembled.

Maybe it won't be as bad as I fear.

Scouts had been sent ahead to assess the strength of their enemy, but they had yet to return. To Vaaler's surprise, Darmmid—the soldier who believed Keegan had cursed him—had volunteered to join them. Shalana had been reluctant simply to turn him loose unsupervised, but Vaaler didn't see any harm in letting him go. Even if he went mad again or decided to betray them, he doubted one man could do much harm.

"Jendarme is coming," Shalana said, pointing back at the long line of soldiers winding out behind them.

The old captain had come along to serve as the leader of the Cheville troops, though Vaaler wasn't certain if Bonchamps had ordered him to do so or if he'd volunteered. He'd feared the long journey would exhaust the old man even though he also rode rather than walked. But Jendarme seemed to have ample reserves of energy, and he'd even taken on the role of liaison between the various factions that had united under their banner.

His horse trotted briskly past the marching ranks until he fell into step beside Vaaler and Shalana.

"A gentleman would let the lady ride," he said by way of greeting, arching one eyebrow.

"I can think of only one good use for a horse," Shalana told him, "and then only if the meat is tender."

"No wonder they call you Barbarians," he grumbled.

His tone was gruff, but in their short time together Vaaler had learned to recognize his deadpan sense of humor. Fortunately, Shalana recognized it as well.

"It could be worse," she answered, the hint of a smile on her lips. "I hear in Torian they say we eat babies, too."

"Torian is no longer one of the Free Cities," Jendarme told her, and this time his anger wasn't for comic effect. "They lost the right to that title when they decided to grovel at the Pontiff's feet."

"Any word from the scouts?" Vaaler asked.

"Not the ones we sent ahead to Callastan," he answered. "But a messenger brings word that troops from Innaca are on their way. They should meet up with us by tomorrow night."

"How many?"

"Only a few hundred," Jendarme replied. "Lady Vennessia is no friend of the Order, but Innaca is the smallest of the Free Cities. I doubt they could spare any more."

Over a thousand troops in total now, Vaaler thought. *Enough to be a threat to the Order as long as the defenders in Callastan are able to hit them from the other side at the same time.*

"Thank you, Captain," Vaaler said. "You are dismissed."

Jendarme bowed low in his saddle, then wheeled his horse around in a tight circle and rode off at a full gallop.

"He handles his horse with more flair than you," Shalana noted as she watched him go. "If I ever want to learn to ride, I think he'd be a better teacher than you."

"I think I'm starting to feel a bit jealous," Vaaler said in mock indignation.

"Relax, my love," she said, patting him gently on the thigh. "I prefer younger men."

When Methodis arrived to find the warehouse empty, his first thought was that Bo-Shing had double-crossed them. But as the minutes dragged by and Cassandra failed to show up, he realized that it was the young woman who had misled him.

He briefly considered rushing to the docks to try to intercept them before they fled the city, but quickly discarded the idea. Cassandra clearly didn't want him to go with her.

She's trying to protect me.

Outside he could hear the distant sounds of battle as the fighting spread slowly through the city. Those who stayed to defend Callastan would neither give nor ask any quarter, and he knew casualties on both sides would be high.

He couldn't help Cassandra anymore, but there were others who would soon need his services. He was one of the few healers who had a shop outside the wealthy merchant and noble districts; it wouldn't be long before a steady stream of wounded began to arrive at his door.

Leaving the empty warehouse, he worked his way cautiously back to his apothecary. Several times he had to backtrack and take an alternate route to avoid streets where soldiers on both sides hacked away at each other, but he managed to reach his shop without incident.

He slipped inside and closed the door behind him but didn't lock it. Then he took a quick inventory of his supplies. He wasn't surprised to see that Cassandra had left everything behind, but he wasn't expecting to find the hastily written chalk note waiting for him.

I'm sorry. But I know you will understand why it had to be done. I can never repay the kindness you showed me. Thank you for everything, and I will pray to the True Gods to keep you safe.

As he read it, his eyes misted up.

May the True Gods watch over you, too, child.

He heard the door behind him swing open and glanced over his shoulder. Two young men stood in the door, covered in dust and blood. One was barely conscious, only standing because his friend was literally holding him up.

"Fell off the wall," the friend said. "Leg's all busted up. Shoulder, too."

Methodis grabbed a rag and wiped away Cassandra's message.

"Bring him over here and lay him down on the floor," he said. "I'll see what I can do."

Keegan was so exhausted he could barely stand when Callastan finally came into view. The city was just barely visible in the rapidly fading light of the setting sun, but it was clear they had arrived too late: The attack had already begun.

Dark plumes of smoke rose from the city, and the gates had been thrown wide. Bodies were strewn along the base of the city wall, and a smattering of slow-moving figures could be seen moving steadily away from the carnage: lucky refugees who had managed to slip past the Order's lines during the fighting.

This is my fault!

Despite his bold claim a few days ago, the toll of his time lost in the Burning Sea had drained Keegan's body, mind, and spirit. Only a few hours after they had first set out, he'd already begun to labor. Neither Scythe nor Jerrod called attention to his weakness, but they both insisted on frequent stops along the way.

"We're too late," Scythe muttered beside him. "We've come all this way for nothing."

"We don't know that," Jerrod told them. "Just because the Pontiff has taken the city doesn't mean she has the Crown. Cassandra is resourceful: She has successfully avoided capture for some time so far."

"She would have tried to find a ship," Keegan said. "To take her to the island where the Keystone is located."

"How would she know where to go?" Scythe asked. "Did your visions show you how to get there?"

The young man shook his head.

"This is all just speculation," Jerrod told them. "We need to get inside the city and find out exactly what happened with Cassandra."

"I don't think the Pontiff is accepting visitors," Keegan said.

"I grew up on Callastan's streets," Scythe told them. "I know every smuggler's tunnel and secret entrance. I can get inside the walls without being seen. And some of my old contacts might still be there. Maybe they'll know something."

Keegan expected Jerrod to object—sending her off alone into an enemy-occupied city seemed incredibly risky.

But instead, he only said, "There is a good chance many of your contacts have been killed or captured. Unless they managed to flee during the attack."

"You don't know Callastan," Scythe replied. "The gangs and crime lords fought too hard to carve out their territory simply to run away. When things get bad, they go to ground. There's no way the Order will find all their bolt-holes and underground lairs."

"What about the Sword?" Keegan asked, suddenly concerned. "Won't the Inquisitors be able to sense its presence?"

"I don't think so," Jerrod explained. "The Sword doesn't radiate Chaos; it devours it. To my Sight it appears nothing more than an ordinary blade."

"Good," Scythe told them. "Because I wasn't going to leave it behind."

"Go," Jerrod told her. "See what you can find out. Keegan and I will wait here for your return."

"I might be gone for a couple days," she warned. "Try not to panic."

As she turned to go, Keegan reached out and grabbed her shoulder. She turned back to him, her eyes wide with trepidation at what she feared he was about to say. But something held Keegan back.

"Be careful, Scythe," was all he said. "And hurry back."

Relief washed over her features.

"After everything we've been through," she assured him, "this will be easier than bribing a politician."

She set off at a run, the Sword strapped across her back. Keegan watched her until she disappeared out of sight.

"She knows how deeply you care for her," Jerrod told him once she was gone. "There is no need to say it. At least not until all this is over."

He's right. My feelings don't count for much against the fate of the entire world.

"What happens if Cassandra was captured?" Keegan asked. "What do we do if the Order has the Crown?"

"I have a feeling we don't have to worry about that," Jerrod said. "Cassandra is like you and Scythe. You are the Children of Fire, and the Pontiff has no idea what she is up against."

Yasmin walked slowly along the main thoroughfare that ran through Callastan's market square as the last rays of the setting sun disappeared behind the sea's distant horizon.

The fighting here had been particularly intense several hours ago, and many bodies from both sides littered the street. The merchant stalls that filled the square had been utterly destroyed: Tents and awnings had been slashed into tatters and been upended and smashed into kindling. All manner of wares from merchants who had been setting up in the early dawn before the attack were strewn about—everything from fruits and vegetables to jewelry to silk scarves and handwoven baskets.

I must tell Xadier to post some guards in the square to discourage looters, she thought.

As if on cue, the Seer ambled into view from around a corner on the other side of the street. Seeing the Pontiff, he hurried over to deliver the latest news.

"The city is ours," he triumphantly proclaimed. "There are still a few pockets of minor resistance, but most of the defenders have retreated or surrendered."

"Or gone into hiding," she cautioned. "Just because they are too beaten to continue the fight today doesn't mean they won't strike back at us tomorrow."

"Of course, Pontiff," he said. "But we now control all the areas of strategic importance in the city."

"Including the docks?" she asked.

"They are secured now," he answered, obviously uncomfortable, "but there were many ships that managed to escape before we took control."

His implication was clear. Neither Cassandra nor the Crown had been located yet.

"And what of our Inquisitors?" Yasmin demanded. "The ones I sent to watch the docks?"

"Most are still missing," Xadier answered, "but we found the bodies of Rezza and Juloss."

"They are dead?" Normally the Pontiff was an expert at controlling her emotions, but the news was so unexpected she couldn't hide her surprise.

"For at least a day, it appears," he told her. "Their throats were slashed and the bodies drained of blood before being stashed away in an abandoned building damaged by the recent earthquake."

Drained of blood?

Had Cassandra turned to dark Chaos rituals to escape them? Or was there some other explanation?

"Cassandra was here with the Crown," Yasmin insisted. "Someone in the city had to see her. Somebody has to know where she went!

"Offer a substantial reward for any information about her. Interrogate every prisoner who surrendered to us. Go to every door in every neighborhood and question every citizen who still remains.

"She may have slipped through our grasp, but we will find her again," the Pontiff vowed. "Someone helped her escape Callastan, and for that this whole wretched city will suffer!"

Chapter 23

SCYTHE HAD LITTLE trouble sneaking past the Order's guards and into the city. Even after centuries of trying, the Callastan authorities had never been able to stop completely the flow of contraband smuggled into and out of the city. It was foolish to think soldiers who didn't even know the city would be able to accomplish the task on their first night of occupation.

Creeping through the night, she made her way to a nondescript section of the east wall. Far from the main gate, she located a small, square section of stone at the base that appeared virtually identical to every other. Atop the wall a pair of guards walked past, not bothering to look down. Even if they had, they wouldn't have seen her in the shadows.

When she lived in Callastan, every thief and criminal knew the guards atop the wall were merely for show—a way to make the nobles inside the city feel like they were taking some action to curb the illegal activities within their city. As an actual deterrent, however, they were completely ineffective.

The more things change, the more they stay the same, Scythe thought as she braced her hands against the cool earth and pushed with both boots against the stone.

It slid into the wall, scraping softly. She scooted forward on her backside and gave another push with her feet, moving the stone enough to reveal a small hole just large enough for a child—or a small, lithe woman—to squeeze through.

Once inside the wall, she shoved and worked the stone back into position, sealing up the secret entrance. She paused to see if anyone had been attracted by the sound, then stood up and darted off down the street once she was confident the coast was clear.

With her heightened sense, she'd be able to hear any soldiers out on patrol early enough to avoid them. She wasn't sure what she'd do if she ran into any Inquisitors: They'd probably sense her before she had a chance to avoid them. Hopefully they'd just disregard her, not wanting to bother with the petty crime of a lone citizen breaking curfew to wander the streets. If not, she was confident she could defeat them with the Sword as long as she didn't have to take on more than four or five at once.

She slowly worked her way deeper into the city until she reached the slums. She suspected the bars, whorehouses, and other natural gathering places would be occupied by soldiers by now—or at least under close surveillance. But she doubted the invaders would have ventured into the tunnels and sewers below the city streets.

It didn't take her long to find a false sewer grate that hid one of the many entrances into Callastan's literal underworld. Sliding it aside, she slithered through the entrance and clambered twenty feet down the rotting wooden rungs built into the wall. The surface of the tunnel was covered with an inch of fetid wastewater, but even after so much time away Scythe was still so used to the smell she barely noticed it.

A maze of twisting tunnels eventually led her to her destination—a large antechamber several hundred feet across. The streets above had the market square; the sewers below had the Pit.

It wasn't unusual to see a crowd of a hundred or more gathered in the Pit on any given night—once the sun went down the real business of Callastan's economy happened here. On this night, however, there were fewer than fifty souls wandering about.

Scythe made her way into the mass of people, looking around for a face she recognized.

"Quint!" she called out. A young man turned in response to his name, then smiled when he saw her.

"Long time no see, kiddo!" he said, rushing over to wrap her in a fierce hug. "Last I heard you had run off with some big Barbarian."

"I'm back now," Scythe said, not wanting to talk about Norr. "By myself."

"Picked a hell of a time for a homecoming, kiddo," Quint said with a grin.

"Where is everybody?" Scythe asked, looking around. "I didn't think that many of our people would cut and run."

"Ah, not many did," Quint answered. "But Grevin and Stitch have their people on high alert, got them all holed up together. And Brinn told her people to lie low for a couple days. Figured the rest of the gangs decided to follow their lead."

"Good to know the Order hasn't broken their spirit yet," Scythe said with a grin.

"You know how we operate, kiddo," Quint answered. "Wait for the enemy to look the other way, then stab them in the back. Twice."

It's good to be home, Scythe thought.

She was surprised to realize that part of her wanted to pretend like nothing had changed—just slip back into her old life as a petty criminal working Callastan's streets. *If it weren't for Norr, I never would have left.*

But she had left, and since then too much had happened. She wasn't a lowly pickpocket anymore; she was destined to save the world.

"I'm looking for information," she said. "Trying to find some-one."

"I keep my ear to the ground," Quint said. "Try me."

"What's this going to cost?" she asked.

"No charge. Consider it my welcome-home present. Who you after?"

"A young blond girl. White eyes, like she works for the Order. But she's not on their side."

Quint laughed. "You hoping to cash in on that bounty?"

Seeing Scythe's confusion, he laughed again.

"You really are out of the loop, Scythe. You ain't the only one looking for her. Ever since that army showed up at our walls, there's been a big reward out for blondie. Must have done some-thing to piss the Pontiff off real bad."

"You could say that," Scythe admitted. "But I'm not after a reward. I just need to know where she went."

"Rumor is she was seen hopping on a ship with some pirates today. Got out soon after the fighting started. No idea where she was going, though."

"Can you think of anyone who might know?"

"The pirate who took her is a man named Bo-Shing. You know him?"

"Name's not familiar."

"Doesn't come around too often. Typical Islander slaver scum. But I heard he used to sail with a healer named Methodis."

"Methodis?" Scythe said, her head spinning.

No, it can't be.

It had been over five years since she'd been forced to abandon the man who'd raised her. Five years since she'd left him chained up in the cargo hold of the pirates who attacked their ship and took them prisoner.

"You okay, Scythe?" Quint said, grabbing her upper arm. "Look like you're about to pass out."

"Where's Methodis?" she snapped. "Tell me how to find him!"

Quint's hand dropped away from her arm and he took an involuntary half step back.

"It's okay, Scythe. Just relax. Didn't mean to grab you like that."

Good to know people still remember I have a temper, she thought, even as she tried to rein in her rampaging emotions.

"I'm sorry, Quint," she said, straining to keep the urgency from her voice. "But I really need to see this healer as soon as possible."

"He's got a shop near the Laughing Donkey. Opened it up about a month after you skipped town."

That's his old apothecary. It has to be him!

"Thanks, Quint," she said. "I know the place."

"Hey, hold on a second," the young man called out as she turned to go. "It's almost morning. You don't want to be out on the streets when it's light. Better wait until nightfall before you go see him.

"Stick around and you can buy me a drink."

"Sorry, Quint," she called out over her shoulder. "This can't wait!"

If Quint thinks there's a connection between Cassandra and Methodis, Scythe thought, *then others must think it, too.*

It wouldn't take long for this news to reach the Pontiff's ear.

I have to find him before they do!

Methodis rubbed his eyes with the back of his hand, blinking in surprise as the morning sun peeked through his window. Since returning to his shop yesterday, he had worked nonstop treating the wounded who were brought to him. He had stitched cuts, set broken bones, cleaned and dressed wounds, and handed out all manner of herbs, poultices, and powders to speed the healing and help control the pain.

Several of the local men and women had come to help him as

best they could, setting up a makeshift triage outside his door. They assessed the severity of the wounds and tried to get urgent cases in first. In some cases they helped carry the severely wounded into the shop and carried them back out once their treatment was finished.

Harsh conditions and long hours were nothing new for Methodis; in his years as Bo-Shing's captive he'd suffered far worse. Still, the endless stream of patients was taking a toll. For all his skill, there were some brought in who were beyond his help; he found those cases to be particularly exhausting. But he could never turn anyone away even if all he could do was make their final moments more comfortable.

"Methodis!" one of his volunteers called out, poking her head in through the door. "They're coming!"

Even in his sleep-deprived state, he knew whom she meant. He'd know the Order would link him to Cassandra eventually, and he'd asked his assistants to warn him when the Inquisitors came.

So soon. I thought I'd have more time. A few days at least.

"Get everyone out of here!" Methodis called back. "But if they try to stop you, don't resist. If they ask you anything, tell them the truth!"

He quickly finished bandaging what remained of his current patient's right ear, then slapped a roll of thin white fabric into the man's hand.

"Keep this clean and use it to change the dressing in two days. Now go. Go!"

Hustling the patient out of his shop, Methodis locked the door. He knew it would only delay the Inquisitors for a few seconds, but that was all he needed.

He turned back to the medicines on his wall and grabbed a blue bottle from the lowest shelf.

How much to take? he wondered.

Behind him he heard someone slam against the door, and the wooden frame cracked.

Yanking out the stopper, he guzzled down the entire bottle.

The door flew open behind him, and he spun around to see three white-eyed agents of the Order—two women and one man—advancing on him. He should have been terrified, but the contents of the bottle were already taking effect, and he greeted them with a wide, glassy-eyed grin.

"The Pontiff wants to speak with you," one of the women said. "About Cassandra."

Methodis opened his mouth to reply, but all that came out was a long, twittering laugh. He was still giggling as the Inquisitors seized him by the arms and literally dragged him away.

Scythe flew down the sewer tunnels with supernatural speed, the Sword fueling her mad dash. A series of sharp turns and narrow passages brought her to an exit back to the street that would emerge only a block away from the apothecary.

Ignoring the wooden ladder on the wall, she leapt and grabbed the ledge at the top and hauled herself up with one hand. The other slapped the grate aside, and she rolled through the opening and popped to her feet.

She took off again, rounding the nearest corner only to see a small crowd milling around in front of Methodis's shop. The door was ajar, knocked off its hinges.

"Where is he?" she shouted, rushing over.

"The Inquisitors took him," a woman said with a solemn shake of her head.

"Which way did they go?" Scythe demanded.

No one in the crowd answered.

"Maybe I can still catch them," she snapped. "Someone just tell me which direction they went!"

"They came twenty minutes ago," the woman said. "You're too late. He's gone."

Yasmin strode down the hall of Callastan's massive city jail with long, quick strides, her pace just slightly faster than normal. As chief Inquisitor, she had performed more interrogations than she could remember, but never had the stakes been so high, and she was eager to begin.

Every second we waste the Crown gets farther beyond our grasp!

They had taken the city; now began the more arduous task of holding it. She had soldiers in every neighborhood, nailing up proclamations as they patrolled the streets so the citizens would be clear as to what was expected of them.

For as long as the Order remained in the city, there were rules that must be followed: Nobody was allowed to leave the city; after sunset no one was permitted on the streets; no one was permitted to venture within a hundred yards of any ship, boat, or watercraft; citizens could not assemble in groups of seven or greater in public or private gatherings; all swords, spears, knives, clubs, bows, and crossbows had to be surrendered to representatives of the Order. Anyone caught violating these rules, the proclamations explained, would be imprisoned and held for trial, as would anyone harboring enemy combatants, known fugitives, or weapons of any sort.

Where they would put any offenders, the Pontiff realized, was another problem they'd soon need to solve. Given its character, the city prison in Callastan was far larger than most. Even so, the cells lining either side of the long corridor she walked were already filled to overflowing with prisoners.

Most were enemy soldiers captured during the fight or refugees apprehended while fleeing the city. Others were looters caught going through shops and abandoned buildings. A few were saboteurs who had struck during the night once the fighting was

done, seized even as they tried to set fire to several buildings the
Order had taken over as temporary barracks for their army.

*But they are all guilty of a much greater crime, as well: They have de-
fied the will of the Order!*

She had briefly considered randomly selecting one of every ten
of the prisoners for a massive public execution. In addition to
clearing space in the jail, the fear of being burned alive might
quell the whispers of rebellion. But Xadier had strongly advised
her against it.

We control the city for now, he'd warned her, *but only barely. The
spirit of rebellion still burns strong in these people. There is no need to fan
the flames.*

In the end, she realized he was right—she'd let her anger over
Cassandra's escape cloud her judgment.

Remember what is important. You are not here to punish the wicked.

Once the city's anger had cooled, most of the prisoners would
probably end up being released ... after questioning, of course.
The bulk of those interrogations would be left to the rank and
file. The Inquisitors would be reserved for those prisoners thought
to have crucial knowledge.

And as for the healer we captured this morning—he is mine!

The reward she offered for information on Cassandra turned
out to be money well spent. Several witnesses had claimed to have
seen a blond-haired woman fighting alongside a band of pirates
near the docks yesterday morning. And though the pirates and the
woman had escaped via ship, there was one of their company left
behind: a local healer who had apparently financed the venture.

Did they betray you, Methodis? Yasmin wondered.

If that was the case, it was possible he might be so eager for
revenge he would immediately tell her everything he knew. Even
if that happened, however, Yasmin would still need to perform a
full interrogation to verify anything he told her.

The Pontiff reached the end of the prison's long hall and

headed down a steep, narrow staircase. The healer was being held in a special cell down in the basement, one where his screams wouldn't be heard by the other prisoners. Yasmin didn't actually approve of the design—in the past she'd found great value in having other subjects know exactly what to expect while waiting for their turn to be questioned. Some Inquisitors actually believed that the fear of torture could be worse than the actual pain inflicted.

Fear can be a useful tool, the Pontiff admitted to herself, *but when properly applied the pain is always far more effective.*

Xadier was waiting for her at the bottom of the stairs. Something about the look on his face bothered her.

"You seem troubled."

"It's the prisoner, Pontiff."

"What about him?"

"He took something when the Inquisitors came for him."

"Poison?" she said, her stomach churning. It wouldn't be the first time someone had tried suicide to avoid her questions.

"Not exactly."

Puzzled, Yasmin let her awareness extend through the heavy door and into the tiny room where the prisoner was being held. Two Inquisitors stood watch over a tiny, elderly man strapped to a chair made of stone. He was completely naked and his wrists, elbows, knees, ankles, shoulders, and head were all held in place by thick leather straps tied to iron loops on the chair. A table against the wall held a number of implements capable of inflicting both intense pain and irreparable harm to the body, and a small brazier of hot coals was burning in one corner. It was all a familiar sight, and Yasmin still didn't understand what Xadier meant as she thrust open the door and strode through.

Methodis greeted her arrival with a prolonged giggling fit.

Yasmin had seen terror express itself as mad, cackling laughter. But this was something different. Despite being strapped naked to a chair, there was no tension in the healer's body. His muscles weren't taut, his eyes didn't dart from side to side, and his breathing was calm and relaxed.

Moving closer, Yasmin noticed that his gaze didn't follow her—he seemed to be staring off into the distance.

"Do you know who I am, Methodis?" she asked. "I am Yasmin the Unbowed, Pontiff of the Order!"

She thought she caught a glimmer of recognition in his glazed eyes, but he didn't show any sign of fear or concern. Instead, he smiled as if meeting an old friend.

Yasmin picked up a set of metal tongs from the table and used them to carry one of the burning coals from the brazier over to the prisoner. She pressed it against the skin of his thigh, and the flesh began to smolder and cook.

Methodis didn't scream. He didn't thrash or strain against his restraints. His muscles didn't even tense. But he did start giggling again.

Yasmin removed the coal, her anger so great she could feel herself trembling. Whatever drug he'd taken before the Inquisitors took him made it futile to continue. As much as she enjoyed inflicting pain in the pursuit of truth, torturing a prisoner who couldn't give information was pointless sadism.

"How long until the drug wears off," she asked through clenched teeth.

"We don't know, Pontiff," Xadier admitted. "We found the empty vial in his shop but have not been able to identify it. It appears to be a unique concoction of his own creation.

"We've induced vomiting and administered all the common narcotic antidotes, but nothing seems to have any effect."

"Come get me the second this passes," she said, spinning on her heel and marching from the room.

As she climbed the stairs, her ears burned with the faint but undeniable sound of the healer's soft, easy laughter.

Chapter 24

"SHE'S COMING BACK," Jerrod said as he sensed Scythe approaching on the fringes of his Sight.

She'd warned them she might be gone for days, but barely twenty-four hours had passed since she'd left.

Beside him, Keegan jumped to his feet and brushed off his clothes with his one good hand. He peered out toward the dim outline of the city, but Jerrod knew in the evening dusk he wouldn't be able to see anything. After a few seconds, he gave up and simply stood awkwardly waiting for her to arrive.

"She's running," Jerrod added, knowing the young wizard would be hungry for any detail. "But I don't think anyone is following her."

It wasn't much longer before she burst into their camp, gasping for breath.

How fast was she going, that even carrying the Sword she's tired?

"I found him!" she sputtered. "He's alive! He's alive!"

"Who?" Keegan asked.

"What about Cassandra?" Jerrod added.

"Cassandra is gone," Scythe blurted, her words running over each other in her haste to get them out. "She left on a pirate ship. And Methodis helped her escape!"

"Calm down, Scythe," Keegan said.

"Who's Methodis?" Jerrod wanted to know. "And how does he know Cassandra?"

Scythe took several deep breaths, collecting her thoughts as she tried to recover from her run.

"Methodis is a healer," she finally said, speaking more slowly. "He raised me. I haven't seen him in five years. I thought he was dead, but he's not—he's still alive!"

"How does he know Cassandra?" Jerrod asked again.

"I'm not sure," Scythe said. "But he helped her escape Callastan. And now the Order has taken Methodis prisoner."

"You are certain all this is true?" Jerrod wanted to know.

"I trust my sources," Scythe answered.

"Cassandra wouldn't leave without the Crown," Jerrod said. "That means the Pontiff failed to find the Talisman."

"You said she left on a ship, right?" Keegan chimed in. "In my visions, the Keystone was on an island. If Cassandra saw the same visions, that must be where she's headed."

"Methodis must have helped her figure out how to find it," Scythe said.

"If the Order has him, then the Pontiff probably already knows all this, too," Jerrod said. "Including the location of the Keystone."

"They only took him this morning," Scythe said. "Maybe he hasn't told them anything yet."

"If not, then he soon will," Jerrod told her. "No one can resist Yasmin's interrogations for long."

"That's why I came back," Scythe said. "We have to rescue him.

"I saw where he's being held," she added. "A prison crawling with soldiers and Inquisitors. Too many for me to try to take them on alone."

"Do you really think the three of us have any chance against those kind of odds?" Jerrod asked.

"We do if Keegan uses the Ring," Scythe insisted. "This can't be any harder than taking out the Danaan patrols that came after us in Ferlhame."

"That was different," Jerrod said, cutting Keegan off before the young wizard could speak. "He was calling on the ancient power of the North Forest."

"But I'm stronger now," Keegan argued. "I stopped the yeti army in the Frozen East, and the Ring will be even stronger here."

But the backlash from stopping the army might have killed Norr, Jerrod thought, but didn't say out loud.

"You still struggle to control your power," Jerrod reminded him. "In Ferlhame, half the city was leveled when you and the dragon fought. And when you cast your curse on Shalana, the backlash created a rift between you, Scythe, and Vaaler, despite all the precautions you took."

He expected Keegan to find some other objection; he knew how badly he wanted to help Scythe. But to Jerrod's surprise, she actually intervened on his behalf before Keegan could say anything.

"White-eyes is right," she agreed, chewing nervously on her lower lip. "I don't want anything bad to happen to Methodis if you rain fire down on Callastan or accidentally wake up some kind of Chaos Spawn monstrosity."

"You don't trust me?" Keegan asked, crushed.

"I know you wouldn't do anything to hurt him on purpose," Scythe said, reaching out to lay a consoling hand on his arm. "But every time you use the Ring, people die."

"That is the essence of Chaos," Jerrod reminded them.

"If neither of you thinks I can safely use the Ring," Keegan snapped, sullen and bitter, "then how do you expect me to stop Daemron?"

"I would have faith in you if you were rested and strong," Jerrod said. "But you still haven't recovered from being lost in the Burning Sea."

"It's nothing to be ashamed of, Keegan," Scythe chimed in. "I was only there for a few hours and it left me physically and mentally drained. You were trapped there for almost two whole days!"

Keegan nodded but didn't speak. His jaw was clenched and he stared down at the ground, refusing to look either of them in the eye.

"We must come up with some other plan to rescue this healer," Jerrod said. "He might be able to tell us how to find Cassandra and the Keystone."

"And we have to do it fast," Scythe added grimly.

She's trying not to imagine the tortures the Pontiff will use during her interrogation, Jerrod realized.

Nobody spoke for several seconds, then Scythe let out an angry shout and stabbed Daemron's Sword into the ground at her feet. The blade dove deep into the hard earth, burying itself almost halfway to the hilt. Then she slumped down beside the Talisman until she was sitting with her arms wrapped around her legs and her knees pulled up close to her chest.

"He was like a father to me. And I abandoned him," she whispered. "I never thought I'd see him again. Now I find out he's alive but there's nothing I can do to save him this time, either."

Keegan looked over at Jerrod, then turned back to Scythe and took a seat beside her.

"Maybe you can turn the city against the Order," Keegan said, his own disappointment and anger forgotten as he tried to console her. "Use a rebellion as some kind of distraction."

Scythe seemed to consider his suggestion briefly before forlornly shaking her head.

"The underworld is waiting for the chance to rise, but they won't fight unless they think they can win. Right now the Order is too strong."

"Now that they've established control over the city, we'd need an army to take them on," Jerrod agreed.

Keegan looked up and gave him an angry glare, and he took a few steps away to give the young couple some space. Dusk had given way to darkness, so Jerrod crouched by the fire pit they'd dug last night. He stacked several small, dry twigs they'd gathered yesterday into an irregular, triangular tower. He slid several handfuls of dry grass inside, then went to the supply packs to grab the tinderbox.

They've both suffered loss before, Jerrod told himself, striking the flint so that a shower of sparks leapt onto the dry grass. *Let them grieve together, then they'll find a way to continue on.*

Keegan had his left arm wrapped protectively around Scythe's shoulders though he was careful to keep the stump where his hand used to be from touching her. With his good hand, he gently rubbed her upper arm.

A short distance away, Jerrod tended to a smoldering fire, shielding it from the breeze coming in from the sea. After a few seconds the flickering flames caught on the kindling. Satisfied, the monk stood up, but he didn't come any closer.

He's letting me handle this, Keegan realized. He wanted to say something to Scythe but couldn't think of anything that would help.

First Norr, and now the man who raised her. How much more can she take?

He'd lost his own father many years ago, and he'd never truly gotten over the loss. The pain was buried so deep that he would go days or even weeks without thinking about it, but it was still a part of him. It always would be. He couldn't bear to imagine what it would be like to feel that not once, but twice.

Part of him wanted to ignore all the risks and warnings and simply try to use the Ring to help her. But they were right. He knew he didn't have the mental strength to focus his will enough to control the power right now. If he unleashed Chaos against the Order, he might end up wiping Callastan completely off the map.

What good is my power if I can't help the people I care most about?

It was hard enough carrying the burden of being the prophesied savior of the world. But being an impotent savior was much worse.

He didn't know if his feeble attempts to console Scythe were helping, but he thought he could feel the muscles in her shoulder and arm starting to relax. And then they suddenly went tense, and her head snapped up even as Jerrod announced, "Someone's coming!"

Scythe was on her feet so fast Keegan was left holding empty air. She snatched the Sword free from the ground and held it out in front of her with both hands wrapped around the hilt.

Jerrod had also reacted before Keegan could even think about moving: The monk had dropped into a low crouch and tilted his head to one side. His brow furrowed in concentration as he pushed out with his awareness. The fire popped and crackled, causing Keegan to jump. And then the monk relaxed and stood up straight though his expression reflected in the fire's glow was one of confusion.

"Darmmid?" he called out into the shadows beyond their camp. "Is that you?"

Keegan couldn't believe his eyes as the bearded soldier stepped into the firelight.

He must have been following us ever since I pretended to put that hex on him.

"What are you doing here?" Scythe snapped, her eyes narrowing suspiciously.

"I did it," Darm said, ignoring her and speaking directly to Keegan. "I brought you an army."

"He's alone," Jerrod said. "There's nobody else out there."

"They're coming, Keegan of the Gorgon Staff," Darm said,

dropping to his knees. "Vaaler is bringing the armies of the Free Cities to Callastan."

Vaaler?

"Where did you hear that name?" Scythe demanded, stepping forward and placing the edge of her blade against the soldier's throat.

"I found him outside the Free Cities," Darm said, though he never took his eyes off Keegan. "With his Barbarian followers."

No, Keegan thought. *This isn't possible.*

"Vaaler is bringing his army to Callastan," he said again. "I came ahead to tell you."

"How did you find us?" Jerrod asked.

"The hex," Darm told Keegan. "Vaaler said he broke it, but I could still feel your pull."

"The Chaos you used in the ritual," Jerrod said. "Remember?"

"That was just for show," Keegan protested. "It was nothing. Just a tiny spark!"

Could this really all be because of the backlash from that one seemingly insignificant act? Keegan wondered.

"You bound me to your will," Darmmid insisted. "And I have done everything you asked. Please—release me!"

"You said Vaaler is leading an army to Callastan," Keegan replied, an idea of how he could help Scythe forming in his head. "Where are they?"

"A day or two behind. I scouted ahead. I knew I'd find you."

"I have one more task for you to perform before I set you free," Keegan told him. "Take us to Vaaler!"

They broke camp and set out immediately, much to Scythe's relief. Every second Methodis was being held inside the Order's prison was one too many.

She was worried about how Keegan would handle the journey,

but he'd had almost a full day to rest while she'd been searching out her contacts in Callastan and he was able to keep up.

If it had just been her and Jerrod, they could have traveled much faster. But they needed Darmmid to guide them, so Keegan wasn't really slowing them down anyway.

The soldier marched out in front, carrying a smoldering torch to illuminate his path through the night. As they walked, Scythe was still grappling with the implications of Darm's unexpected arrival.

Keegan didn't mean for any of this to happen. It was just a tiny flash of magic—a light show to sell his lie. But somehow that was enough to bring an army to Callastan.

His power continued to grow. Scythe had no idea if it was because the Legacy was getting weaker or if it had something to do with all the time he'd spent carrying Daemron's Ring, but he was clearly much stronger than even he realized.

She shuddered to think what kind of havoc he would have unleashed if he'd tried to use magic to free Methodis.

Sometimes White-eyes is right; Chaos really is dangerous.

In the end, Vaaler's army was even closer than Darmmid had guessed. By the time morning broke, she could see the mass of soldiers traipsing across the Southlands, and it wasn't long until a small vanguard broke off from the main army to come and greet them, with Vaaler and Shalana at the head.

The Danaan was on horseback; Shalana on foot beside him. A dozen Easterners followed close behind.

As they drew closer, Vaaler spurred his horse forward and Shalana broke into a run, leaving the others behind.

Pulling up just short of the new arrivals, Vaaler leapt down from his horse and rushed forward to wrap his arms around Keegan in a fierce hug, laughing.

"You never cease to amaze me," he said.

Shalana arrived a few seconds later, her long strides not quite able to keep up when Vaaler's horse broke into a run.

"Where's Norr?" she asked.

Keegan looked down at the ground, and Jerrod shook his head. Vaaler's smile vanished and a somber mood fell over the reunion.

To Scythe's surprise, Shalana stepped forward, bent down, and wrapped her long arms around her.

"I'm so sorry," she whispered. "I know how much you loved each other."

Scythe couldn't answer; she was too choked up to speak. The taller woman held her for several seconds, then let go and stepped back. Scythe could see she was also fighting back tears.

As the rest of the vanguard arrived, Shalana said something in her native tongue that Scythe couldn't understand.

"The Red Bear has fallen," Vaaler translated, speaking softly.

As one, the other Easterners bowed their heads in silent honor of their fallen champion. It was all finally too much for Scythe to take, and the tears began to flow.

After the initial meeting, the group gathered over breakfast to discuss what must happen next. In addition to Shalana, Scythe, Keegan, and Jerrod, Vaaler had asked Andar to join them as well. Darmmid had left them, heading off to join the main bulk of the army after Keegan told him, "You have served me well. I absolve you of your debt to me, and I release you from my hold. You are free!"

Vaaler wasn't surprised that the mad soldier had stumbled across his friends outside Callastan. It was one just one of many events that went beyond the scope of fathomable coincidence. Clearly there was something greater at work, driving them toward a single goal.

We were all born under the Blood Moon. Our fates are inextricably intertwined.

"Callastan has fallen," Jerrod said to start their meeting. "But we believe Cassandra escaped the city by ship with the Crown."

Andar glanced over at Vaaler, who gave him a nod of encouragement.

"We might know where she is going," the High Sorcerer told them. "There is an obelisk of black stone on an island near the farthest edge of the Western Sea—"

"You know about the Keystone?" Keegan exclaimed in surprise, cutting him off.

"The Queen has seen it in her visions," Andar explained. "She believes that is where you must go to fulfill your destiny."

"You've had the same visions, haven't you?" Vaaler said with a knowing smile. "You've seen the Keystone and the island in your dreams."

"I have," Keegan admitted. "But those visions are a trap sent by Daemron to mislead us."

"But Cassandra may not know this," Jerrod interjected. "We think she believes that once she reaches the Keystone, she can use the Crown to restore the Legacy. Instead, she may bring it tumbling down."

"Someone in the city helped her escape," Scythe added. "A man named Methodis. The Pontiff is holding him prisoner. If we free him, he can tell us exactly where her ship was going."

"There may be another way to get to the island," Vaaler said. "Instead of traveling by ship, it might be possible to reach the Keystone by using magic."

"Magic?" Keegan said, eager and excited. "How?"

"Before the Cataclysm," Andar explained, "magic was far stronger than it is now. The most powerful wizards were able to summon enough Chaos to open a portal through space and time. They could pass through this portal to travel instantly from one location to another."

"Rexol had me transcribe several accounts of mages who attempted this during the time of Old Magic," Vaaler said. "But the ritual is extremely complicated and very dangerous. Even Rexol thought it wasn't worth the risk.

"Theoretically, though, it is possible."

"This is fascinating," Scythe interrupted. "But what about Callastan? What about Methodis?"

"If there is another way to get to the Keystone, we may not need his help after all," Jerrod said.

"Methodis raised me!" Scythe snapped. "I'm not leaving him in that prison!"

"We serve a higher purpose," Jerrod reminded her. "You are letting your personal feelings cloud your judgment."

"This is as personal as it gets!" Scythe shot back. "After Norr's death, I tried to be like you. I swore I would bury my emotions and focus only on fulfilling your prophecy, no matter what the cost.

"But I can't do it. I can't sacrifice someone I love for some greater cause even if I know that cause is real!"

"She's right," Keegan chimed in. "We have to save Methodis. Going after Cassandra can wait."

I don't know if it can, Vaaler thought. But he actually agreed with Scythe. Jerrod's dedication to his cause had turned the monk into some kind of monomaniacal zealot. *He's lost his humanity.*

He'd seen the destruction Keegan could unleash. If he lost the ability to feel compassion for others, he'd become a monster. *Is that what happened to Daemron?*

Jerrod was silent, studying Keegan and Scythe with the unsettling gaze of his blind eyes. When he finally spoke, he surprised them all.

"I see how much this means to you. And saving your friend will deal a crushing blow to the Pontiff. Perhaps it will be enough to finally break the Order's hold over the Southlands."

"Do we actually have the numbers to attack Callastan?" Andar asked. "It would be one thing if they were still camped outside the walls. But if they've taken the city, they'll have a fortified position."

"And we can't expect any help from Callastan's forces if they've already been routed," Shalana added.

"There are still those inside the city willing to fight against the Order," Scythe assured them. "If we attack, they'll join in."

"The Order seized control of the city in a single day," Jerrod added. "But they had greater numbers and the element of surprise on their side."

"But we have Daemron's Sword and his Ring," Vaaler reminded them.

"They won't let me help them," Keegan said, his eyes cast low. "They're afraid I won't be able to control my power."

Vaaler knew his friend well enough to realize Keegan believed the same thing.

"There still might be a way for you to help us," Vaaler suggested, the outline of a plan already forming in his head. "You said the Order struck with the element of surprise. We need to do the same thing.

"Maybe you can cast some kind of spell that will hide our forces from them until we reach the city."

"It isn't just the army's scouts who must be fooled," Jerrod reminded him. "You must also blind the Sight of the Pontiff and her followers."

"The spell would have to be subtle," Vaaler agreed. "So that they don't even realize what's happening until it's too late."

"I . . . I don't know if I can do something like that," Keegan said.

"Vaaler can help you," Scythe blurted out, grabbing the young mage by the arm. "Right?"

The Danaan nodded.

"What about the backlash?" Keegan asked. "How can we control it?"

"The Sword," Scythe said. "Remember when you were lost in the Burning Sea? We used the Ring to bring you back, but I used the Sword to keep the Ring's power in check."

"Are you saying the Talismans actually balance each other out?" Vaaler asked, his mind reeling with the potential implications of this new bit of knowledge.

"There is some evidence to support that theory," Jerrod confirmed.

"Maybe if Keegan uses the Sword and Ring together, he can control his power," Scythe said, her excitement growing. "If he can use magic to hide us so we can catch the army in Callastan unprepared, we can take back the city and save Methodis!"

Vaaler looked at his friend and saw a storm of conflicting emotions at play. He clearly wanted to help Scythe, but he was afraid of failing. *Or even accidentally killing the man they're trying to save.*

"I can help you prepare a ritual to hide us from the scouts and the Order," Vaaler told him. "But only if you're strong enough to do this."

Keegan looked over at Jerrod, then at Scythe, his uncertainty painfully clear.

"You can do this," the young woman told him, offering him the hilt of Daemron's Sword. "I know you can."

Reaching out slowly, he took the blade from her grasp and turned to Vaaler. Taking a deep breath, he said, "Show me what to do."

"Shalana," Vaaler said, "you and Jendarme prepare a battle plan."

Turning back to Keegan, he warned, "This won't be easy."

"I'm ready," the young mage vowed, his head held high and his shoulders thrust back.

Even though he was looking directly at Vaaler, it was clear to the Danaan that he was actually talking to Scythe.

"I promise I won't let you down!"

Chapter 25

THE PONTIFF WAS in a foul mood. Three days had passed since the healer's capture, yet he was still in a state so addled it would be pointless to question him. He was no longer giggling uncontrollably; as the drug began to clear his system, his body had gone into extreme withdrawal. He was sweating, vomiting, and shaking uncontrollably as he slipped in and out of consciousness, completely oblivious to his surroundings.

As if echoing her emotional state, the city was enveloped in a dense fog that had rolled in from the sea during the night. It did nothing to hinder Yasmin's Sight, of course, but for some reason she found the thick mists unsettling.

You're just frustrated by the healer, she told herself.

She tried to tell herself that his withdrawal was a good sign; soon his mind would be clear again, and she could begin her interrogation. She just had to remain patient; Xadier would come find her when the prisoner was ready.

Yet for some reason, she felt compelled to go to the prisons to check on him herself. As she marched through the city streets, the vague sense of unease continued to grow.

When she reached the prison, she could immediately tell she wasn't the only one affected by the fog. The guards outside were nervous, anxiously peering into the mists. They tensed up and raised their weapons as she materialized from the haze, but quickly lowered them when they recognized her bald, scarred scalp.

She passed by without a word and made her way past the cells on the upper floor and down to the torture chamber in the basement. The Inquisitors standing guard seemed just as nervous as the soldiers outside.

They stepped aside as she entered the small room where Methodis lay huddled in the corner. The room reeked of his bodily excretions, and the Pontiff crinkled her nose in revulsion. But he was no longer convulsing.

Crouching beside him, she whispered, "Methodis, can you hear me?"

He groaned and twitched in response to his name, but didn't open his eyes.

Soon, she thought. *A few more hours at most.*

A sudden impulse hit her, brought on by a combination of her anxiousness about the fog, her impatience to begin the interrogation, and her disgust at the smell in the tiny room.

"Clean the prisoner up and bring him to my private quarters," she instructed.

Keegan sat atop the back of Vaaler's horse, his right arm fully extended above his head. Daemron's Ring was on his finger, the Slayer's blade clutched firmly in his hand and held aloft. He had been stripped naked save for a loincloth, and arcane tattoos and sigils of power carefully drawn by Vaaler the night before completely covered his skin from head to toe ... though they were much fainter than they had once been.

He sat completely motionless save for a slight trembling of his muscles as he struggled to control the Chaos, summoning it with the Ring, then channeling it through the Sword to project the heavy fog that covered Callastan. Scythe walked at his side on the right and Vaaler on the left, watching carefully to make sure he didn't topple over in the saddle while he focused on maintaining the spell.

He's been doing this for hours, the monk thought. *He can't last much longer.*

They were only a few miles away from Callastan. The bulk of their army, including Shalana and her Eastern honor guard, had already pressed on ahead, outpacing the wizard's slowly walking mount as they moved into position. Reaching out with his awareness, Jerrod could sense the dark gray cloud of vapor that had descended on the city. His Sight pierced the misty veil, but all he saw were the buildings and inhabitants of the town: It was as if the army hidden within did not exist.

Just a bit longer, Jerrod silently implored him. *We're almost there!*

Keegan swayed in the saddle and the Sword drooped, the blade angling downward as the last of his strength left him. The faded markings on Keegan's skin suddenly began to disappear, vanishing in seconds as Chaos ate away at the symbols Vaaler had designed to hold it in check.

Keegan let out a low moan, and the air around him rippled as he was enveloped in a blue aura. Both Vaaler and Scythe staggered back as if they'd been hit, grunting in surprise. Jerrod tried to rush to the wizard's side, only to be knocked off his feet as the invisible wave of power rolled over him.

Scythe was the first to recover, lunging forward as Keegan slumped over in the saddle and Daemron's blade slipped free from his hand. But instead of snatching for the falling weapon, Scythe let it clatter to the ground. The tiny woman somehow managed to catch Keegan, taking the brunt of his weight and easing him gently down to the ground as he slid from his perch.

"Get the Ring!" Jerrod shouted as he scrambled to his feet, but Scythe was already ahead of him.

She slipped the Talisman from his finger, and ahead of them the bank of fog vanished like a puff of smoke in a strong wind, exposing the army that had crept to within a hundred yards of the walls. Horns sounded from their ranks, and an angry roar rose up from the soldiers of the Free Cities as they charged. Bells rang out from inside the city, sounding the alarm. The battle had begun.

Jerrod's attention, however, was focused entirely on Keegan. He rushed to the young man's side, where he lay breathing hard on the ground, Scythe protectively cradling his bare torso. His face was drawn and flushed, his brow beaded with sweat. Despite this, he was shivering, but his eyes were open.

He looked around, momentarily confused, then his gaze focused on Scythe.

"You did it, Keegan," she said, gently wiping her hand on his brow. "You did it!"

"I did it," he whispered through chattering teeth. Then he closed his eyes and rested his head against Scythe.

Vaaler appeared a second later, carrying a heavy woollen blanket.

"Help me wrap this around him," he said, lifting Keegan up with Jerrod's help.

Scythe watched as the two men swaddled him like a child, then scooped up Daemron's blade.

"Go," Jerrod told her. "Find your friend."

"We'll look after Keegan," Vaaler promised.

Scythe didn't even bother to reply. She simply turned and took off, moving so fast she appeared little more than a blur.

It didn't take long for Jerrod to be satisfied that Keegan was exhausted but otherwise unharmed.

Coming to the same conclusion, Vaaler motioned over one of the small company of soldiers who had stayed behind as an escort.

"We'll make camp here," he said. "Set up a perimeter and get a fire going."

As the soldier scurried off, Jerrod turned to Vaaler.

"Keep him safe," the monk said.

"Where are you going?" Vaaler asked in surprise.

"I have something I must do. If I don't return, don't look for me. Once you have Methodis, go after Cassandra."

Before the stunned Danaan could ask any further questions, Jerrod took off. Though not quite as fast as Scythe while she carried the Sword, it wouldn't take him much longer than her to reach Callastan.

And then there will finally be a reckoning.

The Pontiff was so focused on watching her prisoner that she didn't realize the fog had lifted until she heard the ringing of the watch bells.

"We're under attack!" one of the guards who'd brought Methodis to her chambers exclaimed, stating the obvious.

With the unnatural mists dispelled, Yasmin could sense them clearly now: an army swarming over the walls and into the city.

A small army, she silently amended, her awareness giving her a general sense of the size of the force arrayed against them.

If we hold our positions, they have no hope of overrunning us.

"Go to your posts," she snapped at the guards, who saluted, then ran off.

"You, too," she told the Inquisitors who had come with her. "Hold the city and drive the enemy back."

"What about the prisoner, Pontiff?" one asked.

"Do you really think he poses any threat I cannot handle?" she asked.

Rather than reply, the Inquisitors wisely rushed off to join in the defense.

Methodis still wasn't fully aware of his surroundings, but it wouldn't be long now. Without any of her tools, the interrogation would have to be more blunt, but Yasmin was confident she'd soon know everything about Cassandra and where she had taken the Crown.

Scythe never broke stride as she raced toward the battle, heading for the main gate. The defenders were struggling to close them, while her soldiers fought to keep them open as more and more of their army poured through.

Though outnumbered, the enemy was bolstered by a pair of Inquisitors, giving them the edge. Scythe's arrival, however, changed everything.

Fueled by battle lust and Daemron's Sword, she carved through a half dozen ordinary soldiers before the Inquisitors were able to blunt her charge. They came at her with a coordinated attack, striking from opposite sides so one would be guaranteed to flank her.

Their tactics were sound, but Scythe was too quick. Recognizing what they were doing, she threw herself at the closest foe in a reckless assault. Had he simply retreated, he might have survived. But he made the mistake of trying to meet her head-on, throwing up his staff to deflect the first blow from her silver blade. The Talisman sliced effortlessly through the Inquisitor's weapon. Its momentum unabated, it cleaved deep into his torso, severing flesh, bone, and internal organs with ease.

As he dropped, the second Inquisitor lashed out at Scythe from behind. Though she was looking away, the Islander sensed the blow coming and threw herself into a forward roll. The staff whistled harmlessly through the air, throwing the Inquisitor off-balance.

Scythe spun around, crouching low and extending one leg to sweep her enemy's feet out. The Inquisitor reacted by leaping high in the air and jabbing the butt end of his staff at Scythe's face. Throwing her head back, Scythe avoided the worst of it and only took a glancing blow on the side of her chin.

She rolled clear, ready to launch another attack. Before she could, however, four of her soldiers threw themselves at the monk. Hacking and slashing with a mad fury, they brought their opponent down in seconds ... much to Scythe's amazement.

Daemron's Sword doesn't just affect me! she realized. *It inspires my allies, too!*

"Hold this gate!" she shouted, before racing off toward the prison.

The fighting raged all around her as the Free City soldiers pushed into the city, but she was focused only on one goal. Despite this, wherever she passed she sensed an immediate turn in the battle in their favor. Bolstered by the presence of the Talisman, ordinary soldiers fought like berserkers, routing the enemy with their unbridled ferocity.

By the time she reached the prison it wasn't just the Free City soldiers battling the Order. In the streets around the jail, the gangs of Callastan had emerged from the sewers to join the fray.

Several Inquisitors outside the prison had managed to rally their troops, but they were hemmed in on all sides by a mob of armed thugs and violent criminals. In an ordinary battle they might have stemmed the onslaught and even started to push out. But they weren't just fighting an opposing army. The Talisman was a gift from the Gods, and against its power they had no chance.

Within minutes of Scythe's arrival all resistance at the prison was vanquished in an orgy of blood and screams. Leaving it to others to free those in the cells on the main floor, Scythe raced to the stairs that led to the torture chambers below.

The narrow hall was deserted. She rushed toward the heavy door at the end and slammed the Sword into it. The door was wrenched from its hinges by the force of the blow, and a shower of splinters and chunks of wood flew into the room.

Methodis wasn't there. Instead, she saw a young man with a shaved head and pure white eyes.

"Where is he?" she snarled.

"Please," the man said, holding up his hands. "I'm not a warrior. My name is Xadier. I'm just a Seer!"

"Where is he?" Scythe asked again, raising her blade and taking a slow step toward him.

"I can't tell you," he said defiantly. "I won't!"

Scythe removed one of his hands with a casual swipe of the blade. Xadier screamed and dropped to his knees, clutching the spurting stump against his chest.

Laying the flat of her blade on his shoulder, Scythe called on the Sword to heal the wound, instantly staunching the flow of blood before he passed out.

"Where?" she asked again.

This time when he refused, she took his left leg below the knee. By the time he finally told her what she wanted to know, he was little more than a blubbering, limbless torso.

She took just long enough to grant Xadier the mercy of ending his life before turning and racing back up the stairs and out of the prison, heading for the Pontiff's private chambers.

By the time Jerrod reached the battle, the Free City forces had already secured Callastan's front gates. The bulk of the army was already inside the walls and pushing steadily deeper into the city.

As he entered the fray, he felt a sudden burst of adrenaline coursing through his veins. There was an almost palpable energy in the air, an excitement that made him feel as if victory was inevitable.

The Sword.

He felt its pull, drawing him willingly—eagerly—into the battle. But Jerrod resisted its call; he wasn't here to help take the city.

This is as personal as it gets.

Scythe's words had resonated with him. They'd touched something deep inside, something he'd buried for so long and so deep he almost forgot it existed. For over twenty years he'd served his cause, sacrificing everything to find the Children of Fire and help them fulfill their destiny.

But he hadn't worked alone. He'd recruited others to his cause, just as Ezra had once recruited him. Over the years scores—if not hundreds—of men and women, some from within the Order and others from beyond the Monastery's walls, had served with him. Nazir, the previous Pontiff, had worked relentlessly to quash what he called the Heresy of the Burning Savior. And Yasmin had been his most ardent follower.

How many of my friends and followers died by her hand? How many were burned at the stake, or tortured to death in her interrogation rooms?

Rounding a corner, he scrambled up the side of one of the closely packed buildings that lined the streets. Below him the fighting was spreading quickly, and everywhere he looked the Order was losing ground.

Once again he felt the call of the Sword, urging him to leap down from on high and bring death to the enemy. Again, he resisted, setting off along the rooftops toward the center of the city.

Of all those who had sworn to walk Ezra's path, only he was left. Some had given their lives willingly over the years so that he could evade capture whenever Yasmin and her Inquisitors had closed in on him. Others had sacrificed themselves to help him and Keegan escape the Monastery after Rexol and his apprentice were imprisoned. Most had simply been hunted down and slaughtered for daring to defy the Order's doctrine.

He had accepted their deaths as part of the greater good. He had swallowed his anger and sorrow each time, not allowing himself to become distracted from his goal. Now they were nearing the endgame. Soon, one way or another, the prophecy would be fulfilled.

Nazir was gone, slain when the Minions attacked the Monas-

tery. But Yasmin was still alive, and the memories of all those he
had lost cried out for her blood.

This is as personal as it gets.

He knew Yasmin well. He had studied her from afar for years
just as she had studied him, each trying to know the enemy better
in their deadly game of cat and mouse. She was ruthlessly practi-
cal, but she also understood the importance of symbols, especially
for the common masses. Whenever she came to a city or town—
whether as the Pontiff or in her earlier days as an Inquisitor—she
always set up her private quarters in a building right beside the
home of the city's ruler.

*She projects humility by living an austere existence while sitting in the
lap of luxury. She shames those around her for their excess, and intimi-
dates them with her constant presence.*

He knew where he'd find Yasmin. And when he did, only one
of them would walk away.

Yasmin knew that the city was lost. The enemies at the gate had
been joined by rebels inside the walls; the Order's defeat was only
a matter of time.

But even though virtually all her followers were being slaughtered in the streets, there was still hope. If she could find Cassandra
and reclaim the Crown, the Order could rise again. And Methodis
was the key.

He lay huddled in the corner of her otherwise empty room. As
she always did, she'd had all the furnishings removed when she
claimed it for her own.

Material possessions are a sign of weakness.

The enemy would eventually find their way here to the center
of the city. She had hoped to interrogate the healer before that
happened, but now she was having second thoughts. She might
need to flee . . . taking Methodis with her, of course.

She briefly regretted sending the guards away. At the time she thought the attack would be easily beaten back, but now she could have used them to help transport her still-barely-conscious prisoner.

I can take to the rooftops, she realized. *Avoid the fighting. Even carrying him with me I—*

Her thoughts were cut short as she sensed his arrival. For an instant she refused to believe it was true. She'd hunted him for so long, come so close to capturing him so many times, that she couldn't believe he would show up now.

"Yasmin!" Jerrod called from the far end of the hall. "It's time to pay for your crimes!"

"Only a heretic would dare to pass judgment on the Pontiff!" she shouted back, a smile crossing her face.

Jerrod was coming toward her, walking slowly. She could sense he was alone, just as he could sense the same about her.

"I've dreamed of this day more times than you can imagine," she told him as he reached the door to her room.

"Leave the dreaming to the Seers," Jerrod advised.

She ran the fingers of her left hand gently over the scarred skin of her scalp as she studied him: a nervous habit she had broken many years ago returning in the anticipation of what was to come.

He looked much as she remembered from their last meeting several years ago—a fit but otherwise ordinary man. He wasn't particularly broad or tall; there was hardly anything distinguishing about him at all. But she knew he was highly skilled and very, very dangerous.

But so am I!

"You're unarmed," he noted. "Did you lose your staff?"

"The Pontiff never carries a weapon," she reminded him. "But I will enjoy killing you with my bare hands."

He wasn't carrying a weapon, either, but Yasmin knew that didn't make him any less deadly.

In the corner, Methodis groaned softly and Yasmin seized on the distraction to make the first move.

She came at him high, leaping into the air and snapping out the heel of her boot at his head. Jerrod slapped it away as she flew past and spun around as he threw an elbow at her ribs. Yasmin blocked it with her forearm, twisting in the air so that when she landed they were still facing each other, but standing on the opposite sides of the room.

"A pedestrian first pass," she taunted. "I expected something more from you."

"It's never good to reveal too much too early," he answered.

He came rushing forward at a strange angle, and Yasmin instinctively backed up, uncertain of his line of attack. Her retreat took her into the corner of the room as Jerrod jumped at a forty-five-degree angle, planted one foot on the wall for leverage, and kicked off in the complete opposite direction, his fist slamming down at the bridge of her nose.

The unorthodox move happened too fast for the eye to follow, but the Pontiff's senses operated at a higher level. In the instant it took to execute, she realized not only what he was doing but that she had nowhere to dodge. Backed into the corner, her only option was to throw her head forward, absorbing the blow with the top of her bare scalp.

At the last instant Jerrod opened his fist and struck her with an open palm to keep from breaking his knuckles on the hard bone of her skull. The blow hit hard enough to drive Yasmin to her knees, and Jerrod's momentum brought him down on top of her. But as she dropped she rolled onto her back and kicked up hard with both feet.

Her kick lacked any real power, but it was strong enough to throw Jerrod off her. He landed on his feet, legs spread wide and knees bent as he dropped into a fighting crouch just as Yasmin popped back up.

"Unconventional," she told him. "But you weren't quick enough to take advantage."

"I have a few more tricks up my sleeve," he told her.

An empty threat, Yasmin thought.

Though no damage had been done in their two brief exchanges, they'd tested each other's limits. And the Pontiff knew she was quicker.

She threw herself at him full force with a blinding flurry of kicks, punches, elbows, and knees. Jerrod countered the barrage, deflecting, dodging, and blocking each attack. She struck with perfect form and precision each time, but Jerrod couldn't match her. On one of his counters his balance shifted a miniscule amount to his heels, and she seized on the advantage by pressing in close and getting low. With better leverage, each of her attacks packed even more force and she relentlessly drove him back. He tried to disengage, but with her superior position she cut off each avenue of escape and slowly backed him into the corner.

In desperation he threw his hands over his head and spun away, having no choice but to absorb a series of devastating punches to his midsection to break away and create some space. She heard a rib crack and Jerrod grunted in pain as he retreated to the far side of the room, breathing hard.

"Tired already?" she said, shaking her head in mock disappointment. "Maybe you should have been training more instead of running around consorting with wizards and heretics."

Jerrod came at her again, throwing a series of feints and fakes to confuse her into making a mistake. But Yasmin didn't make mistakes. She had spent thousands upon thousands of hours perfecting her technique, and even more meditating and learning to channel her inner spark of Chaos into perfect physical action.

She calmly countered each of his moves, never overreacting or taking a foolish risk that would leave her exposed. And once again she picked away at the tiny imperfections in his form, slowly building up each subtle edge and incremental advantage until she had him once more out of position.

This time she exploited her opportunity far more aggressively, striking for his face and throat with a succession of tight chops and sharp jabs from the edge of her palm. As he slapped her attacks away he overreached just enough for her to seize his thumb and snap it back, dislocating it with a sharp snap.

Jerrod screamed and stumbled back. Instead of pursuing, she let him go, taking a moment to relish his pain.

"You're going to lose," she said. "We both know it. It will take time, but this will inevitably end with you broken and bloody at my feet."

Throwing all caution to the wind, Jerrod came at her with pure, reckless aggression. His rage would have overwhelmed a lesser opponent; against the Pontiff it only opened him up to a brutal beating.

She slid under a wild punch and smashed her forehead into his nose, crumpling it with a sickening thud. Undeterred by the blood gushing down his face, he lashed out with a knee. Yasmin dodged the blow by dropping low and slamming her shoulder into his other leg. Braced against the floor, it buckled sideways, ripping ligaments and cartilage.

Unable to support his weight, Jerrod collapsed. As he fell, she caught his wrist and twisted, dislocating his elbow. Yasmin rolled clear of her broken opponent, kicking him hard enough in the face to knock out a tooth as she did so.

She stood over her wounded foe, staring down at him.

"This is actually your fault," she told him. "You were already a legend when I joined the Monastery. Jerrod the Heretic.

"They told such wild tales of your incredible prowess that I dedicated myself to becoming the greatest warrior the Order had ever known. I vowed that if we ever met, I would destroy you."

She ran her fingers over her scalp again, then quickly snatched her hand back down when she realized what she was doing. At her feet, Jerrod began to cough and choke until he spit out a viscous mixture of blood and phlegm.

"Admit it," she demanded. "I'm better than you ever were. You could never beat me."

"I could never beat you," he said, the words muffled by his rapidly swelling lips and the blood pouring from his broken nose and into his mouth. "But she can!"

Yasmin's awareness had been almost completely focused on Jerrod during their battle. It was only now that he was vanquished that she sensed another's arrival.

Spinning to meet the new threat, she saw a small Islander girl standing in the door, carrying a strange silver blade. And then the girl vanished, replaced by a demon made of steel and rage.

The monster launched itself at her with a speed unlike anything Yasmin had ever faced. The Pontiff threw herself into a back handspring as the blade sliced through the air in too many different directions for her to follow. For an instant she thought she had miraculously escaped unharmed, but as she landed her left foot simply gave way, the tendon in her heel severed so cleanly she hadn't even felt the pain.

As Yasmin crumpled awkwardly to the ground the creature was on her again. This time she actually saw the blow coming though she wasn't fast enough to move out of the way.

Daemron's Sword lopped her head from her shoulders in one smooth stroke, sending it spinning through the air. The Pontiff's consciousness endured just long enough for her awareness to sense the room tumbling around her, and the last image to pass through her brain was that of her own decapitated body toppling forward, a dozen feet away.

Chapter 26

METHODIS COULD FEEL the warmth of a lantern shining on his face, but he wasn't ready to open his eyes yet. They itched and burned, and he knew bright light would only make them worse. His throat was dry and scratchy, so parched it hurt to swallow. His empty stomach was clenching and cramping, as if trying to digest itself to feed his ravenous hunger.

He recognized all the symptoms as signs that the bliss-wort he'd taken was almost completely out of his system.

That means they'll begin the interrogation soon.

Knowing there were far worse torments to come, he let his eyes peek open just a crack. To his surprise he wasn't in some kind of prison or torture room; he was lying in bed in the room at the back of his shop.

Impossible!

Closing his eyes again, he tried to dig up memories from the delirium that had gripped him the past few days. He could remember the Pontiff's speaking to him, but he couldn't recall her torturing him.

Maybe she didn't. I don't seem to be injured or in pain beyond the expected withdrawal symptoms.

He vaguely remembered the Pontiff taking him from his cell, carrying him over her shoulder like a sack of flour as she leapt from rooftop to rooftop.

Did that really happen, or was it part of some bizarre fever dream?

There was a man, he suddenly recalled. He and the Pontiff fought. And then a woman. There was something familiar about her ...

No! It couldn't be. She's gone. It had to be a dream.

But then how did he end up back in his shop?

"Drink this," a woman said, placing a cup up to his lips.

They're trying to drug me to make me talk!

He clamped his lips together and turned his head away.

"You always told me healers make the worst patients," the woman told him. "Now quit being childish and drink!"

Methodis opened his eyes to see Scythe's olive-skinned face hovering over him. The woman sitting on his bed was no longer the fifteen-year-old girl she'd been when he last saw her, but her eyes still had the same spark and spirit he'd seen on the day she was born. She had grown into a beautiful young lady though there was an edge to her features and a hardness in her gaze that made her seem older than he knew she was.

"They told me you were gone," Methodis said, his dry throat making his raspy voice crack.

"I came back," she answered curtly. "Now drink!"

He took a small sip from the cup, and a cool, syrupy liquid dribbled across his tongue.

"Good?" she asked.

"A little more," he said, and this time the words didn't hurt to speak.

This time he drank deeply, letting the elixir coat and soothe his aching throat. But his relief quickly vanished when he remembered the danger they were in.

"You have to go, Scythe," he warned her. "The Order is looking for me!"

"Not anymore," she told him. "They've been driven from the city. Most of the Inquisitors and Seers are dead. Including the Pontiff."

"You killed her," Methodis said, as random images bubbled up from his memory.

"She deserved to die," Scythe told him. "I'm just sorry we couldn't get to you sooner."

Scythe stood up and set the cup on the small table beside the bed.

"When I think of what they did to you . . ."

She trailed off, but Methodis could see the emotions churning inside her.

So much anger. So much hate.

"I'm okay, Scythe," he assured her, sitting up in his bed. "They didn't hurt me."

"You don't have to worry about sparing my feelings," she told him. "If you tell me what they did, we can start trying to help you."

"They didn't do anything," he said, laughing. But this time his chuckle wasn't a mad giggle; it was warm and natural. "I gave myself an overdose of bliss-wort before they grabbed me."

"No wonder you look terrible," she said, clearly relieved. "I'll go find you some golden-stem extract to settle your stomach."

"You still remember your lessons," Methodis said, grinning. "I'm impressed."

"If that impresses you, wait until you hear the rest of what I have to tell you," Scythe told him.

Then she bent down and gave him a fierce hug, squeezing so tight he actually thought he might pass out.

"Scythe," he gasped, "this is no way to treat a patient."

She loosened her grip and gave him a soft kiss on the forehead.

"Sorry. I'm just so happy to have you back; I don't ever want to let you go.

"I'll go get you some golden-stem," she promised as she headed out toward the front of the shop. "And then we need to talk about Cassandra."

She disappeared before Methodis could say anything, but a thousand questions suddenly exploded in his head.

What kind of trouble have you gotten yourself into this time, my little Spirit?

Cassandra had never visited the Western Isles; few in the Southlands had. However, it wasn't distance that kept them relatively isolated from the mainland. Most vessels could make the journey in ten or twelve days. Bo-Shing's enchanted ship took half that time, its dormant magic roaring to life once they hit the open sea.

But on the first day after leaving Callastan the storms began, buffeting and battering *The Chaos Runner*. Mornings were usually calm, but by afternoon the winds would rise and heaving waves would toss their vessel for hours on end, causing Cassandra's stomach to disgorge its contents dozens of times. The storms would continue well into the night, leaving Bo-Shing and his men little time for sleep as they battled to stay afloat and on course.

When they finally reached Pellturna—the Western Isles' infamous pirate port—Cassandra had been only too glad to drop anchor. It seemed a miracle they had made it, and she couldn't even imagine making the journey in an unenchanted vessel.

The storms wouldn't be as strong for ordinary vessels, Rexol had pointed out. *The Chaos that drives the ship forward comes with a price.*

Despite the knowledge that the backlash from Bo-Shing's ship was unleashing terrible storms, Cassandra was eager to resume their journey as quickly as possible. But two days had passed since their arrival at Pellturna, and Bo-Shing showed no signs of wanting to leave anytime soon.

The city—if it could even be called that—was little more than a collection of ramshackle buildings built along the water's edge of a sheltered cove. The inhabitants couldn't even be bothered to maintain a dock: Visitors on larger ships had to drop anchor in the cove and come ashore in rowboats with a shallow enough draw to land directly on the beach.

The entire commerce of Pellturna was built on satisfying the vices of unscrupulous sailors: sex, alcohol, and mind-altering plants and herbs were all readily available for the right price. As Cassandra had no interest in such things, she hadn't bothered to leave the ship. Unlike Bo-Shing and the rest of the pirates, who spent virtually all of their time visiting the local brothels.

They know there is something foul on this ship, Rexol said. *An evil presence. I can feel it!*

Cassandra had gotten used to the mage's paranoid ranting, so she paid him little attention. If anything, he was probably just sensing the Chaos that fueled Bo-Shing's vessel. And the pirates' prolonged absence didn't require some sinister explanation; they were simply filthy beasts eager to satisfy their carnal desires.

The only one in the crew who didn't seem determined to catch some kind of venereal disease was Tork, the navigator. Bo-Shing had told her that Tork possessed the far-sight. Cassandra still wasn't clear on exactly what that meant, but he was clearly suffering from some kind of mental imbalance. While the others engaged in their debauched revelries on land, he seemed content to putter about *The Chaos Runner*, talking to himself.

He didn't even seem to realize Cassandra was there unless she addressed him directly; he was lost in his own private world. On a few occasions she had tried to speak with him about their destination. But whenever she asked about the island or Keystone, he would smile, shake his head, and give her the exact same answer.

"It lies beyond the Kraken's Eye. On the edge of the world. You'll see soon enough."

Her frustration had grown to the point where she had decided to venture out into Pellturna herself. She didn't have a boat to take her to shore, but it was close enough she was confident she could make it if she swam.

She made her way up to the main deck. Before she could dive into the water, however, she sensed Bo-Shing and several others returning to the ship. A second later her ears picked up the sound of several voices loudly singing off-key. The captain stood in the bow of a rickety rowboat as Shoji and several other pirates manned the oars, swaying from side to side despite the calm waters as he led his crew in drunken song.

When they reached *The Chaos Runner* they clambered up the cargo nets draped over the side of the hull, displaying impressive agility considering their inebriated state. Seeing her waiting for them, Shoji laughed and threw his arms wide as he stumbled toward her.

"A kissh from my fav'ritest lady," he slurred.

Cassandra was in no mood for foolishness. She met his clumsy advance with an angry shove, sending him sprawling hard to the deck. Bo-Shing and the others burst out laughing, doubling over with alcohol-fueled mirth.

"Glad to see you finally made it back," Cassandra said.

"Been up for two days straight," the captain told her. "And only a fool sleeps in Pellturna. Good way to wake up robbed of all your clothes and your throat slit wide open."

Cassandra didn't bother to point out the fact that anyone with a slit throat wouldn't wake up at all. "I hope by morning you're sober enough to sail," she snapped instead.

"Why?" Bo-Shing asked, seeming genuinely surprised. "Are we going somewhere?"

"Back into town," Shoji called out from where he still lay on the deck. "Soon as we're rested!"

"You promised to take me to the Keystone!" Cassandra reminded them. "We had a deal!"

"But I never said when we'd get there, did I?" Bo-Shing countered. "You need to learn to negotiate better," he added, his voice rising to be heard over the laughter of his crew.

"You know what I can do if you make me angry," Cassandra warned him, her voice low and menacing.

Unfortunately, Bo-Shing still had enough of his wits about him to call her bluff. "You do anything to me and you lose the only captain who can get you where you need to go," he told her with a satisfied smirk.

When she didn't have an immediate comeback, Bo-Shing turned away and stumbled across the top deck, heading for the steps that led down to his private cabin. The other pirates dispersed, staggering off in various directions to find somewhere to sleep. Shoji simply closed his eyes and lay where he had fallen, snoring almost immediately.

Cassandra followed Bo-Shing down the steps and into his room, shutting the door behind her.

Use the Crown! Rexol urged. *Break his spirit! Bend his mind to your will!*

She'd gotten so used to ignoring him that she barely even registered his words. Bo-Shing looked over at her curiously, then shrugged and began to strip off his clothes.

"What are you doing?" she demanded.

"I sleep naked," he said. "Feel free to get naked, too," he offered, tossing his shirt into a corner.

"Methodis told me about your case of root rot," Cassandra said. "If we don't leave here tomorrow, I'll tell the entire crew how you failed as a man."

"Without the healer around to back up your story," he said as he dropped onto his bed and yanked off his boots, "do you really think they'll believe you?"

"Is that a chance you're willing to take?" she asked.

"I think it is," he answered with a smile.

For a brief instant she considered telling him what was really at stake: the Legacy, the Slayer's return, the fate of the entire world. But she couldn't bring herself to say the words out loud.

Is that because I know he wouldn't care or because I think he wouldn't believe me?

On some level, Cassandra wasn't even sure she believed it herself. Preparing their flight from Callastan, she had managed to convince herself that bringing the Crown to the Keystone was the right thing to do. Now, however, she wasn't sure.

At one time she'd been certain this was her destiny, and she'd embraced it. But looking back, she couldn't help but feel somewhat helpless. She'd fled the Monastery with the Crown, hoping the Guardian would take it from her when she reached his lair beyond the edge of the mountains of the Frozen East. But in the end he'd pushed her away. Then she'd fled across the Southlands, hunted by the Minions and the Order.

Her vision of the Keystone had momentarily given her a true sense of purpose, but the time spent languishing in Pellturna had dulled its edge. In reality, little had changed. She was still alone and on the run. She hadn't really chosen her path; it had been thrust upon her.

"You got something else to say, sweetie?" Bo-Shing asked. "Or you just going to watch as I strip down?"

It doesn't matter if I chose this path or not, Cassandra realized. *I'm on it now, and I have to see it through to the end.*

"You promised to take me to the Keystone," Cassandra said. "We're leaving tomorrow. If we don't, I promise you will regret it."

"I don't respond well to threats," Bo-Shing replied, giving her a wink and fumbling with the drawstring of his trousers.

"Sleep on it," Cassandra advised, turning to go before he started removing his pants. "You might feel differently once you're sober."

The spell that kept Orath hidden in the shadows was beginning to fade. The Chaos that fueled the ship helped mask his presence, but it wouldn't be long until Cassandra sensed him lurking in the cargo hold.

Orath wasn't about to suffer the same fate as the Crawling Twins. While the monk was on the top deck confronting the pirates, he slithered through the porthole and scuttled along the side of the ship's hull.

When Cassandra left the captain's cabin and returned to her own quarters, Orath slowly climbed up the side of the ship and onto the top deck. It was empty except for a single snoring pirate.

The last of the Minions slipped down the stairs and headed toward the captain's quarters. He slipped open the door and approached the sleeping pirate. Just like Cassandra, Orath was eager for them to reach the Keystone. Unlike the young woman, however, he was willing to take action.

Raven had mastered the art of disguise and impersonation; of all the Minions she had been the most skilled at transforming herself into another being. Orath favored a more subtle approach. As with the Danaan Queen, he preferred to manipulate and control his subjects rather than become them. But in this case he couldn't hover at Bo-Shing's side giving him orders.

There were other ways to exert control, however. Wrapping his arms tightly around his own body, Orath began a soft chant. His whispered words were little more than a hiss as he called upon the Chaos. His flesh quivered as his transformation began. Within seconds his tall form had become completely incorporeal; he was no longer a physical being of flesh and blood, but a figure made of dense black mist.

The mist began to shift, the outline of Orath's form dissolving into a cloud that hovered over Bo-Shing before slowly crawling down his throat.

The next morning there was much grumbling and complaining when the captain ordered his men to weigh anchor. But nobody—not even Cassandra—suspected the truth.

Bo-Shing was gone. His body was little more than an empty shell of skin, everything beneath eaten away from the inside so Orath could wear it like a cloak.

Chapter 27

THE ORDER HAD been driven from Callastan. The few Inquisitors who'd survived the attack had fled, as had many of the soldiers fighting with them. Many more had simply thrown down their weapons and surrendered during the battle, utterly demoralized by a combination of the forces uniting against them and the power of Daemron's Sword.

I felt that power myself for a while, Keegan thought, remembering the odd sensation of using two of the Slayer's Talismans simultaneously. Jerrod had been right: They balanced each other out. But Keegan had also felt a powerful synergy between them: Together, they were even greater than the sum of each individual part.

With the Pontiff slain, there was no longer a clear ruler of the city. Most of the nobles had fled during the Order's initial attack, abandoning the ordinary citizens to fend for themselves. The various crime lords who had stayed and joined in the fight were eager to divide up and lay claim to the various districts, but so far the presence of the Free City armies had limited their efforts to petitions and negotiations rather than violence.

I hope Captain Jendarme is as capable as Vaaler claims, Keegan thought.

The leader of Cheville's forces had been given the difficult task of maintaining order within the city streets until a proper ruling body could be established. Over the first two days an uneasy truce had held inside the city walls, the natives and their liberators existing peacefully side by side.

Keegan knew the current situation was precarious. Technically Jendarme and his troops were an occupying force. Eventually they would want to return home, and the people of Callastan would want them gone. Smoothly turning over power to a responsible authority when they left would be no easy task.

I can't worry about that right now, he reminded himself. *There are more important things to focus on.*

Taking charge as he so often did, Vaaler had organized an impromptu council to address the real issue: what to do about Cassandra and the Crown. He'd offered to delay the meeting another day or two, concerned about Keegan's health after seeing the toll that summoning the mystical fog had taken on his friend. But they'd already lost enough time, and the young wizard had insisted on pushing forward as quickly as possible.

Now Keegan and everyone else who knew anything about the Keystone had gathered together in the spacious, and currently abandoned, council chambers of Callastan's city hall.

Vaaler and Shalana were both there, sitting close together. Clearly their relationship had progressed into something more than friendship during the war against the Danaan, and Keegan was happy for his friend.

Andar and several other Danaan were also present; Keegan still found it hard to think of them as allies after all that had happened. But if Vaaler was willing to vouch for them, he wasn't going to turn them away.

Jerrod had also joined them, limping across the room to take a seat on the side of the table beside Keegan, opposite Vaaler and the others. Scythe had used the Sword to heal the worst of the monk's injuries, but he was still moving stiffly as he recovered from the brutal beating he'd received at the Pontiff's hands.

Scythe and Methodis had been the last to arrive, the healer

moving slowly and leaning on the young woman for support. She hadn't left his side ever since rescuing him from the Pontiff. Keegan had never seen her so protective of someone, not even Norr.

She needed this, he thought. *She needed to remember that there are things in this world worth saving.*

Once everyone was seated, Vaaler was quick to get things going.

"We all know why we are here," he said, dispatching with formality by not bothering to rise from his seat as he spoke. "We all understand what is at stake."

Keegan noticed his eyes flick over toward Methodis as he spoke. Scythe answered with a barely imperceptible nod, confirming she had already explained their mission to the healer.

"You need to find Cassandra," Methodis agreed. "And Scythe has assured me you mean her no harm."

"She has to be stopped," Jerrod said. "Hopefully we can convince her of this. If not, I do not know what will happen to her."

Keegan frowned at the monk's brutal honesty, but it didn't seem to bother Methodis.

"I would help you if I could," he said. "But you already know as much as I do.

"She was looking for passage to a remote island marked by a massive black obelisk."

"It's called the Keystone," Keegan said. "It's where the Old Gods created the Legacy."

"Scythe has told me of your quest," the old healer assured him. "But though I helped Cassandra escape the city, I do not know how to find the island. Bo-Shing claimed he would take us there, but he never divulged the location to me."

"I think there is enough information in the ancient Danaan texts for us to find the Keystone," Andar said.

"Even if you're right," Methodis objected, "you'll never catch her. There is no ship faster than *The Chaos Runner.* Bo-Shing might already be there."

"If that was true, the Legacy would no longer be standing," Jerrod insisted. "We still have time to stop her."

"You said there was another way to get there," Keegan said, addressing Vaaler. "Using magic."

"It might be possible to create a portal to cross the Burning Sea in a fraction of the time it would take by ship," he agreed. "But as I warned, the ritual is incredibly dangerous."

"When the ancient wizards used Old Magic to bend the laws of space and time," Andar explained, "they could only travel to a place they had visited many times before."

"None of us has ever been to the Keystone," Scythe noted.

"I've been there in my dreams," Keegan reminded her.

"It's not the same," she insisted.

"No," Vaaler agreed. "It's not. But Andar and I have been studying the passages that reference the Keystone. It may have properties that will make it easier to create a portal that leads to it."

"The Keystone isn't just where the Legacy was born," Andar explained. "It's the foundation the Old Gods used to create the entire world."

"It's the nexus where our world and the Burning Sea connect," Vaaler added. "If we imagine all of our physical reality as a map, then the Keystone would be the zero coordinate."

"Using this, can you open a portal to the Keystone?" Jerrod asked.

"I can't," Vaaler answered. "But I can show Keegan how.

"As I mentioned before, Rexol had me transcribe numerous accounts of wizards who attempted it. The details of the ritual are complex, but I think I remember them well enough to re-create them accurately."

"Quit being modest," Shalana told him. "You never forget anything."

Keegan knew it was true. During the time they both served under Rexol Vaaler had always been the better student. The arcane words and symbols needed to channel Chaos into a specific spell had come easily to him despite the irony that he himself had no magical ability whatsoever.

"How long will it take?" Keegan asked.

"Probably two days to make all the preparations," Vaaler estimated. "Will you be ready by then?"

A fair question.

Just the thought of attempting to summon Chaos again—to try to control the power of the Ring so soon after his last ordeal—brought on a fresh wave of exhaustion. But there was no other who could do this, and they were running out of time.

"I'll be ready," Keegan promised.

"You won't have to do this alone," Andar promised. "I and the other Danaan mages will stand with you. You can draw on our power to help sustain yourself."

"How many can pass through this portal?" Jerrod asked.

"In all the accounts I've read, only the wizard who created it," Vaaler admitted. "But in theory it should be possible to bring along another though it will make the ritual even more dangerous."

"Speaking in my professional capacity," Methodis chimed in, addressing the monk, "you're in no physical state to go with him anyway."

"I'm not the one who needs to go," he answered, and all eyes turned to Scythe.

Keegan saw her jaw clench, and he spoke up quickly before she could reply.

"I'll go alone. I've carried both the Ring and the Sword before."

"Don't be stupid!" Scythe snarled. "The Sword is my burden, not yours. I'm coming with you."

"This is not the time for foolish bravery, Scythe," Methodis chided. "There are others more suited to this than you."

"I thought you told him everything," Vaaler said.

Scythe shot him a fierce glare. Then her face softened as she turned to Methodis.

"Keegan and I share a powerful bond. It's hard to explain, but it's real. Our fates are bound together. I can't let him face this alone."

To his credit, Methodis didn't argue or protest. Whether that was because he simply accepted what she said, or whether he simply knew her well enough to realize she was too stubborn to change her mind, Keegan couldn't say.

"Then it's decided," Jerrod declared. "Vaaler will prepare the ritual, and Keegan and Scythe will go through the portal and fulfill their destiny."

And if we fail, Keegan silently added, *the entire world is doomed.*

Methodis didn't speak as Scythe escorted him back to his shop. Despite their years apart, she knew him well enough to see that he was carefully considering everything he'd heard at the meeting.

"I'm sorry I didn't tell you everything," she said. "I didn't want to overwhelm you."

"It's all a bit much to take in at once," he agreed.

Scythe was relieved there was no hint of anger or disappointment in his voice. But she picked up on his concern.

"I'll be okay," she promised.

"You always say that," Methodis reminded her. "Even when it's not true."

"I have to do this," she said.

"You really believe this is your destiny, don't you?" he asked, smiling softly.

"After all that has happened, I'd be a fool to deny it."

"I care about you, Scythe," he said, "but you're not a child anymore. You don't need my permission to do this."

"No," she admitted. "But I'd like your approval."

"I'm still not sure what I think of all this," Methodis said. "I need time to process it.

"But I trust your judgment, Scythe. If you believe this is something you have to do, then do it with my blessing."

Scythe smiled and took hold of Methodis's arm, wrapping herself around it. He wasn't a tall man, so she was able to rest her head on his shoulder as they walked.

She closed her eyes, allowing herself to slip back into her youth, when Methodis would hold her close, making her feel safe from whatever the world could throw at her.

After a few minutes of comfortable silence, Methodis spoke again.

"You said you and Keegan share a bond."

"We were both born under the Blood Moon," Scythe said, choosing her words carefully as they walked slowly down the street arm in arm. "We are both Children of Fire, each touched by Chaos in our own way. And we share a destiny to save the world."

"I wonder if there's more to it than that," he said.

"Isn't that enough?"

"You clearly care about him," Methodis told her, meeting her evasions with bluntness. "But I can see you fighting against your feelings."

Scythe lifted her head from his shoulder and let go of his arm.

"I lost someone very close to me recently," she answered tersely. "I need time to grieve."

"We need to grieve to heal," the old healer agreed. "But don't use your grief as an excuse."

"An excuse?"

Methodis stepped in front of her and turned to face her, forc-ing her to stop in her tracks.

"I think you're afraid, Scythe," he said, his words earnest but not harsh. "You lost someone you cared about. Now you won't let yourself care about Keegan because you're afraid you'll lose him, too.

"But shutting him out isn't the answer. If you close yourself off as a shield against pain, you'll never know happiness."

"It's too soon," Scythe insisted. "We've been through a lot, but Norr's only been gone a few weeks. I can't just run off and seek comfort in the arms of someone else."

"Why not?"

"It's . . . it's not appropriate."

Methodis chuckled softly. "I've never known you to be 'appro-priate,' Scythe. The pain of his loss might still be fresh, but if being with someone else helps you feel better, you shouldn't fight against it."

"It's more complicated than that," Scythe said, stepping around him and resuming her methodical pace.

"It always is," Methodis said, falling back into step beside her. "But you know me; I can't help sticking my nose in where it doesn't belong."

"I'm supposed to help Keegan save the world," Scythe contin-ued, the words coming out in an unexpected flood. "But nobody has any clue how that's going to happen!"

"And you think you know?"

"What if he has to sacrifice himself? What if Keegan's destiny is to become a martyr to save the world? What if I have to help him do it?"

"All the more reason not to shut him out now," Methodis said gently. "If you only have a short time left, you must make the most of it."

He didn't say anything else, he just walked along with her.

Keegan's not the only one who might become a martyr, she thought, but she didn't have the courage to say the words aloud.

After a few more strides she once again took his arm and laid her head on his shoulder. She still wasn't sure what to do about Keegan, but Methodis was right about one thing: If time was short, she was determined to make the most of her last moments.

Chapter 28

The Chaos Runner's prow knifed through the storm-tossed sea, riding the waves like a living creature. With each rising swell, it seemed to gain momentum despite the ferocious headwinds, leaping forward as the crest broke to attack the next surge.

Cassandra stood on the top deck, braving the wind and rain as Bo-Shing relentlessly drove his vessel through the gale. Any triumph she might have felt at convincing the captain to leave Pellturna had long since been swept away by the storm. She clutched tightly at a length of rope wrapped around her wrist and lashed to the foremast, the mainsail above her pulled taut by the howling wind. The sack with the Crown was secured tightly at her back, tugging at her shoulders with each angry gust.

While his captain manned the wheel, Shoji shouted orders at the crew, his voice barely rising above the screaming of the squall.

That's not his captain, Rexol said. *It's a demon!*

Cassandra was too focused on settling her heaving stomach to argue with him. Knowing that the fierce storms were caused by the backlash of their enchanted ship had actually helped her deal with her nausea—for the first two days after leaving Pellturna she'd been able to keep her food down. But the storms opposing them had grown steadily worse, and this morning she hadn't even tried to eat.

She saw Tork coming toward her, his gait calm as his body

naturally rolled with every wild pitch and cant of the ship. The storm pummeling *The Chaos Runner* didn't seem to bother him. Based on his demeanor, Cassandra wondered if he even noticed it at all.

"The Kraken's Eye!" he shouted in her ear once he drew close. "I told you you'd see!"

Pushing out with her awareness, Cassandra saw that the tempest that assailed them was only the edge of the weather front. The sky above them was already dark and hard and cold rain pelted them like stones thrown from the sky. But ahead the clouds were pitch-black and the deluge was like a solid wall of water.

But Cassandra barely registered the monsoon they were bearing down on. Instead, her focus went to the massive cluster of whirlpools and maelstroms dead ahead. The largest was easily fifty feet across, a whirling vortex crawling across the ocean like a hungry maw. A dozen more, each large enough to swallow the ship on its own, circled slowly around it in seemingly random patterns.

Every few seconds, whirling waterspouts shot up and danced atop the surface before crashing back down with enough force to snap a ship in half. The largest waves crested at well over fifty feet, and Cassandra knew a broadside hit from even one of those monsters would surely sink *The Chaos Runner*.

"We're not seriously going through that, are we?" she shouted.

"Your island is on the other side," Tork answered. Then he smiled. "Done it before. Once."

With that he turned and headed toward Bo-Shing, moving with the same preternatural calm. He reached the captain's side and began giving quick, curt instructions. Bo-Shing never hesitated and never questioned him. With each order, he spun the wheel exactly as Tork demanded.

Cassandra wrapped the rope around her wrist a few more times to guard against a rogue wave sweeping her overboard as they plunged headlong into the Kraken's Eye.

"Twenty-eight degrees to port! Sixteen to starboard! Thirty-seven to starboard. Twelve to port!"

Orath struggled to keep up with Tork's shouted instructions, the ship's wheel fighting against his efforts to constantly change course in the raging waters. When he had devoured Bo-Shing, some of what the man was—including his skill as a sailor—was preserved, passing into Orath's mind. But though he had the technical knowledge, he lacked the pirate's natural instinct and years of experience. Without them, the Minion feared, they'd be swallowed by the sea.

Cassandra and the Crown stood on the deck behind him; so close he could feel the Talisman's power thrumming in his chest above the fury of the storm. For a moment he considered letting the ship sink: If *The Chaos Runner* went down, maybe he could get his hands on the Crown before it plunged to the bottom of the ocean.

But what if Cassandra survives the wreckage? Don't underestimate her like the others did!

"Hard to port! Hard to port!"

He cast the plan aside even as Tork barked out a new course, forcing him to turn the wheel hard to the left. Calling out orders with Bo-Shing's voice, he relayed every new change of direction to the crew, leaving it to Shoji to see that they trimmed the sails and manned the rigging to keep them on course.

Ahead of them a waterspout erupted skyward, then smashed back down like an angry fist, narrowly missing the ship. Had they not changed course, they would have been directly in its path.

Tork can see what is coming before it happens. He can guide us through to the other side!

If they failed, Orath realized, it wouldn't be because of the navigator. The weakest link in the crew was the false captain. If he failed to react to Tork's commands—if he was too slow, or he turned the wheel too far and they missed their mark—all would be lost.

"Sixty-two degrees to starboard!"

Orath knew it was dangerous to summon Chaos this close to Cassandra, even with the terrors of the Kraken's Eye drawing most of her attention. If she noticed what he was doing, she would unleash the full power of the Crown against him. But if he did nothing, they wouldn't survive much longer.

Drawing on the reservoir of Chaos he'd gathered from feasting on the blood of the Inquisitors, Orath reached out to the magical essence imbued within the ship itself. He felt the touch of Old Magic, trapped within the hull, and opened himself up to it.

The Chaos Runner was a creature of the sea. It understood the ocean in ways no sailor ever could—not even Bo-Shing. By forging a connection with the remarkable ship, Orath suddenly became more skilled than any captain since the Cataclysm.

"Forty degrees to port!" Tork bellowed.

Orath reacted with uncanny speed and perfect precision. The crew pulled on the ropes as they tacked hard, and the ship veered just in time to avoid being sucked down into one of the whirlpools that had unexpectedly spun off from the main constellation.

"Sixty degrees starboard!" Tork shouted, and Orath dutifully spun the wheel again, all thoughts of Cassandra and the Crown pushed from his mind as he battled the angry sea.

Keegan kept the hood of his cloak up as he approached the ritual grounds, hoping it would hide his nervousness. Vaaler had spent the past two days meticulously preparing the location: a testament to how complicated and dangerous the spell he was about to attempt could be.

He didn't want to die in a final blaze of uncontrolled Chaos, but that wasn't what he feared most.

They're all counting on me, he thought, staring out at the faces of the friends and allies who'd gathered to wish him well. *They're all looking at me to save them. And what if I can't?*

Scythe was there, too, of course. She wore her typical outfit: tight black trousers and a sleeveless leather vest. The exposed flesh of her face and arms was covered with temporary tattoos that mirrored Keegan's own, painstakingly drawn by the Danaan sorcerers working off Vaaler's instructions.

As he saw Scythe standing there a new fear crept into his mind. It wasn't just his own life he was risking with this ritual.

"You don't have to do this," he told her. "You can give me the Sword and stay behind to look after Methodis."

"Maybe you should be the one to stay behind," she shot back. "Just give me the Ring and send me through the portal."

"You're not a mage," Keegan reminded her. "You've had no training. You don't know how to use the Ring."

"And you're no warrior," she reminded him. "And believe me—you have no clue how to properly use the Sword. So I guess we better just accept that we both need to do this. Together."

She smiled at him, and he felt some of his anxiousness slip away.

"I know you're scared, Keegan," she whispered, leaning in close. "So am I. But I believe in you. I know you can do this."

For an instant, Keegan thought about trying to kiss her again. Fortunately, he resisted the urge. Scythe was a friend, nothing more. But somehow, that was enough.

"I bet you would have made an incredible Chaos mage if you possessed the gift," he told her, returning her smile.

"Save it," she said though not overly harshly. "Everyone's waiting for us."

It was hard to tell for sure, given her complexion and the markings scrawled on her face, but Keegan thought she was blushing.

They stepped forward to where Vaaler was waiting to usher them into their assigned positions.

"You both know what you have to do?" Vaaler asked.

"I just have to stand still and shut up," Scythe answered. "Wish me luck."

"What about you, Keegan. Are you ready?"

"I am," he said.

Vaaler reached out and grabbed them both in a fierce hug.

"I believe in you," he told them before stepping back to stand beside Shalana and Jerrod beyond the edge of the ritual grounds.

"I believe in us, too," Scythe whispered, taking his hand.

The ritual ground covered most of the large cobblestone courtyard inside the city hall's main gates. Over the past two days, Vaaler and the Danaan wizards had transformed the bare stones into a map of the entire known world. The ground along the North Wall had crudely drawn trees to represent the North Forest, while scattered handfuls of coarse sand marked the edges of the Southern Desert. Blocky triangles traced in charcoal reflected the mountains bordering the Frozen East, and a series of curved wavy lines stood for the Western Sea, with a smattering of small circles serving as the Western Isles.

Each of the Seven Capitals of the Southlands was drawn onto the map, as was Callastan. That's where Keegan and Scythe now stood, surrounded by a perfect circle traced in ash. Vaaler had drawn a thick line from Callastan across the imaginary ocean, through the Western Isles and ending at another circle on the far edge of the map. Rexol's gorgon-headed staff stood upright inside the circle, supported by a small stand. Visually it made a suitable representation of the Keystone itself, but more practically, incorporating the powerful staff into the ritual would allow it to be a catalyst for the spell.

He wasn't the only mage who would be invoking the spell. Just outside the map several more circles had been drawn. Inside each one stood a Danaan wizard, including Andar himself. Like Keegan and Scythe, their skin had been covered with symbols to help ward them against the Chaos they were about to summon.

As one, Andar and the others began to chant. For two days they had practiced the incantation Vaaler had given them, and the strange words rolled smoothly off their tongues.

"Lev. Ull. Fer. Shi. Lev. Ull. Fer. Shi."

To his surprise, Keegan recognized the words from his training under Rexol: North, south, east, and west in the Old Tongue.

Stay focused!

As the rhythmic chant continued, the glyphs on Keegan's skin began to tingle. Chaos was gathering, summoned by the combined efforts of the Danaan mages.

Keegan didn't join them; his role was not to summon the Chaos but to draw it into himself, concentrating the power of many into one. He felt the familiar heat of the blue flames building up inside him, and he slipped on the Ring he'd been clutching in his hand.

A tower of blue fire suddenly leapt up around him and Scythe, but the protective circle kept the flames from devouring them. He could feel her tense up beside him, fighting her instinctive response to flee the unnatural conflagration.

Stay focused!

"Lev. Ull. Fer. Shi. Lev. Ull. Fer. Shi."

Augmented by the Ring, the Chaos flowing through him became an unstoppable torrent. But instead of fighting to control it, Keegan let it pass through him and out into the ritual grounds.

The pillar of fire around them grew higher, and a line of flames slowly began to trace its way along the line from Callastan to the Keystone. Keegan struggled to stay calm, resisting the urge to seize the Chaos and try to control it with his will. At this stage of the spell, he was still merely a conduit.

"Lev. Ull. Fer. Shi. Lev. Ull. Fer. Shi."

The line of flames finally reached Rexol's staff, and the empty eye sockets of the gorgon's skull glowed with a fierce green flame. Scythe gasped beside him, and for an instant his concentration wavered as his head turned in response to the sound.

Blue fire leapt from the pillar, engulfing him and Cassandra and spreading rapidly across the map in all directions. He heard Vaaler shouting, his voice panicked. The chant of the Danaan mages had dissolved into cries of pain and fear.

Go! Keegan screamed inside his mind. *Go now!*

The world beyond the edges of the map suddenly vanished into empty darkness. The pillar of blue flame lifted him and Scythe high into the air, and she clutched at his arm.

Keegan ignored the contact, his mind focused entirely on the spell, just as Vaaler had told him. He was no longer just a conduit; now the Chaos was his to control!

Far below them the map began to grow in size. The crude representations of trees and mountains transformed into reality, growing to true scale in a matter of seconds. The wavy lines became an ocean stretching out before them, and Rexol's staff metamorphosed into a massive black obelisk sending up a beam of pure white light to the heavens.

The Keystone!

Focusing on his destination, Keegan wrapped an arm around Scythe's waist, then willed himself toward it. Suddenly they were flying through the air, hurtling toward a tiny island on the far end of the world, propelled along by a massive wave of Chaos.

We're going to make it! Cassandra thought.

The worst of the Kraken's Eye was behind them. They had reached the farthest edge of the whirlpools and the storm; somehow, Tork and Bo-Shing had brought *The Chaos Runner* safely through.

Through the ebbing rain she could see clear skies and smooth waters ahead. In the distance, the Keystone jutted up from a tiny island, shining in her Sight like a beacon.

The ship suddenly bucked as they were hit by a massive wave. But this was not spawned by the sea; as it rolled over them Cassandra recognized the terrifying power of Old Magic.

What did you do? she lashed out at Rexol.

That was not me, the wizard protested.

Tork had stopped shouting orders at the captain. His expression of perpetual calm was gone, replaced by a look of abject terror.

"The Sleeper awakes!" he shouted.

Even as the words left his mouth, Cassandra felt it rising from the depths—a Chaos Spawn so ancient and monstrous the Old Gods had never let it touch the land. Her awareness recoiled from it, refusing to allow her mind to picture fully the horror that was coming for them. Instead, her mind was assaulted with a collage of rapid-fire images: hundreds of wriggling, writhing tendrils attached to a body of immense size reaching up from the depths toward them.

Reeling, her attention fell on Bo-Shing. It was only then that she realized something was very wrong with the captain.

He's hollow, she thought, struggling to comprehend what she was seeing. *And something is living inside him. Something dark and sinister.*

I tried to warn you! Rexol shouted.

Before her dazed mind could make sense of what was happening with the captain, the beast from below struck. Dozens of long, suckered tentacles slithered across the deck of *The Chaos Runner.* Each was as thick around as a man's waist, but they moved with the speed of striking serpents. They snatched up half the crew in seconds and dragged them screaming down into the depths.

Shoji tried to run as another arm snaked its way from the water and lurched toward him. But the deck was covered in glistening slime left behind by the first wave of tentacles, and his feet flew out from under him. Cassandra cast aside the rope that lashed her to the mainmast and leapt toward him, grabbing his hand as the tentacle coiled around his ankle.

Suddenly they were both being dragged toward the edge of the deck. Cassandra managed to brace her feet against the ship's railing, calling on the Crown to give her the supernatural strength to hold on. But the man she was clinging to was made of ordinary flesh and blood, and he shrieked as his arm ripped free from his body and he vanished over the edge, leaving Cassandra holding nothing but a bloody stump.

Repulsed, she tossed the limb aside. Another swarm of the slimy, slithery appendages crawled up over the side, flailing about for more victims. Cassandra jumped clear as one grasped for her ankle, then scrambled up the mainmast to get clear as the few surviving crew members were taken.

Use the Crown! Rexol screamed inside her head.

This time she didn't argue. Instead, she slung the bag from her shoulder and pulled out the Talisman. Just before she placed it on her head a massive tentacle erupted from the deep, twenty feet in diameter and with suckers twice the size of a wagon's wheel. It wrapped itself around *The Chaos Runner* and snapped the hull in half with a single squeeze, sending up a shower of splintered wooden planks and beams.

The front half of the ship vanished; still in the clutches of the gigantic tentacle, it was instantly dragged below the surface. Fortunately for Cassandra she was on the other half, though it was sinking quickly.

She placed the Crown on her head, bracing herself for Rexol's attack. But the wizard didn't try to fight her this time; even he recognized the danger they were in.

A million sounds and images—the thoughts of every person in the mortal world—exploded in her head. But they were pushed aside almost instantly by the looming presence of a consciousness of unfathomable age and power.

Brushing up against the behemoth with her Sight earlier had temporarily stunned Cassandra. But now that she was wearing the Crown, she was no longer overwhelmed by the Chaos Spawn. As magnificent as it was, it was nothing compared to the omniscient power of the Crown.

Sleep, she thought, projecting her will toward the leviathan below. *You are not of this world! Return to the depths and sleep!*

The creature fought her at first; after eons of slumber it had no desire to resume its hibernation. But even the mightiest Chaos Spawn had to bow before the power of the Talisman. Reluctantly, the creature retreated back to the black abyss whence it came.

Still clinging to the mast of the sinking remains of the ship, Cassandra peered out across the water, looking in vain for other survivors.

It was only then that she realized how still the sea had become. The wake of the rising monster had carried them beyond the edges of the Kraken's Eye, leaving her alone on the calm waters a few miles from the island.

I can still reach the Keystone, she realized.

In that instant, Rexol tried to take control. She felt the wizard's consciousness explode into the forefront of her brain, shoving her own awareness aside as it tried to leap from the Crown and into her physical body. The mage had caught her off guard, and for a moment he had the upper hand in their struggle. But Cassandra had cast him out once before, and after a short but violent mental battle she reasserted control.

Ripping the Crown from her head, she let go of the mast as the second half of *The Chaos Runner* sank slowly out of sight. Alone, she bobbed in the calm waters, clutching the Crown in her hand as she tried to recover from Rexol's ambush.

She could see the island only a few miles away, but swimming to the distant shore was not an option. The back-to-back battles with Rexol and the Chaos Spawn had left her so exhausted she could barely keep herself afloat.

With the last of her strength, she managed to wrap her free arm around a shattered plank from *The Chaos Runner*'s hull floating nearby. She could sense there was still power trapped within the wood. If she could just hold on, it would eventually ride the currents and bring her safely into shore.

And what then? Rexol wondered, but Cassandra was too angry with him—and too drained—to answer.

Chapter 29

KEEGAN INSTINCTIVELY BRACED himself for impact as the Keystone rushed toward them, wrapping his arm even more tightly around Scythe's waist as they hurtled through the sky. But they didn't swoop down and land at its base like Gods descending from on high. Instead, the world around them began to blur as they neared their destination and their pace rapidly slowed.

A shimmering blue veil fell over everything, growing brighter until it became so intense Keegan was forced to squeeze his eyes shut. Then his ears popped, and suddenly he could feel that he was standing on solid ground again. Opening his eyes, he saw the black obelisk towering above them, exactly as it had appeared in his vision.

"Look down," Scythe whispered.

Below their feet was a shimmering blue circle roughly four feet across—the same size as the one on Vaaler's map, where their journey had begun. Though translucent, they couldn't see the ground beneath it. It appeared to be a glowing hole plunging down into infinity, but somehow he and Scythe didn't fall through even though they were standing right on top of it.

Keegan gave Scythe a nod and let his arm drop from her waist. Taking a deep breath, she hopped out of the glowing circle and onto the ordinary-looking ground beyond its edge. Keegan joined her a second later.

Even after they had left it, the strange glowing circle remained—a magic portal, open and waiting just for them.

Only you and Scythe can use the portal, Vaaler had explained. *Nobody else will even be able to see it. To return, simply step inside and imagine yourself back in Callastan. Once both of you pass through, it should seal itself behind you.*

"Where's Cassandra?" Scythe asked, taking quick stock of their surroundings.

There wasn't anyplace on the island to hide. Scattered clumps of long, wispy grass that barely reached up to their knees were the only vegetation, and there were no large rock formations or hills. The only notable feature on the entire island was the Keystone itself. From where they were standing they could actually see all the way out to the ocean in every direction.

It can't be more than two miles across, Keegan thought. He made a slow turn, taking in the beach that formed a sandy ring around the entire perimeter of the island.

"She must not be here yet," Keegan said. "We beat her, thanks to Vaaler's spell!"

"I'd say it was your spell, not his," Scythe argued. "Vaaler may have planned it out, but you're the one who actually brought us here."

"If you say so," Keegan conceded modestly, though her words caused a burst of pride to swell inside him.

"I don't see a ship on the horizon," Scythe said, gazing back toward the east—the most likely direction of Cassandra's approach.

"I guess we just have to wait for her, then," Keegan answered uncertainly.

We were so intent on getting here in time to stop Cassandra from using the Crown, he realized, *that we never even thought about what we would actually do once we arrived.*

Scythe glanced back at the shimmering portal on the ground.

"How long will it stay open?" she wondered aloud.

"Vaaler wasn't sure," Keegan said. "He thinks a few days unless we use it first."

"What happens if Cassandra doesn't show before then?" Scythe asked. "Or if she doesn't show up at all? Do you have any idea how to fulfill Jerrod's prophecy and restore the Legacy?"

Keegan turned to look at the massive black obelisk, craning his neck as he let his gaze run all the way up the black stone until it reached the top. Neither the swirling shadows trapped inside the rock nor the strange symbols carved into its surface offered any immediate answers.

"She'll be here," he insisted, recalling his dreams. "And I think we'll know what to do when the time comes."

Orath felt the incredible weight of an entire ocean pressing in on him from all sides. He'd been clinging to the ship's wheel when the Chaos Spawn dragged the bow of *The Chaos Runner* down. As the ship went under the surface, he felt one of the smaller tentacles wrap itself around his ankle.

He struggled in vain to break free from the monstrous grip as he was pulled toward the ocean floor. And then suddenly the beast released him; driven back to its lair by the power of the Crown. He was free but still hundreds of feet below the surface.

At this depth there was no light, and the extreme pressure was more than most surface-dwelling creatures could survive. But Orath was strong enough to endure, for a few minutes at least.

Orath peeled away the living suit of Bo-Shing's skin, tearing the flesh away in long, sinewy strips. Summoning Chaos, he launched himself upward, cutting through the black water like an arrow shot toward the surface.

He was moving fast, but the surface was far, far away. His lungs began to burn; even a Minion needed to breathe. After what seemed like an eternity the darkness slowly receded as he reached a depth pierced by a few dim rays of the sun. The water around him turned from black to green and finally blue, even as his starving lungs screamed out in protest. Just when he thought they'd explode, he breached, his body instinctively gulping in air as fast as it could.

For several seconds he couldn't even think, his mind panicked by the terror of almost drowning. But the fear soon passed and Orath's composure returned. Though he couldn't see Cassandra or the Crown, he could feel the pull of the Talisman off in the distance, drifting slowly toward the island on the horizon.

Orath followed, swimming with long, powerful strokes.

Cassandra was struggling to stay conscious, her mind desperate to sleep so it could recover from her recent mental battles. Clinging to the plank from *The Chaos Runner*'s hull, she floated along in a haze.

When the tide finally brought her into the shallow waters near the island's shore, she didn't even open her eyes. Lacking the strength to stand, she let go of the wood and crawled through the shallow surf on her hands and knees, still clutching the Crown in one hand.

Tiny rocks scraped up her hands and knees, their sharp edges cutting through her clothes. But Cassandra wasn't even aware enough to register the pain. She scuttled forward like a blind crab until she reached the safety of the beach, then collapsed on the warm sand, the Crown finally slipping from her grasp.

"I see something!" Scythe shouted, peering out toward the beach.

Keegan followed her gaze but couldn't pick anything out on the horizon.

"Where?" he asked.

"Someone just crawled out of the ocean," Scythe said, her vision allowing her to pick out the figure at nearly a mile away. "It's Cassandra!"

She broke into a run, heading toward the beach. Keegan tried to follow but was quickly left far behind.

Scythe could see that Cassandra wasn't moving. The Crown lay beside her, the sunlight reflecting brightly off its shining surface.

Keegan was laboring along slowly behind her, but Scythe didn't slow. Cassandra might see them as an enemy; she might try to use her Talisman against them. But if Scythe could get to the Crown before Cassandra regained consciousness, she could nullify the threat.

She was still a quarter mile away when another figure rose from the waves. It was tall and thin, but its batlike features were clearly not human. It fixed its yellow eyes on Scythe as she rushed forward, then flicked them down to the Crown.

Powered by the Sword, Scythe was running so fast her hair flew straight out behind her and the wind whistled in her ears. But the creature was much closer, and it lunged forward and wrapped its long, skeletal fingers around the Talisman while she was still a hundred yards away.

It gave her a look of utter disdain, then placed the Crown atop its head.

Orath saw his opportunity and seized it. Cassandra was helpless, the Crown was his for the taking. The mortal charging toward him carried Daemron's Sword, and Orath knew how deadly the weapon could be. But of all the Talismans, the Crown was the most powerful.

He placed it atop his head, eager to unleash its full power against both her and Cassandra.

Instead, the inside of his skull exploded.

Rexol had tried to take the Crown from Cassandra twice. But she was wary of his presence, and she had been able to cast him out. The creature that wore the Talisman now had no idea he was lurking.

The wizard struck hard and fast, shredding his unsuspecting victim's mind. Bits and pieces of knowledge bubbled up into Rexol's own consciousness as he tore away at the other's identity. *Orath. Minions. A netherworld beyond the Legacy ruled by Daemron the Slayer.*

The mage ripped away everything, wiping out all traces of what the thing once had been. In seconds it was over: Orath, last surviving Minion of Daemron the Slayer, was gone.

Only Rexol remained, his consciousness fully possessing the body of a creature from the other side of the Legacy. With his new eyes he saw a young woman rushing toward him, a blade raised above her head to strike him down. The weapon burned with the power of Old Magic.

But Rexol now possessed Old Magic of his own, and he opened himself up to the glorious power of the Crown.

Scythe was only thirty feet away when a brilliant burst of green light erupted from the figure on the beach. It rolled toward her like a wave, throwing up a swirling wall of sand.

She ducked her head into the crook of her arm to shield her eyes as she held the Sword vertically out in front of her with both hands. The wave of green light washed over her, knocking her off her feet and burying her in the sand.

A booming voice echoed inside her head, and she knew it was coming from the thing wearing the Crown.

I am Rexol, and I am a God! Kneel before me!

Scythe felt her legs buckling as if to comply with his command, but she caught herself before she obeyed.

"Scythe!" Keegan screamed from somewhere behind her. "The Keystone!"

The horror in his voice compelled her to turn away from Rexol. The obelisk was still standing, but a giant crack now ran through the smooth black stone of the side facing her.

I am Rexol, and I am a God! the voice inside her head screamed out again. Even though it was only a thought, Scythe could hear the madness in it.

She snapped her head back to Rexol, but he no longer seemed aware she was there. He stood with his long, thin arms raised to the sky as a bank of dark, purple clouds gathered above him. He was surrounded by a dark green glow that crackled and popped with barely contained energy.

Even Scythe could see he was summoning Chaos, though to what end she couldn't guess.

I am Rexol, he cried out again, *and I am a God!*

He's snapped! Scythe realized. *The Crown is too much for him to handle!*

Something exploded behind her: a wet, horrible sound. Wheeling around, she saw the air thirty feet behind her shimmer and shift. A dark black sphere materialized, hovering a few feet off the ground. At first it was the size of a fist, but it quickly stretched to several feet across. As it grew, the awful noise intensified—the sound of reality itself being torn apart.

The Legacy! Scythe realized. *It's crumbling!*

A misshapen, three-fingered hand emerged from inside the sphere, clutching at the edge as some nameless abomination hauled itself through. The thing stood roughly the height of a tall man, though its arms and legs were disproportionally short and its torso was round and bloated. It was naked and hairless, its gray flesh hanging too loosely on its frame. It had no nose, and its mouth was nothing but a gaping maw of pointed teeth. It had only one eye, perfectly centered in its forehead. In one hand it held a crude axe.

The creature lunged for her, making a clumsy swing with the axe. Scythe easily dodged the axe, then ran the Sword through its eye, felling it with a single blow.

Reality shrieked in protest again as the sphere stretched wider, its lower edge now reaching all the way down to the ground. Another monstrosity came through; this one had the head and torso of a woman atop the body of an enormous black snake. She was bald, and her skin was covered in scales. She carried no weapon, but instead of arms she had two long, segmented appendages tipped with deadly stingers, like a pair of scorpions' tails.

The thing slithered toward Scythe, moving fast. It lashed out with a stinger, but Scythe ducked to the side and responded by slicing the horrifying limb off halfway up its length. The snakelike tail lashed out to sweep her off her feet, but Scythe jumped up at the last second and it harmlessly whipped past beneath her boots.

She lashed out with the Sword, slicing a deep, diagonal wound across the thing's female torso. The woman's head screamed once though it sounded more like a hiss, and the creature collapsed and began to spasm uncontrollably on the ground.

Ignoring the death throes of her opponent, Scythe focused her attention on the ever-expanding sphere. The wet, ripping sound assailed her ears again, and this time two of the living nightmares came through at the same time.

Keegan heard Rexol's voice echoing in his head, but he didn't have time to wonder how the mind of his dead master had returned inside the inhuman body now wearing the Crown.

Rexol had unleashed a powerful wave of uncontrolled Chaos magic, and the Keystone had fractured, opening a hole in the

Legacy. Scythe had already slain the first two creatures to come through the breach, but she was now locked in fierce combat with two more.

He was still too far from the beach to make out any of the horrific details as Scythe hacked and slashed at her enemies, the battle happening much too fast for his eyes to follow. As he ran, he began to draw Chaos from the Ring, summoning it to unleash against Scythe's opponents.

When the gathering Chaos reached a critical mass, he stopped. But instead of releasing it, he hesitated. Scythe already had one of her foes down, the other was sure to follow quickly—she didn't need his help. But he could hear the rising scream that signaled another wave of invaders coming into the mortal world.

He unleashed the Chaos, targeting the black gate that hung in the air on the edge of the beach. Even if there was some kind of spell he could cast to seal the breach, it was beyond his knowledge and skill. But if he couldn't close the passage, he could at least stop the enemy from coming through.

Blue fire shot from his hands, enveloping the two figures just emerging from the breach. They howled in pain as the Chaos incinerated them, reducing them to small piles of ash in only seconds.

Near the water's edge, a massive Chaos storm was building above Rexol. It was already starting to grow beyond his control; Keegan could feel the power rolling out across the island in a slow but steady stream.

I am Immortal! the wizard howled, and his cackling laughter filled Keegan's head.

There was a thunderous crack, and he knew another fissure had appeared in the Keystone. A second sphere materialized near the beach, fifty feet away from the first one, and began to grow.

Scythe had just finished off her last foe, and Keegan opened his mouth to tell her they had to stop Rexol. But his warning was lost in a deafening cascade of cracks and snaps reverberating across the island.

A dozen of the hovering black spheres materialized, scattered and spaced along the edge of the beach. Seconds later, the inhuman horde came pouring through.

There was no time to think; Keegan simply reacted by throwing everything the Ring had at them. Bolts of blue lightning arced from his fingertips, jumping from target to target in the closely packed enemy ranks. Blue fire rained down from the sky, melting anyone and anything it touched. Pillars of flame erupted from the ground like geysers, wreaking havoc.

He was dimly aware of Scythe leaping and spinning through the magical carnage. Protected by the Sword, she had no fear of his spells as she hacked her way through the advancing army. And for a second Keegan thought they might hold the enemy at bay.

And then Daemron the Slayer appeared.

Cassandra was pulled back to consciousness by the clamor of battle and the cackling laughter of Rexol ringing through her mind. As awareness came back to her, she instantly recognized Rexol, despite the unfamiliar form he now wore.

He was standing on the beach less than ten yards away from where she lay, his arms reaching up to the unnatural storm raging above him. As he had in Callastan, he was gorging himself on the power of Old Magic, gathering Chaos until it filled him and spilled out into the mortal world. But this time, Cassandra realized with dawning horror, his madness had actually brought the Legacy down.

Strange, dark spheres dotted the island—passages to a realm far beyond the mortal world. Through them came scores of grotesquely mutated beings, driven by hate and hunger. On the other side of the spheres she could sense thousands more lying in wait; the gibbering masses of Daemron's twisted army.

Two figures fought bravely against the Slayer's vanguard. A young Islander woman wielding a wondrous Sword mowed down wave after wave of the invaders while a young man she recognized as Rexol's apprentice unleashed devastating Chaos magic against them.

But her attention was ripped away from the heroic pair by the arrival of a God. She had never seen Daemron but she recognized him instantly: He glowed with the power of an Immortal.

A red-skinned giant, he stood over eight feet tall, his naked, muscular torso perched atop powerful legs ending in heavy hooves. A pair of thick horns curled up from his head, and he hovered a foot above the battlefield on a pair of massive leathery wings, his long tail whipping back and forth in eager anticipation of victory.

His arrival seemed to rally his troops, and suddenly the tide of battle shifted. The young woman's advance through the enemy ranks stalled, and she was forced into a fighting retreat.

Tilting his head back, Daemron roared to the sky. His voice snuffed out the fiery rain and deadly lightning of the young wizard, and his forces surged forward.

"Rexol!" Cassandra screamed, trying to reach him with both her mind and her voice. "Help them!"

Somehow, her cry pierced the veil of his insanity, and Rexol turned his attention from the sky toward the battle.

"The Crown is mine!" he shouted, his voice echoing across the island and in her head.

He began to laugh, a shrill, high-pitched sound that drove itself into the back of Cassandra's skull. The violet storm clouds gathered above him swooped down and enveloped Daemron and his army, gripping them all in the mage's madness.

The hideous swarm turned on itself. Instead of attacking the

humans, the creatures fell on each other with wild, reckless abandon. They bit and slashed with tooth and claw, furiously ripping
and tearing at anything and everything within reach. Even Daemron was affected: the Slayer landing in the middle of the battlefield
to unleash slaughter on his own followers.

The Islander and the young wizard staggered away from the
bloody carnage, falling back to stand side by side on the edge of
the beach, watching in dumbfounded amazement. Inside Cassandra's head, Rexol's maniacal laughter continued unabated.

The bloodlust that possessed him faded after only a few seconds,
but in that short time Daemron had already butchered dozens.

The Crown is even more powerful than I remember!

Spreading his wings he launched himself skyward, away from
the mindless bloodbath.

Seeing Orath standing on the beach wearing his Crown, he
suspected treachery at first. But then he realized it was not Orath
but a mortal who had possessed the Minion's body.

"I am a God!" he cried out, once more trying to use the Talisman to dominate Daemron's mind. "Kneel before me!"

But this time the Slayer was prepared, and he resisted the com-
pulsion.

"Obey me!" the mortal shrieked. "I command you to kneel!"

Daemron dropped from the sky like a stone, hitting the earth
with a heavy thud. But instead of kneeling, he scooped up a crude
axe left behind by one of the fallen. With a mighty flap of his
wings the Slayer took to the sky again and sent the axe flying end
over end.

The heavy blade buried itself in Orath's long, thin face, cleav-
ing the front of his skull wide open. The force of the blow sent the
Crown flying backward, and the mortal who had dared to use one
of his own Talismans against him toppled over, dead.

Chapter 30

KEEGAN WAS ALMOST grateful when the dull, heavy thud of the axe burying itself in Rexol's face put an end to the wizard's insane laughter inside his head. But with Rexol's death, the purple clouds hovering over the battlefield began to dissipate.

Reinforcements were already coming through the breach, though as they arrived they were struck with the same killing frenzy that had decimated the first wave. But it wouldn't be long before the spell evaporated completely and the Chaos horde once more rallied against them.

We have to strike now! Keegan thought. The Crown had affected Daemron—clearly he wasn't immune to his own Talismans. Together, the Ring and the Sword could take the Slayer down!

"Now's our chance, Keegan!" Scythe shouted as she rushed forward, obviously coming to the same conclusion.

Daemron was still flying twenty feet above the battlefield. Keegan felt him gathering Chaos, possibly to dispel the last of the purple clouds. Seizing on the opportunity to strike while his enemy was distracted, he called upon the Ring to knock the Slayer from the sky.

A ferocious gust of wind sprang up out of nowhere and sent Daemron spinning wildly out of control. Focusing his will, Keegan lashed out again, and a powerful downdraft sent him plummeting toward the ground.

At the last instant he managed to pull up and spread his wings to slow his descent, and he landed heavily but not hard enough to be injured. And then Scythe was on him.

She and the Sword moved as one in a beautiful dance of death. She attacked with a perfect combination of grace, precision, speed, and strength. The Slayer fought back by slashing at her with his fearsome claws and lashing out with his long tail. But his blows failed to make contact; over and over he struck the empty air where Scythe had been a split second before.

First blood went to Scythe, the Sword biting deep into Daemron's thigh. He managed to knock her off-balance by buffeting her with one of his wings and tried to follow up with a vicious butt of his horned head. Scythe ducked at the last instant and drove her blade up toward the Slayer's throat.

Daemron slapped the blade aside, but the edge sliced open his palm. He tried to retreat, but Scythe was too quick and she cut him off. He tried to take to the skies, but Keegan summoned another gust of air to knock him back to the ground.

Scythe leapt forward, but this time Daemron was ready. He dropped into a crouch and wrapped his wings around him in a protective cocoon. The Sword bit into the tough, leathery flesh but couldn't cut through it, catching Scythe by surprise. Taking advantage, Daemron lashed out with his tail, sweeping her feet out from beneath her.

Before he could leap atop his prone opponent, Keegan thrust the Ring to the sky. A wall of Chaos flames shot up between the two combatants, and Daemron stumbled backward. It lasted only a second, but it was enough for Scythe to get back on her feet.

We're winning! Keegan thought, but in the back of his mind he knew they were running out of time. If Scythe didn't finish this soon, they'd once again be fighting both Daemron and his entire army.

Cassandra forced herself to stand. She was still exhausted, but she knew what had to be done. Somehow, Keegan and the Islander were battling Daemron to a standstill, but they needed her to stop the monstrous army from coming to the Slayer's aid.

The Crown had flown twenty feet from where Rexol's body had fallen. She staggered over and picked the Talisman up. Steeling her resolve, she placed it atop her head.

To her shock, without Rexol's intrusive presence battling against her, the Crown didn't threaten to overwhelm her with its limitless power. Instead, it revitalized and energized her, washing away her fatigue.

She also realized that she could suddenly see into the minds of Keegan and the Islander. *Scythe. Her name is Scythe!*

Suddenly she understood why they had been here, waiting for her arrival. They'd come to stop her from accidentally destroying the Legacy.

You are one of us, Keegan said to her, speaking without words as he felt the touch of the Crown brushing up against his thoughts. *We were all born under the Blood Moon. We are all touched by Chaos and bound by fate.*

She saw that it was true, the connection of their birth allowing her to peer inside the young mage's mind.

Leave the Slayer to us, Scythe chimed in. *You just stop the army!*

The purple clouds that had turned Daemron's army against itself were gone, and reinforcements pouring through the still-expanding black spheres had swelled the enemy numbers to over a thousand. They were no longer ripping out each other's throats, but she could sense they were still dazed from what had happened.

Knowing they would still be vulnerable to suggestion, Cassandra pushed out with her mind in a piercing mental scream.

Flee!

Hundreds of the enemy turned and ran, scattering across the island. Others simply dropped to the ground and cowered in fear, buying Keegan and Scythe a few more moments of precious time.

Their terror wouldn't last long. And the next time, Cassandra knew, they'd be less susceptible to the Crown's power. But at least she'd bought them some time.

Still, reinforcements continued to pour through as the Legacy continued to crumble, and Cassandra knew even the Crown wouldn't be strong enough to stop them all.

Scythe heard Cassandra's scream, but it wasn't directed at her and she felt no ill effect. Daemron also seemed oblivious; he seemed to have learned how to protect himself after what Rexol had done to him.

He's getting stronger the longer this lasts, she realized.

She was still the one pressing the fight, but her advantage wasn't what it had once been. With every pass, Daemron seemed to ward off her attacks with greater ease.

He's learning my moves. Studying me and my tactics.

The realization spurred her into an all-out assault, trying to take him down while she still had the upper hand. Daemron was driven back once more, a desperate retreat as he flailed and floundered against the ferocious assault. But somehow he still managed to keep her from dealing any kind of serious damage, dodging or deflecting her blows with his impenetrable wings.

He's gathering Chaos! Keegan warned, his thoughts transferred through Cassandra and the Crown via the bond they all shared.

Scythe stepped back and threw the Sword up in front of her as Daemron breathed out a jet of blue fire. The flames struck the Sword and were swallowed up, absorbed by the Talisman. But the

Slayer wasn't finished. He followed up the thwarted attack by slamming a hoof into the ground.

Scythe's world vanished in a flash of blue light and a ferocious bang. The next thing she knew she was flying backward through the air, swept away by a concussive blast of magic. She landed hard on the beach, a full fifty feet away. Her clothes were torn and tattered from the detonation and the only sound she could hear was a single, high-pitched squeal.

Her mind was dazed from the impact, but some part of her instinctively knew she had broken several bones. Acting on instinct, she called upon the Sword to heal her wounds.

It was only then that she realized she no longer held the blade.

Keegan sensed Daemron's spell an instant before it was unleashed. Keegan lashed out to counter it, striking quickly. He threw an invisible shield up around Scythe, but in his haste he wasn't able to properly call on the full power of the Ring. The Slayer's spell ripped through his shield unabated.

He's getting stronger!

In horror he watched as Scythe was launched through the air by a powerful burst of Chaos. She slammed into the ground hard, where she lay motionless.

He took an involuntary step toward her, then heard Cassandra calling to him.

She's alive. Grab the Sword!

The Talisman lay on the battlefield, pulsing with energy. It had absorbed enough of the blast to keep Scythe alive, but she hadn't been able to hold on.

Daemron was rushing toward it, his own reserves of Chaos temporarily drained. Calling on the Ring, Keegan was able to get to it first.

Hand extended out in front of him, he used Chaos to call the Sword. It leapt from the ground and flew toward him, the hilt slapping itself into his waiting palm.

In a flash Daemron changed course and rushed at Keegan. The young wizard felt a rush of power coursing through his body—his muscles coming to life in response to the Sword's call to battle.

He met the Slayer head-on, confident the combination of the Ring and the Sword would bring him victory. But though his body was faster and stronger than it had ever been, he wasn't anywhere near as skilled as Scythe. Instead of the smooth, deadly dance, he felt disjointed and awkward as he hacked away at his foe.

The Slayer batted his first clumsy attacks aside, then tore open Keegan's cheek with his long, sharp nails. Keegan managed to parry a slash from his enemy's tail but was sent reeling by a fist to the jaw.

Keegan called on the Ring to defend himself, but Daemron was too close. Before he could summon enough Chaos to do anything, the Slayer had picked him up and lifted him above his head.

Daemron slammed Keegan's body to the ground, face-first, stunning him. Somehow, Keegan managed to hold on to the Sword as all the air rushed out of his body. A heavy hoof slammed down on his lower back, shattering the vertebrae.

Scooping the fallen wizard up, Daemron raised him above his head a second time.

Throw him! Cassandra cried out, her command hitting them with a frantic urgency far greater than anything Rexol had been able to muster.

Daemron hurled Keegan through the sky instead of slamming him down at his feet. Still clutching the Ring and the Sword, he landed on the beach at Cassandra's feet.

Attack! she screamed at the cowering remnants of Daemron's army. In response, they leapt to their feet and threw themselves at the Slayer.

"They won't slow him for long," she told Keegan. "Use the Sword to heal yourself and Scythe and give her the Talisman. Together we can defeat him."

In that instant, Keegan finally understood.

"No," he said to Cassandra. "We can't."

Everything finally made sense to him. Jerrod's visions of a savior bathed in flames. His own dreams of being overwhelmed by the Chaos horde. The recurring image of a flaming giant towering over him. At last it was clear.

"It has to be you, Cassandra. You're the Burning Savior!"

Their minds still linked through the Crown, Cassandra experienced Keegan's revelation even as it was happening.

When Scythe fought Daemron, he used magic to defeat her. The Sword alone wasn't enough to protect her.

The Talismans were meant to be used in concert. But simply possessing the Talismans was not enough.

When Keegan had both the Ring and the Sword, he was no match for Daemron physically. He lacked the physical and mental training of a warrior. He didn't know how to use the Sword.

Like all members of the Order, Cassandra had trained in the martial arts. And her flight with the Crown—hunted by the Minions—had given her a warrior's will and strength of spirit.

I can use the Sword.

Rexol had given her training in the ways of magic. Through her dreams, she'd served an entire apprenticeship under the most powerful Chaos mage in the Southlands.

I can use the Ring.

And she already knew how to use the Crown. Her years in the Order had given her the necessary mental discipline to control it, even while wearing the Ring and wielding the Sword.

And you were born under the Burning Moon and touched by Chaos,

Keegan added, still connected to her through the Crown. *You are one of the Children of Fire.*

Cassandra realized that her entire life had been leading up to this moment. Everything that had happened to her—everything she had ever learned and done—had been for this one purpose. Her early days under Rexol as a young child. Her years studying in the Monastery, learning the ways of the Order, ingraining the mental discipline to use the Crown and mastering the martial abilities required to use the Sword. Her endless flight, strengthening her will. Her recent apprenticeship to Rexol, learning the Mage's art so she could control the Ring. No other person had her unique combination of abilities, training, and experience. She was the only one who could stop the Slayer.

"I *am* the Burning Savior," she said aloud.

She took the Sword from Keegan's grasp. Then she slipped the Ring from his finger and placed it on her own.

The infinite power of all three Talismans flowed through her— Old Magic, forged by the True Gods. It was incredible. Exhilarating. Unlike anything she had ever experienced before.

It wasn't like a river of Chaos rushing through her. Not even a flood. She could call upon an entire ocean, drawing on the pure essence of magic from the Burning Sea itself.

With a mere thought and a wave of her hand, she fully healed both Keegan and Scythe of their injuries. At the same time, she created a barrier between her mind and theirs, severing the bond that had linked them through the Crown for their own protection.

The Talismans were drawing their power directly from the Burning Sea—an infinite well of Chaos that could destroy a mortal mind. Despite this, she felt no sense of being overwhelmed. She had no fear of any backlash or losing control. The Ring, the Sword, and the Crown were in perfect, harmonious balance.

Her body spontaneously combusted, but she felt no pain. She

began to grow and change, transforming from an ordinary young woman into a living pillar of fire, twenty feet tall.

On the battlefield, Daemron had cast off the last of the hapless underlings Cassandra had thrown against him. He turned as if about to charge, then hesitated when he saw the flaming figure standing defiantly on the beach.

He roared out his fury and unleashed a powerful blast of Chaos. But instead of targeting Cassandra, he directed it at the Keystone. The obsidian monolith exploded into dust, and the Legacy dissolved completely. The twenty black spheres became a hundred, then a thousand, then ten thousand. As one, the rest of his army crossed into the mortal world.

Calling on the Ring, Cassandra cast a spell that froze the entire horde dead in its tracks. Enraged, Daemron threw back his head and roared, summoning Chaos to use against her.

He's feeding off the power of the Talismans, too, Cassandra realized. *They were bound to him once, and he can still draw on them.*

Despite the realization, she felt no fear. Daemron could only touch a fraction of the Talisman's potential. Her power was that of the Old Gods themselves.

Like Cassandra, the Slayer's form was suddenly covered in flames, and he grew until they were of equal size, two twenty-foot-tall titans engulfed in fire, standing face-to-face. He threw himself at her, but to Cassandra he seemed to be moving in slow motion.

Without even thinking about it, she stepped to her left and brought the Sword up in a wide diagonal arc. Daemron feinted as if he were going to her right, then suddenly changed direction, charging headlong right into the upstroke of the blade.

The Crown lets me see the future, Cassandra thought. *I know what he's going to do even before he does.*

As the Sword struck him, Daemron exploded into a trillion crystals of blue light. They fell over the battlefield like flakes of glittering snow, winking out of existence a few seconds after they touched the ground.

With a wave of her hand, Cassandra released his army from their paralysis. Seeing their leader obliterated and facing a giant made of Chaos fire, they turned and fled back through the dark spheres, running back to their blighted netherworld.

The Slayer was defeated, his army driven back. But Cassandra knew her work wasn't done.

With several massive strides she crossed the island to the spot where the Keystone had stood only moments before. Throwing her head back, she thrust the Sword up to the heavens, calling on the power of Chaos to once more do her bidding.

Keegan and Scythe watched Daemron's fall with awestruck wonder, amazed by what Cassandra had become.

When the Slayer fell, neither dared to speak or look away. As Cassandra released the Chaos horde and sent it scurrying in terror from the mortal world, they remained rapt. And when she went over to where the Keystone had stood and thrust her magnificent flaming sword to the sky, they could only stare, enthralled by the sight of a God walking upon the earth.

The thousands of black spheres began to wink out of existence, disappearing with tiny pops amplified by their sheer numbers. When the last one vanished, Cassandra spoke to them.

As before, they heard her in their heads. But this time she sounded different—hollow and far away, as if calling to them from a great distance.

You must go. Return through the portal before it closes.

"What about you?" Scythe asked. "Aren't you coming with us?"

The True Gods sacrificed themselves to create the Legacy. How can I restore it without doing the same?

"Daemron is destroyed," Keegan argued. "His army routed. You don't have to do this."

The Chaos hordes still live. They will still seek to return to this world if they are not banished. I must see that will never happen. But I must work quickly.

My power comes with a price. I am not an Immortal; omnipotence is too great a burden for me to bear for long. Already I can feel it beginning to devour me. Soon I will cease to exist. I must restore the Legacy before that happens.

"Then we stay until you are finished," Keegan declared. "Whatever you create using the Talismans, someone else might try to destroy.

"We will gather up the Talismans after you are gone and keep them safe to honor your sacrifice."

"That's what the Order tried to do," Scythe reminded him.

The Talismans will not survive this ritual, Cassandra said.

"If the Old Gods couldn't destroy them," Scythe asked, surprised, "then how will you?"

The Talismans were created by the Immortals, but they were forged in our world. Bound to it. The True Gods could not destroy them because, unlike the Talismans, they were not of the mortal world.

Born from Chaos, the True Gods could not break the connection between our world and the Burning Sea. But I can.

Though they were no longer linked directly to Cassandra's mind, Keegan had a sudden glimpse into the true nature of what she was doing.

"You're not just destroying the Talismans," he said, horrified. "You're going to make the Legacy so strong that Chaos will not be able to enter the mortal world at all!"

The essence of Chaos is death and destruction.

"You're going to create a world without magic!"

Magic is the offspring of Chaos. Inevitably it leads to pain and suffering.

"You can't do this!" Keegan shouted. "I won't let you!"

You can't stop me.

Scythe reached out and grabbed Keegan's arm.

"Would that really be so bad? A world without any magic at all? No wizards. No Seers. No more dreams or prophecies."

"If I'm not a wizard," Keegan said, holding up his stump, "then I'm nothing!"

"You're not nothing, Keegan," Scythe told him.

"Without magic," he continued, "what do I have?"

For a second she didn't answer. If Methodis were here, he'd know exactly what to say. He always did. But words weren't her style. Instead, she grabbed Keegan by the neck and pulled him in close for a long, passionate kiss. After a second of stunned confusion, Keegan wrapped his arms around her and responded.

"Well?" she said when they finally broke it off. "What do you think? Are you ready to live in a world without magic after all?"

"I guess it has a few things to offer," he said with a wide grin.

You have to go now, Cassandra told them. *When the Legacy is restored and magic is no more, the portal to take you back to Callastan will cease to exist!*

"How long do we have?"

I can feel the pull of the Burning Sea, calling me to become one with the Chaos. I must start my ritual now or I will cease to exist before it is done.

Scythe pulled at his hand and they broke into a run.

"She didn't really answer my question," Keegan panted as they raced from the beach toward the tall, burning figure and the shimmering blue circle on the ground at her feet.

Suddenly, Cassandra was bathed in bright white light that shot up in a beam toward the clouds. It rose until it disappeared somewhere high above. A second later the sky was filled with a million rays of light—red, yellow, green, and blue—shooting off in all directions.

Keegan slowed, dumbfounded by the spectacle above them. Scythe yanked hard enough to almost jerk him off his feet and he picked up his pace again. By the time they reached the spot where the Keystone had once stood, Cassandra had disappeared, engulfed by the blinding white beam rising up to the heavens.

"Hurry!" Scythe shouted, as he stopped to look in wonder yet again.

Together they crowded into the portal. Keegan closed his eyes and pictured them whisked away back to Callastan.

Nothing happened.

"Come on!" Scythe shouted. "What are you waiting for?"

"I'm trying!" he shouted. "Something's wrong!

"Cassandra!" he called out. "What's happening?"

When there was no response, he knew she was already gone, consumed by the ritual she had set in motion—a ritual that might just have trapped him and Scythe on an empty island on the farthest edge of the world.

"Look down," Scythe gasped.

Below their feet the blue circle was flickering like a flame in the wind, phasing in and out of existence. Keegan watched as it vanished completely, then faded back in, growing steadily brighter.

"Hold on," he said to Scythe, pulling her close. "This could get ugly."

As the pulsing blue light reached maximum intensity Keegan closed his eyes and imagined Callastan, with Vaaler and the others all gathered together waiting for them.

Go now! he thought. The island suddenly vanished, and everything around them turned to black.

This time there was no sensation of flying across a living map of the world. Instead, it felt like they were falling straight down into a deep, dark hole. Keegan had no idea if this was how the return journey normally worked, or if something had gone wrong because of Cassandra's ritual to restore the Legacy.

One way or another we'll know soon enough.

He suddenly felt cold wind rushing over his face, and he caught the outline of tall buildings and high city walls rushing up toward them through the darkness.

It's night, his bemused mind noticed even as they plummeted toward the sleeping city. *The journey must have taken longer this time.*

With horror he realized they weren't slowing down. He reached out, trying to summon Chaos to slow their fall, but he felt absolutely nothing.

It's done. The Legacy is restored. There is no magic left. It happened while we were going through the portal, interrupting the spell. And now we are going to die.

All of this—from feeling the wind on his face to the stark realization that they were plummeting to their doom—took less than a second for his mind to process. And then they hit the cold water of Callastan's harbor, sending up a splash so high it crested above the city wall.

Still clinging to each other, they plunged far below the surface. Keegan panicked as the water closed in around him, clawing and clutching at Scythe and dragging them both down. Then he felt a hard smack on his jaw and he went limp.

A few seconds later he was gasping and flailing on the surface though he had no idea how he'd gotten there. A strong, wiry arm had wrapped itself under his chin in some kind of choke hold.

"Settle down or I'll smack you again," Scythe warned.

It took another second before he realized she was the one with her arm around his neck, holding his head above the water.

"Not much of a swimmer, are you?" she grumbled.

Thankfully, Scythe was a strong enough swimmer for the two of them, and she managed to keep them afloat on the dark waters.

Vaaler stared through the bedroom's tiny window at the night sky, unable to sleep. Shalana lay in the bed, snoring softly despite her insistence that she preferred to sleep out under the stars rather than cooped up inside a building within the city.

What happened to you, Keegan? he wondered.

The Blood Moon no longer hung in the sky; hopefully, that was a good sign. For weeks it had shined its ghastly light down upon them, and the sky looked strange with an ordinary moon. But that was far from the strangest change in the night sky.

As part of his royal upbringing, Vaaler had learned to use navigational star charts. Like everything else he studied, he still remembered them in near-perfect detail. And as he stared upward, he realized there was a new constellation in the heavens. A brilliant cluster of four very large, very bright stars had appeared on the night sky's western horizon.

Is that your doing, Keegan? Is that why magic has disappeared?

Jerrod had been one of the first to realize what had happened, the white veil that covered his eyes vanishing without any warning whatsoever. Vaaler had been standing beside him when it happened, both of them keeping vigil over the ritual grounds in the courtyard as they waited for Keegan and Scythe to return.

To his credit, the monk hadn't panicked when his Sight vanished. Instead, he'd simply stated, "Chaos has been banished from the mortal world."

Andar had confirmed his assessment a short while later; none of the Danaan wizards could feel its touch or summon it in any measure or form.

It was impossible to say for sure if the effect was localized to the area around Callastan or if it encompassed the entire world. But Vaaler suspected the latter.

For the most part, the city had reacted with curiosity and confusion rather than panic as realization spread. Most of the population were like Vaaler: completely blind to Chaos in all its forms. But there were enough magicians and hex witches working in the city—either independently or in the service of various nobles or gangs—for the news to spread quickly.

Despite having his extrasensory awareness stripped away, Jerrod had taken it as a good sign.

"If the Legacy fell, Chaos would grow stronger, not weaker," he'd declared. "Keegan and Scythe must have succeeded in their mission."

But at what price? Vaaler wondered. *If magic had vanished, how would they return?*

His musings were cut short by someone's pounding hard on their door. Roused by the sound, Shalana sprang from the bed, grabbing her spear from where she had propped it against the wall in easy reach.

"They're back!" Jerrod shouted from the other side of the door. "Keegan and Scythe! They're here!"

Vaaler wrenched the door open, his heart pounding with excitement.

"Are they hurt? Where are they?"

"They appear unharmed," Jerrod assured him. "Though they are cold and wet. A patrol found them treading water near the docks."

A thousand questions were racing through Vaaler's head. *What happened? How did they return without magic? Why were they in the harbor?* But none of these things really mattered: His friends were alive!

Vaaler grabbed the monk in a bear hug, lifting him off his feet and spinning him around, laughing with unbridled joy.

Epilogue

Vaaler sat atop his horse, watching as Andar and the rest of the Danaan contingent left Callastan. Nearly half the army of the Free City soldiers marched with them, serving both as an escort and as couriers to deliver a message to Lord Bonchamps: After decades of distinguished service, Captain Jendarme was stepping down as leader of Cheville's city guard.

That didn't mean the old man would be retiring, however. At the official request of the nobles, and with the unofficial sanction of the gang bosses and crime lords, the legendary soldier had agreed to serve as temporary Governor of Callastan until the city's ruling class had reestablished itself.

"Good luck to you," Andar said, reaching up to shake the young man's hand.

"And you," Vaaler replied. "And Keegan and Scythe wanted me to thank you again on their behalf."

Since being fished out of the Callastan harbor three days ago, both Keegan and Scythe had been fighting a nasty cold. Under Methodis's overprotective care, they'd been put on a strict regimen of bed rest and liquids.

"We should all be thanking them," Andar replied. "They saved us all and restored the Legacy."

Vaaler couldn't say for sure, but he thought he picked up a hint of bitterness in his voice.

Would that be so surprising? He's the High Sorcerer. Of course on some level he's going to resent losing his powers.

"Are you sure you won't change your mind?" Andar asked, but Vaaler simply shook his head.

"No matter how many times you ask, it will always be the same answer."

Over the past few days the High Sorcerer had made numerous appeals to Vaaler, trying to convince him to accompany the delegation on their return to Ferlhame. All to no avail.

Vaaler knew there were still many among the Danaan who would brand him a traitor, but he didn't decline out of fear for his safety. From what Andar had told him, the Queen and most of her advisers did not see him that way. But that didn't mean they would welcome him with open arms.

And I'm not ready to see Rianna yet, he thought, watching the Danaan head out through the city gates.

As if reading his thoughts, Shalana asked, "Do you think you will ever forgive your mother?"

"I honestly can't say," he told her.

"The Danaan will have need of a strong leader," she reminded him, "now that they can no longer rely on visions and mages to protect their kingdom. It will be a difficult adjustment for them."

For all of us, Vaaler thought.

He had never considered himself to have any kind of magical ability. Despite the pedigree of his bloodline, Chaos did not flow in his veins. Yet with magic gone, he found his memory wasn't quite what it used to be. It wasn't that he'd forgotten everything he'd learned, but many of the details weren't quite as sharp or as clear anymore.

I was born under the Blood Moon, he reasoned. *Maybe I was touched by Chaos, after all. Maybe it enhanced my skills and abilities in ways too subtle to notice until it was gone.*

That realization was daunting, but Vaaler knew there would be many others who had a far more difficult time adjusting to the new world than he. Magic and visions were ubiquitous in both the Southlands and the Danaan kingdom. To have such a common tool taken away was going to have many unforeseen consequences . . . not all of them desirable.

"You may not be ready to return to the North Forest yet," Shalana noted, interrupting his train of thought, "but one day you will go back. It is your home."

"Not anymore," he assured her. "Once we're done here in Callastan, I'm heading with you to the Frozen East."

"What if I don't want to go back right away?" Shalana asked. "What if I want to explore the Southlands?"

"It will be an interesting time," Vaaler conceded, not quite sure if she was teasing him or not. "Maybe it'll be worth sticking around to see how it all turns out.

"Just as long as we're together," he added, leaning over in his saddle to give her a quick peck on the cheek.

"I finally understand the purpose of that horse," she said with a coy smile. "Now you don't have to get on your tiptoes to kiss me."

As he made the long walk from the kitchen to the bedrooms, Methodis was reminded why he hated treating patients in the mansions of the nobility. Every time he prepared a medicinal mixture—or even made a bowl of soup, like the ones he now carried—he had to traipse from the servants' wing to the private chambers of the owner.

As temporary Governor, Jendarme had commandeered this particular residence for Keegan and Scythe to use while they remained in the city. Officially it still belonged to the original owner, but there were reports that his ship had sunk when he tried to flee Callastan during the Order's attack. He and all his heirs were lost beneath the deep, dark waters.

Yet Methodis had heard a slightly different tale. There were rumors of the nobleman's having an affair with the daughter of one of the local crime bosses that ended badly. Some claimed he disappeared to avoid the wrath of an angry father who also happened to employ several highly skilled assassins.

Of course, none of that had any effect on the health and welfare of the doctor's current patients. He knocked with his foot against the door of their bedchamber, carefully balancing the tray of soup.

"Come in," Scythe called out, her voice still stuffy and congested.

As usual, she was up and about, pacing around the room. She had never taken to bed rest well. Keegan, on the other hand, had made himself comfortable in the luxurious bed, wrapping himself in the down-filled comforter.

"I'm glad at least one of you is following doctor's orders," Methodis said, coming in and placing the soup down on the small, ornate table in the room's breakfast nook.

"Any idea how much longer until we're better?" Keegan asked, punctuating his question with a trio of wet sneezes.

"A few more days," Methodis said. "If you rest up," he added, glaring at Scythe.

"Too bad I'm not a wizard anymore," he groused. "I could just snap my fingers and make this all go away."

Methodis smiled, relieved the young man was able to joke about what he had lost.

He's coming to grips with this. It won't be easy, but he will find his way.

"It's probably for the best," Scythe chimed in. "You were always a bit careless with your spells. Probably turn this cold into a plague that would wipe out half the city."

The young man laughed softly and shook his head.

They're so comfortable around each other, Methodis thought.

He was glad that Scythe had taken his advice and finally opened herself up to the young man. It would help him in his recovery, and Methodis thought it was good for her, too.

Scythe was different since they'd returned. The change was subtle, but for someone who had raised her it was easy to see. She didn't seem as confrontational or quick to anger, as if the fire that had always burned inside her had softened somewhat.

Privately, Vaaler had speculated to Methodis that with the Legacy restored, Chaos was no longer acting as a catalyst for her temper. A possibility, but one Methodis discounted.

He saw the way Scythe and Keegan looked at each other, and he recognized young love. *Hang on to this one, my little Spirit,* he thought.

Another knock came on the door, and Jerrod poked his head inside. It took a moment for Methodis to recognize him. With the white veil no longer covering his eyes, his features were so plain as to be almost generic.

"I came to say good-bye," the former monk announced. "I'm leaving in a few hours."

"I need to go check on my shop," Methodis said, coming up with an excuse to give them some privacy. "I'll be back later tonight."

As a parting shot, he added, "Make sure you eat the soup!"

"He's a good man," Jerrod said, as Methodis slipped out the door. "You are lucky to have him back in your life."

You have no idea, Scythe thought. Out loud, she answered, "There is no kinder or more caring soul in the Southlands."

"I just wish his daughter took after him a little more," Keegan said, earning a snarky glare from Scythe.

"You sure you don't want to wait a little longer before leaving?" Scythe asked, turning her attention back to Jerrod. "Or, better yet, just forget about this crazy plan altogether?"

To Scythe's dismay, Jerrod was determined to wander the Southlands, telling everyone the tale of the Children of Fire.

"Cassandra sacrificed herself to save us all," Jerrod insisted. "People must be told of what she has done. She must be remembered and honored."

"We wouldn't be here now if it wasn't for her," Keegan agreed. "Everything we have—our lives, each other, the entire world—we owe to her. And keeping her name alive is the only thing we can do to repay her."

"And there are others who sacrificed as well," Jerrod added. "Their story must also be told."

Scythe nodded, knowing exactly who he meant. Even though she'd finally given in to her feelings for Keegan, she still cared deeply for Norr. She always would. She wanted people to know about him and what he had done.

"Of course you're right," she admitted. "And I don't mean to sound ungrateful. It's just weird. Almost seems like you're starting some new religion."

"In a way, I am," he answered. "The Order is gone, but people still need guidance. They still need a shining example to inspire them in their daily lives. What better example than Cassandra's courage and selflessness?

"People have seen the new constellation in the sky," Jerrod added. "Already they are calling the cluster the Children of Fire."

Scythe groaned. "Can't you just leave me out of all this? Cassandra's the one you want everyone to worship, anyway. She's the savior, right?"

"Much was asked of you all," Jerrod reminded her. "For a time you each bore a great burden, and you bore it well. The world owes you a debt they can never repay, but at least they should know what you've done."

"Maybe you could just change Scythe's name or something," Keegan offered, trying to find a compromise to satisfy them both.

"I'm sorry," Jerrod replied. "I must tell them the entire truth. I cannot pick and choose what goes in or stays out."

"Why not?" Scythe challenged. "Every other religion does it."

"I hold myself to a higher standard," he told her.

"Great," Scythe grumbled. "So I get to suffer for your principles."

"I wouldn't worry about it," Keegan told her. "Nobody's going to believe him, anyway. They'll just think he's crazy."

Jerrod smiled at the jab, knowing it was delivered by a friend in jest.

It always looks strange when he smiles, Scythe thought. *His features are too harsh and stern.*

Even without the unsettling white eyes, it was easy to guess he'd once served the Order. He still carried an air of grim authority about him.

People are going to believe him when he tells his tale, she realized. *Many of them, at least.*

Jerrod came over to the bed and clasped Keegan's arm. "Good luck to you," he said. Then he turned and offered his hand to Scythe.

On a wild impulse she grabbed him in a fierce hug, just to see how he'd react. To his credit, he endured it with aplomb.

"Just remember," Scythe told him when she let go. "If this religion of yours takes off, I want a cut from the collection plate."

He smiled again, nodded at them both, and left the room, closing the door behind them. Once he was gone, Scythe crossed over to the bed and climbed in beside Keegan, snuggling close under the covers.

"I can't believe you're not more bothered by what Jerrod is doing," she told him.

Keegan shrugged. "I guess I just got used to being told I was some kind of all-powerful savior. Maybe it's hard for me to let that part of my identity go."

Scythe knew Keegan was still struggling to come to terms with losing his gift. But she truly believed he was better off without it. And she needed him to believe it, too.

"You're not letting that identity go," she told him. "You're breaking free from it."

"What do you mean?"

"Our lives were never our own," she explained. "We were controlled and manipulated by Chaos. We were just pawns in some greater plan. Slaves to our fate. But that's over now.

"Now we can be anything we want! Go anywhere we want! Do anything we want! That's an amazing gift, and Cassandra gave it to us."

"I hadn't really looked at it like that," he said, nodding thoughtfully.

"Well, it's time you started," she told him. "The future is whatever we make of it. So let's make it a good one. Agreed?"

"Agreed," he said, flashing her a bright smile.

He doesn't smile enough, she thought. *But unlike Jerrod, it looks good on him.*

"Glad you're on board," Scythe said, satisfied. "So tell me—what is the one thing you want to do more than anything else?"

"This," Keegan said, pulling her close and giving her a long, hard kiss.

Daemron crouches on the cold stone floor of his inner sanctum, his wings wrapped protectively around him. Slowly he unfurls them and stands, every muscle and fiber of his body aching with exhaustion. The spell that he used to transport himself instantly back into his nether realm is draining, even for a God, but it has served him well.

Had he fought with everything in his power, he could have lasted much longer against the mortal who carried his Talismans. But in the end, he knew he would have fallen. She was too strong—better to retreat and live. And so, at the first blow from her weapon, he simply vanished.

He had used the same trick against the Old Gods when the tide of battle turned against him seven hundred years ago, but they had not been fooled. They sensed his retreat and banished him. But as powerful as the mortal who turned his own Talismans against him was, she was no God. She did not see through his trick. She does not know her enemy still lives.

With the Legacy destroyed, he can now cross between the worlds. The Children of Fire are not immortal; they will age and die. Until then he can plot and scheme, gathering followers in the mortal realm. And, when the time is right and there is no one left strong enough to oppose him, he will strike.

Outside his sanctum he hears the return of his followers, an angry army marching into the cramped, grimy city from which he rules his blighted kingdom. He hears them surrounding his castle, searching for the God who deserted them on the battle-field.

In time he will win their loyalty back, but first he must let their anger cool. He senses the horde descending on his inner sanctum; he knows it is time to leave. With the Legacy gone he can cross between realms, but they cannot.

He closes his eyes and reaches out to touch the mortal world, his mind stretching out to it across the Burning Sea. Instead of the tiny island where he left a foothold to draw him back, however, his mind butts up against a dark and forbidding wall.

No! The Legacy was destroyed!

With dawning horror, he realizes what has happened. Like the Old Gods before her, the mortal he fought sacrificed herself to banish him.

He pushes against the reborn Legacy, sensing there is something different about it now. The original Legacy was permeable; a barrier to keep him out but still allow the mortals to touch the ocean of Chaos from which all things were born.

The new Legacy is stronger. More solid. An impenetrable wall between the mortal world and the source of all magic: eternal and indestructible.

No! Anything that can be built can be torn down!

There is a weakness in the wall. There has to be! He only needs time to find it.

A shadow falls across the floor of his inner sanctum. Looking up at the hole in the domed ceiling—the only way in or out—he sees the outline of one of his soldiers in the aperture, clinging to the curved stone.

She scuttles in, invading his inviolate space. Others follow close behind: Those with claws crawl along the stone; those with wings simply fly in. Those that cannot fly or scale the wall are carried in on the backs of others. A dozen. Fifty. A hundred.

They fill Daemron's inner sanctum like insects packed into a hive, their eyes hateful and accusing.

Their God stands motionless at the center of the horde, knowing he is too weak to fight them all. But his reputation keeps them temporarily at bay, and his mind races as he thinks of what to say to win their loyalty back after abandoning them on the battlefield.

As he opens his mouth to speak they fall on him. In seconds Daemron is ripped to shreds, his followers feasting on his entrails.

Chaos is the source of all life and creation, but also all death and destruction. Nothing is eternal. Even an Immortal can die.

Acknowledgments

Chaos Unleashed is the final book in my Chaos Born trilogy— a labor of love that has consumed the vast majority of my creative energy over the last four years. I've spent many, many hours with these characters and this story, and now that the tale is finished I find myself engulfed by a mixture of satisfaction, relief, and even regret. It's part of my life that I will miss, but it's time to move on to other things.

Of course, none of this would have been possible without the help and support of many people. This project never would have gotten off the ground without the help of my agent, Ginger Clark. She championed this series from day one, and I'm proud to have her in my corner. I also want to thank my fantastic editors, Tricia Narwani and Michael Rowley. In any tale that spans across three full-length novels there are going to be some rough bits. As the author, I'm often too close to the story to see where things didn't quite work as I planned, and my worst fear is to have all my efforts undone because I slipped up on some crucial aspect of character development or because I inadvertently left some kind of gaping plot hole. Throughout this process, Tricia and Michael have been there with a steady hand to guide me through the choppy waters that inevitably spring up, and I know this project would have suffered greatly without their input.

I also want to thank those in my family who have given me the love, support, and understanding any creative person needs when undertaking a massive project like this. My wife, Jennifer, has always stood beside me; without her, I wouldn't be where I am today. Many years ago she carried the financial burden when I left my job at the bank and went back to school to pursue my dream of being a professional writer. But that was a minor contribution to my success compared to everything else she has done for me over the years. I write in fits and starts, and she's never complained about the long stretches where I procrastinate and do nothing productive for weeks on end. She's put up with me in the times when my deadlines get closer and I go into crunch mode, working far too long until I'm tired and cranky and short-tempered. She's patiently listened as I've prattled on and on about my half-finished ideas, letting me bounce them off her as I try to shape them into something worthy of sharing with the world. I owe her everything.

I also need to acknowledge the incredible job my parents did in raising me. They encouraged me in my writing, and they were never afraid to tell me how proud they were of what I was doing. And I always knew that if things went wrong, they'd be there to help me pick myself up. They gave me the courage and confidence to work at becoming a writer; they taught me to follow my dream.

My father passed away unexpectedly a month after I finished the first draft of *Chaos Unleashed*. I think it was safe to say he was my biggest fan, but he never got a chance to see the ending of my story. He taught me so much about life that I can't even begin to express it in words. Dad loved people, and people loved him. He understood that everyone has worth and value, and he treated everyone with respect. He taught me that life isn't just what you do, it's who you do it with. Friends and family are what really matter. Though Dad is gone, part of him lives on in the memories and the relationships that those who loved him share with one another.

My mom has shown tremendous courage since his death, and I'm so proud of how she has carried on. She's been an inspiration to me, and though we have come through difficult times I know there are still many good days ahead of us. I've also realized how lucky I am to have had such incredible parents, and I see now that I was taking them for granted. It's awful that it took a personal tragedy to make me fully grasp how much they mean to me, but I intend to treasure the time I have left with Mom.

Finally, I want to acknowledge all the readers and fans who have followed me on this long journey. Obviously, I wouldn't be anything without you. Being able to share my stories with others is a rare honor and a privilege, and I know how lucky I am. So, thank you for everything, and I hope you enjoyed *Chaos Unleashed*!

ABOUT THE AUTHOR

DREW KARPYSHYN is the *New York Times* bestselling author of *Children of Fire, The Scorched Earth,* and *Chaos Unleashed,* as well as the *Star Wars: The Old Republic* novels *Revan* and *Annihilation,* and the *Star Wars: Darth Bane* trilogy: *Path of Destruction, Rule of Two,* and *Dynasty of Evil.* He also wrote the acclaimed Mass Effect series of novels and worked as a writer/designer on numerous award-winning videogames. After spending most of his life in Canada, he finally grew tired of the long, cold winters and headed south in search of a climate more conducive to year-round golf. Drew Karpyshyn now lives in Texas with his wife, Jennifer, and their pets.

Also available from Del Rey:

CHILDREN OF FIRE

Chaos Born 1
By Drew Karpyshyn

For centuries after a devastating battle between the immortals,
humanity has been protected from the Chaos realm by an invisible
barrier known as the Legacy.

But sealed behind the weakening barrier, the traitor Daemron
makes one last, desperate bid for freedom: he casts his most deadly
spell and curses four unsuspecting children.

Born under the Blood Moon, they are destined to
wield Daemron's talismans of power, to either save the
barrier – or bring it crashing down . . .

DEL REY

Also available from Del Rey:

THE SCORCHED EARTH

Chaos Born 2
By Drew Karpyshyn

Beset on all sides by mortal and supernatural enemies,
The Children of Fire – four mortals touched by the
power of Chaos – are in search of the Talismans that
can put a stop to an ancient enemy of the Gods.

But in doing so, they unleash a flood of Chaos magic
on the land – leaving death, destruction and a
vengeful queen in their wake . . .

DEL REY

Also available from Del Rey:

THE THOUSAND NAMES
By Django Wexler

**In the desert colony of Khandar, a dark and
mysterious magic, hidden for centuries, is about
to emerge from darkness.**

Marcus d'Ivoire, senior captain of the Vordanai Colonials,
is resigned to serving out his days in a sleepy, remote outpost,
when a rebellion leaves him in charge of a demoralised force
in a broken down fortress.

Winter Ihernglass, fleeing her past and masquerading
as a man, just wants to go unnoticed. Finding herself
promoted to a command, she must rise to the
challenge and fight impossible odds to survive.

Their fates rest in the hands of an enigmatic new Colonel,
sent to restore order while following his own mysterious
agenda into the realm of the supernatural.

DEL REY

DEL REY UK

The home for the best and latest science fiction and fantasy books.

Visit our website for exclusive content, competitions, author blogs, news from Del Rey HQ at Penguin Random House, musings on SFF and much much more!

 Follow Del Rey on Twitter @delreyuk for weekly giveaways

 Visit www.delreyuk.com

 Sign up to the newsletter

Join the conversation on: